Praise for Sherryl Woods and the Trinity Harbor Trilogy

"Sherryl Woods always delivers."
—*New York Times* bestselling author Jayne Ann Krentz

"A wonderfully charming cast of characters.... [The] story is full of warmth and humor."
—*RT Book Reviews* on *About That Man*

"Clever characters and snappy, realistic dialogue add zest...making this a delightful read for contemporary romance readers."
—*Publishers Weekly* on *About That Man*

"With a true sense of fun and humor, Ms. Woods knows how to write romance that warms your heart and tickles your funny bone."
—*RT Book Reviews* on *Ask Anyone*

"The protagonists and the colorful townspeople are appealing, and Liz's attempts to win back the Spencer family's trust are portrayed deftly."
—*Publishers Weekly* on *Along Came Trouble*

"An engaging story.... You'll enjoy the Spencer clan."
—*RT Book Reviews* on *Along Came Trouble*

Also by #1 New York Times *bestselling author Sherryl Woods*

Chesapeake Shores

Willow Brook Road
Dogwood Hill
The Christmas Bouquet
A Seaside Christmas
The Summer Garden
An O'Brien Family Christmas
Beach Lane
Moonlight Cove
Driftwood Cottage
A Chesapeake Shores Christmas
Harbor Lights
Flowers on Main
The Inn at Eagle Point

The Sweet Magnolias

Swan Point
Where Azaleas Bloom
Catching Fireflies
Midnight Promises
Honeysuckle Summer
Sweet Tea at Sunrise
Home in Carolina
Welcome to Serenity
Feels Like Family
A Slice of Heaven
Stealing Home

The Perfect Destinies

Destiny Unleashed
Treasured
Priceless
Isn't It Rich?

The Calamity Janes

The Calamity Janes: Lauren
The Calamity Janes: Gina & Emma
The Calamity Janes: Cassie & Karen

The Devaney Brothers

The Devaney Brothers: Daniel
The Devaney Brothers: Michael and Patrick
The Devaney Brothers: Ryan and Sean

Ocean Breeze

Sea Glass Island
Wind Chime Point
Sand Castle Bay

For a complete list of all titles by Sherryl Woods, visit www.sherrylwoods.com.

SHERRYL WOODS

ALONG CAME TROUBLE

Recycling programs for this product may not exist in your area.

ISBN-13: 978-0-7783-1989-4

Along Came Trouble

For questions and comments about the quality of this book, please contact us at CustomerService@Harlequin.com.

www.MIRABooks.com

Printed in U.S.A.

Dear Friend,

I'm so thrilled that you're getting a chance to know everyone in Trinity Harbor now that this series is back in print. To everyone's shock, murder and mayhem are currently the talk of the town. This time Tucker's the one stirring up trouble, which isn't exactly the smartest thing for a county sheriff to be doing. Naturally King Spencer, Tucker's father, is in an uproar, but thankfully King's own love life is in so much chaos, he can only do so much interfering in Tucker's.

I hope you'll enjoy this final installment in the saga of the Spencers. I have loved getting to know the residents of Trinity Harbor and sharing them with you, just as I have thoroughly enjoyed hearing from so many of you. That the books made you laugh and made you cry says that the Trinity Harbor folks came to mean as much to you as they did to me.

All best,

Sherryl Woods

ACKNOWLEDGMENTS

A special thanks to the real Westmoreland County sheriff Buddy Jackson, who provided invaluable technical, departmental and jurisdictional information. Sadly, in 2008, Westmoreland County lost this outstanding law enforcement official to lung cancer. My thoughts and prayers are with his wife, artist Diane Jackson, and all of his colleagues.

And, as always, my undying appreciation to editor Joan Marlow Golan, who guided me through the entire Trinity Harbor trilogy when it was first released.

Along Came Trouble

Prologue

Robert "King" Spencer eyed the silent telephone beside his chair, willed it to ring, and muttered a curse when it didn't. He'd never thought he would live to see the day when he actually wanted to fend off a dozen callers reporting trouble with one of his kids, but that day had come. With Daisy and Bobby settled down, it was past time for Tucker, his oldest, to start raising a ruckus around town.

Of course, as sheriff, Tucker was more prone to squelching trouble than stirring it up, but even a saint had an off day every now and then. It was way past time for some woman to come along and lead Tucker astray, but as far as King knew, Tucker hadn't even had a date in months now. Worse, King's elder son didn't seem to give two hoots that he had no social life to speak of.

As for trouble, there had never been so much as a whiff of scandal in that boy's life with the possible exception of the time Mary Elizabeth Swan, his childhood sweetheart, had taken up with an outsider and left Tucker pining away for her. Folks in Trinity Harbor had had a field day with that one, but they'd been sympathetic to Tucker, and eventually the talk had died down out of respect for his feelings.

King should have been proud that his elder son was an honorable man who people looked to as an example, but the truth was, he found it frustrating. A man had to stir things up once in a while or life just passed him by. King considered starting a few rumors of his own, just to get the ball rolling. If nothing else, that would bring Tucker flying out to Cedar Hill to deny them… which would give King an opportunity to deliver a long-overdue lecture on marriage and family.

King was not a patient man. Okay, that was a massive understatement. He liked to be in control, liked to make things happen on his own timetable. He did not like having his plans foiled again and again by the streak of stubbornness that ran wide through his own children. Right now his plan included grandbabies, a whole dynasty of Spencers.

He had one flesh-and-blood grandson, for all the good it did him. J. C. Gates had been kept from Bobby and from King for years. Some of that had been King's own doing, so he could hardly complain now that the boy still hadn't warmed up to him. J.C. was as cautious and fractious as a spooked horse around his own daddy, never mind King. But Bobby was both patient and determined that the boy's attitude would change with time. King was counting on it.

In addition to J.C., there were four more little hellions King could claim, even if they didn't have Spencer blood running through their veins. Daisy's adopted son, Tommy, was turning into a fine boy, now that Daisy and Walker had taken a firm hand with him. And Bobby's stepdaughter, Darcy, was a pistol. She looked real cute, too, now that her dyed-green hair had grown out. King was as proud of his two ready-made grandkids as if they were his own flesh and blood. He felt the same way about Walker's two sons, even though they all saw precious little of them, since the boys lived down in North Carolina with their mama.

But even with all the commotion that brood had brought into his life, King wanted a new generation of full-fledged Spencers he could educate in tradition from the very beginning. He wanted a generation who'd grow up and see to things in Trinity Harbor, Virginia, the way King and his ancestors had from the beginning of time in this little town on the Potomac River. Spencers had a duty and an obligation to folks around here to keep things running smoothly.

Since Daisy and Bobby didn't seem to be in the slightest hurry to give him grandbabies, that left Tucker. Unfortunately, his son seemed to be aware of King's intentions. Tucker had been giving his father a wide berth for weeks now, making up excuses to avoid Sunday dinner at the farm and the pointed questions that King tended to serve along with the fried chicken and mashed potatoes.

Worse, King hadn't been able to corner him in town or at the sheriff's office over in Montross. Tucker was getting to be as slippery as some of those criminals he was always going on and on about.

Now, it was *possible* that Tucker was trying to crack a big case, but King doubted it. The kind of "big" cases that turned up around here tended to begin and end with a drunk-and-disorderly charge or a traffic citation. Oh, there had been that drug business a couple of years back, and an occasional shoplifting incident or shooting, but all in all, the county was fairly quiet and serene. Which should have left plenty of time for Tucker to pursue a woman, in King's opinion.

"I guess that means it's up to me," King said aloud. "Again."

He managed to pull off a resigned tone, but anyone looking would no doubt have seen the glint of anticipation in his eyes. There was nothing on earth that King liked better than a little well-intentioned meddling, especially when it came to romance. He glanced across the room at the silver-framed photos Daisy and Bobby had given him last Christmas. They both had fine-looking families, thanks to him.

Yes, indeed, a little lively romance was exactly what Tucker needed. And King was getting darn good at providing it, if he did say so himself. He'd get on it first thing in the morning.

1

Tucker stood in the doorway of his bedroom and wondered why in hell there was a woman in his bed.

Unless, of course, he was hallucinating. After the kind of day he'd had, that wasn't out of the question. He blinked hard and looked again. Nope, she was still there. Practically buck naked and gorgeous.

Okay, then, he thought, deeply regretting that he hadn't had one last cup of coffee. He rubbed a hand over his face and tried to get his brain to kick in with the kind of quick thinking for which he was known in law enforcement circles. The woman was a reality. That still didn't give him the first clue about what she was doing in his house and, more specifically, in his bed.

He certainly hadn't invited her to share that king-size space, not in years, anyway. He hadn't even known she was there until he'd walked in the house, dead tired from working a double shift and ready for bed himself. If he hadn't flipped on the bedroom lights, he might have crawled in beside her, which wouldn't have been altogether a bad thing under other circumstances.

As it was, he was simply standing here, mouth gaping as if he'd never seen a half-naked woman before… especially this particular woman.

Last he'd heard, Mary Elizabeth Swan had wanted nothing further to do with him. In fact, the last he'd read on the front page of the *Richmond Times-Dispatch,* she was marrying the local delegate to the Virginia house of delegates. Though that was far from the last occasion on which her name had appeared in print, it was the last time Tucker had permitted himself to read any article that mentioned her. He had to skip quite a bit in the local weekly—to say nothing of entire pages in the feature section of the Richmond paper when the house of delegates was in session.

It sometimes seemed to him as if Liz, as she preferred to be called these days, was on the board of every cultural institution in the entire state. Her picture—always taken at some fancy shindig requiring designer clothes—leapt out at him at least once a week, reminding him with heart-stopping clarity of just how susceptible he was to any glimpse of that flawless face and tawny mane of hair.

Of course, he sometimes had a hard time reconciling those sophisticated images with the girl he'd fallen for on a schoolyard playground the day she'd pummeled a nine-year-old boy for trying to sneak a peek at her panties while she'd been scrambling up a tree. Mary Elizabeth had been a tomboy back then, and while she'd eventually outgrown tree climbing, she'd never outgrown her go-for-broke enthusiasm for life. Not while she'd been with him, at any rate. She'd looked depressingly sedate in those newspaper pictures, however, so maybe she'd changed now that she was going on thirty and a force to be reckoned with in Richmond society.

Tucker had finally taken to tossing the feature section aside just to avoid the temptation to sit and stare and brood about what might have been…what *should* have been. What kind of pitiful excuse for a man couldn't get a woman out of his system after six years and a steady diet of gushing reports about the wildly successful man she'd chosen over him?

Lawrence Chandler had high-tech millions and political ambitions. Mary Elizabeth, who'd been born right here in Westmoreland County, came from generations of Virginia blue blood. She'd inherited Swan Ridge, her grandfather's estate overlooking the Potomac. A cynic might have wondered if that stately old house with its manicured lawn and sweeping views hadn't been as much a lure for Chandler as Mary Elizabeth herself. New money seeking old respectability, as it were.

Be that as it may, it was a marriage made in political heaven. If Tucker had heard that once, he'd heard it a hundred times, usually right before people realized they were saying it to the prior man in Mary Elizabeth's life, the one who'd loved her since childhood, the one who'd expected to marry her. Then they'd slink away, looking embarrassed or—even worse—pitying.

According to all those same reports, Chandler intended to be governor by forty, bypass Congress and head straight for the White House by fifty. Not one single political pundit seemed to doubt him.

But he wasn't likely to pull that off, Tucker concluded, if people discovered that his wife was sleeping just about bare-assed in the bed of a small-town sheriff who had once been her lover.

Tucker might have gloated over this turn of events, but he'd been a sheriff a long time now. Things were seldom what they seemed. He doubted Mary Elizabeth had come crawling back because she realized she'd made a terrible mistake six years ago and wanted to rectify it tonight.

Nope, one glimpse at her pale complexion, at what looked like dried tears on her cheeks and the dark smudges under her eyes, and he concluded that she was here because there was some kind of trouble and for some reason she was desperate enough to turn to him. The thought of the strong woman he'd once known being vulnerable and needy shook him as much as her unexpected presence.

He needed to think about this, and he couldn't do it in the same room with a woman who'd once made his blood roar just by glancing at him with her stunning violet eyes. Mary Elizabeth in a tangle of sheets with only one of his T-shirts barely covering her pretty much rendered him incoherent. She always had, and judging from the way his body was reacting right now that hadn't changed.

Tucker retreated to the kitchen and poured himself a stiff drink, thought about it and made it a double. He had a feeling he was going to need it before the night was over.

Liz stretched, then froze as a barrage of ugly memories crashed over her. For one instant, for one brief moment, she'd forgotten everything that had happened the night before. She'd forgotten the discovery that had brought her running to a man she'd abandoned years ago, the only person on earth she could trust to help her.

If he would.

He had to, she told herself staunchly. Tucker was not

the kind of man to turn his back on someone in trouble, even someone he hadn't spoken to in years, someone who'd hurt him. Tucker was the most honorable man she'd ever known. She was counting on that mile-wide streak of Spencer integrity to come through for her, even if she didn't deserve it.

She hadn't expected to sleep at all when she'd gotten here. In fact, she'd expected to spend endless hours answering questions, but with no sign of Tucker on the premises, she'd been left all alone in the dark with her nerves rattled and her thoughts scrambling. She'd waited for a while on the porch, but eventually exhaustion and fear had taken their toll. She had gone inside the unlocked house—a testament to Tucker's faith in his own law-enforcement skills—in search of a much-needed shower to cleanse away all signs of the night's events.

Then she'd found one of his T-shirts tossed over the back of a chair, slipped it on and, like a child seeking the safety of a familiar place, had crawled into Tucker's bed to wait for him, uncertain what shift he was working or even whether he would be home at all. For all she knew, he could be spending his nights in another woman's arms.

Now, judging from the soft gray light spilling in the windows, she'd slept through the night. Alone, which was as it should be.

Some sixth sense told her that she might be alone in Tucker's bed, but she was not by herself. She rolled over and looked straight into eyes that were as familiar to her as her husband's. More familiar, in some ways.

Tucker regarded her with a cool, penetrating gaze that seemed to see straight into her soul. She wondered if he could see the turmoil, if he could read just how terrified she was…how relieved that he was finally there, even if his expression was far from friendly.

"Welcome back seems a little inappropriate," Tucker said with the wry humor that Liz had once decried because it kept her at a distance.

She studied his face, noted the new lines fanning away from the corners of his crystal-blue eyes, the furrow in his forehead that meant he'd spent most of the night thinking hard about how to cope with her unexpected presence. She wanted to touch him, wanted to smooth away that furrow and tell him not to worry, but that was out of the question. He had every reason to worry. She was about to draw him into a quagmire.

Not only was she—the woman who had once dumped him—suddenly back in his bed, but she was in more trouble than even Tucker Spencer with his keen intelligence, sterling moral streak and investigative skills was likely to be able to fix. But, God help her, she needed him to try…for both their sakes.

"Why are you here?" he asked, when she said nothing.

Liz wished she had the kind of simple answer he seemed to expect. "It's complicated," she began finally.

"Not good enough," Tucker said flatly.

His inscrutable gaze never once left her face, not even to stray to the ample amount of bare skin revealed by his twisted, hiked-up T-shirt. She shivered at the sudden chill in the air and drew the sheet tightly around her, embarrassed by her indecent exposure. Once it wouldn't have mattered, but now it did. Things between them had changed. Much as she might hate it, it was an undeniable fact.

She had to fight to blink back the tears that threatened. She wouldn't—she couldn't—cry. If she started, she might never stop. She had made such a mess of things—of her relationship with Tucker, of her marriage, of her life. Right now, though, she had to concentrate on one thing...finding out what had happened last night and who was responsible.

"Still have that rigid self-control, I see," she said, covering her nerves with sarcasm, even at the risk of alienating the only friend she was likely to have in Trinity Harbor, where people might have voted for her husband but had been slow to forgive her for the choice she'd made between Tucker and an outsider.

"It's gotten me through the rough spots," he replied evenly.

"Meaning what I did to you," she said, regretting that they hadn't had this particular conversation years ago and gotten it out of the way. But Tucker, stoic and disdainful, had refused to let her explain anything back then. He'd said it was enough that she was turning her back on everything they'd shared. He hadn't wanted to know the details, hadn't wanted to understand her reasons for choosing Larry over him. Maybe he'd been right. Maybe none of them were good enough to make what she'd done forgivable. Maybe he hadn't needed to know how deeply she regretted having hurt him.

In the years since, even though they lived within miles of each other for part of the year, she'd done her best to stay out of his path. She'd figured she owed him that much. And if she hadn't come to that conclusion on her own, King Spencer had made it a point to remind her every time they'd crossed paths. She'd made a powerful enemy there, no doubt about it.

"Is our breakup the rough spot you're talking about?" she asked.

"That was one thing," he agreed.

It saddened her that there might have been more, that he'd suffered losses, endured crises, she'd known nothing about. "And the others?"

"Liz, you're not here to catch up on old times," Tucker said with a hint of impatience. "Why *are* you here, instead of over at Swan Ridge? Where the hell are your clothes? What kind of trouble have you gotten yourself into, and last—but hardly least—why aren't you turning to your husband for help?"

She shivered again at the cold glint in his eyes and wondered if she'd made a dreadful mistake in coming here. Tucker was, after all, the sheriff. His first obligation would be to the law, not to her. But instinct had brought her to Tucker, and desperation would keep her from leaving. She needed help that he could provide… if he would. It all came down to that.

"I'm afraid Larry can't help me with this one," she told him.

"Why not?"

She risked a look into those hard, unyielding eyes, praying that Tucker would forgive her for the past, praying even harder that he would help her despite it.

"Because he's dead," she said, then added before she could lose her nerve, "and everyone's going to think I killed him."

2

Well, hell, Tucker thought, as Mary Elizabeth's explanation hit him in the gut. He should have known she wasn't here to rekindle an old flame. He *had* known it. A part of him just hadn't wanted to believe it. A part of him, overcome with that same old uncontrollable lust, hadn't given two figs why she was back. He was going to have to try really, really hard to ignore that part of him, at least until he knew what the devil was going on.

If Chandler was dead, why hadn't he heard about it? Surely it would have been big news. She couldn't possibly be telling him it had just happened, could she?

"When did he die?" he asked, trying to ignore the fact that tears were welling up in her eyes and that she was doing her best to keep them from spilling down her cheeks. Mary Elizabeth had always hated to let anyone see her cry, especially him.

"Sometime yesterday, I think. I'm not sure."

He stared at her incredulously. "You don't know?"

"I went to Swan Ridge last night about eleven," she began.

The news just got worse and worse, Tucker concluded. "Am I hearing you right? It happened here, in Trinity Harbor?" he demanded as the ramifications of that slammed into him. He had a dead politician in his jurisdiction and no one knew about it. Dear God, what *had* Mary Elizabeth been thinking?

She nodded at his harsh question. "Yes. I..." She swallowed hard. "I found him. And then I came here."

"Damn it, Mary Elizabeth, have you lost your mind?" Tucker exploded before he could stop himself.

Now the tears were more than she could fight. A steady torrent of them streamed down her cheeks, and Tucker's heart flipped over. He fought the reaction and stayed right where he was.

"I didn't know where else to go, what else to do," she whispered.

She sounded more frightened and helpless than she'd ever sounded in her life, at least around him. Bravado had been ingrained in her from the day she'd arrived to live with her grandfather, a little girl who'd just lost her parents and been left with a man who was a virtual stranger.

"Did you think for one single second about calling the police?" he asked, trying to keep the impatience out of his voice, but not really succeeding.

She stared at him with those huge, watery eyes. "You *are* the police."

Tucker raked a hand through his hair and muttered a curse. Okay, first things first. "You're sure he's dead?"

She nodded, her expression bleak.

He wanted to relent, to reach for her and hold her until those uncharacteristic tears dried up, but he steeled himself against that reaction. He needed to be a cop first, a friend second, at least until he knew more. It might seem cold and unfeeling, but it was the best way to help her.

And to protect himself, he thought bitterly. He couldn't let himself forget for one single second that he'd been burned once by this very same woman. Lust aside, he couldn't let himself trust her, not for a minute. She could have come here just to muddy the hell out of any investigation by the local authorities. Maybe she wanted the state police on the case, for some reason—they would take over if there was any question about whether the sheriff's department had a conflict.

"Did you do it?" he asked, leveling a look straight into her eyes. He would know if she was lying, had always been able to tell, not because she was lousy at it, but because he could see into her soul. He knew her inside out, knew what she was capable of. Or at least he'd once thought he did, and she'd let him believe it, right up until the day she'd announced her engagement to Chandler. He'd missed that one coming.

Now there was a flicker of hurt in her eyes at the question, but then she responded, her tone as cool and impersonal as his. "No."

Tucker held her gaze, but she never once wavered, never even blinked. Something that felt a lot like relief—or maybe more like cautious optimism—rushed through him. "Okay, then, why don't I make some coffee and you can tell me what's going on."

At least that would get her into some clothes and out of this bedroom. Maybe then he'd be able to concentrate, act like a policeman instead of a frustrated ex-lover who wanted to jump the bones of a potential murder suspect.

She seemed surprised. "Just like that?"

He shot her a rueful look. "You knew how I'd react. That's why you're here and not at the station over in Montross."

"That's one of the reasons," she conceded.

"And the others?"

She sighed. "Maybe we'd better save that discussion for another time."

Since Tucker's supposedly rigid self-control had been weakening for the last ten minutes, he knew better than to press her on that. One tiny hint that she was back here because of him, because of something personal, and he'd be in that bed and all over her. It seemed like a really bad idea to go that route, especially if someone had very recently killed her husband.

Which, he noted as he headed for the kitchen to make the coffee, she didn't seem to be all that broken up about. She was scared and shaken, not grief-stricken. He was going to have to ask her about that. Hell, he had so many questions, they might not get out of the house for days.

While the coffee brewed and he waited for Mary Elizabeth to join him, he called the station and told the dispatcher that he wouldn't be in.

"Until later?" she asked, sounding stunned.

"No, I won't be in at all," he told her, understanding her shock. He hadn't taken a day off in weeks, if not longer. Work had been his refuge, especially since Bobby's wedding. He knew that he was on his father's shortlist of projects. Staying out of King's path had seemed like a good idea. "Until further notice, I am officially on leave."

"Well, good," Michele said, rallying. "It's about time. I hope she's gorgeous."

"This is not about a woman," Tucker said very firmly.

"Yeah, right. It's *always* about a woman when a workaholic male finally takes time off out of the blue and in the middle of the week."

"Well, this time it's not," he said, lying through his teeth. The last thing he needed was word getting around that he was holed up at home with a woman. Until he knew what was going on with Mary Elizabeth, he had a hunch no one should know she was even in town, much less hiding out at his place. He told himself he was gathering evidence, not hindering an investigation in which he already knew he would have no formal role. He needed an hour, two at most, to get a firm grip on what the hell was going on. After that, he'd go the official, by-the-book route.

"Have fun," Michele said cheerily, clearly not believing him.

Tucker hung up on her. He looked up to find Mary Elizabeth regarding him with amusement.

"Haven't taken much time off lately?"

"No." He poured two mugs of coffee and handed one to her. He surveyed her from her tousled, subtly frosted brown hair to the pink tips of her perfect toes, noting the shadows in her eyes and the fact that she was wearing another one of his shirts and not much else. "I asked this before, but I think maybe I ought to ask it again—Where are your clothes?"

"In the trash," she said with a shudder.

He stared. "Why? Please don't tell me there's blood all over them."

"Okay, I won't tell you that," she said.

Tucker was forced to admire the stubborn, defiant jut of her chin. He'd leave the issue of the bloody clothes for later. As long as they were in *his* trash, whatever evidence they might provide was safe enough.

"Are you hungry? The cupboard's pretty bare, but I can manage eggs or cereal."

"Nothing for me. You go ahead."

"I had breakfast earlier, while I was waiting for you to wake up." He handed her the coffee, noticed that her hand shook as she accepted it. She was not nearly as composed as she wanted him to believe.

She met his gaze. "Then I guess there's nothing left but to deal with all those questions racing around in your head."

"Just one question for starters," he corrected. "What happened?"

"If only the answer were as simple as the question," she said. She took a sip of coffee, then another, clearly not anxious to get into it. She set the mug on the table; then, as if desperate for something to do with her hands, she picked it up again.

"There are lots of starting places," he told her. "The beginning. The end. Anyplace in between."

Still she hesitated. The color in her cheeks faded and her eyes took on a faraway look, as if she'd retreated to a place where her world had come crashing down.

"I found him in my grandfather's library, in a chair in front of the TV. The news was on. The anchor was talking about some fireman who'd rescued a cat from a roof." She met Tucker's gaze, looking lost. "Funny how I can remember something like that, but I can't remember what it felt like to love my husband."

She sounded so pitiful, looked so fragile, that once again Tucker fought the temptation to reach for her, to offer any sort of comfort. Years of training as a cop told him to sit perfectly still, to wait her out until the whole story had come spilling out. Years of loving her made that almost impossible. His fingers tightened around his own mug of coffee and he waited.

"I thought he was asleep at first, but he was a light sleeper. Usually the slightest sound brought him wide awake. When I spoke to him and he didn't answer, I knew something was wrong. I knew..." Her voice shook, then steadied. "Somehow I just knew that he was dead."

"Did you call for a doctor? An ambulance?"

She shook her head. "I started to. I really did. I walked closer to get the portable phone beside him. That's when I saw it."

"Saw what?"

"The bullet hole." She shuddered. "In his chest. And the blood. There was so much of it. The bullet must have hit an artery or something. I touched him. His eyes were wide open and he was cold." Her gaze sought Tucker's. "That means he'd been dead a long time, right?"

"Probably," Tucker agreed. "Was it a suicide?"

She shook her head. "Definitely not his style."

"That's not an explanation that's going to wash with the police. Any man's style can change if he's feeling desperate enough."

"Okay, then, there was no gun." She regarded Tucker with a helpless look. "That means he had to have been murdered, right? There's no other explanation."

"You're sure about the gun? Think, Mary Elizabeth. Could it have fallen on the floor, slid under the chair?"

Fresh tears welled up in her eyes at his harsh tone. "I looked," she whispered. "I looked everywhere, and then I realized that someone had shot him and that I was going to be the first person everyone thought of. I panicked. All I could think about was coming here and telling you, letting you figure out what happened."

"Why would anyone think you'd done it?" he asked, even though he knew that the spouse was the most likely suspect in a case like this, at least until things had sorted themselves out and more clues had been uncovered.

"Because I was leaving him for good."

Tucker was as shocked by that as he had been by her announcement that Chandler was dead. "You were?"

She nodded. "It was a well-kept secret that we were having problems. I'd moved out of the Richmond house months ago."

"You didn't come back here," he said. He would have known, would have heard if she'd been back at Swan Ridge alone. If nothing else, King would have warned him away from her.

"No, I traveled with a friend. Larry told everyone I was taking an extended vacation, that he'd planned to go along but that pressing matters in Richmond had kept him here."

"Any of that reported in the media, any speculation that you two were splitting?"

"No. His press secretary was very careful. He knew Larry would fire him if so much as a hint leaked out."

"Okay, then, if everything was so hushed up, what makes you think people would suspect you of killing him?"

"I got back to town two days ago. I'd made up my mind to end things. We went to dinner in Richmond, and I told him it was over. We had a really nasty, very public brawl. I had thought it would be better if I told him in public, that he wouldn't risk a scene because of the political ramifications, but I was wrong. He went crazy. He started accusing me of cheating on him."

"Were you?"

"Of course not," she retorted. "I couldn't believe the lies that came pouring out of his mouth. He didn't believe a word he was saying. He was just trying to give me a taste of what it would be like if I went through with a divorce. He wanted me to see that my name would end up being dragged through the mud." She shuddered. "People were staring, starting to whisper. It was obvious that he was already off to a good start at ruining me to save his own political career."

"So there were a lot of witnesses to this scene?" Tucker said. "Anyone you knew?"

"I don't know. I was too humiliated to look around. It was a restaurant that's popular with the movers and shakers in Richmond, so I imagine it's a safe bet that there were people there we knew. Why?"

His mind was already whirling in a dozen different directions. That scene couldn't have done a better job of setting Mary Elizabeth up to take a fall. "Because if one of them had a grudge against your husband and wanted him out of the picture, you had just handed him the perfect opportunity to arrange it and throw greater-than-usual suspicion on you."

She looked shaken by his assessment. "Greater than usual?" she repeated in a whisper.

"You knew you'd be under suspicion," he said. "You said that was why you'd come to me."

"I know. Hearing you say it, though..." Her voice trailed off. "I'm scared, Tucker."

Again, he fought the temptation to offer comfort. She needed real help more than she needed empty reassurances. "Let's get all the facts on the table, okay? How did Chandler end up at Swan Ridge? Did he come back here with you after dinner that night?"

"No. I told him I was coming here and that he should stay in Richmond, that I didn't want him anywhere near me."

"He agreed?"

"He said he'd stay in Richmond and come down here later to pick up a few things. I made it a point to be out of the house all day yesterday to avoid another confrontation."

"Where? Were you with anyone?"

She shook her head. "I took the boat out."

"And stayed on the water till eleven?" he asked skeptically.

"No, till dusk."

"Where do you keep the boat?"

"At the marina at Colonial Beach. I didn't think we should keep it here because of...well, you know."

"Because my brother owns the marina," Tucker said, realizing anew in just how many small ways they had managed to keep their lives from intersecting. "What did you do next?"

"I stopped over there and had dinner."

"Did you see anyone you knew?"

"No. The restaurant was almost empty."

"Would the waitress remember you?"

"I don't know. Maybe. We talked about her daughter and the trouble she's having in school and about standardized testing. I know a lot about it, because it's one of Larry's campaign issues."

"Did you mention Larry? Did she realize he was your husband?"

"No. At least, I don't think so. His name never came up."

"What time did you leave there?"

"Around ten-thirty, maybe a little later."

"Then what?"

"I drove home. When I got to Swan Ridge, his car was in the driveway, so I knew he was inside. I almost turned around and left, but I didn't want to act like a coward, not in my own home."

"So you went in, and that's when you found him?"

"Yes."

"Do you have help working at the house?"

"Just Mrs. Gilman, but she only works when I call her. I hadn't let her know that I was back in town."

"Is that unusual? Wouldn't you normally call her to get the place ready for your return? Maybe to go in and dust, stock the refrigerator, whatever?"

Her face paled. "Yes, but I… I didn't this time."

Tucker could see exactly how suspicious that would look to a jury. "Why?"

"I was too upset after I saw Larry that night. I came straight down here without calling. I just wanted to get away from him, to be alone." Her gaze clashed with his. "It looks bad, doesn't it? Like I didn't want anyone around so I could kill him?"

"That's one interpretation," he agreed. "But your explanation is just as logical. The man had just given you a taste of how vengeful he could be. It's little wonder you wanted to get away from him as fast as possible."

"Will people believe that?"

He met her gaze. "I do."

"Thank you. It's more than I deserve."

"Look, let's get one thing straight," he said bluntly. "I

might hate what you did to me, but I don't think you're capable of murder."

Relief spread across her face, only to fade in an instant. "Tucker, what should I do?"

Because he knew exactly how fast things would spin out of control once word of Chandler's death started to spread, he said, "You need to hire a criminal attorney, someone from Richmond, I think. Do you know any good lawyers down there?"

"The city is crawling with them, though most of the ones I know don't like to get their hands dirty with anything as messy as murder."

Tucker nodded. "Then we should call Powell Knight. If he won't take the case, he'll recommend someone who will."

"Powell Knight who bloodied your nose over me in the fifth grade?" she asked incredulously. "He's a lawyer?"

Tucker chuckled. "He stopped the assaults before law school. He's been walking the straight and narrow for years now. And he owes me. My nose is still crooked."

Liz smiled for the first time since she'd begun talking. "It is not. It just has a little character." She lifted her hand as if to touch it, then drew back with a sigh.

"Why does life have to be so damn complicated?" she asked wistfully.

"Keeps it interesting," Tucker said. He might have said more, but common sense and practicalities kicked in. "Do you have a cell phone with you? Why don't you make that call to Powell? I'll see if I can't rustle up some clothes for you to wear, then I'll call the station and have a deputy meet us at Swan Ridge."

"Do you have a stash of women's clothes around here?" she asked, regarding him with curiosity.

"No. I'll call my sister."

"No," Liz said at once, looking panic-stricken. "Tucker, you can't call Daisy. She already hates my guts for what I did to you. She'll be furious that I dragged you into the middle of this mess."

"I would have been dragged into it one way or another," he said, shrugging off her fears. "It happened in my jurisdiction. If you don't want me to call Daisy, do you have any better ideas?"

She hesitated, her shoulders slumping. It was tantamount to an admission that she'd maintained few real friendships in Trinity Harbor. He almost felt sorry for her, but he steeled himself against the reaction. She'd made her choices. Her grandfather had been an important man in Trinity Harbor. She would have basked in the same respect shown him if she hadn't hurt a Spencer.

"I'll call Daisy, then. You don't even have to see her. And she doesn't need to know what's going on, or even who the clothes are for."

"You shouldn't have to lie to your own sister on my account."

"It's an omission, not a lie."

"I doubt she'll see the distinction once she hears the whole story."

"Let me worry about Daisy. You call Powell."

As soon as she'd gone looking for her cell phone, he called the station and asked for Walker. His brother-in-law had been a homicide detective in Washington before he'd hooked up with Daisy and moved to Trinity Harbor.

He was the best deputy Tucker had, and the only one he wanted on the scene this morning.

"I need you to get over to Swan Ridge," he told Walker. "We've got a problem."

"What kind of problem? That's Larry Chandler's place, isn't it?"

"There's a report that he's dead. I've got his wife here with me. Keep this under your hat until you see what's going on over there. I'll be there right behind you."

"Didn't I hear that you once had a relationship with Liz Chandler?" Walker asked. "Are you sure you ought to be anywhere near the scene?"

"Dammit, Walker, I know better than to take on the case myself. That's why I called you, but I'm not keeping my nose out of it. I want to know everything you find the minute you come up with it. And I want you to do it all by the book, no matter how bad it looks for Mary Elizabeth."

"Do you think she did it?"

"What I think doesn't matter. The only thing that matters is the truth."

"Noble words," Walker said. "But what's your gut telling you?"

"It's your gut that matters. Do your job."

"I'm on my way."

"And try to keep the media from finding out anything, at least until we have a fix on what went on over there."

"Done," Walker promised.

Tucker placed his next call to his sister. "I need some clothes over here—a pair of your jeans, a T-shirt, some underwear, some shoes. And I need it without a lot of questions."

"But—"

"No questions, Daisy. Please, just this once, help me out without giving me the third degree."

"Third degrees are your business," she said with an indignant huff. "Okay, I'll bring everything over there. Want me to leave it in a plain brown bag on the front porch and slink away?"

"Actually that's not a bad idea."

"Fat chance."

"Daisy," he warned.

"Okay, okay, I've got it. Bring the clothes, leave the questions back home."

"Thank you."

"But you'll owe me," she told him.

"I usually do."

As soon as he got off the phone, he retrieved a clean garbage bag and went looking in his trash for Mary Elizabeth's bloodied clothes. She hadn't exactly tried to conceal them. They were right on top, in plain view. He took that as a good sign. Less positive was the fact that there was a lot of blood, more than a person would get checking a man's pulse. Was there as much as if she'd shot her husband at close range, maybe even struggled with him as he bled? Tucker didn't even want to speculate on that. He'd leave it to the experts.

He turned and saw Mary Elizabeth regarding him uneasily. Her gaze shifted to the trash bag, then back to his face.

"Tucker?"

He met her gaze. "What?"

"Are you going to arrest me?"

"I won't even be involved in the decision," he told her.

Something that looked like panic flickered in her eyes. "Why not?"

"Because by coming here, and because we have a past history, you've made sure I have to take myself off the case."

"But—"

He cut her off. "That's the way it has to be, Mary Elizabeth. You know that. I've got my best deputy heading over to Swan Ridge right now."

"Oh, God," she whispered. "What have I done?"

Tucker's blood ran cold. "Why do you say that?"

"I wanted you to handle this."

The icy fist kept a firm grip on his insides. "Because you thought I'd protect you?"

"No. Because I trust you."

Tucker wanted desperately to believe that's all it was, that she hadn't come here hoping to use their past to keep him from delving too deeply into the circumstances surrounding Chandler's death.

"I hope you're telling me the truth."

There was genuine hurt in her eyes when she met his gaze. "I've never lied to you. *Never.*"

"I think maybe that's open to interpretation," he said quietly. "But what's done is done. All I care about is whether you're being honest now."

"I am. I swear it."

He nodded. "Then we'll deal with the rest as it comes."

"Together?"

He thought of the sensible reply and the one that came from his heart. "Together," he agreed.

All he could do was pray that he wouldn't live to regret it.

3

Tucker had made one serious miscalculation when he'd called Daisy. He'd forgotten that Mary Elizabeth's very distinctive car—a Jaguar with vanity plates he'd sometimes spotted driving too fast on the county's back roads—had to be parked somewhere in the vicinity. He hadn't noticed it the night before, but it was a sure bet she hadn't walked to his house from Swan Ridge.

He realized his mistake when his sister came barreling into the kitchen like an avenging angel and tossed a bagful of clothes straight at him. The heavy bag caught him right in the gut. She always had had a great arm, to say nothing of an amazing protective streak when it came to him and Bobby.

"I sincerely hope those clothes are not for Mary Elizabeth," she said, staring him down.

"What makes you think they are?" he replied defensively.

"Because that's her fancy car sitting in plain view in front of your house. I'm not stupid, Tucker. Neither is anyone else in this town." She regarded him with a worried frown. "I hope to heaven you know what you're doing."

"I do," he said, tucking a hand under her elbow and steering her straight toward the door without wasting time on the explanation she was so obviously hoping for. "Thanks for coming over here so quickly."

"Why does a woman with a designer wardrobe need my clothes?" Daisy inquired testily. "You two going somewhere incognito? I hate to tell you this, but it will take more than a change of clothes to pull that off."

Tucker sighed. "No questions, remember?"

"The woman broke your heart," his sister said fiercely. "Have you forgotten that?"

"Not for a minute."

"If you say so," she said, her doubt plain. "In my experience, men can push an amazing amount of past history out of their heads when they start thinking with another part of their anatomy."

He scowled at her. "Don't make me sorry that I turned to you for help this morning."

After an instant's hesitation, she reached up and kissed him on the cheek. "And don't make me sorry I gave it. I love you."

"You, too, kid."

He watched as she walked to her car, shot a disparaging look toward Mary Elizabeth's sports car, then drove off with a distracted wave in his direction.

"Will she go straight to your father?" Mary Elizabeth asked, coming up behind him.

"No," he said with confidence. "Daisy never tattles."

Mary Elizabeth looked skeptical. "That's not the way I remember it. She was the first one to run to King when she realized you and I were having secret meetings out behind the barn."

"Don't go there. That was a lifetime ago." And he didn't want to be dragged down memory lane. The present was complicated enough without it.

Tucker handed her the clothes. "We need to get moving."

"I'll hurry," she said at once.

True to her word, she was back in minutes. Without makeup and with her hair swept into a loose ponytail held up by what looked like one of his handkerchiefs, she looked a whole lot more like the girl he remembered than the sophisticated woman she'd become. The jeans hung loosely on her, and she'd had to roll up the cuffs. She'd tucked in the bright yellow T-shirt, then added one of his belts around her narrow waist. Somehow she managed to make the ill-fitting outfit look stylish.

He studied her pale complexion and worried eyes. "This is going to get rough. Will you be okay?"

"I'll manage," she said stoically. "Let's get this over with."

The drive to Swan Ridge took less than twenty minutes. Mary Elizabeth grew noticeably more tense as he turned through the open wrought-iron gate and onto the cedar-lined drive. Bright green soybean fields spread east and west as far as the eye could see. Up ahead, just around the first curve in the drive, Tucker knew he would catch his first glimpse of the three-story brick house with its jutting wings and majestic sweep of steps. It always reminded him of Stratford Hall, the historic home of the Lees not too far up the road. Same period, same style, only on a slightly smaller scale.

The landscaped grounds were filled with holly trees,

azaleas, towering oaks, magnolias and the sweet, lingering scent of honeysuckle that had apparently escaped the notice of the gardener. The pink, purple and deep red crepe myrtles were just coming into bloom as July edged toward August. In the back, he knew, there was a formal boxwood maze, where he and Mary Elizabeth had stolen many a kiss far from her grandfather's watchful eye.

"It hasn't changed much," he said, glancing at her out of the corner of his eye.

Her hands were clutched tightly together in her lap. She jerked her gaze from the sight of the sheriff's cruiser in front of the house and looked at him.

"Larry loved this house as much as my grandfather did. He insisted we do nothing to change it. He even hired someone to run the soybean operation. When one of the trees got hit by lightning, he brought in a full-grown tree to replace it. It cost a fortune, but he said it was worth every penny." She sighed heavily. "Sometimes I wonder if he cared more about losing all this than he did about losing me."

Since that very same thought had crossed Tucker's mind, he couldn't bring himself to argue with her. He caught the flicker of hurt in her eyes when he didn't utter some platitude denying her speculation.

"You didn't know him," she said stiffly, defending her husband despite Tucker's silence.

"No, but you did, and you're the one who said it, Mary Elizabeth," he reminded her, hitting the brakes too hard and jerking the car to a stop in front of the house. "I knew nothing about Chandler or your marriage. I made it a point to keep it that way."

"And now I've dragged you into the middle of it," she said with regret. "I'm sorry."

"I'm not in the middle. From this moment on, I'm on the sidelines."

She winced at the reminder. "Tell me about the deputy who will handle it."

"His name's Walker Ames. He's good. He was a homicide detective in Washington up until a couple of years ago. He won't miss anything."

"But..." She regarded him with dismay. "Isn't he Daisy's husband?"

"That won't matter," Tucker said with conviction even as she turned to stare out the window. He tucked a hand under her chin and forced her to face him. "It will be okay. I promise. You want the best person available on this, and that's Walker. If there's so much as a hint that he's not being scrupulously impartial, whatever the reason for it, I can call in the state police and turn the whole investigation over to them. I can do that now, if you'd prefer, if you think my department can't give you a fair shake."

"I want to believe you know what you're doing, but I'm scared," she admitted.

"You came to me because you trusted me, right? Then listen to what I'm saying," Tucker told her. "If you're not guilty, then you have nothing to fear."

"*If?* I'm not guilty of anything except wanting a divorce," she declared fiercely.

"And I believe that," Tucker reiterated.

"Do you? Do you really?" she asked, her voice escalating in near hysteria. "Or did you bring someone else in to handle this just so you won't have to be the one to slap the handcuffs on me?"

Before he could respond, she was out of the car and running. Tucker debated going after her, but decided against it. She wouldn't go far. If she'd wanted to take off because she was guilty, she would have done it without ever setting foot in his house. She could have been halfway to Europe or South America before anyone even realized her husband was missing, much less dead. She certainly had the resources to flee to anywhere in the world she wanted to go.

Her accusation that he didn't believe in her stuck in his craw. Surely she didn't believe that. She'd just lashed out at him because her nerves were shot and he was handy.

But what if he was wrong? What if he'd just given her a convenient excuse to take off? He watched as she fled around the side of the house and headed for the river. He found that oddly reassuring. Unless things had changed, there was an old swing hanging from a tree at the edge of the beach. She'd always said that soaring into the sky in that swing was like flying and that the air there made thinking easier. That was where he'd find her when the time came to go looking.

Until then, he needed to go inside, talk to Walker and find out just how much trouble Mary Elizabeth was really in.

King strolled into Earlene's and headed for his usual booth in the back. He'd only made it halfway when he spotted Frances Jackson sitting all alone at the counter, nursing a cup of coffee, her expression glum. He slid onto the stool next to her.

"Does that frown you're wearing have anything to do with me?" he inquired.

Ever since she'd gone off to some spa and gotten herself all fixed up with a new hairdo and a new svelte figure, they'd been dancing around each other like a couple of testy old bears. No matter what he did, he couldn't seem to get things between them back on track.

Now she barely spared him a glance. "Not everything is about you."

"These days, seems like nothing is," he shot back before he could stop himself. "You want me to stop bothering you, Frances? Is that it?"

This time she swivelled her stool around and faced him fully. "Bothering me? When was the last time you asked me to go out? When was the last time you invited me to Sunday dinner with your family? Ever since I got back to town and Bobby got married, you've been all but ignoring me."

"Ignoring you? I'm here now, aren't I?"

She gave him a pitying look. "King Spencer, you are the densest man on God's green earth. Why I ever thought for a single minute that you and I could get along is beyond me. Seems like our fate was sealed years ago when I beat you in that spelling bee and you resented me like crazy. What's been happening between us the last couple of years was apparently just some kind of midlife foolishness."

King bristled. "We'd been getting along just fine, at least until you got some crazy notion in your head about trying to take ten years off your looks."

"You object to me wanting to look nice?" she inquired.

Her tone was only mildly curious, but King spotted the minefield in the nick of time. "Of course not, but I thought you looked just fine before. You're a handsome woman, Frances. Always were."

He'd always approved of a woman with a little meat on her bones, a woman who wasn't afraid to look her age. This new, improved Frances had taken him aback. He was pretty sure the changes were meant to impress somebody else, since things between the two of them were decidedly cooler now than they had been. Just the thought of Frances with another man was enough to rile him, but it seemed like that was the direction things were headed unless he could figure out what was eating at her or who was stealing her attention.

He regarded her with impatience. "Don't know why you couldn't see that I found you attractive. Didn't I make it plain often enough?"

She actually had the audacity to laugh at that. "King, for a normally blunt, plainspoken man, when it comes to you and me, you have always had an amazing knack for reticence."

King couldn't have been more shocked if she'd accused him of cheating on her. "I let you know how I felt. You spent Sundays with the family. You came to Daisy's wedding with me and to Bobby's. I took you to bingo, for goodness' sakes. What man does all that if he doesn't have feelings for a woman? I even broached the subject of taking things to another level, but you brushed me off, if I recall correctly."

She nodded, her expression thoughtful. "Yes, I can see how going to a few bingo games would be a dead giveaway. I'll have to think about that," she said, taking a dollar out of her purse and leaving it on the counter. She snapped her purse shut, then slid off the stool and gave him an unreadable look. "I surely will think about it."

She was about to walk away, when King blurted, "Have dinner with me tonight, Frances. Let's talk this thing through. It's not the kind of thing we can discuss with all these busybodies listening in." He scowled in the direction of the owner. "Earlene's already gotten an earful."

King's breath lodged in his throat as he waited for Frances to respond. For a minute, he thought she actually might refuse him. And maybe that was exactly what he deserved for being such a horse's behind for all these months now. Daisy and Bobby had certainly told him so often enough. Even Tucker, who tended to avoid the topic of emotional entanglements like the plague, had put in his two cents on his father's love life.

"Where?" she said at last.

King's heart finally resumed a normal rhythm. "You name the place."

"The marina," she said at once.

"But—" He wisely cut himself off before he could protest that Bobby would spend the entire evening hovering over them and then reporting every last word they said to the rest of the family. Clearly that was exactly what Frances had in mind. She knew she had allies in his kids, and she intended to make the most of that. "The marina will be just fine. I'll pick you up at seven."

"Six-thirty will be better. We have a lot to discuss." She leveled a look straight into his eyes, one of those piercing gazes that served her well as a county social worker. "And for once, it won't be about your children's love lives. It will be about ours."

"Whatever you say," King said meekly.

Obviously Frances had lost patience. It was put up or shut up time. Maybe, if he had a few spare minutes, he'd wander past a jewelry store and see if there was anything there that would suit her. In his experience, jewelry had a way of saying what mere words couldn't express.

And, he thought with a sigh, with any luck, she wouldn't throw it right back in his face.

Liz ran until she was out of breath. It was no surprise to her that she'd ended up on the banks of the river. It was where she'd always come when she had things to sort through—here or to Tucker. From the time she'd come to live with her grandfather after her parents' deaths in an avalanche on an Alpine ski slope, Tucker had been her sounding board, always listening without judging. He'd been the best companion a lonely girl could have wished for. He'd been her champion when she'd started classes at the tight-knit Trinity Harbor school. He'd asked her to play on his summer baseball team and dared anyone to challenge the selection. For a tomboy like Liz, that had been the ultimate compliment a boy two years older could have paid her. Tucker had been her hero from the day they'd met on the school playground because he'd let her fight her own battles, hanging back and ready to help only if she asked for it.

Times had changed. She'd seen hints of judgment in his eyes more than once this morning, even when he'd managed to say all the right things. How could she blame him, though? She was lucky he hadn't just tossed her out without listening to a single word she'd said.

She'd also noted what he hadn't asked, how careful he'd been to avoid discussing the state of her marriage, but the questions were hanging in the air between them. She'd acknowledged her plans to divorce her husband but said nothing about her reasons. Sooner or later Tucker—or his deputy—was going to want to know what they were. She was going to have to brace herself for the humiliation of admitting that she'd never been enough for Larry, that he'd taken lovers within weeks of the wedding, perhaps even sooner.

Would the police see that as a motive for murder? she wondered. Could she make them see that it would be one only if she still cared, only if she hadn't been worn out from a one-sided fight to save her marriage?

She picked her way along an overgrown path that would have horrified Larry—if he'd ever bothered to walk this far. Fortunately he'd been satisfied to survey his domain from the library windows or the brick terrace. He hadn't known about Liz's secret hiding place, little more than a shady patch of grass beneath a giant oak with a weathered swing dangling by thick ropes from a low branch. The river lapped gently at the shore here, glistening in the midmorning sun.

She sat on that swing now and pushed off idly, letting her thoughts wander. If Tucker was right, if someone had witnessed her scene with Larry and used it as a perfect cover for murder, who could it have been? A political enemy? A spurned lover? An outraged husband? There were plenty of each. Larry's passions tended to draw emotional extremes. He'd fielded his share of threats, but had refused to take any of them seriously. Obviously he'd miscalculated.

There were anonymous letters, though, and tapes of threatening phone messages, all of the sort that many politicians received when they stirred up their constituents. Larry had dismissed them, but he'd been prudent enough to save them just in case one was ever acted on. She could provide them all to the police, which was what she needed to be doing now, not sitting down here hiding out and sulking over the doubts she'd seen in Tucker's eyes. No one had a higher stake in proving her innocence than she did, not even Tucker.

Slowly she climbed the hill back to the house, aware that Tucker was waiting on the terrace, his expression inscrutable, his eyes shaded by mirrored aviator sunglasses as he watched her approach.

"Feel better?" he asked when she neared.

"Not really. I guess the soothing effects of my hideout don't extend to murder." She regarded him curiously. "I'm surprised you didn't come after me to make sure I wasn't taking off."

"The thought never crossed my mind."

"Really?"

"Really." He regarded her worriedly. "Mary Elizabeth, this is going to get out of hand really fast. Walker's had to call the forensics team and get the local medical examiner in here. Once Doc Jones heads out this way, the media won't be far behind. You ready to face that?"

"Can't we leave?" She shook her head and resolutely squared her shoulders. "Never mind. Of course we can't. Can I go inside, put on something more appropriate?"

"No. It's a crime scene."

"Then I guess this will have to do," she said, smoothing down Daisy's ill-fitting jeans. "Your sister's going to be thrilled to see her clothes on TV. She'll probably burn them."

"Or give them away," he agreed.

Then, for the first time since she'd awakened to find

him staring at her, he took her hand in his and gave it a squeeze. The gesture gave her the strength to face whatever was ahead.

"You stay put," he said. "You should be safe enough out here for a time. I'll get you something to drink and be right back. Powell ought to be here soon, too."

She nodded and watched him go. She could do this, she told herself. She'd faced the media a thousand times in the last six years. She was good at it, a natural at spinning a story. She would make Larry proud of her one last time.

An hour later, sheriff's deputies and media were swarming all over the place. Liz stood by and tried very hard to distance herself from the reason for their presence. She didn't want to think too much about the scene inside her home, about Larry—a man she had once loved with all her heart—being dead, about the vicious words he'd hurled at her the last time they'd talked. That exchange would live with her forever. It was a side of her husband she'd never seen before, a side that was ruthless and manipulative.

He'd made it seem as if he'd been devastated by her request for a divorce, when nothing could have been further from the truth. They'd both known for a long time that the marriage was a shell of what it should have been. There had been no passion for years now. There were no kids to distract from the fact that they had nothing in common. Larry had wanted her for her name and connections, and for Swan Ridge, second only to King Spencer's Cedar Hill in terms of a prestigious address in the county.

Even the date of their wedding had been calculated for maximum political benefit, just when the campaign season was heating up. Somehow she had missed that when he'd been courting her with lavish gifts and whispered words of love, when they'd talked far into the night sharing their idealistic dreams for a better world that together they could help to shape. She'd been blinded by his charm and his rhetoric. Somehow she had completely missed the shallowness beneath it.

Her first clue that she'd been conned had been the lover she'd found in his hotel room when she'd unexpectedly joined him on the campaign trail. They'd been married for less than two months at the time. Larry had apologized, said the relationship was over, but the woman hadn't accepted it yet. He'd sworn it would never happen again, and bought Liz a diamond and amethyst necklace he'd told her reminded him of the sparkle in her eyes. Maybe if he'd exchanged the extravagant necklace for a sincere apology, she would have believed him.

Even so, Liz had been determined to make the marriage work. She'd dutifully appeared by his side at every chicken dinner, every small-town parade, every campaign stop. The year of finishing school her grandfather had insisted on had made her poised. Early years in Europe with parents who had too much money and too many interests to pay attention to a little girl had taught her to fend for herself and never let them see how much their neglect hurt. For the rest of the campaign, she had smiled despite the torment.

And on the day after the hard-won election victory, she had insisted Larry fire the campaign manager he'd slept with, denying the woman the prominent place on his staff she had clearly expected.

"She goes, or I will leave you now and tell the whole world why," she had threatened him quietly as he savored the headlines in the local paper. She had grown up over the course of the campaign. Now it was time he did the same.

It had been three months before he'd taken another lover. Another six before he traded that one in. Liz had known about most, if not all, of them, but with each one her will to fight had lessened. Her respect for her husband had vanished, and with it, the last remnants of her love. Her hopes and dreams had faded, including the plans for a family. Even if she hadn't decided against bringing children into such a marriage, Larry's belatedly announced timetable would have precluded it. He wanted his career on a firm footing before any children kept her from devoting her full attention to him, he had told her when she'd dared to broach the subject of starting the family they'd once talked about.

That coldly calculated timetable of his had been yet another reminder that he wasn't the man she'd thought him to be. Even so, it had taken her a long time—too long—to admit defeat.

Now, though, as she watched her husband's shrouded body being removed from their house, she knew the humiliation was finally over.

Or was it? Unless Tucker could find the evidence to save her, even in death Larry Chandler was going to find one more way to rip her life to shreds.

4

Tucker filled a glass with water and ice, then stood staring out the kitchen window at Mary Elizabeth. What had she been through in the last six years? What had driven her to want to put an end to her golden marriage? Had it been bad enough that she'd been driven to take drastic measures? Had she believed, even for an instant, that divorce wouldn't end whatever hell Chandler was putting her through?

The instant the thought crossed his mind, he banished it. He would not let himself consider for one second the possibility that she was guilty of murder. Every person deserved a presumption of innocence, but it was easier for him to get to that point with Mary Elizabeth. Past history, deep feelings, gut instinct all intertwined to assure that he saw her only in the most positive light.

Which was why he'd turned the case over to Walker from the get-go. Tucker didn't have a prayer of maintaining objectivity. He'd blindly rushed to her defense in a math class cheating scandal in tenth grade. He'd done it again on countless other occasions when her grandfather had found fault with one thing or another that she'd done. Each and every time Tucker had believed with everything in him that Mary Elizabeth was the innocent victim. Even after she'd turned her back on him years ago, he believed in her now.

How stupid was that? he wondered cynically. But breaking off a relationship was a far cry from murder. Things would have to be beyond desperate for a strong, deeply moral person to cross that kind of line.

Walker found him where he remained standing at the window, the glass of water still clutched in his hand, continuing to ponder whether things had gotten that desperate for Mary Elizabeth.

"You okay?" his brother-in-law asked.

"I've been better."

"How's she doing?"

"She's a strong woman," Tucker said.

"No hysterics? No grief?" Walker asked.

"She's upset, not distraught," Tucker conceded tightly. "The marriage was on the rocks." He scowled at Walker's immediate show of interest. "That doesn't mean she wanted him dead."

"What about money? That's always a motive for opting for murder over divorce."

"She had plenty of her own."

"You sure about that? It costs a lot to maintain a place like this."

"And she inherited more than enough from her grandfather. The Swans might have been relative latecomers to this area, but they were descended from English aristocracy. The first family member arrived here at the beginning of the eighteenth century, maybe a decade or two after the Spencers. William Swan had a head for business. So did every male descendent who came after, at least until Mary Elizabeth's father. He was better at throwing money around than making it. He and her mother were spending the winter skiing in Switzerland when they died in an avalanche. That's when Mary Elizabeth came here to live with her grandfather. It was the first time she'd seen him since she was a toddler. She barely even remembered him, but he took her in and devoted himself to raising her. He left her everything he had."

"Thanks for the history lesson, but it doesn't have much to do with what went on here last night," Walker pointed out.

Tucker frowned. "Fine. Ignore the past and concentrate on the evidence. What have you got?"

"The forensics guys are working in there now. No signs of a struggle. Nothing out of place. We'll have to ask Mrs. Chandler if anything's missing, but it looks as if whoever did it had only one thing on his—or her—mind, killing Chandler and getting away."

"I strolled around outside. I didn't spot any signs of forced entry," Tucker said. "How about you?"

"None I could see, either."

"Then he let the killer in," Tucker concluded.

"Or the killer had a key," Walker suggested with a pointed look outside where Mary Elizabeth remained, shoulders slumped and sunshine glinting on her hair.

"She has an alibi," Tucker reminded him.

"You checked it out?"

"No, but you will, and it will hold up. I'd bet my badge on it."

Walker regarded him evenly. "What hours does the alibi cover?"

"All day yesterday, till around eleven last night. That's when she found him."

"And after that?"

"She came straight to my place."

"You know that how?" Walker countered. "You were on duty."

"She told me," he began, then faltered, irritated by his own gullibility. "Damn."

"Exactly," Walker said sympathetically. "You don't know for sure what time she got to your place. You don't know for sure what time Chandler was shot. There's a lot of wiggle room in there."

Tucker didn't want to agree with Walker, but he was forced to concede that Mary Elizabeth's alibi wasn't as airtight as he'd hoped. Now that he thought about it, even her alibi of being on the river all day long meant nothing. There was a very large dock at the edge of the property. She could have brought the boat around here from the marina, slipped inside, shot her husband and gone back to Colonial Beach without anyone being the wiser. Hell and damn!

He met Walker's gaze. "You're going to need to ask some questions over at the marina at the beach. She said she was out in her boat yesterday. Someone probably gassed it up, saw her on the docks, something that will confirm her story."

Walker's gaze shot to the dock in the distance. "Dammit, Tucker, who's going to be able to say she didn't make a beeline straight over here?"

"Other boaters," Tucker countered, thankful he'd grasped the same point in time to come up with a plausible counterargument. "This time of year the river's

crawling with them, and not just on the weekends. If you don't want to take the time to track them down, I will."

"You can't," Walker shot back. "Anything you come up with will be suspect, and you know it."

"Why? She and I have a lot of past history, that's true, but a lot of it's bad. Most people around here would believe I have more reasons to want to find her guilty than innocent."

"Maybe if you were a different kind of man," Walker agreed. "But you're a decent guy, and your feelings for people run deep. If you loved her once, that hasn't just disappeared." He leveled a penetrating look straight into Tucker's eyes. "Has it?"

"My feelings don't have a damn thing to do with anything," he said tightly. "You handle this case by the book. That's all I'm asking. If Mary Elizabeth is guilty, if the evidence points to her, I won't stand in your way. But if there's evidence that exonerates her, I expect you to find that, too."

"And you believe she is innocent, don't you?"

Tucker hated his slight and very telling hesitation. "I believe in her, yes."

"Why? Because you want to?"

"Partly that," he conceded, forcing himself to be honest with Walker and with himself. "But mostly because she came to me. Why would she do that if she were guilty?"

"Who better to have in your corner than the sheriff?" Walker said bluntly.

Tucker started to argue, but the words died on his lips. Not once since he'd joined the sheriff's department had anyone had any reason to doubt his credibility or his integrity. Now, in a matter of hours, anything com-

ing out of his mouth regarding this case was going to be considered suspect. Once again, Mary Elizabeth had managed to twist his life inside out.

"I'm going outside," he said curtly. "Let me know what's happening."

"I'm going to have to talk to her sooner or later," Walker reminded him.

Tucker nodded. "She'll be here whenever you're ready."

"She got a lawyer?"

"He's on his way," Tucker said, grateful that she'd insisted that Powell drive straight up from Richmond, rather than waiting. On that score, she'd been thinking more clearly than he had. He'd thought it would be enough to have Powell on standby. Tucker hadn't seriously believed that Mary Elizabeth would be a suspect for much more than a minute, because his own feelings had gotten in the way. He'd wanted to believe that the real murderer would be so obvious that she'd be cleared at once. Was that the first of many errors in judgment he was likely to make? Or was the first not tossing her out on her lovely backside when he'd first found her in his bed?

Walker nodded. "We'll talk when he gets here, then. I'm trying to put together some sort of statement for the media. They're gathering like vultures on the front lawn. You want to look it over?"

"No."

"They're going to ask why you're not involved. What should I tell them?"

"The truth, that Mrs. Chandler and I are old friends and that I wanted this case handled by someone with more objectivity and homicide experience than I have."

"We could leave out the issue of objectivity," Walker said. "It'll be opening a whole can of worms that might be best left shut tight."

"The information is out there. Someone will open it sooner or later," Tucker replied. "It'll be better to be up-front about it."

"Whatever you say."

"Walker?"

"What?"

"Don't do her any favors, but don't try to railroad her, either."

His deputy regarded him with annoyance. "You didn't need to tell me that. I know how to do my job."

"I didn't say that to insult you," Tucker told him. "Under most circumstances, I'd never feel the need to say such a thing, but you're going to hear a lot of things before this is over with, not all of them favorable to Mary Elizabeth. Daisy and my father hate her guts, and that's just for starters."

"What about Bobby?"

Tucker gave a rueful chuckle. "You know my brother. He's a laid-back kind of a guy. It would take a lot of energy for him to hate anybody, so he stays neutral. He takes his cues from me."

"And you don't hate her?"

Tucker thought about just how complicated his feelings for Liz Chandler were, then sighed. "No," he admitted. "I don't hate her." Far from it.

"Anybody else in town going to be anxious to start a lynch mob besides your father and my wife?"

"I'll have to think about that one. In the meantime, try not to let my involvement muddy the investigative waters."

"Just how involved do you intend to be?"

"After we get through today, I'm hoping I can turn my back and walk away and leave the whole mess in your capable hands."

Walker snorted. "Oh, yeah. I'll be counting on that. Tucker Spencer walking away from a lady in distress." He shook his head. "Never going to happen, pal."

Tucker watched Walker leave the room, then glanced back at the woman waiting for him on the terrace. Her vulnerability reached out and tugged at his heart. He hoped to hell Walker was wrong. He needed to run—not walk—away from this mess as fast as he possibly could.

Powell Knight hadn't changed all that much, Liz noted when he walked around the side of the house. He still had the same easy confidence, the same arrogant polish, the same evidence of expensive taste he'd had way back in high school. Only the leather briefcase in his hand and the cell phone plastered to his ear were new additions.

"Yeah, yeah, yeah," he was muttering as he walked toward her. "Just tell your client that we're playing hardball and it will be a cold day in hell before he ever sees one single dime of that money." He snapped the phone shut, then gave Liz a thorough once-over. A smile broke across his face. "Damn, Mary Elizabeth, you're even prettier than you are in all those pictures I see in the Richmond papers. How did I ever let you get away?"

He reached for her and twirled her around until she was breathless.

"Put me down, you idiot," she said, laughing despite the somber occasion and the trouble that was heading her way in the form of an interrogation with Tucker's top deputy.

Powell shot a grin at Tucker. "What's the deal? You're not snatching her out of my arms, leaping to her defense? Not that long ago you'd have punched me out by now."

"Mary Elizabeth can take care of herself," Tucker said. "If I were you, I'd get out of range of her knee unless you want to hobble inside looking a little less than your best for this interview with the police."

Powell put her down and gingerly stepped away. "No interviews, not until she and I have had a chance to talk." He shot a pointed look at Tucker. "Alone."

"He can stay," Liz said at once.

Powell immediately shook his head. "No way, sweetcakes. He's a cop. And in this instance, until you're completely in the clear, the cops are not your friends."

"It's okay, Mary Elizabeth. He's right. I'll go," Tucker said. He scowled at Powell. "For the record, though, I'm not handling this investigation. I've already taken myself off of it."

"Good to know, but I still don't want her blabbing any secrets to you. You're liable to get the idea that you're duty-bound to repeat them to whoever is in charge of the case."

Tucker looked as if he might want to argue the point, but he kept his mouth clamped shut and walked away.

"He wouldn't do that," Liz told her old friend.

"Your old lover might not do it, but you never can tell about the sheriff. Since they're one and the same, I'd rather not take any chances." Powell tucked a finger under her chin. "You doing okay?"

"I've had better days," she said truthfully.

"I can imagine. Tell me what happened," the attorney said. "Beginning to end."

"That could take a long time. I'm not sure how patient Walker Ames is likely to be."

"He'll wait," Powell said confidently. "He doesn't have any choice."

Even so, Liz gave him the condensed version of her marriage. She wasn't surprised to see the shock that registered on Powell's face. She and Larry had done a great job of covering the chasm in their relationship, particularly in Richmond.

"It all came to a head this week." She repeated what she'd told Tucker about the fight they'd had, about her retreat to Swan Ridge, about spending the day on her boat, and about going home to find Larry's body. Powell took copious notes, nodding occasionally but otherwise keeping his expression bland and his own comments to a minimum.

"I didn't do it," she said, because she felt she had to get it on the record with him.

"Doesn't matter," he said at once. "They're not likely to come up with anything more than circumstantial evidence. We can beat it."

Liz felt a shudder of revulsion. "You're not listening to me, Powell—I…did…not…do…it. If you don't believe that, then I don't want you to represent me."

His gaze shot up then and clashed with hers. Eventually, he nodded. "Okay, then. Let's make sure that nobody thinks otherwise for a single second. There's a lot of media out front. I'll get them around here."

"Before I've talked to the police?"

"Preemptive strike," he said succinctly. "We get our message out before they do."

That little chill of dismay ran through her again. "This is all a game to you, isn't it?"

"It's a challenge, a battle of wits," he conceded with a disturbing glint of anticipation in his eyes.

"Same thing. I don't like it."

"Sweetcakes, when you're in this kind of a jam, you need somebody on your side who understands the rules. You don't have to love me. You don't even have to like me. You just have to let me do my job. I am very, very good at it."

A part of Liz knew he was right. The law and politics had a lot in common. Much of the game was about perception. If she was forthcoming with the public, through the media, she could win the first round. She hated it, but it was a fact of life. And the last few years had taught her to be a pragmatist.

But, she vowed, once this was over, she would never again compromise her own beliefs for the sake of expediency. She was going to find the decent, caring woman she'd once been and fit back inside that skin.

Powell regarded her expectantly. "What's it going to be?"

"Get the reporters," she said quietly. "But before you ask, you can forget the fake tears for the benefit of the cameras."

"You'll have more credibility if you come across as a grieving widow."

"I'll have more credibility if I tell the truth," she said adamantly.

"Fine. Do it your way. But leave out the stuff about the affairs. That needs to come from somebody else. It'll make you look more sympathetic."

Liz glanced toward the house and spotted Tucker

watching her from inside. He was going to be furious about this impromptu news conference Powell was about to call. For a moment, the prospect of his disapproval was almost enough to make her call it off, but she was paying Powell for his expertise. And Tucker himself was the one who'd suggested she call him. Surely he knew what a barracuda Powell was. She had to follow the attorney's advice, even if the next few minutes tore her apart inside.

"I know what to do," she said tightly. "Let's just get this over with."

Powell nodded, punched in a number on his cell phone and spoke to someone in a low voice. Within minutes, an entire herd of reporters rounded the side of the house. Tucker had clearly spotted them, because he came charging out the door with a man who had to be Walker Ames right on his heels. Before they could get close enough, Powell had gestured for quiet and began making a statement.

"This is a very sad occasion for this county, the entire Northern Neck of Virginia and the state," Powell intoned solemnly. "We have just learned that Delegate Lawrence Chandler has been found dead in his home, the apparent victim of foul play. As I'm sure you can imagine, his wife is in shock, but I have persuaded her to say a few words. There will be no questions at this time, though I am sure that the investigating officer from the sheriff's office will speak to you when we're through and fill you in on what they have so far."

Liz risked a glance at Walker Ames, saw the barely restrained fury on his face. She could just imagine what he'd have to say when she was finished. She didn't dare look at Tucker.

Liz stepped forward, determined that what she would say now would be only the truth, even if only half the truth. She would not be the one to tarnish her husband's reputation. She summoned her memories of Larry's best qualities.

"The people have lost an ardent champion today," she began softly. "My husband was a dedicated public servant who believed fervently in his ideals. He was a great delegate. He would have made a wonderful governor. This is a senseless tragedy, and I assure all of you that I will not rest until the person responsible has been brought to justice."

She allowed her gaze to meet Walker's, to hold it without blinking. "I am confident that Deputy Ames, who is handling the case, will bring it to a rapid conclusion, for Larry's sake and for the sake of all of us who loved him."

She turned then and walked directly to the deputy. "I'll answer your questions now."

"You'd better believe it," he said tersely. "Inside."

"You don't want to make a statement to the media first?" she asked, surprised that he would let the opportunity to counteract her statement pass by.

He gave her a wry look. "I think the reporters have plenty to chew on for the moment. That was a nice performance. I imagine your lawyer put you up to it."

"I make my own decisions, Deputy."

Something that might have been respect flickered in his eyes for just an instant. "I'm glad to see that you believe in being accountable for your actions."

"Always."

He gestured toward a chair at her kitchen table. It was the first time in years Liz had sat there. Larry had frowned on sitting down to eat in the kitchen. He'd said it was common. In so doing, he'd managed to deprive Liz of a habit begun in childhood, when she'd eaten with the housekeeper more evenings than not. She'd been happier in this room than anywhere else in the drafty old house. It had reminded her of the Spencers' home, where the family tended to congregate in the kitchen, both while Mrs. Spencer was alive and after, when Daisy had been struggling to make everything seem exactly the same despite their terrible loss.

Liz had been accepted as a part of the family back then. Tucker had seen to that. Even Daisy had liked her, had treated her like a sister.

Remembering all that, Liz felt sadder, but stronger somehow. She sat at the scarred oak table, then met Deputy Ames's gaze. "Whenever you're ready," she told him just as Powell came charging through the door. Before he could speak, she waved him to a seat in the background. "It's okay. We're just getting started."

"Okay, Mrs. Chandler, let's make it simple. Why don't you tell me exactly what happened here yesterday?"

For the third time, Liz described the events that had led up to the discovery of her husband's body. She tried to read the deputy's expression as she spoke, but he would have been an excellent poker player. His face gave nothing away.

"And after you found him, what did you do?"

"I panicked," she said. "I knew what people would think, so I went looking for Tucker. I knew he'd know how to handle it."

"Why didn't you just call him?"

The memory of the moment when she'd realized that

Larry had been shot, that he was indeed dead, came flooding back over her. Tears stung her eyes at the senseless waste of a life.

"I…" She swallowed hard. "I couldn't stay here. Not for another minute."

"Because?"

She scowled at his lack of sensitivity. "Because my husband was dead, Deputy Ames. He'd been murdered. I couldn't bear seeing him like that. And for all I knew the person who'd done it was still around here somewhere."

"So you still had feelings for him, even though you intended to divorce him?"

"Of course I did. I had loved Larry Chandler with all my heart. Just because our marriage hadn't worked didn't mean that I wanted him dead or even that I didn't still care about him. In many ways, he was a wonderful man. He just wasn't a very good husband."

"Meaning?"

She glanced at Powell and saw his nod. "Meaning that he was unfaithful."

"He had an affair?"

"There were affairs," she confirmed. "I lost count."

"Did they end badly?"

"You'd have to ask the women that."

"Names?"

"I can give you those I knew about," she said wearily. "I'll make a list. I can't swear it'll be complete."

"What about political enemies? Did he have them?"

"Of course."

"Business problems?"

"None that I'm aware of."

"Is there anyone you can think of who would have reason to want your husband dead?"

She told him about the veiled, anonymous threats. "I believe the notes and answering machine tapes with the messages are in the safe. I can get them for you."

Walker nodded. "Let's do that, then."

He followed her into the library, watched as she pressed a button and a panel of bookshelves swung away from the wall. Behind it was a safe originally installed by her grandfather. She turned the lock, then stepped aside.

Donning gloves, Walker drew out jewelry boxes, packets of papers, then a box that contained the letters and tapes. He took that, placed it into an evidence bag, then returned everything else.

"Have you had a chance to look around?" he asked. "Did you notice if anything is missing?"

"I only came through the foyer and into this room last night. I went out the same way."

"Then let's take a look around. Are there other valuables beyond what's in the safe?"

"I keep a few pieces of jewelry in my room. There's silver that's kept in the pantry."

Liz led the way upstairs. She knew it would be evident when they walked into her room that she hadn't shared it with Larry. There were no masculine belongings, just antique perfume bottles and cosmetics on the dressing table, gowns in one closet, her suits and casual clothes in another. The carpet and iron bed were white, the comforter white with sprigs of violets. Gauzy white curtains billowed at the open windows. It was a very feminine room and not nearly as large as the master suite down the hall. It had suited her as a girl, and she had retreated to it when she no longer wanted to share a bed with her unfaithful husband.

Walker surveyed the room without comment, waiting while she checked her jewelry box.

"Everything is here," she said when she'd counted the few pieces of antique jewelry that had sentimental value to her. The far more expensive treasures, the ones Larry had lavished on her after each affair, were in the safe downstairs. Those, too, had been accounted for—not that she'd cared.

"Let's see if the silver's where it's supposed to be," Walker said.

"It'll be closer if we take the back stairway," Liz told him. It was the way she'd slipped downstairs in the middle of the night for cookies as a girl, the way she'd sneaked outside to meet Tucker as a teenager. Even now she almost expected to find him waiting for her just outside the kitchen door.

He wasn't.

Every piece of silver, much of it from famed English silvermakers of the eighteenth century and earlier, was exactly where it belonged, gleaming on the padded shelves of a special silver closet in the pantry. As a girl, Liz had been awed by the display. She'd even liked the rainy afternoons when she'd sat at the table helping the housekeeper polish every piece. She'd loved imagining tea being poured from this very service by some distant ancestor in London hundreds of years before. She'd read every book in her grandfather's library about the gracious way of life from which she was descended.

Dreaming about a bygone era was a far cry, however, from wanting to live in it. She had balked at the old-fashioned constraints her grandfather had placed on her, stolen every opportunity to break free so that she could follow Tucker on his adventures. He had given her back the childhood that the tragic death of her parents had stolen.

Tucker would have given her the world if she'd let him. But Larry had come along with his charm and his prospects. Her grandfather, one of Larry's staunchest political supporters, had encouraged the two of them to spend time together. He'd believed they shared the same ideals. After several lengthy conversations, Liz had come to believe it, too.

For her, those talks had been intellectually stimulating, nothing more. Spending time with Larry had been the first thing she'd ever done of which her grandfather had totally approved.

Later that had been a huge incentive to say yes when Larry had proposed, that and the promise of the fairy-tale wedding of which every girl dreamed.

"Mrs. Chandler?"

She snapped her attention back to Walker Ames.

"Is all of the silver here?"

She nodded.

"Okay, then, unless you discover something missing, I think we can safely rule out robbery as a motive. I'd appreciate that list of names as soon as possible."

"I'll do it this afternoon," she said.

"Good. Where can I pick it up?"

She was startled by the question. "I can't stay here?"

"Not for the time being," he said. "Once we're sure all the evidence had been gathered, we'll release it, and you can move back in."

"Will I be able to take a few of my things?"

"Of course. I'll wait while you get them, then I can drive you wherever you'd like to go."

"I came with Tucker. I'm sure he can take me…someplace."

The deputy looked as though he disapproved, but he said only, "I'll check with him while you pack. I can have one of the deputies go up with you."

"That's not necessary," she began, but then she saw the look on his face and sighed. "That will be fine."

When Walker had gone off in search of someone to accompany her upstairs, Powell tucked a finger under her chin. "You did just fine. I need to get back to Richmond. Will you be okay?"

"Sure."

"If they call you in for more questioning, don't go until you contact me. Understood?"

"Yes."

"And I'll want to see whatever paperwork you give the police. Make me a copy of those lists and fax it down." He handed her his business card. "The number's on here."

"Thanks for coming, Powell."

"No problem." He gazed into her eyes. "One last piece of advice. Steer clear of Tucker. I know you trust him, but his loyalties are bound to be divided."

"Tucker would never do anything to hurt me," she said with absolute confidence.

Powell regarded her evenly. "He once thought the same about you."

Liz shuddered, despite her conviction that Tucker would always be on her side. Was it possible that he would turn his back on her just when she needed him the most? And how could she blame him if he did?

5

There was some sort of uproar over at Swan Ridge. King spotted the commotion on his way back to Cedar Hill. There were police cars and media vans everywhere, plainly visible from the highway. Probably another one of Lawrence Chandler's press conferences, King concluded. And he'd probably hired all the local off-duty cops to work security. The man did like all the trappings of celebrity.

King was tempted to venture onto the grounds and see for himself what Chandler was up to, but the prospect of bumping into Mary Elizabeth kept him away. He hadn't been able to look the woman in the face without getting riled up since she'd gone and broken Tucker's heart. If it had been up to him, she'd have been chased out of the county, but, sadly, the law wouldn't permit him to run her off. Tucker had explained that on more than one occasion when King had expressed the view that her presence was a blight on the community.

So, instead of going on up to Swan Ridge, King drove on, only to find a bit of commotion at his place, as well. His daughter was pacing back and forth across the veranda with some sort of bee in her bonnet. The instant she spotted him, she came flying down the steps and all but tore the door off the car and dragged him out.

"Have you seen the news?" Daisy demanded.

"Where would I see it?" King inquired testily. "I've been in town all morning."

"And nobody said anything?" she said incredulously. "I can't believe it! For once, the gossip hot line in Trinity Harbor is actually running behind the TV news."

"Slow down, girl. Take a deep breath. I'll get us both a glass of iced tea, and you can tell me what's got you all hot and bothered."

"There's no time for that," she said, shoving him right back toward his car.

"Will you make up your mind?" he grumbled. "Am I going or staying?"

"As soon as I tell you, you're going," she said fiercely. "And I'm coming with you."

"Where?" he asked suspiciously. He hadn't seen her this het up since the night she thought Walker and Tommy were in danger from a gang of drug dealers. To Tucker's dismay, she'd come to the marina armed with a shotgun and a full head of steam, prepared to take on anybody so much as considering harming the two people she loved.

"To Swan Ridge."

"I saw all the commotion. What's going on over there?"

"Somebody murdered Larry Chandler," Daisy announced. "And Mary Elizabeth has gone and dragged Tucker right into the middle of it."

This time, it didn't take any effort on Daisy's part to get King to sit down. His knees felt so weak, he reached behind him and sank onto the driver's seat in the car. "Chandler's dead? You're sure?" He'd never much liked the politician, especially for his part in hurting Tucker, but the thought of someone killing him right here in Trinity Harbor was enough to make his blood run cold.

"It's all over the Richmond news," Daisy said, then scowled. "And that woman is going to break Tucker's heart all over again. I just know she is."

"Tucker's smarter than that," King insisted.

"Is he really?" she scoffed. "Then why was I taking clothes over to his place at the crack of dawn this morning so that Mary Elizabeth could get dressed?"

King stared at her incredulously. "What the devil are you talking about?"

"Can't I explain all this while we drive to Swan Ridge?" Daisy pleaded.

"No," King snapped. "I want the whole story right here, where I can digest it without running off the road."

Daisy described her early-morning mercy mission to Tucker's place. "I wasn't going to tell you. In fact, I promised Tucker I wouldn't say a word to anyone, but things have changed now."

"Did you actually see her?" King demanded.

"No, but she was there. Her car was out front, and Tucker didn't deny it when I accused him of letting her back into his life. He just hustled me right back out the door and told me to mind my own business." She practically shook with indignation. "As if this isn't my business, when a member of my own family is about to get his reputation dragged through the mud."

Daisy was so furious and talking so fast, King was having a hard time keeping up with her. He seized on the first thing that had stuck in his mind. "Why the devil would a woman like that want your clothes?" He looked over the jeans and T-shirt Daisy was wearing. Straight from the discount store, no doubt about it. "I hate to say it, but you two never have shopped in the same boutiques. No offense."

Daisy glared at him but didn't debate the point. "If I had to guess, I'd say it's because she'd arrived there covered in her husband's blood," she said furiously. "Wouldn't that be just like her?"

"Good Lord," King whispered, seeing all his hopes and dreams for Tucker's future going up in smoke. Who'd marry a man who'd been consorting with a murderess? His future as sheriff would be reduced to ashes, as well.

He glanced over at Daisy. "Get out."

"I'm going with you."

"No, you're not. I'll handle this," he said grimly. "You go home and see what information you can pry out of that husband of yours. He's bound to know all the particulars. I'll check with you later, after I've tracked down Tucker and given him a piece of my mind."

"Don't blame him. The woman's a witch."

King almost grinned at that. "Don't go saying that to your brother."

"Why not? It's the truth. Look how she betrayed him—betrayed all of us, for that matter—years ago. Tucker needs to be reminded of that."

"I imagine he hasn't forgotten, any more than you have. But if you start name-calling, he'll just rush to her defense and this whole thing will get even more complicated than it already is."

She started to argue, then sighed. "You're probably

right. I'll temper my remarks." She regarded him worriedly. "Think you can do the same?"

"Not bloody likely." He fingered the jewelry box in his pocket and wondered if he'd ever get the chance to give it to Frances. He was supposed to be picking her up in less than an hour, and the odds of him getting Tucker's life straightened out in that amount of time were slim to none.

Well, Frances would just have to understand…again. He sighed heavily. Not bloody likely.

Trying to stay in the background and out of the way of the forensics team was giving Tucker hives. He wasn't used to sitting on the sidelines in his own blasted jurisdiction. He wanted to get into the library where Chandler had been shot. He knew Walker would eventually fill him in, let him look over all the reports, but that wasn't the same as being on the crime scene.

Despite his frustration, though, the instant Walker escorted Mary Elizabeth out of the house, all of Tucker's attention was riveted on her. Her chin was held high. Her shoulders were squared proudly. But her eyes were dull, her complexion pale. He'd never once in the more than twenty years he'd known her seen her look so thoroughly dispirited.

As they neared, she met his gaze, locking on his face as if it were the first friendly beacon she'd seen.

"You okay?" Tucker asked, pushing aside his anger at that sneaky press conference she and Powell had called.

She nodded, but her eyes welled with tears. She blinked frantically to try to keep them from spilling down her cheeks, but one escaped. Instinctively, Tucker gently rubbed it away with the pad of his thumb, then jerked away when he realized that Walker's steady gaze was fixed on him.

"Since she can't stay here for the time being, Mrs. Chandler and I have been discussing where I'll be able to find her if I need to talk to her again," Walker said.

"You can reach her through me," Tucker said at once.

"No," Mary Elizabeth protested, even as Walker scowled disapprovingly. "I can't ask you to do that."

"You didn't ask," Tucker pointed out. "I offered."

"Can I speak to you privately?" Walker asked in a tone that suggested it wasn't a request. He stepped a few feet away, assuming Tucker would follow. When Tucker joined him, he said, "Have you lost your mind?"

"She needs a place to stay," Tucker said with a defensive shrug. "Think of it as protective custody."

"It is a really, really bad idea," Walker countered. "For reasons so numerous I can't even begin to count them. Given your past history, you invite that woman into your home and I have to place you on the list of suspects right alongside her."

"Do what you have to do," Tucker said, refusing to back down, no matter how black a picture Walker painted.

"Dammit, Tucker, do you want Daisy to kill me?"

"You'll probably have to get in line. I imagine she'll be coming after me first," Tucker said wryly. "This won't sit well with a lot of people."

"Then shouldn't that be a clue it's a mistake?"

"I can't let Mary Elizabeth go through this alone."

"I'm sure a woman in her position has friends," Walker said.

"Maybe so, but I'm the one she turned to."

"And precisely when was that? Last night, correct?

Why exactly did it take so long for you to contact me?" Walker inquired. "What were the two of you doing all that time, getting reacquainted?"

Tucker barely resisted the urge to slug his brother-in-law. He knew what Walker was trying to do. He was trying to show him just how ugly this could get. Tucker refused to take the bait. He understood the risks. He met Walker's gaze.

"Actually, she was sleeping," Tucker said mildly. "I was in my kitchen pondering the funny twists and turns life takes."

"Was that before or after she told you about her husband?"

"Before," Tucker said, just as he'd explained it earlier. "As soon as she told me, I called you."

"Were you anywhere near Swan Ridge last night?" Walker pressed.

"I patrolled the whole county," Tucker told him. "Check my logbook and the mileage on the cruiser."

"Didn't take any breaks?"

"Not a one," he said. "Ask the dispatcher. Michele worked a double shift, too. She and I were having a rather lively discussion about the best place to get steamed crabs. I think Bobby's are the finest around. She's partial to a place across the river in Maryland."

Walker sighed, his exasperation plain. "This is just the tip of the iceberg, you know. The questions are going to start coming at you fast and furious, and I won't be the only one asking them."

"I know that," Tucker said.

"You're a smart man. I have to assume you've weighed the risks."

"Whether I have or not isn't your concern," Tucker

told him. "But I appreciate the fact that you care. If things change after Mary Elizabeth and I have talked, I'll let you know."

"You think she'll object to staying with you?" Walker asked.

"Oh, I imagine she'll have a whole lot more to say than you did." He nodded in her direction. "Take a look."

Mary Elizabeth was tapping her foot and glowering at them.

"What's that about?" Walker asked.

"I'm pretty sure she doesn't like the fact that I made this decision without consulting her. I'm almost certain she's going to tell me to take my offer and shove it."

"And then?"

"And then I'll counter with a few rational arguments. She'll tell me I'm trying to run her life just the way her grandfather did. I'll remind her that she's the one who came to me. She'll tell me that she deeply regrets that now."

Walker's lips began to twitch with amusement. "Now I know you're crazy. You're going to stir up Daisy and your father and have to contend with an irate, ungrateful female."

"That's pretty much how I see it," Tucker said, working really hard to sound like a martyr.

"Good luck."

Before he could get away, Walker called him back.

"What?" Tucker said.

His brother-in-law grinned. "Told you so."

Tucker regarded him blankly. "Told me—?"

"That you'd never steer clear of this. The damsel-in-distress thing gets you every time."

Tucker told his deputy what he could do with his smart-mouthed theories, then went over to explain the plan to Mary Elizabeth.

"You'll stay at my place until we know more," he said. He regarded her with a wry expression. "Though it might be best if you take up residence in the guest room and stay out of my bed, whether I'm in it or not."

"I'm not dragging you any deeper into this," she said flatly. "You've already gone above and beyond what anyone would expect under the circumstances."

"Have you got someplace better to stay?"

"I could go to the house Larry and I have in Richmond."

He shook his head. "Not a good idea. You need to stay here in town."

"I could stay at the hotel."

"The walls would start to close in on you in a day." He studied her thoughtfully. "I suppose I could call Anna-Louise. She'd probably take you in."

"Your minister? I don't think so. Besides, isn't she married to the editor of the *Trinity Harbor Weekly?*"

Tucker feigned an innocent expression. "Would that be a problem?"

"I suppose that depends on whether he's likely to bug the guest room when a suspected murderer is in residence," she said irritably.

"You have a better suggestion?"

"No," she conceded, then added grudgingly, "Okay, I'll stay at your place."

Tucker didn't like the little chorus of hallelujahs that ran through his head at her response. Right up until that instant, he'd been able to convince himself that he was doing his duty as a police officer, his good deed as a human being. That little flaring of excitement was definitely about something else, something that was supposed to be over and dead. Talk about inappropriate, to say nothing of stupid and self-destructive. He shook his head.

When he glanced at Mary Elizabeth, there was no mistaking her amusement.

"Second thoughts already?" she inquired.

He frowned at the question. "I'm doing this because it's the right thing to do—we're clear on that, right?"

"Of course," she said dutifully.

"It has nothing at all to do with..." He couldn't even bring himself to say the word.

"Sex?"

"Us, dammit. It has nothing to do with us. That's in the past."

"Of course," she soothed.

"Your husband just died," he reminded both of them.

"The marriage had been over for a long time. I told you that."

"But you didn't tell me why."

"Do we have to get into that now?"

Tucker glanced over and saw the exhaustion and strain in her eyes, around her mouth. But despite that, despite all she'd been through in the past twenty-four hours, she was beautiful. "No, it can wait," he told her.

She met his gaze. "King's going to go ballistic when he finds out about this. You know that, don't you?"

"I can take it. Besides, what good are old friends if you can't call 'em when you need 'em?"

"We were more than friends, Tucker. And it ended badly. I'm sorrier for that than I can ever tell you. I never meant to hurt you."

He looked into her eyes, then shook his head. "Let's not go there. We just agreed that I'm just helping out an old friend. Don't turn it into anything more."

"Other people will."

"Let them. I can handle that, too."

"But you shouldn't have to defend yourself on my account. I know how it works around here. At the first whiff of scandal, the vultures will start circling."

"I'm not worried."

She gave him a wry look. "You tired of being sheriff?"

"My job's not at risk, as long as I steer clear of this case."

"Completely, or in your professional capacity?"

"Both," he said firmly. "You have an attorney. He'll be more help than I could be from here on out."

"But you're a cop, a trained investigator."

His gaze narrowed. He was pretty sure he could see right where she was heading with this. "So?" he asked cautiously.

"I need to find out who killed Larry. I won't be able to rest until I know. Since you insist on letting me stay with you, I might as well take advantage of your expertise."

"Walker will figure out what happened here yesterday. Your husband was an important man. The sheriff's department will be highly motivated with or without my involvement."

She regarded him with a wry expression. "So highly motivated that they'll want to wrap up the case by arresting the first decent suspect that comes along?"

To Tucker's everlasting regret, she had a point. Even if he stayed on Walker's back, it was possible that the quickest solution would be the one people would grab onto. "If it comes to that..."

"It'll be too late. Don't they say trails go cold very quickly?"

"Mary Elizabeth, I already have a job. If you want someone besides the police looking into this on your behalf, hire an investigator. I'm sure Powell can recommend a good one."

"He could, but I trust you."

He sighed heavily. "I thought you regretted drawing me into this. And I am absolutely certain I heard Powell tell you not to trust me."

She regarded him solemnly. "He did. And I do regret getting you involved, but you're in it now. And it was your choice to keep me underfoot where I can pester you. I might as well take advantage of that fact."

"And my job? What do you propose I do about that?"

"You said yourself you haven't taken any time off in forever. Since you need to avoid this case and I doubt there's much else going on in Trinity Harbor, take a vacation or a leave of absence, whatever makes you comfortable. I'll pay you the going rate to work for me as an investigator."

"Liz—"

"Two weeks," she pleaded. "If nothing turns up in two weeks, you can turn it over to another investigator."

Tucker had weeks of vacation time coming to him, but talk about a busman's holiday. This was hardly the kind of relaxing break he needed. A couple of weeks doing nothing but fishing, that was a vacation. This... this was a disaster waiting to happen. Add in Walker's reaction to having him poking around in his investigation, to say nothing of the personal complications from working closely with Mary Elizabeth, and it was asking for the kind of trouble any sensible man shunned.

"Please," she coaxed. "I need you, and you know I would never say that unless I was desperate."

That was certainly true. Mary Elizabeth had always prided herself on needing no one. The fact that she'd been shedding tears all day like Niagara Falls was testimony to her level of stress and panic.

"Two weeks," he agreed finally. "And not a minute longer."

"Thank you."

"Don't thank me," he said, shifting to meet her gaze. "Just figure out how we're going to keep my father from finding out about this and killing us both."

6

It was two hours after his encounter with Daisy by the time King tore into the sheriff's office. He'd missed Tucker by minutes everywhere he looked…and he had pretty much covered the whole blasted county.

Walker had been downright evasive when King had demanded to know where his son had gone when he'd left Swan Ridge.

"You just tell me one thing," King had demanded when he arrived at the neighboring estate. "Is he with *that* woman?"

"Can't say," Walker said, annoyingly poker-faced.

"Can't or won't?"

"Why are you here?" Walker countered. "Or do I even need to ask? Daisy's behind it, right? Tucker said you two were going to get all worked up over him having any contact with Mrs. Chandler."

"Well, do you blame us?" King had retorted indignantly. "Not five minutes after her husband dies, she's sniffing around Tucker again."

"I don't think it's like that," Walker said, defending

Tucker with brotherly loyalty. "She turned to a friend for a little help."

King snorted. "Then you're as blind as my son where that she-devil is concerned."

Walker didn't take the bait. "You got any other questions? I have a whole lot of things I could be doing around here, like helping the forensics guys gather hard evidence."

"You ought to start with locking up the prime suspect," King had groused.

"I would if I had one," Walker countered. "Anything else?"

"Where's she staying?"

Walker looked him directly in the eye and said with a perfectly straight face, "I don't know."

King regarded his son-in-law with disbelief. "You're in charge of this investigation, am I right? Tucker is sensible enough to leave it to you?"

"Yes."

"And you don't know where in the hell your prime suspect is staying?"

"I repeat, nobody has said she's a suspect," Walker shot back.

"If she's not, then you're a fool," King declared. "A woman who would cut the heart right out of a man like my son is capable of anything."

"That's not the kind of thing you need to be running around town saying to just anybody," Walker admonished him.

"Why not?"

"You ever heard of slander?"

"Last I heard, you can't accuse somebody of slander when they're speaking the truth."

"As you see it. Unless you've got investigative skills I know nothing about, you don't actually know a damn thing."

"Facts are facts," King had said stubbornly.

"Go home," Walker advised. "Have a mint julep or something else that'll settle your nerves. Talking to Tucker when you're all riled up like this will be counterproductive."

"I'll talk to my own son when I damn well please."

"First you have to find him, and my hunch is he won't be anywhere you're likely to think to look."

Walker had certainly been right about that. King had checked Tucker's place as well as the boardwalk, and now he was going to the most obvious place of all, the sheriff's office. Maybe Tucker had come to his senses and locked Mary Elizabeth away behind bars. King could always dream.

"Where is he?" he asked Michele, already pushing open the door to Tucker's office.

"Not in," Michele told him. "He's on vacation."

King stared at her, mouth agape. "Since when?"

"Since an hour ago. He called in early this morning to take the day off, then called back to say he was taking two weeks off. Walker's in charge, but he's not here, either, in case you're wondering."

King sank down on a chair beside the dispatcher. "What the devil is my son thinking?"

"He was overdue for a vacation," Michele pointed out. "He'd been getting downright cranky lately. I, for one, am relieved."

King frowned at her. Either she was completely unaware of the reason for King's sour mood, or she was deliberately choosing to ignore it and play dumb by acting as if this vacation were nothing out of the ordinary.

"Maybe so, but something tells me he's not on a beach in the Caribbean," he snapped.

In fact, King was one hundred and ten percent certain he would find Tucker somewhere in the vicinity of the widow Chandler. When he was calm enough to think rationally, a part of him couldn't blame Tucker. The boy had been raised with a sense of decency and honor. The woman he'd once loved was in big trouble, and she'd come to him for help. What kind of man would turn his back on her at a time like that, no matter how devastated he'd been years ago when she'd walked out on him?

And, to be honest, there had been a time when King had liked Mary Elizabeth just fine, a time when he'd hoped for a union between her and his son, but every bit of sentiment he'd felt toward her had died the day she'd rejected Tucker so she could marry that weasel Chandler. King was not inclined to welcome her back into the family fold, especially not when she was caught up in a murder investigation that could wind up with mud being slung at anyone around her.

He shot a sly look at Michele, a big woman with a bigger heart. She was every bit as protective of Tucker as he was, the only difference being that she was willing to protect him against King. In fact, she considered it her solemn duty.

"Do me a favor. Try that beeper thing of his," he suggested casually.

"I told you, he's on vacation."

"Darlin', you and I both know that man hasn't spent a day in years without that beeper turned on. If it's with him, he'll answer you."

"And then?" she asked suspiciously.

"You let me talk to him."

She was already shaking her head. "I don't think so."

"Why not? What's the harm?"

"For one thing, he's my boss. You're not. For another, he left very specific instructions that he wasn't to be disturbed."

"By anyone?"

"No, by you," she said bluntly, then shrugged. "Sorry."

Just then a call came in on the nonemergency line. Looking relieved, Michele reached for the phone. "Yes, he's here," she said, sounding resigned. She turned to King. "It's for you. It's Daisy."

King took the phone eagerly. Maybe his daughter had been able to use her powers of persuasion on Walker to get some information. "Yes?"

"Have you talked to him?"

"I can't find him," he admitted.

"Try the marina. I just talked to Bobby and tried to get him on our side. He was acting all weird, you know, the way he gets when he disagrees with me but doesn't want to stir up a ruckus. I'm betting Tucker and Mary Elizabeth were right there, hiding in plain sight, as it were."

King stood up, grateful for the tip. "I'm on my way. I'll keep you posted. By the way, you need to tell that husband of yours that he's a Spencer now. We expect loyalty from family members."

"Actually, I'm an Ames now," Daisy reminded him. "But I get what you're saying. Unfortunately, Walker is an independent thinker, especially when it comes to work. That's the one arena where my influence is limited."

"More's the pity," King muttered. He handed the phone back to the dispatcher. "If my son happens to show up here, tell him I'm looking for him."

She grinned. "Oh, I think he's already well aware of that."

King frowned at her. "Do you sass him like that?"

Her grin spread. "Whenever I get the chance. You have a good evening now, you hear?"

King shook his head. If he'd had a woman like that working for him, he'd have fired her by her second day on the job. Of course, he conceded, if a woman like Michele were working for him, she probably would have quit within the first hour.

Bobby tilted his chair back on two legs and looked from Tucker to Mary Elizabeth and back, then shook his head. "I don't get it. Why aren't the two of you bolting for the door? I just told you that I think Daisy figured out that you're here, which means Daddy knows it by now. I give him five minutes, maybe less, to come storming in here."

"You worried the commotion will be bad for business?" Tucker asked.

"Actually, most of the customers like a little diversion with their crabs and rockfish," Bobby said. "Of course, if you're staying, I highly recommend the halibut tonight. It's cooked with lemon and capers and served over a rice pilaf."

Tucker snapped his menu closed. "I'll have that. Mary Elizabeth?"

"I'm not especially hungry."

Tucker regarded her intently. "You'll need to have some food in you if you're going to face down King."

"I could hide in the ladies' room until he leaves," she suggested. It was plain the remark wasn't being made in jest.

"And leave me to handle him? I don't think so." Tucker gave her hand a squeeze. "We might as well get this over with. Besides, there is an up side to this. If we can win him over, let folks see that he doesn't have any doubts about you, it will go a long way toward quelling whatever gossip is getting stirred up around town."

"I think it's going to take more than one evening and some casual chitchat over the halibut special to accomplish that," Mary Elizabeth responded ruefully. "I'm not sure a lifetime's long enough. You know how King loves to hold a grudge. He hasn't spoken to your uncle in how long? Twenty, maybe thirty years? Does he even remember what the feud was about?"

"In detail," Tucker said regretfully. "He still talks about the prize bull his brother stole out from under him at an auction."

"Then I don't hold out a lot of hope for tonight," she said.

"The key is to get him into an appropriately mellow frame of mind," Tucker said thoughtfully. "Bobby, have the waiter set two more places at the table."

"If you think I'm sitting here to play referee, you're crazy," Bobby said, standing up at once. "And I've already warned Jenna to stay home tonight. I called the second you walked in the door."

"The places are for King and Frances." Tucker pulled his cell phone out of his pocket and punched in a number. "Didn't you tell me she and Daddy had a reservation here tonight until he called to cancel it?"

"Yes, but—"

"Frances, this is Tucker." He winked at Bobby, who shook his head and went in search of a waiter. "I'm at the marina, and I understand that you were planning to meet Daddy here tonight. I'm almost a hundred percent certain he's on his way over here right now. Why don't you join us? You'd be doing me a huge favor."

Frances chuckled. "Yes, I imagine I would. Your father's on the warpath over you getting mixed up with Mary Elizabeth's problems, isn't he? It didn't take a genius to figure that one out once I saw the evening news." She sighed. "Not that he said a thing about it when he canceled our date."

"Will you come over here and protect me? Please," Tucker coaxed.

She hesitated.

"I'd really, really appreciate it."

"Mary Elizabeth is there?"

"Yes."

"That poor girl," Frances said, clearly wavering. "She must be beside herself. Okay, I'll be there in fifteen minutes. But keep in mind I am doing this for her, not to protect you from that meddling, know-it-all father of yours."

Tucker grinned and gestured to the hovering waiter to go ahead and set the places. "Understood," he assured Frances.

When he'd hung up, he looked at Mary Elizabeth. "She's on her way. She's worried about you."

Tears filled her eyes, but this time she made no attempt to keep them from spilling over. "She said that?"

"Sweetheart, I told you that not everyone in Trinity Harbor is going to think you're guilty of a crime."

"But the few who don't suspect me of killing Larry are going to blame me for hurting you."

"Which is one reason we're here tonight, instead of at my house. People need to get the message that they don't need to worry about me, that you and I are getting along just fine, despite past differences."

She studied him intently. "Are we, Tucker? Are we really getting along okay?"

"Have you heard me say anything to the contrary?"

"No, but you always were the most polite man I ever knew under the most trying circumstances. A lot of men would have plucked me out of bed and dumped me on the front lawn, rather than get involved in any way with a woman who'd abandoned them."

Tucker glanced up and spotted his father coming in the door in full battle mode. "I think we'd better postpone that discussion for later and prepare to defend ourselves."

Mary Elizabeth turned pale. Her hands were clenched together so tightly in her lap that her knuckles were white. Tucker reached over and gave them a reassuring squeeze. He withdrew hurriedly, because the jolt of awareness that shot through him had little to do with comfort and a whole lot to do with attraction.

"Just smile and leave the rest to me," he said, then lowered his voice, "And remember, if he gets really contrary, I still have my gun with me."

She laughed at that, just the way he'd hoped she would. By the time King reached the table, she'd squared her shoulders and faced him with a smile that only someone who knew her well would recognize as forced.

"King, it's lovely to see you again," she said.

Tucker noted his father's startled reaction and waited to see what he'd do next. King wasn't constitutionally capable of being outright rude to a woman's face.

"Mary Elizabeth," he finally acknowledged with a curt nod.

Satisfied that for the moment his father would remain on good behavior, Tucker gestured toward a chair. "Have a seat and join us. Bobby says the halibut is especially fine tonight."

"I didn't come here to have dinner," King grumbled, but he sat just the same.

"No, I imagine you came here to tell me what a mistake I'm making," Tucker said, getting the issue out on the table.

King seemed surprised that Tucker had grasped that. "As a matter of fact, that is exactly what I intended to say." He frowned at Mary Elizabeth. "No offense."

"None taken," she said, her lips twitching with amusement. "And I can understand why you might not want Tucker mixed up in my husband's murder investigation."

"The investigation's not what has me worried," he said pointedly. "It's this." His gesture encompassed the two of them. "You two, out here in public when her husband hasn't even been buried yet."

"We're having dinner in a public place," Tucker pointed out. "Not dining all alone by candlelight at my house. You think that would be better?"

"No, dammit. I don't think you should be dining together at all. In fact, I think you should be steering completely clear of each other. Otherwise, a tragic situation is likely to turn ugly with speculation and innuendos running rampant around town."

"I'm sure you'll set people straight, won't you, King?" Mary Elizabeth said, her gaze steady. "After all, who knows the two of us better than you do, and you certainly don't think there's any hanky-panky involved, do you?"

"Of course not," he blustered. "My son's not a fool."

"Well, then, you should be able to shoot down all that nasty speculation, shouldn't you?" she challenged.

"Of course I can."

She beamed at him. "We'll be counting on that."

King's gaze narrowed. "'We'?" he echoed. "You're already referring to you and Tucker as if the two of you are a pair? Woman, you cannot just waltz back in here and expect to pick up with my son right where you left off. Let's call a spade a spade, why don't we? That is what you're really after, isn't it?"

Tucker had heard enough. "Daddy, that was uncalled for. Mary Elizabeth has no expectations of a personal nature where I'm concerned. I think you owe her an apology, along with your condolences. She's just lost her husband."

"To tell the truth, she doesn't look all that broken up about it," King noted. "Why is that, I wonder? Does it have something to do with the fact that she has you waiting in the wings to fill his shoes?"

Tucker shot to his feet. "That's enough! If you can't keep a civil tongue in your head, you can leave."

In his fury, he hadn't noticed Frances's approach just as King had all but declared war on Mary Elizabeth.

Frances marched up to the table and scowled down at King. It was apparent that she had heard every word.

"King Spencer, you ought to be ashamed of yourself," she told him. "You've known Mary Elizabeth for most of her life. You knew her granddaddy and her father. You know the kind of woman she is. And you certainly know how honorable your son is. How dare you suggest right out here in public where anyone can hear that there is anything improper going on between them? If there are rumors flying tomorrow, you'll be the one responsible and no one else. I'm embarrassed for you."

Bright patches of color crept up King's neck and turned his cheeks red. "Frances, where did you come from? I thought I told you I couldn't see you tonight after all."

"So you did, but Tucker invited me to join him and Mary Elizabeth. I knew she would be in need of a friendly face tonight, so I came. I am very glad I did, because it has given me a chance to see just how low you can sink when it comes to meddling in your children's lives." She leaned down and gave Mary Elizabeth a hug. "Pay no attention to this old coot. I certainly don't."

"Frances," King protested.

Tucker winced. He certainly hadn't expected to make things worse between his father and Frances by inviting her here tonight. He liked her, liked the way she stood up to King and refused to let him bulldoze over her. Few women—few people—had ever had the nerve to challenge him the way Frances did. And he could see by the worried look on his father's face that King was afraid this time he'd pushed her too far.

King stood up. "Frances, why don't you and I go to

another table, where we can have that talk we planned on having tonight?"

"Absolutely not. I'm here to support a friend. You can do whatever you want."

Bobby appeared from the kitchen just then. Tucker saw him take note of the fact that three of the people at the table were standing, regarding each other warily.

"So, who's having the special?" Bobby inquired cheerfully. "And who's dining on crow?"

King scowled at him. "Very funny."

"Well?" Bobby prodded. "The special's going fast."

"I'll have that," Tucker said, taking his seat. "Mary Elizabeth?"

"Fine," she said without much enthusiasm.

"The halibut sounds lovely," Frances agreed, pushing aside King's hand when he would have pulled her chair out for her.

King sighed and retreated to his own chair. "Might as well make it four."

Bobby's smile spread. "See now, the four of you can agree on something. Isn't that nice?"

Tucker bit back a chuckle at King's stormy expression. "A smart man would retreat to the kitchen about now," he advised his brother.

"A *smart* man would have run like hell an hour ago," Bobby retorted. "Guess we know what that makes you."

Sadly, after a glance around the table at his stony-faced companions, Tucker concluded that his brother was exactly right.

7

Despite all of the awkwardness and tension, which should have been enough to give her a raging headache, Liz thoroughly enjoyed dinner once she got through the initial sparring with King. Obviously her life lately had been worse than she'd realized, if dining with a cranky man who hated her, the woman who seemed likely to be his ex-ladyfriend and a man she'd once dumped could make her feel this cheerful less than 24 hours after her husband had died.

She smiled as she sank back on the seat in Tucker's car. "That was wonderful," she said with a contented sigh.

"Bobby will be delighted you enjoyed the meal," Tucker said, his jaw still set, his anger radiating from him in palpable waves.

"I meant all of it, every single second of sitting around that table with you, your father and Frances."

Tucker turned and stared at her, clearly astonished by her claim. "Are you crazy?"

"It was just so normal."

"Sweetheart, if you thought that was normal, then

dysfunctionality must have reached new heights in your life."

Her smile vanished at the all-too-accurate observation. "It had," she said quietly.

Her solemn response clearly stunned him. Something that looked an awful lot like pity shadowed his eyes. "I'm sorry."

"Don't be sorry for me," she snapped. "I made my own choices. I chose Larry. I chose to stay with him even after I knew he was cheating on me."

She had blurted the comment out without thinking, but now she was glad it was out in the open.

"He cheated on you?" Tucker asked.

The incredulous expression on his face would have been laughable if the topic hadn't been so serious. "Over and over," she said flatly, refusing to show even an ounce of self-pity. She was done with feeling sorry for herself. That was the past, and she was going to put her life back on track, no matter what it took.

"Then why in hell would you stay with him?" He rubbed a hand across his face. "Sorry. That's none of my business."

"It's okay. I promised I'd explain why I'm not more upset about him being dead. You're not the only one who's going to think I'm totally insensitive, not that I'll ever tell anyone else the reason why. That particular truth will be buried with Larry."

Tucker shook his head. "That may not be possible, not when he's been murdered. For one thing, the media's going to be all over this story. For another, the police—and I, for that matter—will have to explore every angle to try to find out who did this."

"There's no way...?" she began, regarding him hopefully.

"None I can see. Once everyone starts digging around in your husband's life, if there are skeletons, they will be found."

She drew in a deep breath as reality set in. Her life was going to be exposed to intense scrutiny. Everyone would know that her husband had humiliated her time and again with his other women. Was that too high a price to pay to discover the person responsible for his death? Of course not. The real hurt had come with the cheating and with the lies to cover it up, lies that had eventually led to an inability to trust one single word that her husband had uttered. She wondered if she would ever be able to trust any man again.

One glance at Tucker answered that question. She could trust him with her life. She *was* trusting him with her life.

Liz caught his worried expression. "What?" she asked.

"Are you going to be okay with that?" he asked. "Is there anything I need to know?"

"Are you asking if there are skeletons in my closet that are going to come tumbling out?" she asked, refusing to take offense at the question. "No, none. No affairs. No secret deals. I didn't embezzle money from any of the charities I raised money for. Larry was the only one with secrets he wanted hidden."

"Okay, then," Tucker said with unmistakable relief. "Start at the beginning. When did you first discover he was cheating?"

Maybe it would be easier to get into all this in the dark interior of a car on the quiet streets of Trinity Harbor than it would be under the glare of lights in Tucker's living room. She took a deep breath and began.

"Only a few weeks after the wedding," she told him, determined to betray absolutely no emotion. "I don't know how long it had been going on, probably from the beginning. At that point he was involved with his campaign manager, a woman named Cynthia Miles. She was young, blonde and ambitious."

"Was she in love with him?"

"Hard to say. She was very good at hiding her emotions. Seeing the two of them together, I would never have suspected a thing, if I hadn't walked into his hotel suite and found them in bed."

Tucker's jaw clenched again. "Why the hell didn't you leave him then?"

Liz shrugged. "The usual reasons, I suppose. He apologized and swore it would never happen again. I was still starry-eyed and in love. I wanted to believe him. As soon as the campaign was over, he fired her because I insisted on it."

"How did she take that?"

"Not well, I gather. I wasn't there."

"Did she vow to get even?"

"If she did, it would have been with me, not Larry."

"I'll need to talk to her. Is she in Richmond?"

"Of course, that's where the power is in this state," Liz said dryly. "Cynthia would never stray far from that."

"Did you cross paths often?"

"Not if I could help it, but yes, she was often at political rallies for various party candidates. She was good at her job. She had no difficulty finding work."

"So she could hardly have resented Larry—or you—for ruining her career," he said thoughtfully.

"I don't see how," Liz agreed.

"Were there more lovers after this Miles woman?"

She nodded, embarrassed but determined to be totally honest.

"Yet you stayed. Why?"

"I don't know if you can possibly understand this, but here it is. I chose to play the docile, loving wife because that's what was expected of me. It was a role, and I gave an Academy Award caliber performance for years."

"Why?" he persisted.

She thought back on the decision she had wrestled with time and again, always coming down on the side of trying to save her marriage. There had been more to it, though. She could admit that now.

"Because I didn't want to acknowledge, even to myself, what a terrible mistake I had made," she said quietly. "It would have meant I'd hurt you for nothing."

She slanted a look at Tucker across the car's dark interior. The only light came from the dashboard, but she could tell that he was biting back a curse. She plunged on. Now that she'd started, she wanted him to know it all. "In many ways, Larry was a lot like my father, charming and immature and totally irresponsible in his personal life, but you only figured that out on close inspection. The casual observer seldom saw past the fact that he was handsome and witty and a brilliant politician. When I realized I'd made the same mistake my mother had, I did exactly what she did. I accepted it as my due. I'd made my own bed, so to speak, and just as she had, I was determined to lie in it. A Swan would do nothing less."

"Family tradition?" Tucker asked mockingly. "Or penance?"

"Penance, probably."

"A miserable life is a high price to pay for one mistake," he pointed out.

"My *life* wasn't miserable," she insisted, determined to make him see that it wasn't as black and white as he was trying to make it. "I had everything money could buy. I had the time—in fact, I was encouraged—to get involved with a lot of high-profile, worthwhile causes, to make a real difference in people's lives. That can be incredibly rewarding." She sighed. "All that was missing was love."

"Some would say that's the most important thing of all," Tucker pointed out.

"They'd be right," Liz agreed. "I finally realized that. That's why Larry and I started leading totally separate lives, why I left on that trip and ultimately why I told him I wanted a divorce. I wanted more than a big house, a fancy car and a lot of acquaintances."

"What about kids? You always talked about wanting a large family."

She sighed at the reminder. "Before the wedding we had talked about having kids and I desperately wanted them, but after I discovered Larry was cheating, I thought it would be wrong to bring a child into the mess we'd made of our marriage. Besides, despite his promises before the ceremony, Larry flatly refused to even consider starting a family because he thought it would interfere with my devotion to his needs."

"So, he got everything he wanted and you got what?" Tucker asked.

When the question was phrased like that, Liz couldn't come up with an answer that made any sense.

"What you deserved?" Tucker prodded.

"Yes," she said, realizing now that her acceptance of that had been no one's fault but her own. "I will never allow that to happen again. When—*if*—I ever marry again, it will be because someone genuinely wants to be with me, to share my life."

She felt his gaze burning into her.

"I can't be that someone, Mary Elizabeth."

She shivered at the certainty in his voice. "I know that," she acknowledged, though she couldn't help the twinge of regret it made her feel. King was right about one thing. A part of her did want Tucker in her life for more than his help in solving Larry's murder. She just didn't know if she deserved him.

"Do you?" Tucker asked, slowing the car to look directly into her eyes. "Because if my father was right, if you came to me because you wanted more than my help, then taking you back to my place is a lousy idea. Things between us can never go back to the way they were."

"Can you at least be my friend?" she asked, unable to hide the wistful note in her voice.

He hesitated so long, she was sure he was going to say no to that, too.

"I already am," he said finally. "I suppose I never stopped."

Being Mary Elizabeth's friend and nothing more was going to take some getting used to. Tucker handed her sheets and towels for the guest room and left her at the door. No way in hell was he stepping across that threshold and straight into temptation.

His declaration in the car that there could be nothing more than friendship between them had been a warning to himself, as much as to her. Despite all claims to the contrary, she was a suspect in her husband's death. She had a funeral to plan, a role that she had to continue to play until the moment they put Larry Chandler into the ground, until they found his killer and brought him or her to trial.

Whatever her differences with the man, she wasn't going to sully his reputation now by airing them in public unless circumstances forced her to. At the very least, Larry Chandler would go to his grave as a fair-haired rising star of politics, not as a philandering husband. As badly as he wanted to, Tucker couldn't fault her for permitting that illusion to continue.

There was going to come a time, though, when she would have to face some hard truths, if only to save herself. She was going to have to permit Tucker to delve into all the dark nooks and crannies of Chandler's life looking for other suspects who might have had a motive to want him dead. Clearly Cynthia Miles was only the tip of the iceberg.

Tucker spent the rest of the night tossing and turning, blaming his restlessness on all the unanswered questions taunting him when the blame belonged right down the hall with the woman who was as out of reach now as she had been when she'd first married Chandler.

He must have fallen asleep eventually, because he awoke to the scent of coffee drifting from the kitchen and something else, something with cinnamon in it. Since he doubted he even owned that particular spice, that meant someone had come calling—Daisy, most likely. And that meant an explosion was likely to erupt in his kitchen any second now.

Tucker shot out of bed and dragged on his pants. He was haphazardly yanking a wrinkled polo shirt over his head when he bolted into the kitchen to find Mary Elizabeth sitting at the table with Anna-Louise Walton, his pastor and Daisy's best friend. It was a marginal improvement over finding his sister there.

"Look what Anna-Louise brought," Mary Elizabeth said happily, biting into a gooey cinnamon roll.

"Courtesy of Daisy," Anna-Louise said.

"Have you checked them for arsenic?" Tucker inquired. He met Anna-Louise's disapproving gaze. "Sorry, but she's not exactly happy about Mary Elizabeth's presence here."

"So I gathered," the pastor said wryly. "We've discussed her feelings at length."

"Did you come over here to share them?" he asked testily. "If so, you'll have to wait till I've had my coffee."

"Actually I came to see if there was anything I could do," Anna-Louise retorted, completely unintimidated by his lousy mood.

"We were discussing the funeral," Mary Elizabeth told him. "I asked her to conduct the service, and she's agreed."

Tucker bit back a sarcastic query about whether Anna-Louise's church would be large enough to hold all the politicians who'd want to be seen at the occasion, given the likely media circus. He merely nodded. This was not a conversation he wanted to participate in. Given what he'd learned about Lawrence Chandler the night before, it would be the height of hypocrisy to pretend that he cared about the man's passing.

"I'll leave you to it, then," he said, downing the remainder of his cup of coffee even though it scalded his throat. "I want to get over to the station and run some checks on the computer there."

"About Larry?" Mary Elizabeth asked.

"Yes."

"You are investigating his death, then?" Anna-Louise asked. "Richard told me Walker was doing it."

"He's doing the formal investigation. I'm acting on my own. And before you start questioning my ethics, you should also know that I've taken a two-week leave of absence from the department."

"Tucker, I would never question your integrity. Neither would anyone else around here," Anna-Louise declared fiercely.

"I hope you still feel that way when this is over. Something tells me it's going to get ugly. Not everyone will like what I find when I start turning over rocks," he said, his gaze on Mary Elizabeth.

She paled, but said nothing.

"Will you talk to Richard if you come up with anything?" Anna-Louise asked. "The *Weekly* is the local paper. He ought to get a scoop, don't you think?"

"That'll be up to Mary Elizabeth and Walker. They get first crack at whatever I find."

Anna-Louise opened her mouth, then clamped it shut again.

"What?" Tucker demanded. "Go ahead and spit it out. It's not like you to keep your opinions to yourself. You're likely to bust a gut."

"Okay, forget the integrity issue for the moment. There's more at stake. Do you really think this is wise?" she asked.

"Not the point," Tucker retorted. "Mary Elizabeth asked me to help, and that's that."

"I admire your loyalty," Anna-Louise said. "But how are your constituents going to feel about you running around second-guessing your own deputy?"

"I'm not second-guessing anybody," Tucker countered. "I'm just conducting an independent investigation to make sure that no stone is left unturned."

Mary Elizabeth winced. "Even to me that sounds like second-guessing." She looked at Anna-Louise. "Will people really get upset if he does this?"

"They could. I've already heard some gossip about you and Tucker being out to dinner last night. It was the hot topic at Earlene's this morning."

"We should have been more discreet." She looked at Tucker. "I'm sorry."

"Stop apologizing. Dinner was my idea. I can live with the fallout."

"And this?" Anna-Louise asked with an all-encompassing sweep of the room. "If they were upset about dinner in public, how do you think they'll feel when they discover that Liz is staying here, sharing a cozy little breakfast in your kitchen?"

Mary Elizabeth looked appalled at the implication. "I'm sharing breakfast with you," she reminded the minister.

"Anyone driving by and spotting your car out front won't know that." She gave Mary Elizabeth's hand a squeeze. "Appearances are important. You know that. And this doesn't look good. Why not come and stay with Richard and me for a while, at least until after the funeral and things settle down again?"

"I don't know," Mary Elizabeth said. "Maybe it would be best."

"Hey, you two," Tucker said, drawing their attention back to him. "I invited Mary Elizabeth to stay here. This is my call. I'm not worried, so there's no reason for either of you to be."

"But I would never forgive myself if my staying here—if having you do this investigation—cost you votes next time you run for sheriff," Mary Elizabeth said, regarding him with concern.

"And I could never forgive myself if I walked away from this, so there you have it," Tucker retorted, putting an end to the discussion, or at least trying to.

"I can fire you," Mary Elizabeth said.

"Doesn't mean I'll stop working," he shot back. "I never walk away from a case until it's over. As for the rest, it's up to you. I'm comfortable with you staying here, but if you're not, move to Anna-Louise's. Of course, you'll be having a journalist watching your every move if you do that."

Anna-Louise scowled at him. "Would that be any worse than having a cop watch her every move?" she inquired tartly.

"Probably not," he conceded.

"I'll think about it," Mary Elizabeth told the pastor. "May I call you later?"

"Of course," she said.

Tucker regarded Anna-Louise with curiosity. "So, what's the speculation at Earlene's about the killer? Any theories?"

"Aren't policemen supposed to be more interested in facts than theories?" Anna-Louise asked.

"Sometimes the best theories contain a nugget of

truth. I'll take my leads anywhere I can find them," Tucker responded. "What's Richard heard?"

"Nothing he's passed on to me, more's the pity," the minister said with a hint of disgust. "He's been working 'round the clock to get out this week's edition. I do know this, people around here are very nervous. Earlene says she hasn't heard this much talk about alarm systems and guard dogs since that banker was killed a few years ago. Trinity Harbor has always been a quiet, safe place to raise a family. This has shaken everyone, reminded them that the real world is encroaching. Next thing you know, there's going to a backlash against any and all attempts at development or tourism. People don't want to give up the peaceful way of life that's been theirs for generations."

"I doubt we can hold it back," Tucker said honestly.

"I agree," Anna-Louise said. "But isn't it a shame we can't?"

"Amen to that," Tucker said, his gaze on Mary Elizabeth. He certainly wished he could turn back the clock—say, six years or so—to a time when this woman had been his to love. Maybe, with a second chance, he could have figured out some way to keep her from making what had clearly turned out to be the biggest mistake of her life.

8

Liz thought she'd been doing a pretty amazing job of holding herself together. All those years of deceiving everyone into believing that she was leading a charmed life had served her well. No one, with the possible exception of Tucker, had seen just how terrified and alone she felt. But Anna-Louise's reminder that she was going to have to go to the funeral home and make the arrangements for Larry's burial brought reality crashing down on her.

This wasn't just some terrible nightmare or TV soap opera. Larry Chandler—the most vital man on earth, albeit a philanderer—was actually dead, and she was going to have to bury him without letting a single soul see the disdain she had come to feel for him. The realization set off a trembling deep inside her that wouldn't stop. She had already buried too many important people in her life—first her parents, then her beloved grandfather, who'd died less than a year after her marriage, content that he was leaving her in capable hands. If he'd only known…

"Are you all right?" Anna-Louise asked, regarding her worriedly.

"It just hit me," Liz said, feeling suddenly shell-shocked. "Isn't that crazy? Everything happened so fast that it just hit me that my husband is gone forever, that he won't be coming back."

"It happens that way sometimes," the pastor said. "Sometimes the mind keeps the truth at a distance until we're ready to cope with it."

"What if we're never ready?" Liz asked, thinking of the huge void Larry's absence would leave in her life. Granted, she'd been preparing for that ever since she'd decided to divorce him, but it wasn't the same. It couldn't be, when the void was so...permanent.

"We're ready when we need to be," Anna-Louise insisted. "God gives us the strength to do the things we have to do. Would you like me to call someone to go with you to make the arrangements?"

Liz bit back a hysterical sob. "There's no one. Isn't that funny? A woman who once knew everyone in this town has no one to call for help." Once she would have called Daisy, but that was out of the question now.

"Except Tucker," Anna-Louise said quietly.

"I can't ask him to do this," Liz said firmly. "I can do it. The people at the funeral home are old family friends. They'll make it easy for me. I just need a few minutes to pull myself together."

"I'll come with you," Anna-Louise said decisively. "I won't let you do this alone."

"Thank you, but I can't ask you to spend your time that way."

"It's what I'm here for, to assist you in any way I can."

Liz thought of Frances's offer to help. "No, it's okay.

Actually there is someone I can call. Frances will meet me there, I'm sure. She and my grandfather were dear friends. She'll do it for his sake."

"Of course she will," Anna-Louise said at once. "Why don't I call her, while you get ready?"

Liz realized then that she was still wearing her robe, an expensive silky confection that bared too much. No wonder Anna-Louise had been appalled by her presence in Tucker's kitchen. "I'm sorry," she said, gesturing to her attire. "It's all I had."

"I'm not judging you. It's not my business to judge anyone."

"Then you're a rarity," Liz said.

"Only because I take my job seriously. I counsel. I never judge. I leave that to a higher authority."

Liz smiled at the comfortable, easy way the minister had of speaking about God. "Wouldn't it be nice if everyone had the same relationship with their boss that you have with yours?"

Anna-Louise grinned. "Oh, we've had our share of squabbles," she assured her. "But in the end, I'm usually forced to admit He knows what He's doing."

"I like you," Liz told her impulsively. "I wish we were getting to know each other under other circumstances."

"We have lots of time," Anna-Louise said, regarding her with a serene expression that had the power to soothe. "Something tells me you're home to stay."

Home, Liz thought. How long had it been since she'd allowed herself to think of Trinity Harbor as home? She could trace it to the moment she'd walked down the aisle at Anna-Louise's church—long before Anna-Louise's arrival there—and said her vows to Larry. At that instant, when she'd severed the final tie to her past with Tucker, she had known that for her Trinity Harbor would never be the same.

At the time, she'd had few regrets, beyond the knowledge that she'd hurt a man who hadn't deserved it. She'd always wanted to live in a big city with all of its cultural opportunities. Knowing that they would live in Richmond for much of the year, with only duty calls back to see Larry's constituents in Trinity Harbor, had been part of his appeal. That Washington might be their next stop was even more appealing.

She had known what turning her back on Tucker and Trinity Harbor meant. People here had long memories, and they loved Tucker. Taking their cues from King, they'd been distant with her from that moment on. They'd behaved exactly as she'd anticipated.

Was it possible after all this time to win back their affection, to earn a real place for herself here? Would it be fair to Tucker? Would she even be able to bear spending all her time in a community that held so many memories if the man who was central to them kept her at arm's length?

Liz sighed. None of those questions could be answered today, or even in a week. All she knew for sure was that Richmond had lost its glamour. Time would tell if Trinity Harbor would be enough for her. Luckily, she had nothing but time on her hands.

Walker scowled when Tucker strolled into the sheriff's office on Courthouse Square in Montross. "What are you doing here?"

Tucker frowned right back at him, pointedly taking note of the fact that Walker was sitting in *his* chair, behind *his* desk. "Unless there's been a coup, it's still my office. I've taken a leave of absence. I haven't quit. You getting power hungry already?"

"No way," Walker said fervently. "You can have this job back anytime you want it. Just so you know, though, I may never forgive you for tossing me this particular political hot potato." He waved a stack of messages in Tucker's direction. "These are the media calls." He picked up another stack. "These are inquiries from Chandler's cronies in the house of delegates." He reached for another batch. "And these are from the concerned citizens of the county, who wonder if they're going to be shot while they're watching *Jeopardy* some night. Any suggestions what I should do about them?"

Tucker gathered up all three stacks and tossed them in the trash. "Just do your job. Solve Chandler's murder, and the rest will take care of itself."

"If only," Walker retorted. "Try telling that to the media hounds who have tired of waiting for my calls and started gathering outside."

"I noticed," Tucker said with little sympathy. "I had to duck around back to get inside."

"Somebody's going to have to talk to them sooner or later. They're not going away," Walker lamented.

"Send Michele out," Tucker suggested. "She's pretty good at fending off annoying pests."

Walker finally grinned. "Not a bad idea. I'll be right back. Sit tight. As long as you're here, we need to talk."

Tucker sat in the visitor's chair, leaving his own seat for Walker. For once he was glad to relinquish it. Despite his refusal to display any overt sympathy for Walker's plight, he didn't envy his brother-in-law the position he'd put him in.

Walker came back in, a smile splitting his face. "Michele's out there now, giving them a bunch of double talk drenched in honey. They're lapping it up, especially those jaded guys from the papers up in D.C. Won't be till after she's back inside that they realize she hasn't actually given them any news." He met Tucker's gaze. "Now, then, why don't you tell me just how deep you plan to dig in this case?"

"Till I hit pay dirt," Tucker said.

"Are you going to work with me or make my life hell?" Walker asked bluntly.

Tucker laughed. "Your call."

"Okay, then. Just don't tamper with any evidence, share whatever you find and we'll be okay."

"You'll do the same?"

"As much as I can," Walker agreed. "I won't keep anything from you unless I feel it could compromise the investigation."

"In other words, if it involves Mary Elizabeth."

"Pretty much."

"Fair enough. What do you have so far?"

Walker flipped open a file. "He was shot at point-blank range. Doc James figures that means whoever shot him was someone he knew and allowed to get right in his face. We'll see if the medical examiner in Richmond agrees. No sign of a weapon anywhere on the premises. We've got about a million sets of fingerprints we're checking out. Too bad Mrs. Chandler didn't have the housekeeper clean before she came back to town. It would have made our lives easier. As it is, there are prints there from their last visit, when they apparently threw some sort of fund-raiser. Richard tells me the place was crawling with bigwigs from all over the state.

He's promised to bring over all the pictures he took at the event, but I seriously doubt we'll find anything that will do us a bit of good."

"Can I see the crime-scene photos?"

"Sure." Walker handed him a thick envelope. "Maybe you'll spot something I missed."

Tucker sifted through the pictures, most of which showed a room that was as tidy as if nothing untoward had taken place there. Only the photos of the victim himself betrayed any evidence of the violent attack. "Three gunshot wounds?" he asked, startled. Mary Elizabeth had mentioned only one.

"Yes," Walker confirmed. "Whoever did it wanted to make very sure he was dead. The shot that clipped an artery accounts for all the blood. That's probably the one that killed him."

"Does that suggest something to you?" Tucker asked.

"Revenge comes to mind," Walker conceded. "But so does panic."

"I like revenge better," Tucker said grimly. "At least it gives us something to look for. You run across anybody who hated Chandler yet?"

"Not me. You're in a better position to assemble a list of suspects like that than I am. Mrs. Chandler hasn't given me that list of names she promised yet. So far all I have are those unsigned letters and anonymous answering machine tapes. Has she been any more forthcoming with you?"

"Just one name so far, a woman who used to work as Chandler's campaign manager—Cynthia Miles."

"Why would she want him dead?"

"Mary Elizabeth discovered they were having an affair and had Chandler fire Ms. Miles right after he was elected to office. She also made sure her husband broke off the affair."

"That gives us motive, assuming she carried a grudge for what, six years or so? It doesn't give us much else to go on. I'll track her down, though. She still in Richmond?"

"According to Mary Elizabeth, she is."

"Anything else?" Walker asked.

"Not so far, but I haven't really started to dig. The thing I do know is that there's not even one viable political opponent here in the county who might be desperate to land Chandler's seat in the house of delegates. He's had a lock on it since he won that first election. Ken Willis went up against him once and was destroyed by a landslide. Nobody's wanted to challenge Chandler since that debacle."

"How about business enemies?"

"I'll look into that today," Tucker said. "Walker, you're the homicide expert. Do you think there's any chance in hell this could have been a random killing, a robbery that went awry, maybe?"

"It doesn't look that way to me, not with no signs of forced entry, and Mrs. Chandler hasn't come up with anything that's missing."

"Maybe the killer heard her coming back to the house and took off before he could take anything," Tucker said. "Is there an estimate yet on the time of death?"

"Sometime between eight o'clock at night and two in the morning. Doc James says the state M.E. might be able to narrow it down a little further than that, but so far that's his best estimate."

Unfortunately, Mary Elizabeth had returned to the house right smack in the middle of that range, according to her story that she'd gotten home during the eleven o'clock news. If she was telling the truth, that would narrow the time of death to the hours between eight and eleven.

If she was lying, she could have been there right when her husband was being shot…and she could have been the one pulling the trigger.

Tucker looked up to see Walker regarding him sympathetically.

"Yeah, I know," his deputy said. "That keeps Mrs. Chandler right at the top of the list of suspects. We *know* she was there during that time frame, because she's admitted it. And so far, she's the only one we know of who had both motive and opportunity."

Tucker couldn't deny the obvious. That didn't mean he had to accept it. "I know in my gut she didn't do it," he told Walker. "That may not be good enough for you, but it is for me."

"I'm sorry, but I can't let it be good enough for me," Walker said. "Tell her to keep that sleazebag attorney's phone number handy."

Over the next few hectic days, Tucker kept his conversation with Walker to himself. Unfortunately he couldn't prevent it from popping into his head every time he looked at Mary Elizabeth. Could she have done it? Could she have changed so much in the last six years that she could have shot her own husband, then coolly walked away and crawled into Tucker's bed?

Absolutely not, he told himself over and over. But how well did he really know her anymore? She was calm under pressure. He'd seen that for himself when

Powell had called that impromptu press conference as a preemptive strike over at Swan Ridge.

Granted, she had little if anything to gain from Chandler's death. If her goal was to get him out of her life, the divorce she was planning would have accomplished the same thing...unless he'd intended to fight dirty, the way that argument in the restaurant implied. She didn't need her husband's money...unless, of course, she had managed to squander her entire inheritance. Much as he hated it, Tucker knew he was going to have to check into all of that.

That could wait, though. The funeral she'd arranged was this morning, and he'd promised to be there, at her side. Frances was planning to accompany them, as well. That ought to make his father's blood boil. In fact, he had to wonder if King would even come to the service, though years of doing his duty as a Spencer would probably compel him to make a pretense of showing respect for the region's most prominent politician.

Tucker glanced up and found Mary Elizabeth hovering uncertainly in the doorway to the kitchen. She was dressed in black from head to toe. It was not her best color. It drained her already pale complexion and emphasized the increasingly dark circles under her eyes that not even expertly applied makeup could conceal.

"You okay?" he asked quietly. "Sit down and I'll get you something to eat."

"I'm not hungry," she said, but she did sit. She regarded him with a plaintive expression. "How am I going to get through this?"

"By remembering who you are and by doing what your grandfather would have expected of you. You can do it. You're stronger than you realize."

A faint trace of a smile touched her lips. "Ah, yes, the Swans excel at doing the right thing in the face of adversity. My grandfather never shed one single tear when he buried my parents."

"Which meant you couldn't, either," Tucker guessed. It was something they'd never discussed. The funeral had taken place before they'd even met, and for years she'd never wanted to talk about her parents at all.

She nodded. "Every time it seemed as if I might cry, he'd look at me with that disapproving frown that, I swear, could dry up the entire Atlantic. I knew better than to let one single tear escape. He considered tears a sign of weakness."

"You were a kid," Tucker said angrily.

"Didn't matter. I was a Swan."

"Do you ever wonder what your life would have been like if your parents hadn't been killed in Switzerland?" he asked.

"I didn't need to wonder. I knew. It would have been carefree and exciting and filled with interesting people. That's certainly the way it was for the first nine years of my life." She regarded him with a wry expression. "Of course, for the most part, I was on the outside looking in. I can remember sitting at the top of the steps in some house we'd rented for the winter, listening to the music and the laughter downstairs, wondering what sort of exotic food they were serving that night and who was there. I used to daydream that a handsome prince—and there was almost always a handsome prince around—would spot me and whisk me downstairs and dance with me."

"It sounds lonely," Tucker said.

Mary Elizabeth looked surprised that he had grasped

that. "It was. Being here, even under those terrible circumstances, was so much better. Swan Ridge was a real home. My grandfather actually paid attention to me. He could be strict and difficult and undemonstrative, but there was never one single second when I wondered whether or not he knew I was around, not one moment when I doubted that he loved me."

She regarded Tucker with a sad smile. "And then there was you. I had never had a best friend before. We never stayed any one place long enough. I knew at first that you thought I was a pest, but I was determined to make you like me."

Tucker grinned. "That explains all those boxes of chocolate-chip cookies I was always finding on the front porch with my name on them."

"I knew you loved them, because your mom, and later Daisy, were always baking them for you."

"But theirs weren't burned crisp at the edges," he teased, finally earning a full-fledged smile.

"I'm better in the kitchen now. One of these days I'll whip up a gourmet meal and amaze you."

"Not necessary," he said quietly. "You've always amazed me."

Their gazes clashed, and something heavy with longing sizzled in the air. Tucker knew it was wrong, knew it could lead to nothing but trouble, but he couldn't bring himself to look away.

"Ah, Mary Elizabeth," he whispered at last.

"I know," she said, finally breaking the eye contact. "We can't do this."

"No," he said firmly. "We can't." He made a point of looking at his watch. "I think we should get over to the church. Frances said she'd meet us in Anna-

Louise's office. We can wait there until it's time for the service to start."

In the car, Mary Elizabeth looked over at him. "You don't have to sit with me. I know it could be awkward."

His jaw set with grim determination. "I can deal with awkward."

"You shouldn't have to. Not on my account."

"Mary Elizabeth, we're not having this discussion again. It's settled. Unless you don't want me there, I'll stay with you."

"Dammit, Tucker, I'm trying to do the right thing. Don't make it any harder than it already is. Please," she pleaded. "Your father would be outraged. So would a lot of other people in town. What's the point?"

"The point is, you need someone," he said.

"I'll have Frances. She's been a godsend the last few days. So has Anna-Louise. I'll be fine."

"You're sure?"

She nodded.

"All right, then. I'll stay at the back of the church. If you need me, all you have to do is look my way."

"I'm already leaning on you too much. I can get through this on my own."

"As long as you know you don't have to," he said.

"I know."

He pulled into the lot behind the small, white-steepled brick church that had been built in the late eighteenth century. So far the parking lot was blessedly free of media and mourners. He helped Mary Elizabeth from the car, then escorted her quickly inside just as the first television satellite truck from Richmond pulled onto the street behind the church. He saw the reporter leap out and sprint in their direction, but Tucker very firmly shut the church door in the man's face and flipped the lock for good measure.

Anna-Louise and Frances met them in the hall. Frances enveloped Mary Elizabeth in a hug.

"She's in good hands now," Anna-Louise reassured Tucker as Frances led Mary Elizabeth into the pastor's office.

"She won't let herself fall apart," Tucker said. "I'm not sure that's healthy."

"She's grieving, don't make any mistake about that," Anna-Louise said. "I may not know everything that was going on in her marriage, but I've gathered there was trouble. She's facing a lot of conflicting emotions today—grief, guilt, maybe even a twinge of relief. You can't help her with any of it, Tucker. She has to work through this in her own way. The best thing you can do for her now is to find out who killed her husband."

He cast one last look after Mary Elizabeth, then nodded. "What did you decide about the TV cameras?"

"They won't be inside the church or on the cemetery grounds. No other cameras, either. Walker says he's got that covered. I can't keep 'em away from the street, so I'm sure they'll be swarming everywhere out there."

"And Richard?"

She gave him a rueful look. "Yes, that was a tricky one," she admitted. "But I told my husband the church was off-limits to his camera, too. He's outside milling around somewhere, probably muttering about marrying the most hardheaded woman on the face of the earth."

Tucker chuckled. "I'll go look for him."

"Feed him some juicy tidbit about the investigation, if you can. It might make things go better at home tonight."

An edge in her voice worried him. "You didn't fight over this, did you?"

"We don't fight," she said indignantly, then grinned. "We have noisy discussions and ultimately agree to disagree, especially when it comes to matters related to our careers. When we got married, we accepted the fact that sometimes our ethics were going to bump smack into each other and cause problems. Knowing that in advance relieves some of the tension when it happens."

"That actually works?" Tucker asked skeptically.

"It has so far," she said. "By the way, I also saw your father milling around outside earlier. He didn't look any happier than Richard. Maybe you can pacify him while you're out there."

Tucker groaned. "You don't expect much, do you?"

"Only what you're capable of doing," she said with an innocently pious expression.

"Yeah, right."

Tucker left her and slipped out the back door of the church, then wandered around the walkway to the front. King spotted him before he'd taken two steps across the grass.

"Couldn't you at least have had the good sense to stay away from here today?" his father inquired testily.

"You didn't," Tucker pointed out.

"It's my duty as a Spencer to be here," King retorted.

"And it's my duty as Mary Elizabeth's friend to show my respect for her loss."

His father snorted. "As if that's got anything at all to do with you being here."

"Don't go there, King. Not here and not now." He glanced pointedly at the TV cameras aimed their way as well as at Richard, who was approaching with the grim determination of a man on a mission.

"You," King said with a sniff. "Might have known you'd be poking around here."

"Ditto," Richard said without rancor. "Tucker, could I talk to you a minute?"

"He's got nothing to say," King snapped.

"I imagine Tucker is capable of answering for himself," Richard said with a hint of exasperation. "Tucker?"

"Out back," Tucker said. "Daddy, if you want to wait till I get back, I'll sit with you."

"Don't do me any favors," his father retorted with a scowl. "You insist on coming inside and making a fool of yourself, steer clear of me."

Tucker sighed, fully aware that Richard had taken note of every word. The instant they got around the corner, the editor of the *Trinity Harbor Weekly* studied him with piercing intensity.

"Mind telling me what that was all about?"

"You know King," Tucker said with a shrug. "His children seldom do what suits him."

"Sounded to me as if there's some specific reason he thought you should be steering clear of the funeral," Richard said. "Does it have something to do with the fact that you and Liz Chandler used to be involved? Several people have taken great pleasure in filling me in on that, and on how she dumped you to marry Chandler. True?"

Since most people in town already knew that whole story, Tucker saw little reason to deny it. "Yes," he said tersely. "Are we on the record here?"

"Unless you object," Richard told him.

"No. I can live with that. I just want to be sure I understand the rules before I answer you."

"Fair enough. We're on the record." Richard glanced at his notes. "So, is your past with Liz the reason you've taken a leave of absence from the sheriff's office? Because of the potential for a perceived conflict of interest?"

"Yes."

"Couldn't you just steer clear of any involvement in the investigation?"

"I could have," Tucker said. "But Mary Elizabeth asked me to help her. If I'm going to do that, I have to do it in an unofficial capacity. I don't want to do anything that could be detrimental to a case against whoever did this."

"And you think that's someone other than Liz?"

"Yes."

"How did you come to that conclusion? Is there any evidence so far that points in another direction?"

Tucker scowled at him. "Whatever happened to printing nice little stories about school bake sales and the upcoming arts and crafts festival over at Colonial Beach?"

"Trust me, I have room enough to get those stories in, too," Richard assured him. "Surely you don't expect me to ignore the murder of a prominent politician that happened right here in Trinity Harbor?"

"I can always dream," Tucker responded.

"You gonna answer my question or not?" Richard prodded. "Are there any other suspects?"

"There are *no* suspects at this time," Tucker retorted emphatically, then added, "in my opinion. You want an official statement, you'll have to track down Walker. He's in charge."

"Is there any chance you can get Mrs. Chandler to talk to me?"

"None," Tucker said. "Because I won't even ask."

"Her attorney seems to be more media savvy than that," Richard pointed out.

"Then talk to Powell, but if he's half as smart as I think he is, he's going to advise Mary Elizabeth to keep her mouth shut from here on out. That statement she made the other day at Swan Ridge is the only thing she'll be saying on the record until we have the murderer locked away."

"Is she stonewalling the police?"

"Ask Walker."

"Is she cooperating with the investigation?"

"Ask Walker."

"Has she given them any leads?"

"Ask Walker."

"Can she explain her whereabouts on the night her husband was killed?"

Tucker shook his head. "How many more of these questions are you going to throw at me before you catch on that I'm not going to answer them?"

"I was hoping you'd get irritated and slip up," Richard said, shooting him an unrepentant grin. "I should have known better."

"Well, at least you got the irritated part right," Tucker consoled him. If the friendly publisher of the local paper was going to be this annoying, then with all those Richmond journalists crawling around outside the church, it was going to be a very long afternoon.

9

Because Swan Ridge was still considered a crime scene, the reception after the funeral was held in the church's parish hall. A Richmond caterer Liz had worked with in the past had provided the food, which she realized at once was far too fancy for the occasion. There was no mistaking the surprised expressions and the whispered comments as Trinity Harbor's residents came upon finger sandwiches and elegant tarts, rather than sliced ham and molded Jell-O salads provided by concerned neighbors.

As she had all afternoon, Frances was quick to offer consolation. "Pay them no mind. They're just looking for something to talk about."

"I should have known better. They think I'm putting on airs," Liz lamented.

"Give them a few minutes till they've had a chance to taste those little pecan tarts. They'll be begging for the recipe," Frances reassured her.

"I suppose," Liz said, searching the mobbed hall for a glimpse of Tucker. He'd stayed within view all afternoon, grounding her. Now, though, there seemed to be no sign of him. Instead, she turned to stare squarely into the tear-blotched face of Cynthia Miles.

"Have you even shed one tear?" the woman asked loudly, weaving on her feet. "Don't you owe him that much?"

The words were like a slap in the face. Liz reacted with anger and hurt and an overwhelming desire to strike back. Instead, before she could say or do anything, Tucker appeared at her side.

"Everything okay?" he asked mildly.

"Who's this?" Cynthia demanded. "Larry's replacement?"

Steadied by Tucker's presence, Liz said, "No. This is Sheriff Tucker Spencer, Cynthia. He's helping me find out who killed Larry. Perhaps you'd like to share some thoughts with him. Tucker, this is Cynthia Miles."

"Ah," he said. "Ms. Miles, perhaps we could talk outside." Before Cynthia could make a scene, he tucked a hand under her arm and steered her toward an exit.

Only when they were out of sight did Liz breathe a sigh of relief.

"Don't mind Cynthia," Ainsley Hayden said as he joined her. "You know how protective she was of Larry."

Liz turned to her husband's former chief of staff, a brilliant man who had sincerely had Larry's best interests at heart. "A bit of an understatement, don't you think?"

He didn't pretend not to understand. "The affair was over a long time ago, Liz. Once Larry fired her, they rarely had any contact."

"For which she has always blamed me," Liz reminded him. "I had the audacity not only to have her fired, but to insist that he end their relationship. She's obviously still very bitter about that."

"He would have ended it sooner or later on his own," Ainsley insisted. "Cynthia's not stable. Any number of people on his staff had warned Larry of that. They told me that they could all see the signs that she was making way too much out of the time they spent together."

"How comforting," she said wryly. "Should I have waited for him to figure out what the rest of Richmond already knew?"

"No. Your timing was impeccable," he said with a faint grin. "That's when he hired me."

She managed a laugh. "So it was. How did I ever forget that?" She sobered at once. "Do you realize that you're one of the few people who will genuinely mourn his death? He came to think of you as a brother."

"The love and respect were mutual," Ainsley said. "I know he treated you badly, Liz, but in his own way, he did love you."

"His way just wasn't good enough anymore," she said with genuine sorrow.

"Then it's true? You were going to divorce him?"

"Did he tell you that?" Liz asked, curious to see if Larry had shared the information even with a man he considered his best friend.

"No. The rumor has been making the rounds in Richmond the last few days."

"Any idea who started it?" she asked, thinking of Tucker's opinion that someone in the restaurant that night could have used her fight with Larry to try quite literally to get away with murder.

He regarded her curiously. "Does it matter?"

"It could," she told him.

"Okay, let me think a minute. Pauline told me," he said, referring to his executive assistant. "She said it was all over Richmond that the two of you had had a huge fight at Chez Dominique. She'd fielded several media calls asking for confirmation by the time I got into the office that morning. She referred them to the PR office we kept on retainer. Before he left for Trinity Harbor that day, Larry notified them to respond to any query with no comment."

"Did any of the reporters mention who'd tipped them off?"

"You'd have to ask Pauline to be certain, but my guess would be that none of them revealed a source."

Liz sighed. "You're probably right. Has the information been reported in any of the papers? I've been avoiding reading any of them."

"Not so far. I think they're showing restraint for the moment. Larry was well-respected by the media in Richmond. Now that the funeral's over, though, I imagine the kid gloves will come off." He peered at her intently. "Is there anything I can do for you? Do you want me to have the PR people contact you and field any media inquiries in your behalf?"

Liz shook her head. "I can refuse to comment as well as a spokesperson can. And I imagine whoever's appointed to fill Larry's seat will want you there for the transition. You'll have your hands full with that."

He nodded. "Call if you change your mind. Officially, Pauline and I may have worked for Larry, but we considered you part of the team. We're happy to do anything we can to make this time easier for you."

Tears stung Liz's eyes at the sincere offer. "Thank you. I haven't seen Pauline. Is she here?"

"Probably in the rest room, crying her eyes out.

She's been inconsolable since the moment we heard the news."

"I'll look for her there," Liz promised.

Pauline Taylor's first job had been on Ainsley's staff as a clerk. Because of her sharp mind and loyalty, she had quickly risen to become his executive assistant. She was only in her mid-twenties, but she understood Virginia politics and the delicate balancing act of building power bases as well as anyone in Richmond. What made her even more valuable was her own total lack of personal ambition. She was completely dedicated to the fortunes of the two people she worked for: Ainsley and Larry. She would have walked through fire for either one of them. It was little wonder that she was grief-stricken.

Liz turned back to Ainsley and saw that his expression had turned speculative. "What?" she asked.

"Any possibility you'll consider taking over the seat, at least until the next election? You'd be a natural. You helped to mold Larry's agenda on the issues. You're fantastic on the campaign trail. In fact, I think you'd be a shoo-in if you decided to run for the office down the road."

"Not a chance," Liz said fiercely. "I've had my fill of politics. I'm staying right here and becoming a private citizen again."

"Don't be so quick to say no," Ainsley pleaded. "You'd be good at it. Everyone knew you were the one who had a genuine rapport with Larry's constituents."

"That's very nice of you to say, but no thanks. I won't be going back to Richmond in any capacity."

"Not even to finish out your terms on the various charity boards you're on?" he asked, clearly startled.

She hadn't considered that. All those charities might

not want her around, at least until her name was completely cleared. But for those that did, she would continue to help in any way she could. "I can commute for that," she told him.

"That's that then," he said with what sounded like real regret. "If you change your mind..."

"I'll call you," she promised.

"Any idea who might be good as a replacement? The governor's going to want some ideas. I might as well have a few suggestions handy."

"I'll think about it," she said. "If I come up with any suggestions, I'll get back to you."

"The last person to express any interest in the job was Ken Willis. What do you think of him?" Ainsley asked.

"If there's another way to go, choose it," she said at once, glancing across the parish hall at a cluster of people that included Willis, his wife, Arlene, and a few local political party bigwigs. Ken and Arlene had been classmates of Liz's, but she hadn't liked them much better then than she did now. Though Ken had preached a lot about cleaning up campaign rhetoric and financing, there had been a number of accusations of sleazy actions that surfaced during his one primary campaign against Larry. He'd sworn at the time that he'd had no part in them, but there was little question that the buck stopped with him.

"Willis isn't capable of running an effective campaign, much less doing the job that's required," she said bluntly. "And I don't think he's especially trustworthy."

Ainsley chuckled. "Nothing lukewarm about that response. I'll keep looking."

Relieved that he'd gotten the message about a man

who could never adequately fill Larry's shoes, she nodded. "And, Ainsley, if you have any thoughts at all about who might have wanted Larry dead, let me know."

"Absolutely," he said, his expression grim. "I want the bastard who did this caught as badly as you do."

Tucker sat silently while a drunken Cynthia Miles sobbed her eyes out. If he hadn't known the whole story about her relationship with Chandler, he might have felt sorry for her. She seemed genuinely grief-stricken.

The woman looked to be in her mid-thirties. She had what was probably stylishly cut brown hair when it wasn't in tangled disarray. She was a little too thin and angular to suit him, but she wore her clothes well. He was no expert, but today's severe black suit looked as if it came with a designer label. Her handbag and shoes were made of fine leather. Managing campaigns must be a lucrative business, even on the state level, Tucker concluded as he waited for her to regain her composure.

Eventually her sobs died away. He handed her a clean handkerchief from his back pocket.

"Sorry," she said as she dabbed her eyes and blew her nose. "I don't know what came over me."

"It's an emotional occasion," he said.

"I suppose you already know that I loved him," she said.

"I know you had an affair with him," he corrected.

She was smart enough to catch the distinction. Her gaze narrowed. "I *loved* him," she repeated emphatically. "No matter what *she* says."

"Are you sure that declaring your love for a married man who's just been murdered is wise?" he inquired.

"Are you suggesting that I killed him because I couldn't have him?"

Tucker shrugged. "I'm not suggesting anything. I'm just pointing out that you could be taking a risk."

"Why would you care about that?" she taunted him. "Wouldn't you like to find someone to pin this on so you can get your girlfriend in there off the hook and close the case?"

"Mrs. Chandler is not my girlfriend," he said firmly. "And I just want the truth to come out, Ms. Miles. I want justice to be served."

"Then I suggest you look a bit more closely at Ms. High-and-Mighty in there. She's the one with the ax to grind against Larry."

Tucker restrained his desire to leap to Mary Elizabeth's defense. "Oh?" he said blandly. "Why is that?"

"Because of all the other women in his life."

"If you loved him, as you've just said you did, weren't you equally angry about that?"

"I understood that he had needs," she insisted.

"Really? Few women can turn a blind eye to their mate's infidelity. Why were you able to? I would think it would be that much harder to take the fact that there were other women after he'd dumped you at his wife's request."

She pulled a pack of cigarettes from her purse, stuck one in her mouth and lit it with a match that trembled in her unsteady grasp. "I was the one she felt threatened by, because he loved me," she insisted.

"Unfortunately, we have only your word for that," Tucker said. He decided to change tactics before he alienated her. "Since you did know him so well, though, any ideas about who might have wanted to kill him?"

"Besides Liz?"

"Besides her," he said, refusing to be drawn into that argument again. "Did he have any business competitors? Any political enemies?"

"Of course," she said at once. "He was a powerful man. Power always draws enemies. Take a look at the chairman of the house education committee, Devlin Rowe. There was bad blood between them over a bill that Rowe sponsored and Larry got defeated last session. The governor was none too happy about that one, either. And I imagine you can find a number of people in the tech world who weren't happy with the fact that Larry had succeeded where they had failed."

Cynthia Miles studied him with a penetrating look. "Of course, there's also someone right here in your own backyard," she said slyly. "The man who lost Liz to Larry." She feigned dismay. "Oh dear, that would be you, wouldn't it? Sorry."

He regarded her evenly. "It's good to know you're up-to-date on old news," he commended her. "I'll make sure to pass along your suspicions to Deputy Ames."

"Who's he?"

"The officer in charge of the investigation."

"I thought that was you," she said, clearly startled.

"As you pointed out, that might be viewed by some as a conflict. I'm on a leave of absence from the department at my own request."

"But Liz said you were investigating the murder."

"I am," he told her. "For Mary Elizabeth. Have a good day, Ms. Miles."

Her indignant sputters followed him all the way back to the parish hall. Tucker smothered a grin as he went inside. He did love it when smart-mouthed individuals fell on their own sword.

* * *

When Tucker went back inside, he found Mary Elizabeth accepting condolences from a steady stream of well-heeled individuals, some of whom he recognized from the front page of the Richmond paper as being prominent politicians, some completely anonymous. Mary Elizabeth caught his eye and pointedly began to mention names for his benefit. When Devlin Rowe came along, Tucker immediately took a closer look.

The state delegate from the Roanoke area was a tall, distinguished-looking man with graying hair and a mild manner. He'd also been one of the primary proponents of school vouchers, which Chandler had opposed and mustered the votes to defeat.

"Sir, could I speak to you for a minute?" Tucker asked him once he'd expressed his condolences.

"Who're you?" Rowe inquired with a trace of impatience. "I've got a car waiting to take me back to Richmond."

"Then I'll walk outside with you," Tucker said. "I'm helping with the investigation into Larry Chandler's murder. I'd like to ask you a few questions."

The delegate's steely gray eyes chilled. "You with the police?"

"I'm working privately on this case, but I'm the sheriff of this county."

"How the devil did you land in a situation like that?" he asked.

Tucker grinned. "Long story. Mrs. Chandler and I are old friends. She asked for my assistance."

"And you had the good sense to take a leave so you could do it, rather than getting embroiled in a controversy about conflict of interest," Rowe concluded.

"Good for you, young man. Too few public servants take such precautions these days."

"Was Chandler one who knew the distinction?" Tucker asked him.

Rowe's expression grew thoughtful. "You know he and I didn't get along, I imagine?"

"I'd heard you disagreed about one particular issue."

"More than one, as it happens, but I respected him. He was an honorable man. Made his position clear from the outset, so I always knew where he stood. Hard-headed as they come," he noted. "But that's not a sin, I suppose, just a danged nuisance."

Tucker laughed. "I imagine it would be."

"You're looking to see if we were sworn enemies, I imagine," Rowe said. "Well, sorry to disappoint you, but we weren't. We disagreed about how some things ought to be done for the good of the people, but we never had words over it, never called each other names in public or in private. You dig as deep as you want, Sheriff, you won't find any bad blood between me and Chandler—just honest differences of opinion."

"Can you say the same about his relationship with all of your colleagues?"

Rowe hooted at that. "Now that is another kettle of fish entirely. Not all politicians take the pragmatic view of the world that I do. Some take defeat of their bills downright personally, and when it comes to that and Chandler's leadership role in those defeats, well, you could say the man had a whole legion of enemies in Richmond. Yes, indeed, a whole legion of them."

"Care to name a few?"

"I wish I could. I surely do, but the governor's waiting right over there. Since I want to talk him into supporting a bill of mine, I don't want to start the ride back to Richmond with him being annoyed about me being late. You check the record from the last legislative session, Sheriff. I'm sure you'll find yourself a whole passel of suspects."

"I'll do that. Thank you for your time," he said, and watched as Devlin Rowe strode over to the black Cadillac waiting in the no parking zone in front of the church. He had half a mind to go over and write a ticket, but since he was officially off-duty, he figured he'd better restrain himself.

He was about to go back inside when he was joined by Walker.

"You finding out anything interesting?" Walker asked.

"No hard leads," Tucker said. "You?"

"Nothing. The bad thing about dealing with a whole passel of politicians is that they're used to lying their heads off. I did spend a little time with that Miles woman. I was a little surprised she had the guts to show up here."

"Not me," Tucker said. "She had the guts to sleep with Chandler right under his wife's nose only weeks after the wedding. Showing up here is nothing compared to that. She's got a lot of anger in her, but most of it's directed at Mary Elizabeth."

Walker nodded. "That was my take, too." He sighed. "And now here comes Richard. That man may run a small-town weekly, but those years at the *Washington Post* have made him as tenacious as the rest of these media pests."

"I heard that," Richard said. "Since you have so little

respect for what I do, I guess that means you don't want to know what I heard a few minutes ago."

Tucker scowled at him. "Don't play games. I'm not in the mood. I'll tell your wife."

Richard laughed. "Now *there's* an ingenious threat for a lawman to pull out. Damned effective, too. Okay, here's the deal. I talked with a guy named Ainsley Hayden. Liz introduced me. He was Chandler's chief of staff. The guy is smooth as silk, said all the right words about his boss, dropped a few hints about how he'd like to persuade Liz to take over Chandler's seat, but something didn't ring true to me, so I asked around. Some of the other delegates thought Hayden was getting tired of staying in the background. One even said he suspected he was planning his own run for office."

Tucker frowned at that. "From here? I've never even heard of him. He's never lived in the district."

"Maybe not, but he knows the politics. He'd have to as Chandler's right-hand man. All he'd have to do is buy a place around here, spend a little time hanging out at Earlene's and some other local spots where the movers and shakers congregate. Next thing you know, he can slide right into the job, especially if the governor were to appoint him to fill the position till the next election."

"Wait a minute," Tucker protested. "How likely is that? The governor's going to want his own person in that seat. He's reportedly miffed that Chandler didn't work with him on the voucher bill. That same animosity is bound to carry over to Hayden."

"Ah, you'd think so, wouldn't you?" Richard agreed. "But my source told me that Hayden practically jumped through hoops trying to bring Chandler around on that bill. They fought over it just before the bill came to the floor for a vote. And he apparently he made sure that their exchange was very public, so naturally the governor heard about it."

Tucker held up his hand. "Okay, enough. That's exactly the reason I hate politicians. You can't tell what sort of backroom deals are being made at any given moment."

"Hold it," Walker said. "Richard could be onto something. What if Hayden used that incident to ingratiate himself with the governor, then saw to it that Chandler conveniently was taken out of the picture to set up his own advancement?"

Mary Elizabeth joined them just in time to hear Walker's speculation. "You can't be serious?" she said, then blinked at his unyielding expression. "You are, aren't you? You honestly think Ainsley had something to do with killing Larry?"

"I'm just saying it's possible," Walker said. "We can't rule out anything at this point."

"That's almost as ridiculous as saying I did it," Mary Elizabeth countered. "Ainsley Hayden was the most loyal man in Richmond. He would have done anything for Larry. He certainly didn't shoot him."

"In your opinion," Walker pointed out quietly.

Mary Elizabeth's chin rose. "Yes," she said with dignity. "In my opinion, and I've known him a whole lot longer than any of you have."

"What kind of relationship did you have with him?" Walker asked.

Fury stained her cheeks red. Tucker decided he'd better intercede before Mary Elizabeth slapped the acting sheriff silly. She was capable of doing it if he riled her enough.

"Okay, enough, both of you," Tucker said as if he were dealing with a pair of squabbling five-year-olds. "This isn't getting us anywhere."

"I think maybe it is," Walker retorted. "Well, Mrs. Chandler? How close *were* you and Hayden?"

"How close are you and Michele?" she shot back.

Walker stared at her with obvious indignation. "What the hell has that got to do with anything?"

"You work together," she snapped. "So did Ainsley and I. Period. That was the extent of our involvement."

"You sound a little defensive," Walker challenged.

"So did you when I asked about your relationship with the dispatcher," she reminded him. "That doesn't make either one of us guilty of anything."

Richard, who had listened to the entire exchange without comment, turned to Walker. "I think she's got you there."

"She gets my vote, too," Tucker said.

Walker regarded the whole lot of them with a sour expression. "Then isn't it a damned good thing that I'm trying to solve a murder, instead of running for office?"

With that he turned and walked away. Tucker winced. "That was probably not the smartest thing we've ever done."

Mary Elizabeth sighed. "Probably not, but I am so tired of people twisting things to suit them, your buddy Walker included. I just want to go home."

"Fine," Tucker said at once. "I'll take you back to my place."

"No," she said at once. "I want to go *home.* Walker told me earlier that they've finished at Swan Ridge. I'm free to go back there."

The thought of Mary Elizabeth rattling around all

alone in that huge old house with all of its past and recent ghosts bothered Tucker. "Do you really think that's wise?"

"I think it's a whole lot smarter than prolonging my stay with you," she said. "The sooner I settle back into something that passes for a normal routine, the better. Besides, it will make King happy."

Tucker should have expected his father's involvement, but he'd actually hoped that for once the old man would manage to keep his opinions to himself. "What did he say?" Tucker asked wearily.

"Nothing that I didn't already know," she said. "Don't blame him, Tucker. He's right about this. It's enough that you've taken a leave from your job to help me. I don't want to ruin your reputation on top of that."

"My reputation can withstand a few knocks."

"But it shouldn't have to," she insisted. "Will you take me to Swan Ridge, or should I ask Frances to drive me? She's waiting to see if I need anything else before she leaves."

"I'll take you," he said tightly.

Mary Elizabeth looked at Richard then. "And will you report that I am now living in my family home?"

"Of course."

"Good. Even King ought to be satisfied with that," she said.

"Yeah, right," Tucker said skeptically.

He had a hunch the only way his father would be totally satisfied was if Mary Elizabeth moved halfway round the world without leaving a forwarding address. And *that,* Tucker decided, was only going to happen over his dead body.

10

Liz knew she was doing the right thing by leaving Tucker's and returning to her own home, but as she stood at the bottom of the steps at Swan Ridge, she hesitated. With dusk starting to close in around them, the place looked dark and imposing, not welcoming at all.

"You don't have to do this tonight," Tucker said. "Tomorrow would be soon enough. You've already had a stressful day."

"I have a hunch it's just one of many stressful days I'm likely to face in the coming weeks," Liz told him. "I might as well get this over with."

"Why don't I go inside first, take a look around and make sure the police haven't left too much of a mess?"

She smiled at the gallant offer. "No matter how they tidied up, they couldn't wash away the memories," she said.

"Maybe you should call the housekeeper, get her over here to give the place a thorough going over before you come back," he suggested. "I'm sure Mrs. Gilman won't mind."

"Same problem," she said. "It won't change the memories. I have to do this, Tucker. It's my home. I'm the only one who can reclaim it. Maybe giving the place a good, thorough cleaning myself will help me do that."

He sighed. "Darlin', I know you have to move back in here, but it doesn't have to be tonight."

"We're talking in circles," she said, then chuckled as a memory came flooding back. "Remember, we used to do that whenever we didn't want to separate at the end of the day? You'd say you had to leave. I'd ask you to stay a little longer. You'd say you had to go sometime. I'd plead for a few more minutes. We managed to prolong the good-nights for a half hour or so, but for what? You still had to go home and I had to go inside alone, and those extra minutes were wasted arguing."

"I think this is a little different," Tucker said dryly. "Your husband was murdered inside this house just a few days ago."

Liz's knees wobbled at the blunt reminder. Tucker caught her around the waist and steadied her.

"See?" he said with a hint of impatience. "You're not ready for this."

"I'm as ready as I'll ever be," she said, stiffening her resolve. There was only one way to do it…quickly. She broke free, marched up the steps, put her key into the lock and turned it. But when it came time to open the door, she froze again.

"I can do this," she muttered under her breath before Tucker could use her inaction to once again push for retreat. She drew in a deep breath and stepped across the threshold.

The air was still and hot inside. Someone had cut off the air-conditioning. The house smelled musty, as if it had been shut up and empty for months rather than days. And yet, cutting through the stale air, there was the lingering scent of the roses she'd brought in from the garden on her return that first day before everything had fallen apart.

She turned to Tucker and said staunchly, "You can go now. I'll be fine."

"I am not leaving here until we've been through the place and checked it out," he said stubbornly.

"Tucker, the killer's not hiding out in a closet," she said.

"You know that for a fact?"

A little twinge of alarm made the hairs on the back of her neck stand up. "You don't seriously think…?"

"Humor me. I'll feel better when I've been over the place from top to bottom."

She nodded finally, hating the relief that flooded through her. It was a sign of weakness, something she'd been taught to ignore. "I'll make some iced tea," she said a little too eagerly.

In the kitchen, she flipped on the bright lights, filled the teakettle with water and put it on to boil. She found the tea bags in the cupboard and a pitcher in the cabinet above the sink. Everything was exactly where it had always been, yet it all felt different.

Once upon a time, in the early days of her teenage romance with Tucker, they had spent a lot of late-night hours sitting at the round oak table in this room, confiding their hopes and dreams for the future. Ironically, the man with whom she'd eventually shared her future had seldom set foot in here. He'd considered it the housekeeper's domain.

Struck by a sudden need to recall something that had once been as familiar to her as breathing, she poked around in the refrigerator until she found a package of already prepared chocolate-chip cookie dough. She'd developed an addiction to chocolate-chip cookies years ago because of Tucker, and it had been the one thing she'd clung to during the years since. Whenever she was feeling down, she baked chocolate-chip cookies. It was her secret way of going back to a happier time. Mrs. Gilman had been instructed that there was always to be a package of ready-to-bake dough in the refrigerator.

Liz broke the pieces apart and placed them on a cookie sheet, then popped them into the oven. By the time Tucker finally joined her, the room was filled with their sweet scent.

Tucker regarded her with surprise. "You're baking at this hour?"

She gestured toward the package. "I'm cheating, but yes. I wanted to do something that would remind me of simpler, happier times." She met his gaze. "Will you stay a little longer?"

"As long as you want," he said, pulling out a chair, then gesturing toward the oven with a grin. "But if you burn those, I'm out of here."

Liz sniffed the air. Sure enough, the aroma was subtly shifting to something less appetizing. "Blast it all," she said, whipping open the door, grabbing the sheet of cookies, then yelping in pain. "Blast and damn!"

Tucker was on his feet at once. "What?"

"No oven mitt," she muttered, her teeth clenched.

"Sit," he ordered. "Where's the first-aid kit?"

"I'll get it. You save the cookies."

He pushed her none-too-gently back into the chair. "I can do both."

The cookies Tucker scooted onto a plate were a little

dark and crisp around the edges, but looked edible, she concluded, then suddenly grinned. "Maybe my skill in the kitchen hasn't changed all that much, after all," she said.

Tucker joined her at the table and cast a critical eye at the cookies. He plucked one off the plate and took a bite, his eyes twinkling with merriment. "Obviously you were subconsciously going for the nostalgia factor. For a long time, I didn't know chocolate-chip cookies weren't supposed to taste this way."

"Of course you did. Daisy's never turned out like this."

His gaze met hers and the amusement faded. Something familiar sizzled between them as he said quietly, "Why would I eat hers, when I had yours?"

Tears stung Liz's eyes. "Oh, Tucker," she whispered.

Before she knew it, great, gulping sobs were rising up in her throat and hot, salty tears were splashing down her cheeks. Tucker reached for her.

"Oh, darlin', don't cry," he whispered, holding her close. "It's going to be okay. I promise. Everything is going to be okay."

"How can it be?" she choked out between sobs. "I've made such a mess of everything."

"And we're going to fix it," he told her, smoothing her hair back from her face, his gaze locked with hers.

"But—"

"No buts," he insisted. "We're going to find out what happened here, and then you're going to put that part of your life to rest and move on."

"To what?" she asked, swiping at the tears with the back of her hand. "I'm obviously an emotional mess. I haven't cried this much in years."

"Then you're long overdue," he told her. "And you are not a mess. Anyone would be distraught after what you've been through. Deciding to ask for a divorce is a big step in anyone's life. Having your husband murdered is beyond what most people ever have to deal with. You're a strong woman. You'll find your way again. What were you planning to do after the divorce?"

"I'm not sure," she admitted, choking back another hysterical sob. "I should have had a plan, but I didn't. It took everything in me to rehearse telling Larry that I wanted a divorce. That was as far ahead as I could think."

Tucker moved her hand aside and dabbed at the tears with his handkerchief. "Then you'll make a plan now. You have all the options in the world," he said, as he concentrated on putting first-aid cream on her burned fingertips. "You can do whatever you want. You can travel. You can get a job. You can marry again, have the children you always wanted. It's up to you."

"I can barely think ahead to tomorrow," she said, though an image of toddlers underfoot crept into her head and wouldn't leave. They all looked exactly like the man seated across from her. For so long, with Larry's insistence on putting off a family, she hadn't allowed herself to think of children at all. She sighed heavily.

Tucker gave her hand a gentle squeeze. "Hey, it's okay. Right now all you have to do is think ahead to the next minute or the next hour. Tomorrow will take care of itself. So will the day after, and the day after that."

"When did you get to be so wise?" she asked, studying his face. Before she could stop herself, she reached out to trace the lines fanning away from the corners of his eyes. "The wisdom shows right here."

He chuckled. "I thought that was old age creeping up on me."

"Don't be ridiculous," Liz said fiercely. "You're not old. Neither am I, though right at this very moment I feel ancient."

Tucker captured her hand and pressed a kiss to her knuckles. "Darlin', if you're what ancient looks like, people would stop carrying on about staying forever young."

She managed a wan smile. "You're still good for me, Tucker. I don't think anybody else could have made me laugh today."

"Yeah, I'm a regular comedian," he said, getting to his feet and putting the first-aid kit away. "Let me make that tea you promised me and then I'll get out of your hair."

She sighed as he moved away, wishing that he hadn't broken the spell, knowing it was best that he had.

When he returned to the table, he had two tall glasses of iced tea. As she took a sip of hers, she realized he'd already sweetened it just the way she liked it.

"How's your hand feel?" he asked. "Any blisters?"

She examined the reddened tips of her fingers but saw no sign of blisters forming. "I think I'll live."

"Never any question about that," he said. His gaze locked with hers. "You're a survivor, Mary Elizabeth. Don't ever forget that."

Whenever he said her name—Mary Elizabeth—in that lazy, honeyed tone, she felt as if she were thirteen years old again and first realizing that she was falling in love with the boy who'd been her best friend. Larry had been the first person to call her "Liz" and the name had stuck with their circle of friends in Richmond. She'd been glad that Larry had used the shorter nickname, because in her head she'd been able to remember the way her name had sounded on Tucker's lips.

She was even happier that Tucker hadn't adopted the nickname since her return. It would have seemed symbolic of the distance between them. Now, whenever he drew her name out with slow deliberation, she felt as if he might be accepting her back into his life. Maybe not in the same intimate role she'd once played, but at least as his friend.

And one thing she'd come to realize over the last six years was that being Tucker Spencer's friend meant more to her than any other relationship in her life. Maybe they could never have more, but she wanted to earn his trust and respect again.

After that…well, time would tell.

King was still seething over the public spectacle Tucker had made of himself the day before by hanging around that blasted Chandler woman after the funeral. It had taken every ounce of will he possessed to make himself brave the likely gossip that would be running rampant at Earlene's this morning.

But a Spencer never let a little idle talk make him turn tail and hide. He'd taught his children that, and Lord knew they had put it to the test often enough. King walked into the riverfront restaurant and headed straight for his usual table in the back. Along the way, he spotted Frances sitting all alone in a booth pushing scrambled eggs around on her plate, her gaze distracted.

He was annoyed as the dickens at the woman, but

he couldn't very well ignore her. He waved at Pete in the back, then slid into the booth across from Frances. She barely glanced at him before returning her gaze to something only she could see.

"You okay?" he asked finally, after Earlene had poured his coffee, cast a worried look at Frances, then shrugged and left.

With a heavy sigh, Frances turned back and met his gaze. "Does it matter?"

"Dammit all, woman, of course it matters," he retorted, then realized that he'd said it loudly enough to draw stares. "Sorry," he apologized to Frances. "But you surely know that I care what's going on with you."

"Do you really?"

"Didn't I just ask you…" His voice trailed off as he realized that he never had gotten around to asking her to marry him the way he'd intended to the other night. All that commotion at the marina with Tucker and Mary Elizabeth had pushed any thought of a proposal right out of his head. And after that, he'd been too irritated by Frances's protectiveness toward Mary Elizabeth to schedule another private dinner when he could pop the question.

"Ask me what?"

Well, he certainly wasn't going to ask her here and now with all those people looking on and the ring he'd bought back home in his pants pocket. "Nothing."

She sighed again, and her gaze drifted back toward the window.

"What the devil's so fascinating out there?" he demanded irritably.

"Nothing," she murmured, but she didn't look back.

"But even nothing's better than looking at me?" he asked.

She did face him then, her jaw set. "Sometimes, yes."

Obviously he needed to do something to make things right. "It's Tuesday, you know."

She blinked and stared. "I suppose it is. Is that important for some reason?"

"You usually like to go over to Colonial Beach for bingo on Tuesday. Do you want to go tonight?"

"I was planning to," she said. "There's no need for you to come along."

"Frances, I am asking if you would like to go to bingo *with me* tonight." He had to fight to keep an edge of impatience out of his voice. Why did she have to go and make this so blasted difficult?

A clearly reluctant smile tugged at the corners of lips. "Such a gracious invitation," she murmured. "How could I possibly refuse?"

He regarded her warily. "Is that a yes?"

"Yes, old man, I'll go with you. Thank you for asking."

"All right, then. And while we're at it, will you plan on having Sunday dinner out at Cedar Hill this week?"

She seemed startled by that. "You haven't asked in a while."

"And now I have," he said. "Well?"

"I don't think I will ever in a million years understand you, King Spencer."

He chuckled at the plaintive note in her voice. "Keeps things lively, don't you think?"

"That is not the word I would use," she retorted. "I have to be going to work." She slid out of the booth and stood, then hesitated. Her gaze met his, and her stern look softened ever so slightly. "I'll see you later, then."

"I'll look forward to it, Frances."

She leaned down, and for an instant King thought she was going to kiss him right there in public, but, instead, she whispered in his ear, "If you stand me up again, you old coot, it will be for the last time."

He bit back a laugh, because he could tell by the fire in her eyes that she was dead serious. Damn, but the woman was a pistol. Always had been. A man would be a fool to take a chance on losing that kind of fire and passion at this stage in his life, and one thing King prided himself on was not being a fool. He was going to seal this deal with Frances tonight. In fact, he had an idea that was going to turn this proposal into something she wasn't likely to forget.

He was still sitting there plotting when Anna-Louise slid into the booth opposite him.

"What are you up to?" she asked, inspecting him suspiciously.

"Nothing I'm likely to tell you about," he retorted. Speaking of pistols, the preacher was as fiery as any woman he'd ever met. He thoroughly enjoyed butting heads with her—not that he ever intended to let her know it. Now he studied her expression and thought he detected something a little sad about her. What the devil was going on with the women around here this morning?

"You okay?" he asked eventually.

"Fine," she said without her usual sparkle.

"Anna-Louise, it is not proper for a parson to flat-out lie to a parishioner, especially me. You and I have been through a lot together. I think I know you well enough to listen if you're having a problem."

"You? Listen?" she said with exaggerated shock.

"I'm darned good at it, when called upon," he insisted. "Now, *talk*—or I'll recommend that the church elders send you on a vacation till your spirits are lifted."

"My spirits are just fine," she said with a little more spunk. "I was just thinking about Liz Chandler."

King bit back an oath. "Does everybody in this town have to obsess over that woman?"

"I am not obsessing over anybody. I'm just thinking about how quickly her life changed. None of us can count on tomorrow."

King had a hunch that Anna-Louise's distress had less to do with Mary Elizabeth than it did with something she was regretting...or maybe wishing for. He never had understood why she and Richard hadn't filled that house of theirs with babies.

"Is this really about Mary Elizabeth?" he inquired. "Or are you having some regrets about something you've let slip away?"

She stared at him in apparent shock. "I haven't let anything slip away. Nobody understands the value of living each day to its fullest more than I do."

"Is that so? You and Richard planning on getting around to having a family one of these days? Neither of you is getting one bit younger."

"King Spencer, that is an incredibly personal question, even for you," she said indignantly.

"Maybe so," he agreed. "But it's a fair one. You don't have to answer me if you don't want to, but if that is what's on your mind, you should be talking it over with your husband."

Suddenly, to his absolute astonishment and dismay, her eyes welled up with tears. "I can't," she whispered. She drew in a deep breath and then the words came pouring out of her. "Richard flatly refuses to discuss it. All those years he was a foreign correspondent in those awful places left him absolutely convinced that he would never bring a child into such a world."

"The man's an idiot," King said fiercely. "I know I've said that before, because we've had our share of disagreements over the way he likes to poke his nose into everything around here, but I always thought he had at least half a brain. Now I'm not so sure. I've never heard such poppycock in all my life! This is Trinity Harbor, not some hellhole on the other side of the world. Can't he tell the difference?"

Anna-Louise swiped ineffectively at her tears, grinning at King at the same time. "I should have known you'd use this as one more excuse to disparage my husband."

"I'll have a talk with him," King said, ignoring her comment. "We'll get this straightened out."

Dismay spread across her face. "King, you cannot talk to Richard about us having a baby."

"Why the devil can't I?"

"Because it's my problem, not yours."

"I'm making it mine," he said, ready to fix this just the way he had to fix everything else in this town. Besides, he thought of Anna-Louise as a daughter, even if she did annoy the daylights out of him from time to time. Come to think of it, maybe that was exactly why she did feel like family.

"Don't you dare!" she said as he slid out of the booth. "Where are you going?"

"To find your husband."

"If you do, I swear I'll use every bit of my influence to get your soul consigned to hell," she said with what sounded like total sincerity.

That stopped King in his tracks. He'd never heard her say such a thing before.

"Sit," she ordered.

King sank back down with a sigh. "Okay, it's your problem," he conceded grudgingly. "How are you going to fix it?"

"I don't know," she admitted.

"You could just do what women have been doing through all eternity," he suggested, but even as he said it he knew that she'd never go for that solution.

"King!"

"I know. I know," he said, backpeddling. "Be direct, then. Lay it on the line. Make him talk it out. If ever a woman was meant to be a mother, it's you. As for Richard, he won't be half bad as a father. The man has an honorable streak, I'll admit that."

"I'm sure he'll be pleased that you noticed," Anna-Louise said wryly. She reached across the table and patted his hand. "Thank you for listening. It really did help. I hadn't let myself admit to anyone, least of all myself, how much this was weighing on me."

"Anytime," King told her. "Just don't forget that I'm the one who gets to hear the news first when something comes of this."

"I imagine I'll want to tell my husband first," she teased. "But you'll be second. I promise. Who knows? Maybe I'll even consider naming you godfather."

"I'd be honored. And in this case, coming in second

will do," King told her. "But make it soon. I'm not getting any younger."

"Who are you kidding? You're going to live forever. You're too ornery not to."

"I hope you're right. I have big plans."

"Oh?"

He winked at her. "I'm not talking."

A grin spread across her face. "I'll bet I know. I saw Frances leaving here earlier."

He laughed. "Come to think of it, you might, but keep it to yourself. She probably ought to know about this before the rest of the world finds out."

"Do you have a plan?"

"A surefire one," he said.

"Then I'll pray it works out," Anna-Louise promised.

"You concentrate on your own plan," he advised. "I've got this one under control, and I don't want His attention diverted from you."

"Oh, I think He can keep an eye out for both of us," she assured him. "In fact, I'm counting on it."

"Then throw in a prayer for Tucker while you're at it," King requested. "That boy can surely use all the divine help he can get, especially since I've got other fish to fry today."

"Done," Anna-Louise said. "Good luck."

"Luck's got nothing to do with it. Confidence, that's the ticket. Keep that in mind."

She laughed. "I surely will. In fact, I think I'll go track down my husband right now."

11

Liz was sitting on the deck with her second cup of coffee trying to work up the energy to tackle the cleaning she intended to do when Frances came around the side of the house.

"I hope you don't mind me dropping in like this, but I wanted to make sure you're doing okay all alone out here." She glanced around. "You are alone, aren't you?"

Liz chuckled at her worried expression. "Tucker's not hiding in the bushes, if that's what you're asking."

"I was thinking more about him strolling out here half-dressed," Frances retorted, then blushed. "Sorry. I have no right to say such a thing, but you two do seem to be getting close again. I suppose it's just wishful thinking on my part. You made such a lovely couple once."

Liz wasn't ready to discuss her relationship with Tucker, even with someone who'd been as kind to her as Frances had. "Could it be that you have romance on your mind?" she asked. "How are you and King getting along?"

"We're going to bingo tonight," Frances said without much enthusiasm.

"I thought you loved bingo."

"I do, and the first time he asked me, I'll admit I thought it was charming, since I knew it was about the last place on earth he wanted to be. Now, I just wish he'd get on with things."

Liz regarded her with surprise. King Spencer wouldn't be her first choice for a woman as lovely as Frances, but there was no accounting for taste. And even though the man riled the daylights out of Liz lately with his harsh, judgmental attitude, she had once been able to see his good points. In fact, she had to acknowledge to herself, she had adored him.

"Is this relationship more serious than I realized?" she asked Frances. "Do you want to marry him?"

Frances's cheeks turned bright pink. "Do I sound like an old fool?"

"Absolutely not. The great thing about love is that it's never too late to find it. At least that's what I want to believe," Liz said, regarding Frances sympathetically. "So what's the problem with you and King?"

"I wish I knew," Frances said, her frustration evident. "We seem to be stuck in a rut. I tried to shake him up by changing my hairstyle and color, and by losing a few pounds, but all that did was make him grumpier than usual."

Liz considered the implications of that. Frances had done so much for her the last few days, she wanted to be able to return the favor...even if it did mean matching her up with a stubborn old coot.

"Does King have any competition?" she asked.

Frances looked shocked by the question. "Do you mean am I seeing anyone else?"

"Exactly."

Frances's expression turned thoughtful. "Well, there is Mr. Mayberry. He's relatively new in town, and he has shown some interest in getting to know me, but I've been putting him off."

Liz grinned. "There you go. Why not see him? He could be a better match for you than King. And if he's not, well, maybe a little gossip about you seeing another man, will get King's attention."

"You're a clever girl, Mary Elizabeth. I just might do it," Frances said with some evidence of her usual spunk. "Perhaps I'll mention to Mr. Mayberry that I'm going to bingo tonight. King will be there and I'll get to see if Mr. Mayberry is any quicker than King to take a hint."

Liz uttered a little sigh of satisfaction as she watched her friend bustle off. Definitely two birds with one stone. She'd helped Frances realize there was more than one fish in the ocean, and with any luck she'd redirected King's energy toward his own love life...and away from her relationship with Tucker.

Tucker breathed a sigh of relief when he spotted his father leaving Earlene's just as he approached. He'd called Walker the night before and suggested they meet there for coffee. He hoped that seeing them together would put to rest any notion in the community that his integrity or his role as sheriff were in question.

Earlene met him at the door. "We don't usually see you in here at this hour not wearing your uniform," she said, an icy nip in her voice. "I'm not sure I like it."

"It's just a temporary situation," Tucker assured her.

"You see that it is. I like Walker just fine, but he's not one of us the way you are. Trinity Harbor counts on having a Spencer keeping us safe."

"Earlene, aren't you one of the first people to tell my father that he does not run things around here?"

She grinned. "I do, and I take great pleasure in it, but that's not the same thing at all. Sit down over there with Anna-Louise and I'll bring your coffee."

"I'm meeting Walker."

"Is there some reason he can't sit with her, too? With all the tourists around, we're crowded at this time of the year. I like to make good use of the space I've got."

He held up a hand. "Okay. I get it. I imagine Walker will enjoy getting Anna-Louise's perspective on things as much as I will."

Earlene nodded approvingly. "You always were a sensible man, which is the only reason I'm not about to start lecturing you about watching your step with Liz Chandler."

Tucker sighed. "Thank you for exercising such great restraint."

She frowned at him. "Doesn't mean I'm not worried sick about you, though."

"Just bring my coffee, okay?" He moved to Anna-Louise's booth and noted with relief that she seemed to be about to leave. "On your way out?"

"I can stick around," she said, putting her purse back down and studying him intently. "What's up?"

"Actually, I'm meeting Walker to talk things over about the Chandler murder. Earlene directed me over here."

Anna-Louise chuckled. "I guess she wanted to make sure I got my fill of Spencer men this morning. Your father just left."

"No wonder you looked a little shell-shocked," Tucker said with genuine sympathy.

"Don't blame King for that. I've just got a lot on my mind. How's Liz, by the way?"

"I haven't talked to her this morning. I'll head out to Swan Ridge when I'm done here."

"She went back there after the funeral?" Anna-Louise asked, clearly shocked.

"She insisted on it."

"I'm surprised you went along with that."

Tucker gave her a rueful grin. "Obviously you don't know Mary Elizabeth all that well yet. She's not an easy woman to control."

Anna-Louise studied him. "You've tried?"

"Not in years. I learned that lesson before I hit puberty." Before she could pursue that, he said, "What are you hearing in here this morning? Are people talking about the murder or the funeral?"

"What you really want to know is whether they're gossiping about you and Liz," she guessed. "I haven't heard anything, but then I've been preoccupied. Ask Earlene."

"Ask me what?" Earlene inquired as she set his coffee down in front of him.

"Are people obsessing about the Chandler situation?"

"They're concerned about the murder, no question about it," Earlene reported. "But they're also talking about all the fancy food and fancy people at the funeral. And some people are speculating about who'll run for Chandler's seat. The smart money's on Ken Willis. He'd already started campaigning at church yesterday. The vote's evenly divided on whether that was tacky or timely."

Tucker grinned at the summary. "Anything else?" he inquired dryly.

Earlene scowled at him. "Yes. They're about to start taking bets on how long it will be before you and Liz get back together."

"I hope to hell King hasn't heard that," Tucker said. "He'll be all over me before the day's out."

"Your father has other things on his mind today," Anna-Louise said. "But don't get too complacent. The second he does hear, he'll find the time to tell you you've lost your mind. Now that Daisy and Bobby are happily settled, your love life is his top priority, and he's clearly concerned about this latest turn of events."

"I don't have a love life of any kind, much less with Mary Elizabeth," Tucker said emphatically, hoping the sharp denial would put the silly speculation to rest. His relationship with Mary Elizabeth was strictly—well, almost strictly—professional.

Anna-Louise had the audacity to laugh. "It's no better for a lawman to fib than it is for a preacher. Even I can see the sparks between you two."

"Only because someone planted the notion in your head," he argued.

Earlene shook her head. "Delusional," she said in an undertone to Anna-Louise.

"That would be my call," the pastor agreed.

Tucker scowled at the pair of them. "Don't you think there's something the slightest bit unseemly about speculating about my relationship with a woman who's only been a widow for a few days?"

"From what I've gathered, her marriage was over long before that," Anna-Louise said. "And nobody's saying you're doing anything inappropriate, just that all the elements are there for the sparks to start flying."

"Oh, for Pete's sake," Tucker grumbled. "Is it any

wonder men will never be able to figure out the female mind?"

"Certainly not my wife's," Richard agreed, appearing at the booth and leaning down to give Anna-Louise a kiss. "Where'd you disappear to this morning? I thought you wanted to talk."

Color bloomed in Anna-Marie's cheeks. "I did, but I needed to get my thoughts in order first."

"So, what's up?" Richard asked, starting to slide into the booth next to her.

"Not here," she said, pushing him right back out. "Let's go for a walk."

"I just finished my run," he protested. "I'm starved."

"Earlene, fix him some coffee and a couple of doughnuts to go," Anna-Louise instructed. "I want him in a weakened state for this."

Richard's gaze narrowed. "I'm not going to like this, am I?"

"That depends," Anna-Louise said neutrally. "Are you on any sort of deadline?"

"No."

"Got any interviews lined up?"

"No."

She beamed at him. "Good, then we have plenty of time for a nice serious chat."

Tucker chuckled at Richard's bemused expression. "Just go with it, man. When a woman gets in a mood like this, it's always best to just go along. She's going to get her way anyway."

"That's what I'm afraid of," Richard said, but he followed Anna-Louise to the counter, retrieved his coffee and doughnut and left, passing Walker on the sidewalk outside.

"Any idea what's going on with those two?" Walker asked when he reached Tucker's booth.

"Not really, but Anna-Louise looks like a woman on a mission, sort of the way Daisy looked when she was campaigning to keep you from taking Tommy away from her."

"Poor Richard," Walker said with heartfelt sympathy. He took a sip of his coffee, glanced pointedly around the restaurant at the clearly fascinated patrons, then looked Tucker straight in the eye. "Other than the PR value of your being seen with me, what are we doing here?"

Tucker grinned. "Comparing notes, of course. Anything new back from forensics?"

"They found some fibers at the scene that might be promising," Walker said readily. "They're running further tests now."

"What good are fibers? I thought they'd be just as useless as fingerprints, given that shindig the Chandlers threw on their last visit."

"They might have been," Walker agreed. "But these were on Chandler's pants. And not on the cuffs, if you know what I mean."

Tucker's heart began to thud. "He was intimate with someone right before he died?"

"In a manner of speaking. At least that's the way it looks."

Tucker had to force himself to ask the obvious. "Do they match those clothes I gave you that Mary Elizabeth was wearing that night?"

"The lab's checking that now. I should know more by the end of the day."

"It won't be enough to arrest her," Tucker said, his mind sifting through all the possible explanations for the least damning one. "We know she was there. We know she touched the body. She's admitted that."

"I'm not going to do anything precipitous, no matter how this turns out," Walker said impatiently. "Come on, Tucker. I know how to do my job, how to build a case. Once I get around to making an arrest, I sure as hell want it to stick. And it won't be based solely on something as flimsy as a few stray fibers."

"Is that so?" a man asked, standing beside the booth and regarding both of them with an angry expression. "You sure about that? Or are the two of you planning to cover up the truth to protect that slut Chandler was married to."

Tucker was halfway out of the booth, his blood pounding, when Walker snagged his arm and dragged him back.

"I'll handle this," Walker said calmly. He rose slowly and faced the man. "Who are you?"

"Doesn't matter who I am," he said. "The bottom line is that you small-town hicks intend to hide what really happened down here, and I'm here to tell you that you won't get away with it."

"No one's going to hide anything," Walker countered. "If you think you know something that would help us solve this case, tell me, and I guarantee you that I'll follow through on it."

"Oh, really?" the man asked skeptically, then gave a nod toward Tucker. "He'll let you do that?"

"Sheriff Spencer is not in charge of this investigation. *I* am," Walker said emphatically. "Now why don't we step outside and discuss whatever leads you think you have?"

"No need to go outside. I'll say it plain right here. The Chandler woman is guilty."

Walker shot a warning look at Tucker. "And you know that how?" he asked.

"It's obvious. She wanted out of the marriage but didn't want to lose access to all that money. I heard the two of them fighting down in Richmond. Hell, the whole damned restaurant heard them."

"Emotions tend to run high when divorce is on the table," Walker said.

"But she said, plain as day, 'I'll kill you first.' I heard her myself," the man said triumphantly.

Tucker's pulse began to beat unsteadily. If true, it was a damning remark for Mary Elizabeth to have made. She'd certainly never suggested to him that anything remotely like that had been said in her heated exchange with her husband. He had a dozen questions and no right at all to ask them, not when this was Walker's witness and Walker was right here to do the questioning himself. Sitting on the sidelines was eating him up inside, though, especially knowing that half the town would know all about this by lunchtime. Even if the man's testimony was ultimately proved false, Mary Elizabeth would have a hard time living down the accusation.

"Let's go over to the station and get this on the record," Walker said to the man. "I'll have someone take an official statement."

The man paled at the suggestion. "No way."

"Why not?" Walker asked. "You want me to pursue this, don't you?"

"I'm not getting involved."

"You're already involved," Walker pointed out.

"I came in here to do my civic duty. Had to chase all over hell and gone just to find you."

"You could have called it in and saved yourself some time," Tucker pointed out.

"Not something this big. I wanted to look this man in the eye when I told him, make sure the significance registered. Now I've told him what I heard and that's that."

"Unless you want to make it official, it pretty much loses all credibility," Walker told him. "Anybody can hurl around unsubstantiated accusations. The fact that Mr. and Mrs. Chandler argued in public has been reported. You could be making the rest up."

"It's the gospel truth," the man insisted. "You do whatever you want with it."

That said, he whirled around and headed for the door. Walker strolled along behind him, clearly in no hurry to catch up. Tucker grinned as he watched Walker take note of the car the man got into, jot down the tag number and stroll right back inside.

"Chances are he's a crackpot, but at least we can get an ID on him," Walker said, using his cell phone to call Michele and ask her to put a trace on the tag.

"Unless…" Tucker began thoughtfully.

"Unless what?"

"Unless he was sent here by someone intent on stirring up trouble for Mary Elizabeth."

"In other words, the real killer," Walker surmised.

"Or someone who's afraid she might decide to step into Chandler's political shoes and take over his seat until the next election," Tucker said.

"Is she thinking of doing that?"

Tucker shook his head. "She hasn't said anything to me about it. From everything she has said, I'm pretty sure she intends to sit tight right here in Trinity Harbor. No way to tell how long that will last. She was always attracted to city lights. I thought that was part of Chandler's appeal—the promise of a sophisticated lifestyle sort of like the one her folks led till they died."

"I'd sure like to know who else was in that restaurant the night they fought," Walker said, "but I can't spare anybody to go down to Richmond and check it out."

"Subtle, Walker. Real subtle. Okay, I'm on it. Let me know about that lab report on the fibers as soon as you have it."

"Will do. And Tucker?"

"What?"

"Watch your back. If somebody's seriously trying to frame Mrs. Chandler, you could get in the way—and we already know they're not averse to murder."

"Nobody knows that better than I do," Tucker told him.

The thought stayed with him all the way to Richmond. It was only when he was halfway there that he realized that other than Walker, Earlene, Anna-Louise and Richard, not one single resident of Trinity Harbor had spoken to him. They might like and respect him, but they were clearly reserving judgment when it came to the way he was handling his life and his job these days. It was the first time it sank in that King was right about all this: Tucker could very well lose the next election thanks to his decision to stand by Mary Elizabeth.

He sighed heavily. If that happened, so be it. He was doing what he had to do.

When she tired of her own company and went looking for Tucker, it required a little detective work, but

Liz quickly discovered that he was on his way to Richmond without her, hoping to find some leads at the restaurant where she and Larry had fought. Fortunately, she had a lead foot and she knew a shortcut. She arrived at Chez Dominique just as Tucker walked through the front door. She caught up with him just outside the manager's office.

"You surely didn't think I was going to let you do this without me, did you?" she inquired sweetly. His stunned expression gave her a great deal of satisfaction.

"What the devil did you do, tail me?"

"Hardly. By all accounts, I left a good twenty minutes after you did."

"Then how the hell did you get here at the same time?"

"You're in law enforcement. You don't want to know."

He dragged her away from the office door. "Mary Elizabeth, why are you here?" he demanded in an undertone.

"Because I know Dominique Gerard and you don't," she said at once. "And it's my life that's on the line."

"I thought you trusted me to handle this."

"I do, but there are some things I can do perfectly well for myself, and this is one of them. Watch and learn."

She tapped on the office door and swept inside. Dominique, a statuesque beauty from a tiny island in the Caribbean, rose to greet her.

"*Ma chérie,* I am so sorry for your loss," Dominique said at once, enfolding her in a jasmine-scented hug. "I was devastated when I heard."

"I'm sure you were," Liz said. "I know that Larry was one of your favorite customers."

"Tsk, tsk," Dominique chided. "You know that I do not have favorites. It is not sensible in this business."

Liz grinned. "And you are, above all, a smart businesswoman, *n'est-pas?*"

"One of the best," Dominique agreed with no attempt at all to feign modesty. "I imagine you are here about the reservation list for the night you and Mr. Chandler fought." She pulled the reservation book from a desk drawer. "I brought it in here to make sure it did not fall into the wrong hands."

"Have others been by to see it?" Liz asked.

"Several reporters have called, and one customer asked if it would be possible to have his name removed. He said he did not want to be drawn into the media frenzy that was bound to surround that night."

"What did you tell him?" Tucker asked.

Dominique turned her attention to him for the first time and blatantly surveyed him from head to toe. "And you are?"

"He's a friend," Liz told her. "He's helping me try to solve Larry's murder. Dominique Gerard, this is Tucker Spencer. He's one of the last remaining good guys."

"And a handsome one, too," Dominique said after another frank assessment.

Tucker, bless his heart, blushed. "About this man who called," he reminded her.

"Ah, yes, it was Charles Foley."

Tucker shook his head. "I don't recognize the name. Should I?"

"He's an aide to the governor," Liz said. "I'll bet you'd recognize him if you saw him. He's in almost every bill-signing photograph taken in the governor's office and he's usually on or near the podium when he speaks. Governor Hastings seldom goes anywhere without him."

"Was the governor here with him that night?" Tucker asked Dominique.

"No, I heard that he was meeting with a delegate. I believe it was someone the governor hoped to win over on his health-care initiative."

"And Foley? Who was he with?" Liz asked.

"I did not see him when he arrived or when he left," Dominique said. "My maître d' seated them. Perhaps Jacques will remember."

"I'll speak to him," Liz told Tucker.

"Does that mean the governor was home that night, since Foley's presence wasn't required?" Tucker asked.

"Or working late in his office," Liz replied. "He has a habit of staying past business hours. It drives his staff and the delegates crazy, since he's constantly calling them in at all hours of the night to go over legislation and plan strategy."

"But wouldn't Foley be around for that?" Tucker persisted.

"Not if the governor had sent him on another mission," Liz said thoughtfully. "Which meant this dinner was important, and since Foley wanted his name taken off the reservation book, it was no doubt something he didn't want widely known."

"Then why come here?" Tucker asked. "You told me yourself this place is usually crawling with movers and shakers."

"But our booths are very private," Dominique explained. "And if one wishes not to be disturbed, there is the private dining room. That is where Mr. Foley was dining that night."

"Mind if I take a look at the layout?" Tucker asked. "I want to see what he could see or overhear from that room."

"Surely," Dominique said. "Liz, will you show him or shall I?"

"I know the way," Liz said. "And we've already taken up too much of your time. Could you make me a copy of that night's reservation pages?"

"Of course," Dominique said at once. "I'll have it ready before you leave, though I don't know how much luck you'll have reading my handwriting. As for Jacques's..." She shrugged eloquently to express her dismay over the legibility of her maître d's scribbles.

"We'll manage," Liz assured her. "Thanks so much for your help."

"Will you be returning to Richmond soon?" Dominique asked. "I'm sure there are many here in town who wish to express their condolences in person."

Liz exchanged a look with Tucker. "No. I'm hoping to stay on in Trinity Harbor, at least for the time being. I've been away from home for far too long."

The other woman chuckled. "Yes, I can understand the allure," she said with another of those disconcerting surveys that clearly rattled Tucker.

He all but ran from the office. Liz caught up with him at the entrance to the dining room.

"Don't tell me she made you nervous," she teased him.

"Nervous? Me? Don't be ridiculous," he grumbled, but his neck was slowly turning a dull red.

"Dominique is a very attractive woman, isn't she?" Liz prodded.

He frowned at her. "What are you trying to do? Set me up with her?"

Just the suggestion of anything like that brought her pulse skidding to a halt. It was way too soon to know exactly what she wanted where Tucker was concerned, but she definitely didn't want to set him up with a woman like Dominique. The restaurateuse had a reputation for going through men like tissues, discarding them without thought.

"No, absolutely not," Liz said fervently, telling herself it was only her protectiveness where Tucker's emotions were concerned that made her so vehement.

He grinned at last. "Glad to hear it," he said, leveling a look at her that made her knees go weak. "Now show me where you were when you and Larry fought."

"Over here," she said, leading him to the table with its heavy damask cloth and floral centerpiece. Chez Dominique had first-rate Old World style and ambience. That, and Dominique's penchant for discretion, kept its lofty clientele coming back again and again.

"And the private dining room is where?" Tucker asked.

Liz gestured to a door less than twenty feet away. There were only a few tables in between.

"So it's entirely possible that this Foley character could have heard every word the two of you shouted without you being aware he was around," Tucker surmised, his expression thoughtful. "What does this guy look like?"

"Tall, a little heavy around the middle, usually a bit disheveled," Liz said. "Why?"

"Brown hair, thinning a bit? Ruddy complexion?"

"Yes," she said slowly. "You do know him, don't you?"

"Unless I'm mistaken, he was in Trinity Harbor just this morning."

Liz couldn't hide her shock. "He was? Why?"

"Trying to make sure that we arrested you for your husband's murder."

12

It was all way too easy, Tucker thought as he considered the discovery that the man who'd come to tip Walker off about Mary Elizabeth was the same man who'd tried to get his name erased from the Chez Dominique reservation book.

Of course, amateurs were often sloppy, he reminded himself.

"Let's go," he said, grabbing Mary Elizabeth's hand. "We'll pick up those copies and then head over to the Capitol."

"You want to pay a visit to Foley," she guessed at once.

"Just a little get-acquainted call," he confirmed. "If I'm right about him being in Trinity Harbor this morning, it ought to rattle him to have me turn up on his doorstep a few hours later, especially with you in tow. How well do you know him?"

"Better than I'd like to," she said with a wry grimace. "He's a very friendly man, if you get my drift."

"He's made a pass at you?" Tucker didn't like the possessive feeling that stirred in him.

"He's made a pass at anything in skirts walking around Richmond. He's a bachelor who's made excellent use of his power to draw the attention of women who otherwise might not give him the time of day."

Tucker was astonished. "Why does the governor put up with that?"

"Because Foley is also very good at his job," Liz explained. "He gets things done without the governor having to get his hands dirty. The expression 'backroom politics' was coined for men like Charles Foley. He exerts pressure. He makes deals. And he plays dirty when he has to."

"Dirty how?" Tucker asked.

"I know of at least one delegate he allegedly tried to blackmail to get the vote the governor wanted on an environmental bill. It was defeated by a margin of one vote, and that margin was provided by a man with a previously strong record on environmental issues. There were rumors in the paper for a month about why he would have changed his vote on such an important bill, and all of them kept coming back to a meeting he had with Foley just hours before the bill went to the floor. Since no one else was at that meeting, we'll probably never know what really happened, but it certainly raises suspicion."

"Make a mental note. I'll want that name."

"Absolutely."

"You get those copies, and I'll meet you outside," Tucker told her. "I need a couple of minutes to process all this." He had a feeling it would take days, not minutes, to make sense of just the few shenanigans Liz had described. Small-town politics were convoluted enough. What she was describing was downright Machiavellian.

When Mary Elizabeth had retrieved the reservation-book pages from Dominique and joined Tucker in the parking lot, he gestured toward his car. "I'll drive."

She shook her head. "I'm the one with the parking pass. Let's go, Spencer. Surely you can handle being a passenger for once."

"I let other people drive all the time," he retorted. "It's you behind the wheel I'm worried about. You've always liked to push the limits."

"Check my record, Sheriff," she challenged with a grin. "No tickets."

"Oh, well, then, that's certainly reassuring," he said. "What it tells me is that you've managed to sweet-talk your way out of them. I know you've dazzled a couple of my deputies a time or two."

"Maybe," she taunted. "Are you going to risk it or not?"

"Let's go," he said, and followed her to the luxury sports car with its vanity plates that had given away her presence at his house just over a week earlier. It seemed like a lifetime ago. It was also disconcerting to realize that in a few short days she had managed to wash away years of anger and hurt. He wasn't sure he'd ever be able to trust her entirely, but he no longer felt that sick sensation in his gut when he looked at her. No, in fact, what he felt was something a whole lot more dangerous.

Tucker studied Mary Elizabeth as she expertly wove through the congested streets of downtown Richmond. She drove with a relaxed posture, as if she hadn't a care in the world. In fact, he thought he detected genuine excitement sparkling in her eyes.

"You're enjoying this, aren't you?" he asked.

She glanced at him. "As long as I don't think too hard

about why it's necessary," she told him with apparent candor. "Then it makes my skin crawl."

"You don't have to come along. You could let me do the job you asked me to do."

"I could," she agreed. "But I'm the one with everything at stake. Besides, why should I sit at home at Swan Ridge worrying about you and what sort of trouble I've sent you into, when I could be right here to protect you?"

He chuckled at the notion of Mary Elizabeth with her soft heart doing what it took to protect anyone in the kind of situations they might encounter. She'd carried on so loudly about her grandfather even keeping hunting rifles in the house that he'd finally gotten rid of them. That was yet another reason why the idea that she had shot Chandler was so completely ludicrous.

"I can handle trouble," he reminded her. "I've been a cop for a long time now."

"And just how many high-profile murders have there been in Trinity Harbor?"

"Okay, not that many, but the county has had its share of murders." He turned the tables on her. "How many have you investigated?"

"None, but I'm a whole lot more familiar with the high-powered backstabbing that goes on down here than you are. Face it, Sheriff, you need me." She met his gaze with an unflinching look. "If I truly get in your way, you can send me home. Deal?"

Tucker considered the offer, then nodded. Better that she was where he could keep an eye on her, than poking around on her own, which she would do, no question about it. For a woman who'd had major self-esteem issues as a kid, she'd not only gotten over them in a big way, she was now evidently confident and stubborn as a mule.

"Fair enough," he said finally.

At the Capitol, Mary Elizabeth breezed past the security guards with a smile, barely pausing to acknowledge the condolences that several of them expressed. She marched past the receptionist in Foley's office, rapped on his door and walked in before the woman could even react.

"Wait," the receptionist demanded, but Mary Elizabeth was already inside.

Tucker gave the woman an apologetic shrug. "I guess she's in a hurry," he said, and followed Mary Elizabeth through the door. Foley was just in the process of slamming the phone down, clearly agitated over the interruption. When he spotted Tucker on Mary Elizabeth's heels, his complexion paled.

"You!"

Tucker gave him a jaunty grin. "Since you had so much to say about Mrs. Chandler earlier today, I thought we'd drop by so you could say it to her face."

Foley sputtered, but couldn't seem to think of a single thing to say now that the target of his venom was smack in front of him.

"Ah, cat's got your tongue now, I see," Tucker said. "Shall I repeat what you said this morning?"

"No need," Mary Elizabeth said sweetly. "I can just imagine what Mr. Foley had to say. My only question, Charles, is why you would be so anxious to see me locked up?"

"Because your husband was a fine man and you shouldn't be allowed to get away with murder."

"Come on," Mary Elizabeth chided. "You can do better than that. You hated Larry's guts, because he didn't go along with the governor's agenda. You're probably relieved that he's gone, because he was a major obstacle in your plans for the next session."

"Don't be absurd," Foley said, clearly shocked. "Our legislative differences didn't mean I'd want him dead. You, however, had what? Several million reasons to kill him?"

Mary Elizabeth looked equally aghast. "Is that what you think? That I killed him for his money?" Then, to Tucker's shock, she started to laugh. It was a brittle sound that echoed in the cavernous room. "Oh, Charles, all those big bucks you thought Larry had obviously dazzled you. But surely even you must be aware that the tech stocks have taken a beating in the last couple of years. Larry's fortune, which was once quite large, at least on paper, took a beating right along with everyone else's. And even if it hadn't, I'd signed a prenuptial agreement. If we ever divorced, he kept what was his and I kept what was mine. There were no exceptions."

Relief flooded through Tucker as he listened to her explanation. It would be easy enough to check out, but at least for the moment it put to rest the last of his lingering doubts about money as a motive for Chandler's murder.

"You're telling me that Larry's fortune was gone?" Foley asked. "Every penny?"

"Not every penny, but he was no longer a multimillionaire," she said. "He'd managed to keep the losses from becoming widely known, but if you don't believe me, check out his tax records for the last two years. I'm sure you have access to them."

"What about if he died?" Foley asked, looking triumphant. "Who got what was left then?"

"Every dime of his business fortune stayed with his business partner, Roland Morgan. His personal funds went to a few charities," Liz said.

Foley looked shaken. "But if you had nothing to gain, why would you threaten to kill him?"

"I didn't," she said flatly.

"But I heard..."

"You misunderstood," Mary Elizabeth said. Then with a hint of impatience, she added, "That's the point, I didn't. That begs the question—why were you so anxious to pin it on me? Were you trying to tie up loose ends and wipe the slate clean before the next legislative session? Or was it something more? Were you protecting someone?"

"Don't be absurd," he snapped. "Who would I be protecting?"

"The governor comes to mind," she said at once. "I've always suspected you'd throw yourself into a raging inferno to save his political butt."

Even Tucker was astounded by the implications of that. "Mary Elizabeth, surely you're not suggesting..."

"She's slandering the governor, that's what she's doing," Foley said, quivering with indignation.

"No worse than you slandered her earlier today," Tucker pointed out. "What say we all back off from all the mudslinging and try to make some sense of this?" He avoided Mary Elizabeth's gaze and looked straight at Foley. Maybe this was a chance to make the man an ally, rather than a venom-spewing enemy. "Who would stand to gain the most in terms of political clout with Chandler dead?"

Foley ticked off several familiar names, then added, "But none of them are killers. I'd stake my life on it."

Mary Elizabeth sighed. "So would I."

"Which leaves us exactly where?" Tucker asked.

"Looking at business colleagues and others with a personal vendetta against him," she said. "Let's go by the house here and look through his papers. Maybe something will jump out at us."

"Fine by me," Tucker agreed.

Foley regarded Mary Elizabeth with something that looked like genuine regret. "Liz, I'm sorry if I jumped to the wrong conclusion."

"I suppose I should be grateful that you cared enough to get involved, but I'm still not entirely certain that you didn't have some personal ax to grind. If you did, I'll figure it out, I promise you that," she told him.

"I suppose I deserve that," he said. "But you won't find anything, I assure you."

Tucker couldn't gauge Mary Elizabeth's reaction, but he believed the man. He kept his opinion to himself, though, until they were once again cutting through heavy traffic and heading toward the outskirts of town.

"What did you think?" he asked eventually.

"That he's the same calculating, self-serving pig he's always been, but that there was no real malice behind the accusations he came to Trinity Harbor to make." She glanced at Tucker. "You?"

"Ditto. You want to grab some lunch before we start on the papers at the house?"

"What I really want to do is stop the car, get out and scream bloody murder, but lunch will do."

"I recommend a glass of wine to go along with it," Tucker said.

She chuckled. "It will take more than a glass of wine to keep me from wanting to scream."

"A whole bottle would probably be too much, since you're the one behind the wheel," he said judiciously. "I'll drink the rest."

She slanted a look at him. "You having a bad day, too?"

"I've had more productive mornings."

"I think we've learned a lot," she countered. "We have a list of names from the reservation book at Chez Dominique. We've eliminated a few suspects, and we've gotten Charles Foley off my case. That means he won't be tossing around allegations to incite the local media."

"Temporarily, anyway," Tucker agreed. "Okay, the trip hasn't been a total waste of time." His expression brightened. "And there's Mexican food."

Liz spotted the fast-food restaurant. "There? You want to have lunch there?"

"Why not? One thing's for sure, we're not likely to run into any of your friends in this place, right?"

"I suppose that is a blessing," she said and turned into the parking lot. "I hope you realize you can forget about the wine here."

"Go through the drive-through. We can take the food to the house. I'm sure you can find a bottle stashed in that wine cellar I've read about."

"Boy, Sheriff, you sure do know how to show a girl a good time." She slanted a look at him. "You've read about the wine cellar?"

He grinned. "Hard to miss. It was on the front page of the feature section of the paper. As for the rest, I pride myself on knowing how to treat a woman right. Just wait till you see the place I've picked out for dinner."

"The prospect boggles my mind," she said, her eyes sparkling with amusement.

"Stick with me, Mary Elizabeth. I'll remind you of how real people live."

"Is that a challenge?"

"Maybe," he said. "You up for it?"

"Hey, I used to follow you anywhere," she reminded him. "There's no reason to stop now."

Something in her tone, a hint of the daredevil girl he remembered, sent a shiver of warning down his spine. He was playing with fire here. How stupid was that for a man who'd already been burned?

Liz drove into the gated community where she and Larry had bought a brick home on a two-acre lot when he'd first been elected to the legislature. Even though his official duties took only a few months of the year, they had both wanted to spend their time in Richmond in a place where they could entertain and live comfortably. Liz had also believed that a real home—rather than the hotel accommodations and rental units other delegates often shared—would keep them here most of the time, rather than in Trinity Harbor where memories and Tucker would always be underfoot.

Over time she had come to hate the pretentious house with its lavish decor and that well-publicized, temperature-controlled wine cellar. Rather than the simple lines and cherished antiques of Swan Ridge, this house was filled with high-profile objets d'art that said more about the decorator Larry had insisted they hire than about their personal tastes. Of course, she also hated it because it was a constant reminder of yet another woman with whom her husband had carried on a less than discreet dalliance.

She stood in the entry and tried to judge Tucker's

reaction to the too-busy wallpaper and elaborate, glistening chandelier.

"This is..." His voice trailed off as he looked around, then faced her. "This is so not you."

Liz chuckled. "Glad you noticed. Larry liked it. He liked the decorator even more, and she was out to impress him. Wait till you see the study. I'm never sure whether to find a gun and shoot the moose head on the wall just to make sure it's dead or to light up a cigar and pour a brandy. Thank God, Grandfather's taste was less blatantly macho. His study is a testament to restraint by comparison."

"I didn't get a good look in there the other day, but I seem to recall it being pretty dark and dreary," Tucker said.

"Not compared to this," Liz warned as she led the way. "I'm only taking you in here because it's where we'll find the papers we need. I hope you don't lose your appetite."

To her amusement, Tucker's mouth gaped when he saw it.

"You thought I was kidding, didn't you?" she asked.

"I thought you had to be. My God, what was he thinking?"

"I don't think he actually looked at it until it was too late. He was too busy focusing on seducing Ms. Highsmith, of the Hampton Highsmiths."

"Is that supposed to impress me?"

Liz shrugged. "It impressed Larry."

Tucker's expression softened. "I'm sorry."

"Don't be. I got used to it eventually."

"Really?"

His steady gaze demanded a truthful answer. "Okay,

no, I never got used to it," Liz admitted. "It just ceased to matter." Because she didn't want to dwell on how humiliated she had felt for years, she gestured toward the sacks of food Tucker was carrying. "Which one's mine? I'm starved."

Thankfully he took her cue, dropped the subject of Larry's infidelities and doled out the food. "I think we can forgo the wine. You have any sodas around here?"

"I'll get them."

Liz bolted for the kitchen, relieved to have a few minutes to herself. She poured them each a soft drink, then paused to take a deep breath. Being here again brought back so many memories of lonely nights waiting for her errant husband to come home. Being here with Tucker brought back other memories, far more bittersweet, of nights when they'd shared take-out food, eaten in a rush so they could move on to more pleasurable pursuits. Liz sighed. There would certainly be none of that today.

She returned to the study to find the food spread out on the marble-topped coffee table. She bit back a laugh just thinking about what Ms. Highsmith would have had to say about that.

She met Tucker's worried gaze.

"You okay?" he asked.

"Fine," she said as she handed him his drink and sat down beside him on the oversize dark brown sofa. She'd always hated this piece of furniture, with its images of what Larry and his decorator friend had likely spent their time doing on it, but having Tucker here somehow chased all of that away. She reached eagerly for her food.

As it turned out, the tacos were surprisingly good,

the burrito even better. Tucker grinned as she licked the last of the fiery sauce off her fingers and sighed.

"You always did have a cast-iron stomach," he teased.

"What's the point of eating Mexican if it's not spicy?" she asked.

"You can taste the actual food, for one thing," he pointed out.

"You're a culinary wimp," she retorted. "You always were. Until I came along, I doubt you ever ate anything more exotic than crab cakes or fried chicken."

"And what's wrong with those? You try telling King that there's any better food on earth than crab cakes or fried chicken. He's still appalled that Bobby dabbles with anything else at the marina restaurant. He says if that food was good enough for his ancestors, it ought to be good enough for us."

"Until the other night, I had never eaten at the marina," Liz said, unable to hide her regret. "I'd heard that the food was fabulous, but now I've discovered for myself how well-deserved all the glowing reviews are. King should be proud of your brother. Bobby's reputation even extends down here to Richmond. I have several friends who are weekend regulars there."

"I'm surprised you hadn't tried it before," Tucker said, then sighed. "No, of course you wouldn't go there."

"I didn't want to risk running into you and making you uncomfortable," Liz told him. "Larry and I fought about it more than once. He thought I was being ridiculous, especially after Bobby earned a reputation as the best chef in the Northern Neck. It infuriated him that I wouldn't agree to take our guests there."

"You didn't have to do stay away on my account," Tucker said.

"It wasn't entirely compassionate," Liz told him. "I was afraid."

"Afraid of what? I would never have caused a scene, and Bobby certainly wouldn't have."

She shook her head and met his gaze. "I was afraid you'd be able to see that my marriage was in trouble. I didn't want you to know that I'd thrown everything we had away for nothing. I don't think I could have stood that. It was hard enough living with my mistake without having your pity on top of it."

He regarded her with obvious dismay. "What can I say?"

"That I deserved it?" she suggested.

"I would never say that," he chided.

"No, you wouldn't," she agreed, filled with regret over her failure to see what a treasure she'd had and tossed aside. "Because you are a better man than that."

"Don't go making me into a saint, Mary Elizabeth. I've got a whole passel of flaws."

"Name one," she challenged, only partially in jest.

"I snore."

She laughed. "You do not."

"How would you know? We did precious little sleeping when we were together."

Suddenly, just like that, her memory was filled with provocative images of the two of them together. He'd come in after working the evening shift and slide into bed beside her. No matter how late it was or how soundly she was sleeping, she would automatically curve into all that heat. She would fit her curves to his solid strength even on those rare occasions when he hadn't awakened her to make love.

She could still remember the way his hands had

felt on her body, the way he'd set every inch of her on fire, the heat in his eyes as he'd slipped inside her, then pounded away until they'd both come in a blissful agony of shuddering surrender. Just thinking about it now made her skin as sensitive as if his hands were all over her. She felt the heat climbing into her cheeks and carefully avoided his gaze.

"Darlin', where'd you go just then?" he asked, his voice sounding choked.

She forced herself to look him in the eye. "To another time, another place."

He gave her a rueful grin. "Yeah, I've been there a time or two myself the last few days."

"I wish—"

He cut her off before she could finish the thought. "We can't go back, Mary Elizabeth, much as either one of us might want to."

She sighed heavily. "I know." It was too soon, and she'd hurt him too deeply.

But maybe in time…

One glance at the unyielding set of his jaw put that idea to rest. He might be giving her a second chance at friendship, but he'd never give her another chance at his heart, not after she'd gone and broken it the first time. Tucker was a good guy, but asking him to put aside what she'd done to him would be asking too much.

But even knowing all that couldn't stop her from meeting his gaze, letting him see the yearning that she felt. For an instant, a desire as needy as her own darkened his eyes, but then he looked away and the moment was lost, perhaps forever.

13

King didn't have much time. He'd promised Frances dinner and bingo tonight, and if he blew it this time, he had a feeling he'd be blowing it forever. She'd evidently lost patience with him, and to be perfectly truthful, he supposed he couldn't blame her. He'd been behaving like a man who had all the time in the world to move on with his future. Worse, he'd been treating her as if she didn't deserve any better. Any Southern gentleman worthy of the title knew better than to treat a woman that way.

Well, he'd fix that tonight, he thought, fingering the small velvet box in his pocket. First, though, he had to have a family powwow and make sure everybody was on the same page about getting Mary Elizabeth out of Tucker's life. The first thing he'd heard at Earlene's this morning was that Tucker had gone chasing off to Richmond to do some investigating and that Mary Elizabeth had left town right on his heels. It was not the kind of monkey business that tended to make a good impression on the people who'd elected Tucker because of his upstanding moral character. Tucker could put any spin he wanted on what he was doing, but folks around here knew exactly what was going on. King had heard about the bets that were being taken, and not all of them could be described as friendly. A few people were going to use the whole blessed scandal to kick his son out of office.

An hour ago he had summoned Daisy and Walker, Bobby and Jenna and Anna-Louise out to Cedar Hill. Anna-Louise might not be family, but he was counting on the pastor to remind them of the difference between right and wrong, in case the others had forgotten.

The first of them should be arriving any second now. King poured himself a tall glass of iced tea, well aware that his throat was likely to get parched by the time he'd said his piece and got things settled. He supposed he could bring up his intentions about Frances, but he didn't want anything sidetracking everyone from the business at hand. Besides, he wasn't sure she was going to say yes, and he didn't want to face his family if things didn't go the way he wanted.

Daisy was the first to arrive, skidding to a halt in the driveway and stirring up a cloud of dust. She flew out of the car, looking thoroughly disheveled and just a little bit panicky. When she spotted King in his rocker on the porch, tea in hand, she stopped and pressed a hand to her chest.

"What on earth? I expected to find you lying on the floor," she said with a hint of asperity in her voice. "You made it sound urgent."

"It is urgent, dammit. We have to do something about Tucker and Mary Elizabeth."

"King Spencer, I could wring your neck," she said. "I have half a mind to get right back in my car and go home. I thought you were dying."

"It's only the Spencer reputation that's in danger of dying," he retorted. "And that's no small thing."

"Oh, for pity's sake, don't you think you're exaggerating just a little bit?"

He studied his daughter intently. "You happy about Mary Elizabeth being back in Tucker's life?"

"No, of course not. You know exactly how I feel. Any fondness I felt toward her disappeared when she left Tucker."

"Well, then, what are we going to do about it?"

"Short of running her out of town, I'm not sure there is anything we *can* do," Daisy said with obvious regret. She fanned herself with a seed catalogue that was stuck in her purse. "Is there any more of that tea?"

"Right over here," King said, knowing he had her hooked at last. "Come on up and sit a spell. The others should be here soon."

"I hope you were more straightforward with them than you were with me," she scolded him.

"Is there anything wrong with a man inviting his family to come for a visit?" he inquired crankily.

"There is when he implies it might be the last time they see him alive. One of them might be inclined to see that it is."

"Well, at least Anna-Louise will be here to pray over my dead body," he said unrepentantly.

Daisy shook her head. "Yes, indeed, that is a comfort."

King saw another car kicking up a plume of dust on the long, winding drive. Given its speed, he assumed it was Walker. Bobby never moved faster than a snail's pace. The flashing blue light was the real giveaway, though.

"Looks like your husband's coming," he noted. "Why the devil is he using his flashing light?"

"I imagine because he thought it was an emergency," Daisy said. "You have any food around? It's going to take more than tea to settle him down."

"There's a plate of sandwiches in the refrigerator. I didn't want to bring 'em out in this heat till everyone got here."

"I'll get them," Daisy said. "I'm not sure I want to hear what Walker has to say about your sneaky tactics."

"Coward," King accused as she scooted inside.

Walker took a real long time exiting his car. King had a hunch he was trying to persuade himself not to draw his weapon. King counted on him doing the right thing eventually.

"Oh, come on up here," he called out. "You're not going to shoot me."

"Don't bet on it," Walker said, but he came on up on the porch and accepted the iced tea King handed him, then settled into an adjacent rocker. "Let me guess—this is about Tucker."

"Smart man."

"I have nothing to say. Tucker is a grown man and my boss. He's handling this in the most professional way he knows how. Beyond that, it's none of my business."

"Of course it is," King scoffed. "You're family now. We Spencers look out for each other."

"No, *you* look out for everybody," Walker corrected. "Or, rather, you meddle in their lives."

"Got you and Daisy married, didn't I?" King demanded. "You complaining about that?"

The beginnings of a smile tugged at Walker's mouth.

"Not with my wife standing in the shadows listening to every word I say," he retorted.

"Damn," Daisy said. "I thought I could find out something to hold over your head."

"Not a chance, darlin'. I have only good things to say about you and our marriage."

King regarded them with satisfaction as Daisy slipped onto Walker's lap and gave him a kiss. Yes, indeed, he'd done all right by those two.

Jenna and Bobby arrived next, walking up to the porch hand in hand, still looking thoroughly besotted with each other. Another success story, King concluded with satisfaction.

"Now Anna-Louise is the only one who's missing," he said.

"She's not family," Bobby pointed out. "And I don't think she much likes you using her to do your dirty work."

"I just want her here to remind everyone of what sort of role models we're supposed to provide for this town," King said. "Besides, if there was ever a woman who could hold her own against me, it's Anna-Louise. She doesn't do anything she doesn't think is right, even if I'm the one doing the asking."

Daisy and Bobby exchanged an amused look. King scowled at the pair of them. "Watch it, you two."

"I'm just surprised at how much respect you seem to have for a woman who doesn't always listen to you," Daisy said.

King shrugged. "Have to take the bad with the good. Anna-Louise knows her stuff. Don't know much of anybody in Trinity Harbor who doesn't try to live up to her ideals. She doesn't order people to do the right thing.

She just points it out and expects them to make the right decision."

"Unlike some people we could name," Daisy said dryly.

Walker seemed to choke on that, quickly turning his head as if that would keep King from seeing his amusement.

"You know, son, you're beginning to annoy me," King told his son-in-law.

"Does that mean I can take off?" Walker inquired. The fact that he was picking up a ham sandwich as he asked suggested he didn't hold out much hope of getting a favorable response.

"No!" King bellowed. "Nobody leaves until we come up with a game plan." Fortunately he spotted the last of his expected guests barreling up the driveway. "Here's Anna-Louise now."

"Oh, brother," she said when she emerged from the car. "I came out here to pray over your near-dead carcass, and instead, I can see I'm about to be asked to do something I'm not going to like."

"Oh, can it," King retorted. "I listened to you bellyache about your problems earlier. You can listen to me now. We have to do something to save Tucker. This situation is getting out of hand."

Before he could get in another word, Jenna and Daisy were turning to Anna-Louise.

"Is everything okay with you?" Daisy asked.

"What sort of problems was King talking about?" Jenna asked.

Anna-Louise shot him a triumphant look. "Nothing I care to discuss in front of everyone," she said sweetly. "Could we go inside?"

With that, all three women disappeared into the house. King stared after them with dismay, knowing he had no one to blame but himself for the hasty defection.

"Nice going, Daddy," Bobby said, not even trying to hide his amusement.

"It could be hours before they come back out here," Walker grumbled.

"Probably will be," King agreed, resigned to the situation. "Oh, well, you two will just have to do. Walker, can't you do something to get Tucker off this investigation he's doing for Mary Elizabeth?"

"Beyond solving the case myself, I don't see how, and I'm short on solid leads at the moment."

"Well, find some," King demanded unreasonably.

"Believe me, I'm trying. Nobody wants this murder solved more than I do. I love being a deputy. I do not like being the one everyone complains to when the crimes don't get solved fast enough."

King frowned at the response, but accepted it for the moment. He turned to his son. "Bobby, talk to your brother," King ordered. "Make him see the light."

"Since when has Tucker ever listened to anything I had to say?" Bobby retorted. "He's just like you—stubborn as a mule once he gets an idea in his head. And he learned all about rushing to the aid of a lady in distress from you. If he thinks Mary Elizabeth needs his help, then he's going to give it to her."

"No matter what it costs him?" King said, then made another attempt to dole out an assignment. "Walker, you tell Tucker how folks in town are taking his leave of absence from the department."

"Seems to me like most of them understand it, even if they're not too happy to have me acting in his place,"

Walker said. "In fact, all I've heard people say is that it's exactly what they would expect him to do, given what an honorable man he is. He's putting ethical considerations first."

"If his ethics were the only thing involved, I'd let well enough alone," King snapped. "We all know it's his hormones. That woman always could twist him up in knots. He stopped thinking straight around her before he even hit puberty."

"I don't think he'll let that happen again," Bobby said. "She ripped his heart out when she married Chandler. A man doesn't forget a thing like that."

"Not if he's thinking with his head," King agreed. "You think Tucker's using his?"

"Absolutely," Walker said.

"I agree," Bobby added.

"Hmm," King murmured thoughtfully. He looked at Walker. "And I suppose you never got distracted by a kiss during all those months when you and Daisy were being all logical and sorting things out about the best thing to do about Tommy?"

Walker muttered something indiscernible under his breath.

"I thought so," King said, then stared at Bobby. "You kept your head the whole time Jenna was pursuing you about developing the boardwalk?"

Bobby frowned. "Okay, okay, you've made your point. What do you want us to do?"

"I think we need to sit down and have a talk with him, one of those intervention things I keep hearing about on TV. How's tomorrow night suit you?"

"What's wrong with tonight?" Bobby asked. "I

thought you were in a hurry. I'd just as soon get this over with."

"I have my own plans for tonight," King said.

"More important than getting all this off your chest?"

"Yes," King said defensively. "Not everything in my life revolves around my children."

Walker chuckled. "He's got a date with Frances. Want to bet?" he asked Bobby.

"Nah," Bobby said, grinning. "That's a no-brainer. It's definitely something to do with Frances. And since I've seen firsthand how much trouble he's in with her, I think he's pretty smart not to stand her up tonight."

"Okay, that's enough. Let's not get sidetracked," King said, pounding his fist on the arm of the rocker. "We're agreed then. We'll all meet at Tucker's tomorrow night. You'll see to it that Daisy and Jenna are there?"

"We'll be there," Walker said. "Bobby?"

"I wouldn't miss it for the world. I'm sure it will be the highlight of my week, maybe even the entire month."

"There's no need for sarcasm," King told him. "Now go in there, retrieve your wives and get on out of here. I've got things to do."

Walker and Bobby rolled their eyes, but did as King had ordered. Filled with satisfaction at a job well-done, he watched the whole lot of them head for their cars. He was about to duck into the house and get ready for his big evening, when Bobby leaned out the window of his car and hollered at him.

"Hey, King, I recommend some of that fancy after-shave for tonight. The women go wild for it."

"Boy, it's not too late for me to disinherit you," King shouted back.

READER SERVICE—**Here's how it works:**

Accepting your 2 free Romance books and 2 free gifts (gifts valued at approximately $10.00 retail) places you under no obligation to buy anything. You may keep the books and gifts and return the shipping statement marked "cancel." If you do not cancel, about a month later we'll send you 4 additional books and bill you just $6.74 each in the U.S. or $7.24 each in Canada. That is a savings of at least 16% off the cover price. It's quite a bargain! Shipping and handling is just 50¢ per book in the U.S. and 75¢ per book in Canada.* You may cancel at any time, but if you choose to continue, every month we'll send you 4 more books, which you may either purchase at the discount price plus shipping and handling or return to us and cancel your subscription. *Terms and prices subject to change without notice. Prices do not include applicable taxes. Sales tax applicable in N.Y. Canadian residents will be charged applicable taxes. Offer not valid in Quebec. Books received may not be as shown. All orders subject to approval. Credit or debit balances in a customer's account(s) may be offset by any other outstanding balance owed by or to the customer. Please allow 4 to 6 weeks for delivery. Offer available while quantities last.

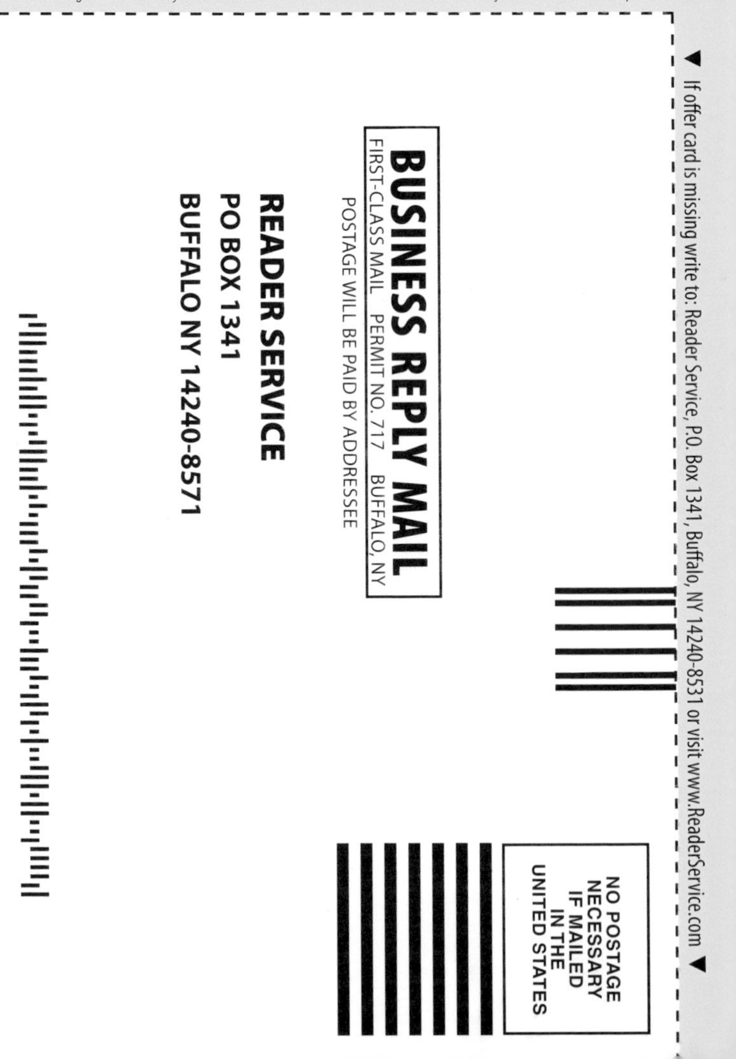

Bobby merely grinned. "I thought you did that years ago."

King sighed as he watched them drive off. He was going to have to come up with a better threat than that. It was evident to him that not a one of them really gave two hoots about inheriting Cedar Hill or anything else he'd worked his whole life to accumulate. Nobody could ever accuse his kids of being nothing but greedy parasites the way some offspring were.

Which, of course, meant that they came around because, despite all the wisecracks, they loved him.

"Well, I'll be damned," he muttered with a hoot. A man couldn't get much richer than that.

Tucker was having trouble concentrating. Every time Mary Elizabeth handed him another file, every time she reached across in front of him to pick up another stack of papers, he caught a faint whiff of the exotic, seductive scent she wore. Her perfectly sedate blouse stretched tight across her breasts, which were encased in a thoroughly provocative scrap of lace that was enough to drive a man to drink. He was beginning to regret his decision to skip the wine and stick with soda. Then, again, he'd probably been really, really smart not to do anything to lower his inhibitions.

"Are you okay?" she asked, studying him intently. "You look a little flushed. If it's too hot in here, I can turn up the air-conditioning."

Unless she set it on freezing, it wouldn't help, Tucker concluded. "I'm fine," he said tersely. "Are you making a list of all these names we're finding?"

She gave him an inscrutable look, then nodded. "Of course. You asked me to, didn't you? It's right here."

She waved a legal pad under his nose. "I've got the business associates on one. Political cronies on another. And there's a third list with all the women I suspected him of having affairs with."

"Okay, then, how many more files are there?"

"Just one drawer left and whatever's in the safe," she told him.

Tucker groaned. "There's a safe?"

"Yes."

"Why the hell didn't you say so? Anything he's trying to keep secret would be much more likely to be kept in there."

"I didn't say so because you asked for his files," she retorted with exaggerated patience. "Besides, I had access to the safe, so how secret could anything in there be?"

"What about safety deposit boxes?"

"None I know about."

"Did he have a safe in his office?"

"Probably."

"Who at his company would have access to that?"

Liz hesitated. "I'm not sure. I didn't have the combination, but someone must have it. Maybe Roland Morgan."

"Remind me again. Roland is?"

"His partner at Chandler Technologies."

"Right." His head was spinning from all the names that had been accumulating since they'd started a few hours earlier. He wondered if he'd ever get them sorted out, much less manage to prioritize the ones most likely to want Chandler dead. This Roland fellow seemed like a good place to start, though.

"Was he at the funeral? Did I meet him?"

"He was there, but he scurried out right after the service. Roland is not a social creature," Mary Elizabeth said, smiling. "You'll see."

"You suppose he's still at the office?" he asked. "It's after five."

"I'll call," she said. "Should I ask him to stick around until we can get there?"

Tucker gauged how long it would take to skim the remaining files, check the safe and drive to the company offices, which he'd seen on the way to the house. "Tell him we'll be there about six-thirty."

"What if he says he has plans?"

"Tell him to cancel them."

Mary Elizabeth nodded and picked up the phone. He heard some of what she was saying as he continued scanning papers. Apparently Roland wasn't giving her a hard time.

"He'll be there. He says anything he can do to help us find out who killed Larry, he's happy to do."

Tucker was relieved by the eagerness to help, though he'd seen plenty of guilty people try to divert suspicion by making a pretense of cooperation.

"Okay, I've made notes of the names from these files. Check the safe, and we can get over there."

Mary Elizabeth returned with a copy of Chandler's will, a few stacks of cash that amounted to a couple thousand dollars and several jewelry boxes.

"That's it?" he asked.

She nodded.

"Have you read the will? Do you know what's in it?"

"Like I told Foley, unless he changed it recently, he's left the business and its assets to Roland and his personal money to the charitable foundation he and I started a few years ago." She regarded Tucker with a hint of disappointment. "I was telling the truth when I said that I had nothing to gain from either divorcing him or killing him."

"Sorry."

She sighed. "I suppose I can't blame you for being suspicious. Despite all the downturns in the market, Larry was still a relatively wealthy man. But whether you believe me or not, it was never about the money with us. We both took great precautions to make sure that we each understood that. Larry loved Swan Ridge, but he accepted that it was my inheritance. I had my own money. I didn't need his."

Tucker wasn't sure how he felt about knowing that Mary Elizabeth hadn't been bowled over by Chandler's wealth. That meant there had been something more between them, something deeper and more personal. He'd been able to accept the idea that she'd chosen a rich man over him, but knowing that he'd fallen short in some other way rankled. At the time he hadn't thought her reasons for choosing Chandler were important, but apparently they'd been eating at him for years now.

"Okay, let's get out of here," he said, unable to hide his suddenly foul temper.

Before he could rise, she put a hand on his arm. He felt the muscle twitch beneath her touch.

"Tucker, I know it hurts you to hear all this, but I did love him at the beginning. I got caught up in the idea that together the two of us could make a real difference in people's lives. When we first met, we talked about all of his plans and ideals. We were on the same wavelength. I didn't even realize it was more than that for a long time. Ironically, it was Daisy who saw it. What I saw as intellectual compatibility, she realized covered a deeper passion. I think that was why she was so furious with me. She thought I was deliberately cheating on you, when in my mind that was far from true. Only after she told me what she suspected did I take a good hard look at what I was feeling and realize that I had deep feelings for Larry. I swear to you that I broke it off with you before I acted on those feelings. We were never sneaking around behind your back."

He knew she thought he would find comfort in that, but it still hurt. He clung to the bitterness because it kept the other, more dangerous, feelings at bay.

"And you could be much more important as the wife of a big-time politician, right? You could do good works on a much grander scale than you could being the wife of a small-town sheriff," he said angrily. "Even if he was a Spencer."

"Yes," she said, regarding him with an unflinching look. "I thought I could. I know now how wrong that was on so many levels it would take the rest of the night to get into all of them, but at the time, yes, that was my thinking. I'm sorry."

Tucker withdrew from her touch. "Yeah. So am I."

"I just keep on hurting you, don't I?" she asked, regarding him with what appeared to be genuine misery. "Do you want to drop this investigation? If that would be easier for you, I'll understand."

Tucker bristled at the suggestion that he couldn't take being around her. "I started it, I'll finish it," he said tightly. "Let's get out of here. This place is starting to give me hives."

Mary Elizabeth chuckled at that. "It has that effect on me sometimes, too."

After a beat, Tucker laughed, too, and just like that the tension was broken.

Outside the soft, sultry air was refreshing compared to the air-conditioned sterility inside. He took a deep breath, as much to clear his head as cleanse his lungs. He could do this. He could be around Mary Elizabeth for however long this investigation took without going crazy and hauling her into his arms.

Just then, though, he glanced down into those petal-soft violet eyes of hers and completely lost his train of thought…and his common sense.

"Tucker—"

Before she could finish whatever she was about to say, he leaned down and covered her mouth with his, catching her gasp of surprise. Fire licked through his blood with the speed and power of lightning. Desire and need rocketed along right behind.

He had wanted this for so long, dreamed about it. The taste of her was always with him, as unforgettable as his name, as sweet as ripe watermelon.

His breathing was ragged, his body hard, by the time his brain finally kicked back in. When he forced himself to release her, to take a step back, her little moan of protest was almost enough to ruin his resolve.

"We're not going to do this," he said, half to himself.

"We just did," she pointed out reasonably.

"I mean again."

"Ever?"

"Ever," he replied emphatically.

Hurt flickered in her eyes. "Your call," she said mildly. "But, Tucker, it really would be too bad if we didn't."

And, Tucker thought, it would be devastating if they did.

14

Roland Morgan had a brilliant mind for technology, but little business acumen. Liz recalled Larry's opinion as she and Tucker walked into Roland's office and found him totally absorbed by something on his computer screen, his desk littered with empty foam coffee cups, his hair disheveled and his eyes bleary behind his thick-lensed glasses. He was dressed for comfort rather than success in jeans and a rumpled T-shirt it looked as if he'd slept in.

Roland blinked hard when Liz spoke to him, then greeted her with a distracted smile. "You're here already?"

"It's been over an hour," she pointed out with amusement. "Obviously you lost track of time. You must be working on something new."

"Just trying to get a bug out of a program that we thought we were ready to start marketing for Christmas." He gazed around as if he hadn't noticed the state of his office before. "Sorry about the mess. I came straight back here after the funeral, and I've been up for more than twenty-four hours. If I can't get this cleaned up, we'll never get it into production. Marketing's having a cow. They've bought hundreds of thousands of dollars in magazine space and TV spots to push this for the holidays."

"How about Larry? Was he having a cow?" Tucker asked, drawing a startled look from Roland.

"Roland, this is Tucker Spencer," Liz explained. "He's investigating Larry's death for me."

Roland stood and held out his hand. Liz noticed then that he was wearing socks but no shoes. She spotted a pair of well-worn running shoes across the room. She had to bite back a grin at the contrast he made to her designer clad, perfectionist husband, who seldom had a hair out of place even after hours on the campaign trail.

"Good to meet you," Roland said to Tucker. "Anything I can do to help, I'll try, but Larry and I pretty much went our separate ways around here. He left the tech stuff to me, and I left all the rest to him."

"Mind if we sit over here?" Tucker asked, gesturing to a sofa and chairs. "We'll try not to keep you from your work for too long."

"The break will probably do me good," Roland acknowledged. "My brain's pretty much fried right now. Anybody want coffee?"

"How about bottled water and some food?" Liz suggested instead. "I'll check the fridge in Larry's office. There's usually some fruit and cheese in there. You look as if you could use some nourishment, as well, Roland."

"Sure. That would be great."

"Tucker, bottled water for you, too?"

"Sounds good," he said.

She could hear the murmur of their voices as she went through the connecting door to Larry's office.

Inside the spacious room with its plush carpet, shiny mahogany desk and expensive furnishings, she paused. For an instant it almost seemed as if she could smell a lingering hint of Larry's aftershave. Though he had spent increasingly less time here in recent months, this office—this entire sedate brick building on a tree-lined street—had meant a lot to him. It had been the first concrete proof of his accomplishments, a new structure built to look as if it had endured through the centuries. Visitors were always stunned to learn that the building was less than ten years old.

In an odd way, that summed up Larry. The image, the facade, were coldly calculated for effect. Few people knew the man underneath. She certainly hadn't, and she had known him as well as anyone.

Born in a failing coal mining town on the western fringes of the state, he had developed a fire inside to achieve something extraordinary. In an ironic way his mother and father had fanned that flame through their own indifference to their poverty. They'd been stunned by the heights he'd attained.

His mother had died shortly after the dedication of this office, his father a year after Larry had been sworn in for his first term in the house of delegates. Neither had attended these events. Larry hadn't invited them. Only later had Liz learned that the omissions had been deliberate. He'd been embarrassed by them. He hadn't wanted anyone to see his humble beginnings. He'd preferred that his business associates and his constituents identify him with the generations-old respectability of the Swans of the historic Northern Neck.

Liz had never met Mrs. Chandler. His mother had died before she and Larry had been introduced. She had met his father only once, briefly, before the wedding. Shortly after the wedding, Martin Chandler had fallen gravely ill. Later Larry went alone to the funeral, taking less than half a day off from his second campaign to attend and then only because he'd understood that television cameras were bound to record the moment.

So many signs that he was emotionally bankrupt and she had missed them all, she thought sorrowfully as she retrieved the food from the refrigerator and carried it back to Roland's office.

She found him and Tucker discussing baseball, of all things. Both, it turned out, were ardent fans of the Atlanta Braves, whose minor league players were based in Richmond. Either Tucker had already found out everything he needed to know from Roland or he'd determined that there was nothing to be learned.

She dispensed the food and sat back to try to figure out which. It took only moments to realize that Tucker was just cleverly putting Roland at ease. Once Larry's partner had distractedly eaten half a dozen crackers with cheese on them and an apple, Tucker's expression turned serious.

"Look," he began, "to get back to the reason we came by, can you fill me in on how the company's doing?"

"You'd be better off talking to the chief financial officer for that. Like I said before, I don't pay a lot of attention to the business details." Roland shrugged and pulled off a wry grin. "No head for numbers."

"Surely Larry filled you in when there were ups and downs," Tucker persisted. "You received financial disclosure reports, something, right?"

"I suppose I did," Roland said, gazing helplessly at

a row of file drawers along one wall. "I imagine Selena put them in there. She's very efficient."

"Selena is?"

"My secretary, Selena Velez."

"She worked for Larry, too," Liz told Tucker.

"She was a lot more useful to him than she was to me. About all I had her do was take messages and keep marketing off my back."

"Did Larry keep any important papers in a safe?" Liz asked. "Or would everything be in his files?"

"Oh, no, there's a safe," Roland said at once. "State-of-art security. I lock a lot of my stuff in there. Corporate spying being what it is these days, Larry convinced me I had to be careful to protect whatever I was designing."

"Could you show us?" Liz asked. "There are some papers of Larry's I can't seem to locate. I thought they might be here, locked away for safekeeping."

"Sure," Roland said, leading the way to what looked like a built-in bar in a small hallway between the two offices. He pressed a hidden button and the bar swung open, revealing the heavy steel door of a walk-in vault.

"Hold on," he said sheepishly. "I have to check the combination."

"You haven't committed it to memory?" Tucker asked.

"It's electronically programmed to change every few days. Larry set it up that way, because I tended to write the combination on scraps of paper, which wound up in the trash or sitting in the middle of my desk. He concluded that he had to have a way to counteract my forgetfulness."

"How on earth do you figure out what it is if it's always changing?" Liz asked.

"I keep the code in a secure file on my computer. Now if I can just find the piece of paper I used to get in there a couple of days ago, I should be able to figure this out."

While Roland went to work out the current combination for the vault, Tucker looked at Liz. "Is he for real?"

"He's brilliant and single-minded. It made him a perfect match for Larry, because he was completely willing to have Larry handle everything except the technological stuff."

"So Larry wasn't a technology whiz himself?"

"He could hold his own up to a point," Liz said. "But Roland is definitely the genius behind the company's success."

"You don't suppose he got tired of being the behind-the-scenes guy while your husband basked in all the glory, do you?"

Liz promptly shook her head. "Does he look as if he cares about that?"

"Were they fifty-fifty partners in terms of profits?" Tucker asked.

"I believe so, but you'd have to ask Roland."

"Ask me what?" he said, coming back with a scrap of paper in hand. He worked the lock with nimble fingers and the heavy door swung open.

"What was your partnership agreement with Larry?" Tucker asked.

"We each owned an equal share of the stock, and between us we held controlling interest in the company. The remainder was sold publicly on the New York Stock Exchange starting last year. Before that we were on Nasdaq. Larry was ecstatic when we had enough assets to make the jump. He said it finally put us in a league with the big guys like Microsoft and AOL Time Warner."

"Any merger or takeover offers on the table?" Tucker asked.

"If there were, Larry would have turned them down flat. This company was his baby," Roland said.

Liz nodded in agreement. "This company brought him the kind of respectability he'd craved. He would never have sold it."

"Not even if he was short on cash for his next campaign?" Tucker persisted.

"Not even then," Liz said.

"Could you have forced him to sell?" Tucker asked Roland.

Roland regarded him with complete bafflement. "Why would I?"

"Debts," Tucker suggested. "The desire to move on to a new challenge?"

Roland laughed. "I've earned more money since we started up than I ever dreamed of having. I live a very simple life. No fancy car. No fancy house." He gestured toward his clothes. "No designer clothes…and definitely no political aspirations."

"What about a new challenge?"

"Every day around here is a challenge," Roland insisted. He gestured toward the open vault. "Take a look around. Maybe you'll find those papers you were looking for. If you don't need me for anything else, I'm going to get back to work."

Liz glanced at Tucker. "Any more questions for now?"

He shook his head. "No. Thanks for your time. We'll let you know when we're on our way out."

"Sure thing," Roland said, his expression already distracted as he headed back to his computer.

"Any idea where we should start?" Liz asked, studying the unlabeled files stacked from floor to ceiling in the vault.

"Apparently Selena's organizational skills didn't extend to the safe," Tucker commented. "Why don't we start at the back. I'll work my way around to the right, you go to the left."

The search yielded incorporation papers, financial records, Security and Exchange Commission filings for the company's initial stock offering. To Liz's untrained eye, it seemed as if there was nothing out of the ordinary. It was when she came to the fifth stack that she realized that a thick manila envelope was sandwiched between the files. She pulled it free, broke the seal and extracted a sheaf of letters written on pale peach vellum. She recognized the handwriting on the envelopes at once.

"Tucker," she said, extending the letters toward him with a trembling hand. "These are from Cynthia Miles to Larry. I don't want to read them, but they could be important."

Tucker regarded her worriedly. "You okay?"

"It's like bumping up against the past. All those old feelings of hurt and disgust and anger that I'd thought were over came flooding back through me."

"We'll take these with us and I'll look them over later. No need to do it now." Handling them carefully by the edges, he stuffed them back in the envelope and set it aside.

"Why did you touch them that way?"

"Because there could be fingerprints we'd find helpful," he explained. "You feeling any better now? How about some water?"

She shook her head, eyeing the envelope warily. "I'll be fine. After all, none of it matters anymore, right?"

"That's exactly right," he said, reaching over to give her hand a reassuring squeeze. "Neither one of them can hurt you ever again."

She drew in a deep breath and went back to sorting through the remaining files. She found absolutely nothing that offered so much as a clue, much less anything likely to incriminate anyone.

Tucker rocked back on his heels at the same time. "That's that. I didn't find a damned thing."

"Me, either," she said. "Let's get out of here. I need some fresh air."

"You head on outside. I'll lock this vault and let Roland know we're leaving."

Liz accepted the offer and hurriedly left the building, relieved to be away from all the ghosts. She couldn't help wondering, though, just how many more she would have to face before this investigation ended.

It was late when Tucker got back to Trinity Harbor. He'd followed Mary Elizabeth from Richmond to Swan Ridge, made sure that she got inside safely, then left before he risked a repeat of that kiss they'd shared just outside her Richmond house.

Since he was still wide-awake and wound up and the contents of those letters were nagging at him, he drove on to Montross, hoping to scare up Walker. He found him behind his desk. Like Roland Morgan, Walker was surrounded by littered coffee cups. Of course, being Walker, there were also several empty food containers, probably provided by an increasingly irritated Daisy. One of these days, Tucker knew, he was destined to hear a long tirade about how he'd dumped this case on her husband.

"Any wheels turning in that brain of yours?" he inquired as he sat down and propped his feet on the desk.

"Not that I've noticed," Walker conceded.

"Maybe these will help," Tucker suggested, tossing the envelope across to him.

"What is it?"

"A whole passel of letters from Cynthia Miles to Chandler."

"Where'd you find them?" Walker asked suspiciously.

"In the safe at Chandler's office," Tucker told him. "Either the man was very sentimental and couldn't bear to part with them or they're blackmail attempts he wanted to hang on to."

Walker whistled at the blackmail theory. "You haven't read them?"

"I didn't want to do it in front of Mary Elizabeth. Just the sight of them sent her tripping down memory lane to a very bad place." He shrugged. "Besides, I figured the fewer fingerprints on them the better."

"Ah, a cop's instincts," Walker said, searching Tucker's drawer for a pair of tweezers.

"First, last and always," Tucker confirmed. "Do I get to look over your shoulder?"

"How about I read them aloud?"

"As long as you can stomach it, I can," Tucker agreed, leaning back and closing his eyes.

"Hey, wake up. These aren't going to be some damned bedtime story," Walker grumbled. He extracted the first letter from its pretty envelope and laid it flat on his desk. "Okay, here goes.

"'My dearest…
I don't know why you're not taking my calls. I thought we had something really special between us. I know that I love you and want to be with you. I will never forgive your wife for keeping us apart. I understand why you feel you must stay with her, but really, Larry, you and I are such an extraordinary team. There are no limits to what we could accomplish together. Think about that, and dream of me tonight, as I will of you.

All my love,
Cynthia'"

"Now isn't that pretty?" Tucker said. "I'm all misty over it."

Walker rolled his eyes at the dripping sarcasm. "It's dated November twelfth, six years ago."

"Right after Chandler won his first election," Tucker said. "That matches Mary Elizabeth's story that she had Chandler fire the Miles woman right after the election."

"Seems to," Walker agreed.

The next three letters, dated for the next few weeks, were more of the same, appeals to Chandler to ditch Mary Elizabeth and team up with his former campaign manager for endless matrimonial bliss and the achievement of his ambitious political goals. Tucker also thought he detected an increasingly impatient edge to them. It was the fifth letter, though, in which the tone changed. Written a year later, it had a note of desperate hysteria to it.

Why won't you even take my calls? I feel as if my whole world, my entire reason for being has collapsed. I have nowhere to turn. You're the only man for me, yet clearly I am not the only woman for you. I saw you, Larry. I saw you with her. How could you do that to me? How could you take her to our special place? I can forgive you for many things, but not that. I will never forgive you for that.

"She didn't sign this one," Walker noted. "I wonder what his response was?"

"If he was half as smart as he was reported to be, he didn't respond at all," Tucker said. "He'd have been fueling her obvious obsession."

"Let's see," Walker suggested, opening another letter dated only a few days later. In it, too, Cynthia berated Chandler for not contacting her. "Looks like you were right. He decided to stay the hell away from her."

There were six more letters, some dated months apart, some only days, each one increasingly desperate. The last two were filled with more accusations about unnamed other women and with threats to get even.

"Isn't this a nice, tidy package providing motive?" Tucker said when Walker had read them all.

"Just one problem," Walker pointed out. "The last one was written two years ago. Why would she wait this long to make good on the threat?"

"Only one reason I can think of," Tucker said, meeting Walker's gaze.

"Chandler went back to her," Walker guessed.

"Seems like the only logical answer to me," Tucker agreed. "Clearly, ignoring her hadn't worked. She was unstable and he needed to keep her quiet. The only way to accomplish that would be to throw her a bone, spend a little time with her."

"I'll talk to the county attorney tomorrow and see if these give us cause to search the Miles woman's home to look for a weapon," Walker said. "If not, at the very least, I can set up an interview. I have a whole slew of questions I'd like to ask her. You have any angles you'd like me to explore beyond the obvious?"

Tucker thought back over the contents of all the letters, then nodded slowly. "Just one. Ask her to name some of the other women. Did you notice she was very careful to omit their names in every letter? Seems to me like she'd caught him with a whole slew of them, but maybe not. Maybe there was one in particular who pushed her over the edge because she thought it was serious."

Walker raised an eyebrow at the suggestion. "More serious than his wife? Liz didn't seem to make her too hysterical."

"She'd already won against Mary Elizabeth," Tucker said, recalling his conversation with Cynthia Miles. "Chandler was having his affair with Cynthia even after the wedding. She probably considered the marriage just a little bump in the road, a political strategy that would pay off with a win in November, which it did. The only thing she hadn't counted on was being fired right afterward."

"So, she did lose to Liz," Walker pointed out.

"Only temporarily," Tucker countered. "She believes to this day that the marriage was only a political maneuver, that Mary Elizabeth never really mattered to

Chandler. The other women followed, proving once more that the marriage meant nothing to Chandler."

"What I don't understand is why the hell Liz didn't dump him right after she found out about his first affair," Walker said. "If I ever cheated on your sister, she'd be out the door in a flash, right after taking a strip out of my hide, more than likely."

"That was my reaction, too," Tucker said.

"And? I assume she told you why."

"Because she didn't want to admit having made a mistake, especially after she'd walked out on me to be with him. Her pride kicked in. She decided to suck it up and stay, because she thought she deserved it as punishment for hurting me. It took her five years to realize that there was nothing to be gained by that except misery."

"Five years? I thought they'd been married six."

Tucker nodded. "She decided the marriage was over a year ago. She'd moved out, but she didn't make the break final until she got back from her trip to Europe the day before Chandler was killed."

"Not exactly the storybook marriage everyone thought it was, was it?" Walker shook his head and stood up. "I'm going home."

"Good. You look like you could use about two days' worth of sleep."

"Forget sleeping," Walker retorted with a grin. "I'm going to wake up my wife and show her how grateful I am that we have a very uncomplicated marriage. We both understand all the rules and live by them."

Tucker groaned. "Could you not tell me things like that? You're talking about my sister."

"We've been married almost two years now. You do know we sleep together, don't you?" Walker taunted.

"Go away. Get out," Tucker ordered.

"You're just jealous because there's no one waiting at home in your bed," Walker accused.

But there could be, Tucker thought, his memory seizing on the passion behind that kiss he and Mary Elizabeth had shared earlier. There definitely could be.

But only if he lost every last grain of sense he possessed, he concluded with a heavy sigh.

"You could be right, Walker. Maybe I am jealous as hell."

"Then do something about it," Walker advised.

How could he? Tucker wondered. Especially when the only woman who could erase the loneliness gnawing at him was Mary Elizabeth?

15

An entire week went by with nothing more than an occasional phone call from Tucker asking Liz if she was doing okay. Because she knew it was what he wanted to hear, she dutifully said yes each and every time. She asked none of the questions that were on the tip of her tongue, because the one time she had, he'd been abrupt to the point of being rude. He wouldn't even say if he was still making trips to Richmond, working unofficially with Walker right here in town or off on the river fishing with Bobby.

While Tucker was doing who-knew-what, Liz was going stir-crazy at the house. After years of maintaining a jam-packed schedule, she didn't have nearly enough to keep her mind occupied. She'd made so many calls to Frances just to see how things were progressing with King that Frances had finally come to see if she was truly all right.

Two days ago Mrs. Gilman had come back to work full-time as housekeeper at Swan Ridge, and between them, they had cleaned the place until every piece of glass sparkled, every surface shone and all traces of the violence in her grandfather's study had been erased. There was only a certain amount of satisfaction to be derived from a spotless home that hardly anyone ever visited.

Thoroughly frustrated, Liz finally broke down and did what she'd sworn she wouldn't—she called Tucker, determined to find out exactly what was going on and to insist on participating. Even during her lousy marriage, she had never passively sat back and done nothing. She'd devised her own life and lived it to the fullest. She refused to do any less now.

"Hello, Mary Elizabeth," Tucker said, his tone resigned.

Blast caller ID, she thought, wishing she'd been able to take him by surprise. "Hi," she said with forced gaiety. "Just thought I'd check in and see what's happening with the investigation. Any news?"

"None I can share," he said, still sounding distant.

The last of her patience snapped. "Tucker, what's going on?" she demanded.

"I just told you—"

"I meant with us," she said impatiently. "Why are you acting like this? Is it because of the kiss?"

His heavy sigh was answer enough.

"It is, isn't it?" She had to choke back the desire to laugh. "That kiss scared you. And ever since we got back from Richmond, you've been stewing over it, blaming yourself for letting down your guard, haven't you? You've probably even told yourself you were taking advantage of me."

"Wasn't I?"

"Absolutely not."

"Well, it should have scared the tar out of you, too,"

he said, sounding embarrassed and disgruntled by her ability to read him so well.

"Sorry, it didn't," she said mildly. "But if you're that uncomfortable with it, we can make sure it doesn't happen again. We're not a couple of randy teenagers anymore. We can control our hormones."

He muttered something that sounded like "speak for yourself."

This time she did chuckle. "Oh, Tucker, I never thought of you being a coward."

"I'm being sensible," he corrected.

"Doesn't seem that way to me. May I remind you that I am paying you to conduct an investigation? You owe it to me to report in occasionally."

"You're not paying me," he corrected.

That was an unexpected wrinkle. "Of course I am," she insisted.

"No, Mary Elizabeth. This is on the house. I won't take money from you. Not ever. Not under any circumstances."

Liz sighed. They'd fought about exactly this countless times in the past, when Tucker had flatly refused even to share expenses on a date and had growled unappreciatively if she'd given him a gift he thought was too expensive.

Though King Spencer was rolling in money, Tucker refused to accept any handouts from him, either, insisting that he could live just fine on his paltry starting salary as a deputy sheriff. Even as sheriff, he wasn't exactly rich. But what he lacked in income, he made up for in pride. There were plenty of times when Liz found that damned annoying. This was one of them.

"Then I suppose I'll have to find someone else to

pick up from here," she told him. "You're a professional, Tucker. I won't let you do this for nothing."

"Too late. You dragged me into this. You can't get rid of me now."

"I'm firing you."

He laughed. "Doesn't mean I'll stop working."

"Oh, for goodness' sakes, can't you just come over here and fill me in on what's been going on? I promise I'll keep my hands to myself."

"It's not your hands that give me trouble," he said.

"Oh? What is it, then?" she taunted.

"You know perfectly well."

"Is it my mouth?" she asked in a deliberately provocative tone.

Tucker groaned. "Don't do this to me, Mary Elizabeth. It's not smart."

"I don't know," she said thoughtfully. "I think it could be the smartest thing I've done in the last six years."

Tucker didn't respond, but he was still on the line. She could hear him breathing and imagined that familiar worry line forming across his brow. She decided to let him off the hook for now.

"If you won't come over, will you at least promise to take me to Richmond the next time you go? You have to admit I was helpful last week. We found those letters together, didn't we?"

"Yes," he conceded grudgingly. "But I think you should keep your distance from here on out. You don't want whatever I find and turn over to Walker to be tainted because you were involved in the discovery. It could look as if you're trying to set someone up."

"Is that really the reason, or is it just more hogwash to keep some distance between us?"

"A little of both," he finally admitted with more candor. "Everybody's worried about my reputation if we're seen together, but it won't be good for yours, either. You're recently widowed. What will people think if it looks as if you're taking up with another man this soon?"

"As if I care about that," she said.

"Well, I do."

Liz sighed. If he was determined to be gallant, there wasn't much she could do about it. "Just tell me this, then—were the letters helpful?"

"Walker's following up on them now," he said, clearly relieved that she'd changed the subject.

"Has he interviewed Cynthia?"

"That's scheduled for this morning."

"Will you be able to sit in?"

"Doubtful, though I'm going to try. If that doesn't work out, I'm sure he'll show me a transcript of everything she says."

"Will you come by afterward, or at least call me?"

"I'll let you know what happens," he promised.

She grinned at his refusal to commit to the means by which he'd let her know. If it was up to him, he'd probably send a note by carrier pigeon.

"Is your family bugging you?" she asked, changing the subject.

"They always bug me."

"I meant about me."

"Actually, they have been strangely silent, but maybe that's because I've been hard to track down."

"Hiding from them, too, huh?"

"Pretty much," he said cheerfully. "It's amazing how peaceful things have been. I'm thinking of hiding out more often. I gather from Walker that King had a big family meeting scheduled for one night last week, but I spoiled his sneak attack by not going home that night."

"Staying with a girlfriend?" she asked in what she prayed was a casual tone, even though her stomach was twisted in knots as she awaited his reply.

"No, Mary Elizabeth," he said with exaggerated patience. "If there were a serious girlfriend in my life, do you think King would be so nervous about you?"

"Probably." She thought of a conversation she'd had with King during one of her infrequent visits to Swan Ridge shortly after her marriage. She'd run into him in town. He'd marched right up to her, gotten in her face and told her point-blank that if she ever did anything to exploit the hold she'd once had over his son, he would personally make her life a living hell. She'd believed him. And from time to time, when her marriage had begun to fall apart, she'd clung to King's admission that she had a hold over Tucker.

Recalling that, she added, "I'm sure no matter how wonderful another woman was, King would be terrified that I was going to mess up the relationship somehow."

"Yeah, you're probably right," Tucker conceded. "But King's opinion isn't important. If he tries to give you any grief, just ignore him."

"Have you ever known anyone in Trinity Harbor who was able to ignore King Spencer when he has something to say? It's not like he'll let you get away with turning your back and walking away."

"But you have an advantage few others have," Tucker reminded her. "Out of respect for your grandfather, he won't cause a scene with you in public. Of course," he continued wryly, "if he turns up at your front door, you might want to consider bolting out the back."

"I'll keep that in mind."

"So, what are you going to do today?"

"Now that you've turned me down, I have no idea," she said, unable to keep the plaintive note out of her voice.

"Go into town. See some old friends."

"And risk bumping into your sister? I don't think so."

"The two of you need to mend fences. You can't do it if you keep avoiding each other."

"Tell that to Daisy."

"Believe me, I have."

"And?"

"She's just as stubborn as you are. Come on, Mary Elizabeth. If you're going to come back here to stay, it's time to start getting out and renewing old acquaintances. You can't stay holed up at Swan Ridge forever."

To her deep regret, he had a point. If she'd just accused him of being a coward for not facing his fears head-on, she could hardly let herself get away with being one. "I'll think about it," she promised. "But don't think for a second that I don't know that this is just a way for you to get me off your conscience because you're leaving me out here all alone."

"Could be, but that doesn't make the advice any less sound."

"Tucker..." Her voice trailed off.

"What?"

Liz sighed. "Nothing." She couldn't say what she was really feeling, that just hearing the sound of his voice was healing her in a way that nothing else possibly could.

"Bye, then."

"Goodbye, Tucker."

"I will be in touch when I have something to report, Mary Elizabeth."

"I know."

She heard his muttered oath and a rueful chuckle.

"Saying goodbye's not one bit easier now than it used to be, is it?" she whispered.

And then, to make it less stressful on both of them, she slid the receiver back into its cradle. But it was a long time before she could make herself release the only connection to him she had.

Tucker slammed the phone down, cursing the fact that after all of his careful attempts to keep things between them cool and distant, he'd given himself away at the end. It *was* hard to say goodbye. He'd never been able to do it, not when they were together and it was just for a night, not after she was gone for good.

It was a darned good thing that interview with Cynthia Miles was scheduled for ten o'clock. He planned to try his best to convince Walker to let him go along. He wanted to hear firsthand what she had to say about those letters and her subsequent attempt to blackmail Chandler about their relationship.

If he planned to pull that off, he had to get over to Walker's and try to intercept him before he left Trinity Harbor. That meant having a run-in with Daisy, more than likely, but maybe he could tell her again what he'd just told Mary Elizabeth—that it was time to put the past behind them.

As he drove to Walker and Daisy's, he recalled the friendship that had bloomed between Mary Elizabeth and Daisy years ago. There had never been any question that Mary Elizabeth was his friend first, but the two girls had spent an awful lot of hours behind closed doors giggling and experimenting with makeup and talking about who-knew-what. Him, more than likely.

In those days, Daisy had been a staunch supporter of Mary Elizabeth's. She'd already loved her like a sister, and when Mary Elizabeth had told Daisy of her plans to marry Larry Chandler, Daisy had felt every bit as betrayed as Tucker had. Mary Elizabeth's plea that Daisy be her maid of honor had fallen on deaf ears. Daisy had refused even to attend the wedding, much less participate in it.

"I won't object if you want to be in the wedding party," Tucker had told her honestly. "I know how close the two of you are."

"Were," Daisy had corrected emphatically.

"I appreciate your loyalty," Tucker said. "But—"

"It's not just about loyalty," Daisy said, cutting him off. "I won't stand up and watch her make the worst mistake of her life."

And that had been that. On the day of the August wedding, Daisy had shown up at his house at seven in the morning and proposed an outing to Kings Dominion amusement park. "We can eat hot dogs and cotton candy and ice cream and ride the roller coaster until we get sick."

Tucker had laughed at the suggestion. "And that's supposed to make me feel better?"

"It will certainly take your mind off what's going on over here," she had insisted.

Because getting drunk was never a solution to anything, Tucker had agreed to her plan. To his amazement, Bobby and King had come along in a show of solidarity. They'd ridden every ride in the park, eaten till their stomachs ached and even laughed a time or two, especially at the sight of King's astonished expression when he'd gotten unexpectedly soaked on the water ride.

How could Tucker berate his sister for choosing sides now, when he'd thanked her for it back then?

He was halfway up the walk when Daisy came out to meet him.

"Are you thinking of going with Walker this morning?" she demanded.

"Yes."

"Why?"

"Because I want answers every bit as badly as he does."

"You told him—you told everyone—that this was his investigation," she reminded him.

"It is."

"How do you think it looks if you're shadowing his every move? A lot of people around here still think of Walker as a come-here. They don't entirely trust him to know his job. You're contributing to their doubts."

Tucker started to protest but stopped himself. She was right. He might see this as doing the job he'd been hired by Mary Elizabeth to do, but others might view it as a lack of faith in Walker's expertise.

"I figured you'd be here before I could take off," Walker said with an air of resignation as he joined them before Tucker could tell Daisy he'd reached a decision.

"I just came by to wish you luck," Tucker said.

It was harder to tell who was more surprised, his sister or Walker.

"Really?" Walker said as Daisy silently mouthed, "Thank you."

"You'll do better without me interfering," Tucker

said. "Cynthia knows I'm working for Mary Elizabeth. Seeing me would just put her on the defensive."

"I'll call you with any news," Walker promised. "You can see the transcript the minute we get it typed up this afternoon."

"Good enough," Tucker said, then turned to his sister. "Any chance you can rustle me up some blueberry pancakes?"

She cupped his face in both hands and planted a kiss on his cheek. "You can have anything you want. Just let me say a proper goodbye to my husband."

Tucker held up his hands. "I don't need to see this. Where's Tommy? Maybe he'll play some catch while I wait for you to get breakfast on the table."

"Tommy's a late sleeper. You can have the pleasure of trying to roust him out of bed," Daisy said. "Tell him about the pancakes. That might get him moving."

Tucker waved to acknowledge the advice as he went inside.

Ten minutes later, a cranky Tommy in tow, he returned to the kitchen to find Daisy spooning pancake mix onto a sizzling griddle. She turned to face him.

"Thank you for what you did out there."

"Don't mention it. You were right."

She grinned. "Words every sister lives to hear. While I'm on a roll, can I offer a piece of advice?"

"No."

She frowned at him. "Listen anyway. Let somebody else help Mary Elizabeth. You can't possibly be objective."

"My objectivity's just fine."

"Oh, really? What was your first reaction when you found her at your house?"

Tucker thanked heaven that Daisy did not know exactly where he'd found Mary Elizabeth that night. "Surprise," he told her.

"Oh, right," she said skeptically. "And I'm the tooth fairy."

"Sometimes you are," Tommy volunteered.

Daisy frowned at him. "Stay out of this and drink your juice."

Tucker hid a smile. It would not help the situation to let Daisy see his amusement. She was trying to protect him, not entertain him.

Apparently his effort was less successful than he'd hoped, because she turned her scowl on him next.

"This is not a laughing matter," she said.

"Never said it was."

"Can you look me in the eye and tell me that not one tiny little hip-hip-hooray crossed your mind when you discovered Mary Elizabeth at your place?"

He could tell her that, maybe even keep a straight face while he said it, but he couldn't look her in the eye and they both knew it.

"I thought so," she said. "Stay away from her. Even after all this time, you're still way too susceptible to her."

"What does that mean?" Tommy asked, regarding them both with curiosity.

"Drink your juice," Tucker and Daisy said in a chorus.

"Geez," Tommy said with disgust. "You'd think I asked about sex or something."

Tucker couldn't help the chuckle that slipped out. One glance at Daisy told him she was having an equally difficult time choking back laughter.

"What is wrong with you?" Tommy demanded. "All I said was—"

"We know what you said," Daisy said, flipping a stack of pancakes onto a plate and handing them to him. "Eat your breakfast before it gets cold."

"How's a kid supposed to learn anything if he can't ask questions?" Tommy grumbled as he poured syrup over his pancakes.

"He has a point," Tucker said.

"Then you explain about 'susceptible,'" Daisy said, stripping off her apron. "I have errands to run. I'm going into town before it gets too hot."

"Hey, where are my pancakes?" Tucker demanded as she flew out the door.

"Fix 'em yourself," she hollered back. "I have better fish to fry."

"See what you've done," Tucker said, nabbing Tommy's plate. "Guess I'll just have to finish yours."

Tommy grabbed the plate right back. "I'm a growing kid."

Tucker sighed and stood up. He could make pancakes in a pinch. How hard could it be when the batter was already made and the griddle was hot? He poured four pancakes onto the flat surface and watched them intently, trying to decide when it was time to flip them. Was it before the bubbles popped or after? Better not take any chances, he decided, flipping them and winding up with a soggy, misshapen mess.

Sighing, he tossed the whole batch into the garbage disposal and turned to Tommy. "Where's the cereal?"

Grinning, Tommy shoved his chair back and headed for the cabinet. "Maybe I'd better fix it. You don't seem to be such a whiz in the kitchen."

"You know, kid, I'd watch that mouth of yours, if I were you. Since Daisy just took off, it looks as if you're stuck with me till she gets back. I'm thinking that my car could use washing."

"And I'm thinking that I'm real tired," Tommy said with a grin. "I'm sure I'll feel a whole lot better after a nap."

"You just got up," Tucker said, catching a handful of T-shirt as Tommy headed for the door.

"Isn't making me wash your car like violating some kind of child labor laws or something?"

Tucker laughed. "I can live with that."

"But you're a cop," Tommy protested.

"Not today. I'm on leave. And my best deputy is out of town for the day. Looks like you're out of luck."

"Okay, I'll make you a deal," Tommy said. "I'll wash your car if you'll go out in my boat with me after."

Tucker hesitated. "Is that thing seaworthy yet?"

"Bobby and Walker say it is," Tommy assured him.

"Have they been out in it yet?"

"They say the paint's not dry."

"When did you paint it?"

"Weeks and weeks ago." Tommy regarded him with a perplexed look. "How long does it take paint to get really, really dry?"

"Months," Tucker said firmly. "Definitely months."

When Liz couldn't stand being housebound for another minute, she took Tucker's advice, drove into Trinity Harbor and went exploring.

A lot had changed in the last six years. There were more shops, including a wonderfully cozy bookstore where she whiled away most of the morning in the mystery section, hoping it would give her some ideas about how to solve Larry's murder. Leaving all of the investigating in Tucker's hands was beginning to chafe. It was past time she stopped heeding his advice and tried to figure this whole mess out for herself. After all, who had a more vested interest in finding answers than she did? And which of them had better insight into the potential cast of suspects?

Not only that, she was the only one who knew for an absolute fact that she was not the killer. For all of his protestations that he believed in her, she knew that even Tucker probably had his occasional doubts. How could he not?

After scanning the mystery section for more than an hour, she took a brisk walk on the boardwalk and wound up at Earlene's, once their favorite hangout for milk shakes and burgers. She hesitated at the door, knowing she was bound to run into familiar faces inside, then took a deep breath and walked in, her head held high.

When she finally risked a look around, the first familiar face she spotted was Daisy's. The lack of welcome in her one-time friend's expression was not a good sign. Apparently she'd been right. Daisy wasn't interested in renewing old ties. Thinking of Tucker's advice, Liz ignored the scowl and went over anyway, grateful for the fact that Anna-Louise was there, as well.

"Daisy, thank you for coming to the funeral," she said. "I'm sorry we didn't get a chance to speak that day. It's good to see you again. Marriage obviously agrees with you. You look fabulous."

"I wish I could say the same," Daisy responded stiffly.

Her curt reply drew a frown from Anna-Louise, who was already sliding over to make room for Liz.

"Have a seat," Anna-Louise commanded gently.

Liz hesitated. "Daisy?"

"Oh, go ahead and sit. Anna-Louise won't be happy if I chase you away. But just because she makes forgiveness her business doesn't mean that I go along with her," Daisy said irritably.

Liz bit back a sharp retort about her lack of manners. Instead, she held firm to her determinedly friendly attitude. She was going to try to bridge the gap between them if it killed her. "I also wanted to thank you for bringing those clothes over to Tucker's. It was a huge help. I'll get them back to you as soon as they're laundered and ironed."

"Burn them, for all I care," Daisy said.

"Daisy Ames!" Anna-Louise scolded. "You should be ashamed of yourself."

"That's okay," Liz said. "Let her speak her mind."

"You don't want me to get started," Daisy said tightly.

"Okay, let's just get it out in the open. You know that I never meant to hurt Tucker," Liz said, cutting right to the problem. "My friendship with Larry during the time Tucker and I were dating was totally innocent."

Daisy sniffed.

"It was. When you pointed out that you thought otherwise, I took a step back and examined my feelings and realized you could be right. The instant I discovered that, I told Tucker. If I'd realized it sooner, I would have told him sooner, but there was nothing to tell. He knew Larry and I were friends. We were never sneaking around. I was always as honest with your brother as I could possibly be."

"But you still hurt him," Daisy said, her expression unrelenting. "He didn't deserve it. And now all the signs point to the fact that you're going to do it again. Why him, Mary Elizabeth? Why couldn't you have gone to someone else for help?"

"Because Tucker is very good at what he does, and I needed the best," she said, even though it was only part of the truth.

"There's no quicker way to a man's heart than acting needy," Daisy said, putting the worst possible spin on Liz's motives.

"Daisy!" Anna-Louise said, looking shocked by the accusation that Liz was using her husband's death to get back into Tucker's life.

Daisy regarded the minister defiantly. "You know it's true." She turned back to Liz. "Are you really under suspicion for murder, or do you just want Tucker to think that you are?"

Liz understood the anger behind Daisy's skepticism, but that didn't make it any easier to take. "Do you really think so little of me?"

"There was a time when I didn't," Daisy said. "But that was before you left Tucker the minute something better came along. Being the wife of a small-town sheriff's deputy wasn't good enough for you back then, not when you could have a man who had his eye on the governor's mansion."

"It wasn't like that," Liz protested.

"You might be able to convince my brother of that, but you'll never convince me." Daisy glanced apologetically at Anna-Louise and slid out of the booth. "I'm sorry, but I've suddenly lost my appetite."

Liz watched Daisy walk away and sighed.

"Is she right?" Anna-Louise asked.

"About what?"

"Any of it?"

"No. Long before Larry was killed, I knew I had made a terrible choice six years ago. I was already in the process of doing something about it when this happened."

"So you were already planning to come back here?"

Liz nodded. "I'd had my fill of city living and of politics."

"And Tucker? Did you want him back, as well?"

Liz nodded again, unable to tell Anna-Louise anything less than the truth. She hadn't realized it herself at first, had convinced herself she was coming back to Swan Ridge simply because it was her home, a safe haven after so many years of turmoil. But the minute she'd seen Tucker, she'd known that she had been drawn back by him, as well.

"I wonder if Tucker will ever believe that, though," Liz asked plaintively.

Anna-Louise reached across the table and squeezed her hand. "Give it time. Let all the rest of this sort itself out. When it's right, love can triumph over just about anything."

"Even betrayal?"

"Even that," Anna-Louise assured her.

For the first time since she'd come home to Trinity Harbor, Liz felt the faint stirring of hope. And meeting Anna-Louise's concerned gaze, she realized something else, as well. She might have lost Daisy as a friend, but she had a new friend who was willing to overlook everything she'd obviously heard about Liz and give her a chance.

16

King was still carrying that blasted engagement ring around in his pocket. His dinner with Frances had gone well enough, but when the time had come to pop the question, it was almost as if she'd anticipated it. Looking vaguely panicked, she'd taken off for the ladies' room. Five minutes later, she'd claimed she wasn't feeling well and asked him to take her home. She'd even insisted on skipping bingo. A man couldn't ask a woman to marry him when she was almost literally turning green around the gills.

She hadn't been responding to his phone calls since then, either. He was almost as annoyed by that as he was by the fact that Tucker was steering clear of home these days. Talking some common sense to his son was yet another mission that was being foiled.

First things first, though. For once he had to make Frances a priority. He had to give her some sign that he was putting her ahead of his children. Since she wasn't answering her phone or turning up at Earlene's, the one place he could be sure of catching up with her was her office. She couldn't very well duck him there.

He drove over to Montross and went straight to the Social Services building on the outskirts of town. As he strolled down the hall, fingering the jewelry box in his pocket, he heard peals of laughter coming from Frances's office. When he got to the doorway, to his complete shock, he saw her laughing her fool head off with Chauncey Mayberry, a slick character if ever there was one.

Mayberry had come to Trinity Harbor just a few months back, a widowed retiree with money in his pocket and an eye for the ladies. It was apparent from the scene King had walked in on that Frances was his latest target.

"What the devil is going on here?" King demanded, drawing a startled look from Mayberry and an embarrassed, guilty expression from Frances.

"Chauncey just dropped by with some fresh peaches," Frances said, her cheeks blooming with patches of bright pink. "Wasn't that sweet of him?"

"If you wanted peaches, why didn't you say so?" King grumbled. "There's a stand every few miles around here. I would have picked some up or taken you over to the Westmoreland Berry Farm for one of those fresh peach sundaes you love."

Frances regarded him with a pitying look. "But I didn't have to ask Chauncey to do this," she responded mildly.

King's temper flared at the subtle reproach. So that was the way it was? Chauncey, with his snow-white hair, tanned skin and fancy seersucker suit that made him look a lot like TV's Matlock, was taking advantage of Frances's fondness for the Andy Griffith character.

He was going to *aw, shucks* his way right into her life with these out-of-the-blue gifts.

"But has he bought you a diamond ring?" King demanded before he could stop himself. He drew the velvet jewelry box from his pocket and slapped it on Frances's desk. "Has he told you he loved you? Has he asked you to marry him?"

The last of the color drained out of Frances face. She eyed the jewelry box as if it might contain something lethal. "What is that?" she asked, her voice quaking.

King felt a great satisfaction at having taken her by surprise. Even Mayberry looked shell-shocked, and it took a lot of rattle a man who'd retired from the marines.

"It's the ring I bought you," King said, flipping the box open to display a two-carat, emerald-cut diamond set in platinum with baguettes on either side.

"But why?" she asked, regarding him with bewilderment. "I thought you didn't want to marry again."

"Did I ever say that?" he asked irritably, then answered himself. "No, I most certainly did not. I never said any such thing. In fact, I was the one who thought we should consider taking our relationship to a new level. Do you recall that conversation, or have you conveniently forgotten it?" He glowered at her. "So what's it going to be, Frances? Yes or no?"

With that, Frances burst into tears and ran from her office, leaving King and Mayberry staring at each other.

"Well, you certainly made a mess of that," Mayberry said, his eyes twinkling merrily. "A piece of advice, old man? If you want a woman like Frances, you need to court her with a little class."

"And I suppose peaches qualify better than diamonds?" King said snidely.

Mayberry shook his head, regarding King with a level of pity that topped Frances's earlier display. "I suppose we'll have to wait and see about that, won't we?"

"Oh, go on and get out of here," King muttered, unwilling to admit to the competition that he had screwed up royally. He hadn't so much proposed to Frances as he had dared her. Under other circumstances, that might be an effective tactic, but not when marriage was on the line.

"A smart man would retreat and give her some time to recover from his monumentally stupid behavior," Mayberry said as he plucked his straw hat from a bookcase and headed for the door. "But I imagine *you'll* be staying."

"You imagine right," King said, ignoring the fact that he'd just been insulted. Mayberry might think he knew a thing or two about courtship, but King knew Frances. Leaving her alone to ruminate on all this was exactly the wrong thing to do. He needed to apologize for bungling everything and he needed to do it now, while the incident was still fresh and the damage could be repaired. That, at least, was one lesson he'd learned when he'd let her run off to Maine a few months back and hadn't gone after her.

When Mayberry was gone, he sat down to wait. It didn't take long for Frances to return, her eyes red and puffy. She peeked into her office, spotted him and almost turned tail.

"Get in here, woman. Let me say my piece."

"I think you've said quite enough for one morning," she retorted, retreating to sit behind her desk.

"I'm sorry."

She regarded him with suspicion. "For?"

"Bulldozing in here and making an ass of myself and embarrassing you."

"Good start," she said approvingly. "Why did you do it?"

"I saw Chauncey wooing you with those peaches and it made me crazy."

"Jealous?" she asked, studying him with mild curiosity.

"Me? Jealous of a man like that? I don't think so," he snapped.

"King Spencer!"

"Okay," he admitted, backing down from the blatant lie. "Maybe I was a little jealous. What's going on between the two of you, anyway? You interested in him?"

"He's a nice man. Unlike some I could name, he's both thoughtful and considerate."

King grated at the compliments. "That's not what I asked," he grumbled.

Frances sighed. "No, I am not interested in him. You're the only man I care about, heaven help me."

"Then let's talk about the ring."

"Let's not," she said, her expression grim and determined. "I think before you bring that up again, you ought to ask yourself why you want to marry me."

"Didn't you hear me say I love you?"

"I heard it, but under the circumstances, since you and Chauncey were engaged in some sort of male ritual for staking out turf, I didn't exactly buy it."

"I meant it, dammit! I had the ring with me, didn't I?"

She stood up and rounded her desk. Before he realized her intention, she slid onto his lap and kissed him, pretty much taking his breath away. At his age, that was a risky business, but he had to admit he liked the sensation. He'd been waiting a long time for her to let her passion overrule her head. Her breath was hitching and her cheeks were flushed again by the time she stopped.

"*That* is how you prove you love me," she said, as she stood up and smoothed down her skirt, then went back to the safety of her seat across the room. "Words alone aren't going to do the trick, not when I know you have such an easy way with them."

King's pulse began to pound. "I can do that, woman. Get back over here."

"Not here and not now," she said, suddenly prim as she folded her hands atop her desk like some prissy old schoolmarm.

"When?"

"Call me. I'll see when I can fit you into my schedule."

King crossed the room in two strides, leaned down across her desk and met her gaze. Her eyes were sparkling with amusement. "I'll pick you up tomorrow at six," he said. "Wear something daring."

She began to laugh, evidently delighted with herself. "You sure your heart can take it?"

"I suppose we'll have to see," he said. "But trust me, Frances. I am definitely willing to take the risk."

Tucker waited impatiently for Walker's return from Richmond. Just when he was about to jump out of his skin from all the caffeine he'd consumed, he saw his deputy pull up in front of the sheriff's office. He was waiting for him when he came inside.

"Well?" he demanded.

"Can't you give me five minutes to get something to drink?" Walker grumbled.

"Here." Tucker shoved his half-empty coffee cup into his brother-in-law's hand. "Finish this. I've had too much anyway."

Walker took a sip, shuddered and handed it back. "I'll have something that's meant to be cold, thanks all the same. Settle down. I'll be right back."

"Can't you at least tell me if you think the woman's guilty?" Tucker called after him.

"No," Walker replied as he disappeared around the corner.

Tucker took off after him. "No, what? No, you don't think she's guilty, or no, you can't tell me?"

"Do we have to carry on this conversation out here where anyone can wander in and listen?"

Tucker glanced around. "There's not a soul in sight."

"But there are reporters lurking in the bushes outside," Walker pointed out.

Tucker crossed to the window. Sure enough, there were brightly marked television vans on the street and strangers with cameras and microphones jockeying for position in front of the building and across the street on the courthouse lawn. "Geez-oh-flip," he commented with disgust. "What did you do, lead them right on back to town like the Pied Piper?"

"Apparently so. Someone had Cynthia Miles's house staked out. When I came out, there were half a dozen television satellite trucks and reporters waiting. They didn't seem to like my refusal to comment, so here they are, ever hopeful." Walker retrieved his can of soda and headed back to his office, where Michele was waiting.

"The natives are getting restless," she pointed out,

sounding decidedly cheerful about the prospect of being involved in another confrontation. "They're calling every five seconds requesting a comment. A few have ventured inside, but I had Deputy Williams escort 'em right back outside. And Richard is right in the thick of it. He looks like he's about to burst a blood vessel, which would probably upset Anna-Louise."

"What do you expect me to do about that?" Walker grumbled.

"Ever heard of a pool reporter?" she asked. "Invite Richard in. Tell him what you want the hordes to know, then send him back out."

"Brilliant idea," Walker said. "Except I don't think the TV guys are going to be happy without film of an actual sheriff's department spokesman."

Michele looked disappointed. "You're probably right. You've got to give 'em something, though, or they'll hang around out there all night. Not that I would mind. That guy from the CBS station is awfully handsome, and he's the first guy I've met in ages I actually have to look up to. Better yet, I think we really hit it off the last time he was here."

Tucker shook his head. "Sweetheart, I don't think this is the time for you to be making friends with a member of the media. At some point, you might be forced to question his motives."

She regarded Tucker with disdain. "Don't you think I know that? It doesn't mean I can't admire the view and practice my flirting. There aren't a lot of guys around town who can help me improve my technique."

Walker merely shook his head. "Go, keep 'em at bay," he advised. "Tell them I'll make a statement as soon as Tucker and I have talked. As for Richard, tell him he can come inside. We can use his input on spinning this."

Tucker winced. "I don't think Richard's going to be thrilled at being used to spin a story."

"He will be if he gets first crack at the information, with a few little exclusive tidbits thrown in," Walker said confidently.

"I suppose that would provide motivation," Tucker agreed.

Richard joined them then, regarding the two of them with wariness. "Okay, why am I in here, while everyone else is outside?"

"I need your help," Walker said.

"I can't help you," Richard protested.

"Just a little advice," Walker coaxed. "And in return you get a bit more information you can use. Is the promise of a scoop sufficient to gain your cooperation?"

"That depends," Richard said cautiously. "Start talking."

Walker nodded. "Okay, but from this moment on, we are off the record until such time as we hammer out what we want released."

Richard squirmed uncomfortably. "I don't know if I can go along with that."

"Would you rather wait outside with everybody else?" Walker asked. "You're not working for the *Washington Post* anymore. This is Trinity Harbor. You're a part of this community, not just editor of the *Trinity Harbor Weekly.*"

"There are still ethical considerations," Richard said. "I'm a journalist first and foremost. You're a source, who at the moment is withholding public information."

"And I'm asking you to do this as a favor to a friend,"

Walker said, "*because* you are a journalist and know the ropes better than I do."

Richard continued to look doubtful, but he finally nodded. "Okay, but if I start getting really bad vibes about this, I'll stop you and the deal's off."

"But you won't use anything you've heard up to that point, correct?" Walker said to clarify the point.

"Correct," Richard said tightly, still obviously unhappy about the deal.

"Okay, then, I interviewed Cynthia Miles today in Richmond," Walker told him. "She admitted to having had a relationship with Chandler before and during the first months of his marriage. She also admitted having threatened to blackmail him, but swears that she never followed through and that he never gave in to the attempt. She says it was a ploy to try to force him to start seeing her again."

"And did he?" Tucker asked.

"She says no. She says by then he was involved with someone else, someone serious, someone who really was a threat to the Chandler marriage—and a whole lot more, because she knew too much."

Tucker stared at Walker. "Too much about what? His personal shenanigans?"

"No. There were plenty of women, alright, but this was about his business dealings. Cynthia claimed she didn't know all the specifics, just that Chandler had played a little fast and loose with his SEC filings. Cynthia said if the information had come out, it would have destroyed not only his company, but also his political future."

"If she knew all this and wanted ammunition to use against Chandler, why didn't Cynthia pursue all this herself?" Tucker asked, not buying a word of what she'd said. "Are you sure she wasn't making this up just to throw suspicion off herself?"

"Possibly." He glanced at Richard. "And here's where I need your help. Do I release anything at all about having a new lead to follow up, and if so, how much?"

"You honestly think this lead is credible?" Richard said.

"We know there was a woman there the night he was killed," Walker said, then held up his hand to prevent the question that was clearly on the tip of Richard's tongue. "I won't say how, but we have forensic evidence."

"And it's not tied to Mrs. Chandler?" Richard asked, looking at Tucker.

"We're waiting for confirmation one way or the other on that, but according to the preliminary reports, probably not," Walker said.

Tucker regretted that his deputy didn't sound more convincing, but at least Walker was beginning to accept the possibility of Mary Elizabeth's innocence. He glanced at Richard. "What are your thoughts about revealing this new lead? How far should Walker go?"

"That depends," Richard said. "If you think this woman is a solid suspect, that's one thing, but if you're just hoping to worry her, maybe get her to make a mistake, that's another thing entirely. I'd be real cautious, if I were you, especially without any concrete evidence."

"Cautious how?"

"No name, no specifics beyond the fact that you've been given a promising new lead, a woman with ties to Chandler. That's vague enough to keep it legal and specific enough to make a guilty person nervous."

Tucker nodded.

"Makes sense to me. Does it work for you, Walker?"

"I can do that." He glanced pointedly at Richard. "Especially if I have a prepared statement to read and don't allow any follow-up."

Richard groaned. "I don't suppose there's any question about who is supposed to draft this prepared statement."

Walker grinned. "Think of it as getting a jump-start on your story for this week."

"You guys are too good to me," Richard said. "Get up. If I'm going to do this, I need your computer for a minute."

"By all means," Walker said, moving out of his way.

"Tell me again what my exclusive is," Richard said as he began to type.

Walker's gaze met Tucker's. "That we've all but cleared Mrs. Chandler of suspicion."

That Walker would say such a thing on the record startled Tucker. "Why would you say that without the lab report? Do you honestly believe it?"

"You do, don't you?" Walker asked.

"Of course, but you wanted solid proof."

"And if you're right, I should have it when that lab report comes in," Walker said. "Besides, the real killer is obviously hoping that all suspicion points to Mrs. Chandler. Once we've ruled her out, it will add to that person's panic, don't you think?"

"In that case, why not make that part of your statement, get the word out far and wide, instead of just here in the county?" Richard asked.

"Because he doesn't want to be too embarrassed if he's wrong," Tucker guessed, watching Walker's reaction. The faint tightening of the deputy's jaw suggested Tucker was right.

"Okay, yes," Walker admitted grudgingly. "I should know for sure in a day or two at most. That's about when that little bombshell will begin to drift down to Richmond. By then our new suspect will already be getting antsy. It could be just the thing to push her right on over the edge."

"If she's guilty," Richard cautioned.

"Yeah, well, there is that," Tucker agreed wryly. "Mind if I run all of this by Mary Elizabeth? Maybe she can provide a name so we can start staking this woman out."

"I already have a name," Walker said quietly. "And before you ask, no, I'm not giving it to either one of you."

"Why the hell not?" Tucker demanded.

"Because I don't want you charging down to check her out and because I don't want any leaks that will stir up media scrutiny of this woman. I want her to get jumpy and make a mistake. I don't want her to panic and run."

"Have you talked to her?"

"Nope, but I have people keeping an eye on her. We'll know if she so much as sneezes over the next few days."

Tucker muttered an oath under his breath.

"You have something you want to say?" Walker inquired, leveling a look straight at him.

"Not a thing," Tucker said at once. "You're doing this exactly right, even if being left out of the loop does annoy the hell out of me."

"Thank you." Walker frowned at Richard. "You?"

"Not me," Richard said with forced cheer. "I'm happy as a clam."

"Good," Walker said with obvious satisfaction. "Then let's go outside and stir things up. I want to get home in time for dinner just once this week."

"Be sure to tell Daisy your conclusions about Mary Elizabeth," Tucker said. "That will make her day."

"I think I'll save that till after dessert, if you don't mind. I want to eat my dinner, not wear it."

Liz answered the door just before six and found Tucker on the porch. It took all of her willpower not to throw herself straight into his arms. She studied his somber expression, but for the life of her she couldn't read it.

"You found out something, didn't you?"

He nodded, shifting uncomfortably. "You want to come out here and talk about it?"

Liz shook her head. "The breeze is nicer out back, and I've just made some lemonade. I'll pour you a glass on the way."

"Fine."

"Just tell me this," she said, scanning his face. "Is it good news or bad?"

"Promising," he said.

She clung to that as she led the way into the kitchen, fixed his lemonade with an extra scoop of sugar the way he liked it, then handed the ice-cold drink to him.

Outside, she returned to her seat on an old-fashioned glider, then watched in amusement as Tucker struggled to decide whether to join her there or sit in one of the nearby rockers. To her disappointment, he chose a rocker, then gazed out over the rolling lawn toward the river.

"It's a peaceful night," he said.

"It won't be if you don't tell me what you found out," Liz said with a hint of exasperation.

Her comment drew a grin from him. "Okay, here's the most important thing. Walker's finally coming around. He admitted that he has doubts about you being the person who killed Chandler."

Liz wasn't nearly as astonished by that as Tucker seemed to be. "He's a sensible man, so I expected that," she said. "But you evidently didn't."

"I'll be honest, Liz. I don't trust my judgment where you're concerned."

"Well, that's certainly blunt enough," she said, not sure why it hurt so much to have his low opinion of her confirmed.

"I'm sorry."

"I wish you'd believed in me without waiting for a man who doesn't even know me to validate your opinion. No one on earth knows me better than you do. How can you not know that I'm incapable of murdering someone?"

"I do believe that," he said fiercely. "But there was a time when I believed in your love, too."

The bitter comment hit its target. "And I *did* love you," she said. "Not that I expect you to believe that. And if I'm being perfectly honest with myself, I can't really blame you. It just…" She met his gaze. "It makes my heart ache."

"I'm sorry."

"So am I." She forced aside the anguish. "You said that was only part of the news. What's the rest?"

As he described Walker's interview with Cynthia Miles, Liz's pulse began to race. "Selena Velez," she whispered at last. "It has to be. I knew they were involved. I could always tell, but she was always so unfailingly sweet and sympathetic to me that in her case I brushed my suspicions aside."

"Are you talking about his personal assistant at the firm?" Tucker asked.

"Yes. And it wouldn't surprise me one bit if she was the one who planted Cynthia's letters in the safe, knowing I'd find them and send the police off after her." She regarded Tucker with excitement. "Does it help that we know who it is? Can you interview her?"

"No," he said at once. "I promised Walker I'd let him handle this. We don't want to do anything to scare her off." He eyed her with worry. "You said she was always nice to you. Did you ever get any indication at all that she had a temper or a dark side of any kind?"

"No, why? Do you think she might not be the one, after all?"

"No, I just want to be sure she's not likely to come after you once she realizes the police no longer suspect you."

"If she is guilty, isn't it more likely that this was a crime of passion, something she did on the spur of the moment?" Liz asked. "I can't see her committing a premeditated murder, any more than I could."

"Unless Larry kept guns in the house, which we know he didn't, she—or whoever the real killer was—came down here with a loaded gun with one purpose in mind," Tucker reminded her. "To kill your husband."

Liz shuddered.

"Just be on guard if she calls or shows up, Mary Elizabeth. We don't know if she's guilty, but I don't want you taking any unnecessary chances."

"Maybe you should move in to protect me," she suggested, only partially in jest.

His gaze turned dark. "And who'd protect you from me?"

"Maybe I don't want to be protected from you," she said, keeping her gaze even with his.

The evening air seemed to crackle with electricity, though there was no sign of lightning in the sky. For an instant, Liz thought she might have cut through his carefully crafted resolve, but then he stood up and set his drink down on the table.

"I need to get home," he said.

"Somebody waiting?" she inquired sweetly.

He frowned at her. "No, Mary Elizabeth."

"Then stay for dinner, at least. I hate eating alone."

He hesitated, then shook his head. "Bad idea."

"Don't think you can keep your hands to yourself, Sheriff?"

"I know I can't," he responded. "And until this investigation is over and your name is formally cleared, I am not going to touch you again."

"Because you don't want to be romantically linked to a suspected murderer?"

"No, dammit, because people talk, and it won't win you any friends here in Trinity Harbor if it seems you're turning to another man this soon after your husband's death. Not everyone knows Chandler was cheating on you. Not everyone knows you were planning to divorce him. All they'll see is that you're being awfully quick to jump in the sack with someone new."

"Not new," she reminded him.

"You know what I meant."

"Okay, let me read between the lines here," she said. "You're not saying never, correct?"

Tucker sighed heavily, as if his regrets were too many to be counted. "No, I am not saying never."

A slow smile spread across her face. "I can live with that," she said. Maybe Anna-Louise was right, after all. Maybe there really was reason to hope for a future with Tucker. She met Tucker's gaze, then added, "For the time being, anyway."

A grin touched Tucker's lips, then vanished. "Trying to motivate me to get this case solved in a hurry, Liz?"

"You bet," she said without hesitation. "I want to get back to living my life, not sitting on the sidelines and watching it pass me by. How about you?"

His gaze met hers and held it. Once more the air crackled with electricity.

"No comment," he said eventually.

She laughed. "Chicken."

"No, darlin'. I've known you a long time. If I give you an inch, you'll take a mile, and the next thing I know you and I will be inside and in bed, living in the moment and saying to hell with everybody else."

"Would that be so awful?"

"That depends. You intending to stick around Trinity Harbor?"

She nodded.

"Then it would be a disaster," he said flatly.

Much as Liz wanted to argue, she knew he was right. Rushing into something with Tucker right now would only stir up more trouble for both of them.

"Do you know how annoying it is to have to admit you're right about everything?" she groused.

"Oh, I've been wrong a time or two," Tucker said, then grinned. "Just not in recent memory."

"Go home, Tucker."

He laughed at that. "See, I knew I could bring you around to my way of thinking. You're actually kicking me out now. That's good," he said approvingly as he stood up and went inside.

Liz frowned at him, but she followed him to the front door. To her astonishment, he leaned down and pressed a hard, unforgettable kiss to her lips before jogging off into the night.

"Sweet dreams," he called back as he climbed into his car.

Liz touched a finger to her burning lips. Sweet dreams, indeed. She'd be lucky if she slept a wink.

17

Sitting on the back patio at Swan Ridge, sipping lemonade and talking over his day with Mary Elizabeth was just a little too much like old times for Tucker's comfort. The only things missing were the soft, lingering kisses, stolen whenever her grandfather's watchful gaze was turned the other way. And as Tucker had told Mary Elizabeth very firmly, he did not intend to lay a hand on her until the matter of her husband's death was resolved.

Okay, five seconds later he'd broken his own vow, but that momentary lapse on his way out the door never should have happened. That was twice now he'd lost his head, which just went to prove that he couldn't trust himself around her. Steering clear of her entirely was definitely the way to go, much as they both might hate it.

It had nothing to do with respect for the dearly departed or the ritual mourning period. He simply was not going to stir up idle gossip that could hurt her, or risk having his heart broken a second time by the discovery that Mary Elizabeth had been merely using him—or his expertise, at any rate—to keep herself out of jail. He felt better on that score after learning today that even his skeptical, consummate professional brother-in-law had doubts about her guilt, but Tucker still wasn't willing to take any chances.

That was why he'd made sure he bolted from Swan Ridge before the sky turned dark and filled with stars, before the silvery allure of the moon on the river filled the night with memories. It was getting harder and harder, though, to tear himself away from her.

But after he had—and thanks to that ill-advised kiss goodbye—his nerves were jumbled and he was far too restless to go straight home. He drove into town, walked along the boardwalk that his brother and Jenna had designed and developed, and mingled with the crowd of summer tourists. He bought a corn dog and a grape snow cone, sat on a bench where he could hear the music of Bobby's infamous antique merry-go-round and pretended that times were simpler.

While he was sitting there, he was acknowledged by half the people who passed. If their friendly greetings were indicative—and contrary to his father's fears—the locals didn't seem all that disturbed about his decision to remove himself from the Chandler case. There were no speculative glances, no obvious whispered comments, once they'd strolled by. In fact, he felt reassured by their outward acceptance. Whatever reservations they'd had on first hearing the news, they were apparently getting past it. It reminded him that one of the reasons he'd chosen to stay in Trinity Harbor was the sense of community and belonging. This was Spencer territory, despite the newcomers who were slowly changing the town from a sleepy rural village to a unique summer retreat.

He wondered if Mary Elizabeth would find the new Trinity Harbor more to her liking. In the old days she had been tempted by bright lights and glamour. She had chafed at his refusal to compromise and relocate to a big city. Would she be any more eager to stay here now? he wondered. Was he setting himself up for even more disappointment by believing she had changed, that her coming back here now was about more than her disenchantment with her marriage?

Pondering such unanswerable questions was one reason it was pitch-dark by the time he finally got home. That was no doubt why he didn't notice the cars in front of his house, that and the fact that his head was filled with thoughts of Mary Elizabeth and just how desperately he wanted her, despite—or perhaps because of—his resolve to do nothing about it.

"Getting in a little late, aren't you, son?"

Tucker's heart thumped unsteadily at the unexpected sound of King's voice cutting through the still, sultry August air. It carried him back to his teens, when King had often waited in the shadows of the porch at Cedar Hill until the last of his children wandered in past curfew. He was no less defensive now, but he held his tongue and settled for a nonconfrontational response.

"Daddy, what brings you by?" he inquired mildly.

As if he didn't know. Tucker cast a quick glance back toward the street and noted the lineup of cars he'd missed before. Daisy's and Bobby's were there plain as day, as well. King had obviously mustered his troops and planned on a full-scale assault. Tucker had been warned about this, but he'd hoped by now that King had moved on to other things. He should have known better.

"Does a man have to make an appointment to see his own son?" King asked, sounding cranky. Before Tucker could say a word, he answered his own question. "Apparently so, since I've been hanging around here just about every night for the past week or so. Where the devil have you been keeping yourself till all hours?"

"I've been busy," Tucker said, finally drawing close enough to see the enemy. King was looking rather pleased with himself at having caught Tucker off-guard. Daisy and Bobby were keeping their expressions determinedly neutral. "So, where are Walker and Jenna? I'm sure they'd like to add their two cents to this family discussion."

"Walker's at the station," Daisy offered. "He said he's not getting involved in your personal business."

Tucker grinned at her obvious exasperation. "Is that so? That must be driving you crazy. Did he also happen to mention his new theory about Mary Elizabeth?"

"If you're referring to his gut feeling that she's not guilty, he told me," Daisy said. "I'll wait for him to actually arrest somebody else before I buy that, if it's all the same to the two of you."

"Damn, but you're hardheaded, sis," Tucker said. "Give the poor woman a break."

"Why should I?" Daisy asked with a touch of defiance.

"Because you were as close as sisters once," Tucker reminded her, then added softly, "and because I asked you to."

"Only because you're not thinking straight," King said.

"That's a matter of opinion," Tucker responded. "So,

whose idea was this ambush? Yours, Daisy? You didn't get your fill of bugging me this morning? Daddy usually prefers to schedule this sort of thing for his own turf."

"Don't blame any of this on your sister," King scolded. "It's your doing and nobody else's that all of us are out later than we'd like to be."

"Then go home," Tucker suggested. "I can live without having this conversation. You've said it all before anyway."

"I'm not leaving till I've said my piece and you've listened to it," King said.

"Like I said, you've made your opinion plain."

"Not plain enough, apparently. You're still mixed up with that woman."

"I'm not 'mixed up with her,' as you so eloquently put it. Mary Elizabeth is in a little trouble. I'm helping her out. I've said that so many times, I thought for sure even someone as thickheaded as you would have gotten the message by now."

"You make it sound as if she got a parking ticket," King snapped irritably. "The woman's under suspicion of murdering her husband. I would think that would give even you, her faithful defender, pause."

"She didn't do it," Tucker said. "Not even Walker believes she did it."

"The two of you know that for a fact?" King shot back.

"Yes," Tucker said. "I do. And so do you. Mary Elizabeth would never intentionally hurt someone."

"She hurt you bad enough," his father reminded him.

"That's old news," Tucker said. "And hardly the same thing."

"Is it really?" King said with an edge of sarcasm.

"Okay, that's enough," Daisy said, scowling at Tucker. "You're wasting your breath, Daddy. Whether we understand it or not, I'm sure Tucker is doing what he thinks is best. Nothing we say is going to change his mind. In fact, he's just more likely to dig in his heels to defy us."

Tucker couldn't stop the grin that spread across his face. "Daisy, believe it or not, my actions have absolutely nothing at all to do with any of you. I'm doing what's right, what you'd want me to do for any one of you if you landed in a similar mess."

"Oh, hogwash! Right for whom?" King demanded. "Is it right for Mary Elizabeth to come back here and stir things up?"

"This is her home," Tucker pointed out. "When she ended her marriage, where else should she have gone? And you can't blame her because a killer snuck into her house and killed her husband while she was out, can you?" He scowled at his still-silent brother. "What about you, Bobby? Do you have an opinion about this you'd like to share?"

"Nope," Bobby said cheerfully. "I'm just along for the ride."

King scowled at his younger son. "Dammit, boy, I was counting on you to tell Tucker that what he's doing is crazy."

"I don't know what he's doing," Bobby pointed out reasonably. "Neither do you, for that matter. Maybe we ought to ask."

King frowned. "Okay, I'm asking. What are you up to with that Chandler woman?"

Tucker held onto his temper by a thread. "When did she become 'that Chandler woman'? She used to sit around our table for Sunday dinner. You and her granddaddy were friends. You used to fish together."

"And then she dropped you like a hot potato when she thought something better had come along," King said bitterly. "Nobody treats a member of my family like that and gets away with it."

"I think that's for me to decide," Tucker said. "What are you really so upset about, anyway? Is it because I'm helping Mary Elizabeth out of a jam, or is it that you're afraid I'm falling in love with her again?"

King looked as if he'd swallowed a fly and was about to choke on it. "Don't even say that," he ordered, as if Tucker had uttered a blasphemy.

"Well, guess what, Daddy? I never stopped loving her. Now, go home, old man. It's been a long day and I'm tired."

It was plain that his declaration had shaken both his father and his sister, but Bobby shot a warning look at Daisy that kept her silent. Naturally King wasn't as prudent.

"I'm going," King said, standing up. "But not before I say one last thing."

"As long as it *is* the last thing you say on this subject," Tucker warned.

King shook a finger under his nose. "You watch your step, Tucker. She used you before. She'll use you again. And the rest of us will be left to pick up the pieces, same as before."

Tucker sighed as his family left. It wasn't as if that were the first time that thought had occurred to him. Sadly, his heart didn't seem to give a damn about the risks.

Liz faced the prospect of another idle day with nothing but her own troubled thoughts for company and concluded that she'd probably tear her hair out. She needed to be doing something, *anything,* to help her own cause. That meant talking to Selena.

Okay, Tucker had said it was a bad idea, and she really did hate to go against his wishes when things between them were just getting back on an even keel, but it wasn't *his* life on the line. At least that was how she justified setting off for Richmond shortly after 9:00 a.m. Besides, who would think twice about her turning up at the Chandler offices? She could be there to see any one of dozens of people. If she happened to bump into Selena, well, that was pure luck.

Even so, she parked down the block, plunked a wide-brimmed straw hat on her head, hurried down the street and slipped in the employees' entrance in the back. Proud of her evasive tactic, she took the elevator to the executive suite, removed the hat and ruffled her hair, then looked up and straight into Tucker's amused gaze.

"Well, hell," she murmured, trying not to notice how totally masculine he looked in his snug, worn jeans and white polo shirt. His tan had deepened in recent days, making his eyes appear even bluer than normal. "What are you doing here?"

"Darlin', I've known you forever. I knew you'd never be able to resist coming to Richmond to talk to Selena."

"You could have saved me the drive and picked me up," she grumbled.

His grin spread. "I thought I'd let you have your fun. Sneaking around was always great sport to you. I never did believe your grandfather objected to the time we spent together. I was always convinced you just liked slipping out a window late at night to meet me by the river."

"So what? You have to admit that the fear of discovery added a certain thrill to our meetings."

"I was thrilled enough when we met in plain sight," Tucker insisted.

She frowned at the comment, then asked, "So, are we going or staying?"

"Now that is a quandary," he conceded. "I did promise Walker that I'd steer clear of Selena."

"But I didn't," Liz said, sensing an opening. "I could go on in and pick up a few papers, see how she's acting. I don't have to cross-examine her." She regarded him hopefully. "Well?"

"Can you make it sound credible? Are there papers you need?"

"The incorporation papers," she said at once. "We know they're in the safe. And I could tell her that the lawyers want to see how things get divvied up in the event of the death of one of the partners."

"The lawyers would probably know that," Tucker pointed out. "Just say you want to know, so you can make sure everything is handled the way Larry would have wanted it."

Liz knew then that she had won. "She'll buy that. She thought all of us lived to do whatever Larry wanted."

"All right, then, let's do it," Tucker said, turning toward Larry's office.

Liz balked. "You can't come in with me. It will make her suspicious."

"And I'm not letting you go in there alone," he responded calmly. "Besides, you need a cop's perspective on her behavior."

She supposed she could see the value of that. "But you can't tip her off that you're a cop," she said thoughtfully. "I'll tell her you're just a friend who drove me down."

He regarded her with amusement. "The strong, silent type, huh?"

She patted his arm. "You'll be good at it. Besides, once she gets a look at those biceps, she won't be interested in your brain, anyway."

He laughed. "Is that what drew you to me?"

"Twenty years ago, you didn't have biceps or much of a brain, Tucker, but I loved you, anyway."

"Why?"

"Because you had character."

He shook his head. "Just what every man wants to hear."

"Don't knock it. Besides, the brains and biceps effect kicked in later."

"How reassuring. Let's go, before I get all weak-kneed," he said.

Liz walked into the reception area for the executive suite, waved a greeting at Barb Prescott, who was on the phone, and went into Larry's outer office. Selena's head snapped up from the papers she was feeding into a shredder. Alarm flared in her dark eyes. Liz walked over and gently removed the remaining pages from her hand.

"Anything important?" she inquired sweetly.

"Just some old documents we no longer need," Selena said without missing a beat, but, fingers visibly trembling, she nervously brushed a strand of stylishly cut black hair away from her cheek. "I didn't expect to see you down here. I thought you were living in Trinity Harbor now."

"I am," Liz said distractedly, while scanning the

pages she'd saved from destruction. She repeated the request she and Tucker had agreed to, asking for the incorporation papers. "Would you mind getting them for me?"

Selena hesitated. "I'm not sure—"

"Please," Liz said firmly enough to make her point that it was an order.

Temper flared in Selena's dark eyes. "I don't work for you," she said heatedly.

"Which raises an interesting question," Liz said. "Who exactly *do* you work for now that Larry's dead?"

"Roland, of course. He's in charge now."

"He told me he doesn't have much use for an executive assistant. He only needs someone to take messages. I imagine Barb can handle that just fine. We probably should think about cutting expenses around here now, anyway."

"You wouldn't dare fire me," Selena said fiercely, clearly trying not to let them see how shaken she was by the threat. "You don't have the authority, for one thing. For another, I would make a very bad enemy."

"Why is that?" Liz inquired, trying to sound only mildly curious rather than outraged by the sudden shift in Selena's demeanor.

"Because I can destroy this place," Selena said bluntly.

"Really?"

Selena smiled, but it wasn't a happy expression. "You have no idea how much I know."

"About?"

"All of Larry's shady dealings with the SEC, about the way he lined up investors with a phony prospectus, about the insider trading that went on."

"So that's what you were holding over Larry's head? Were you blackmailing him?" Liz asked, being very careful not to turn to look at Tucker and give away her sense of triumph.

Selena looked genuinely horrified by the idea. "Of course not!"

"Did he know just how much you were aware of?"

"Of course. He trusted me with everything."

"And you never once hinted at how much damage you could do to him if, say, there were to be a change in your relationship?"

"Absolutely not. I loved him, which is more than I can say for you."

Ah, the gloves were definitely off now. Selena no longer had any reason to feign even mild pleasantries for the wife of her lover. "You know nothing about my relationship with my husband," Liz countered.

"I know that you were a cold, heartless bitch," Selena shot back.

Liz chuckled. "Is that what he told you? It must be what he told all of the others, as well."

Selena fell silent at that.

"You didn't know about the other women?" Liz persisted. "Funny. For a long time, neither did I. I suppose that's something we have in common. Larry made fools of both of us."

"He did not make a fool of me," Selena said, though she looked as if she were about to cry.

"He convinced you to keep silent by telling you he loved you, didn't he? And at the same time he was sleeping with who-knows-how-many other women." Liz nodded. "Yes, I'd say that makes you a fool."

"Dammit, get out of here," Selena said. "I did not

have to blackmail him into staying with me. I won't listen to this."

"Because in your heart, you know it's true," Liz said more gently. "Don't you, Selena? How long have you known that you weren't the only other woman in his life?"

"I don't believe it," Selena insisted.

"I can show you a list of names and dates," Liz told her. "The police are looking into the names on that list. They're all considered possible suspects in Larry's death. I started writing them down a few weeks ago in case I needed them for the divorce."

Selena paled, looking seriously shaken for the first time. "You were divorcing him?"

Liz nodded. "I told him the day before he was killed. I'm sure you heard about the fight at Chez Dominique."

Selena nodded.

"That's what it was about. I told him I was leaving him for good."

"He said you'd never agree to a divorce," Selena whispered, looking shattered.

"He never asked for one. That was one more lie," Liz told her gently, reminding herself that Selena was only a naive young girl. It must have been incredibly easy for Larry to manipulate her and keep her in line. "I'm sorry."

Selena stood up slowly, swiping viciously at the tears tracking down her cheeks, her expression grim. "I'll get you those papers," she said tightly, and hurried from the room.

Liz started to speak to Tucker, but he held up a silencing hand. She nodded and waited for Selena to return.

"Here," she said, shoving the papers into Liz's hands,

then reaching into a desk drawer and removing her purse. "I'm taking the rest of the day off."

"Selena?"

"What?" She stood stiffly, her back to Liz.

"I really am sorry."

Selena turned slowly, her cheeks once again damp with tears. "And I'm sorry for what I said to you before, for what I called you," she whispered. "And I'm even sorrier for what I did, you know…"

"I know," Liz said, and watched her go.

"Let's get out of here," Tucker said. "There's something about the atmosphere in here that makes me sick to my stomach."

"Me, too," Liz agreed, and followed him out.

Outside in the fresh air, she dragged in a deep breath, then faced Tucker. "Do you honestly think that girl could have killed Larry?"

"She blackmailed him, didn't she?"

"She says not."

"Cynthia Miles thought otherwise."

"Now there's a reliable source," Liz said sarcastically. "Maybe Selena didn't even realize that once she knew so much she could hold it over his head. As for murder, I can't imagine it. Tucker, she loved him."

"Right up until the second she found out about the other women," Tucker pointed out.

"Exactly my point. She didn't know until I told her."

"Or so she'd like you to believe," he responded. "Let's assume for a minute that Cynthia was right about her. Anyone calculating enough to commit blackmail has to have a strong stomach for lies and deception. On top of that, what kind of love is it that justifies blackmailing your partner to keep him?"

"I suppose," Liz said, but she couldn't bring herself to believe that Selena was guilty of anything beyond loving the wrong man and using desperate measures to keep him in her life. "Larry obviously inspired strong feelings in the women around him. Look at Cynthia."

"And you," Tucker pointed out quietly. "You hated him at the end, didn't you? I can only imagine how much he put you through to make that happen."

Liz thought back over the years of humiliation. Even with all of that, hate hadn't come easily. Time and again, she had accepted the apologies and the excuses, because she'd wanted to believe in the fantasy.

"Well, it's over now," she said wearily. "But even in my worst nightmare, I didn't want it to end this way."

Tucker cupped her chin in his hand and looked straight into her eyes. "You're better off."

"But Larry's not. He's dead."

"If you believe in a kind and merciful God, then he's in a better place now."

Liz sighed. "I'm not sure what I believe anymore."

"Believe in today. Believe in the future," he told her.

She nodded and managed a tight smile, purely for Tucker's benefit. "That's what I'm hanging on to."

18

Walker threw down the latest forensics report in disgust and met Tucker's anxious gaze.

"Nothing," he said. "Not one damn thing we can use."

Tucker received the news with mixed feelings. He wanted Chandler's murder solved, but the fact that nothing in that report implicated Mary Elizabeth was good. It was one thing to believe in her, quite another to have positive proof that someone else had killed Chandler.

"You're sure?" he asked Walker. "I thought those fibers would amount to something."

"I'm sure they do, but right now we don't have the first clue what they might match other than a piece of clothing that we don't have in our possession."

Tucker fully released the breath he'd been holding. "Then they can't be linked to the clothes Mary Elizabeth was wearing that night?"

"Not even close, according to the experts. Of course, we only have her word those were the only clothes she had on that evening," Walker pointed out.

Tucker wasn't crazy about even the hint of skepticism behind Walker's comment. "If she was going to change clothes and get rid of evidence, then why would she wear clothes splattered with Chandler's blood to my house?"

"A diversion," Walker suggested. "It makes her look as if she's being forthcoming."

"Dammit, Walker, you know she's not that devious," Tucker retorted. "Less than twenty-four hours ago, you admitted you thought she was probably innocent."

Walker gave him a rueful grin. "I've been encouraged to reconsider."

"By whom? Daisy and my father?"

"They certainly don't have a very high opinion of Mrs. Chandler."

"Only because they're being overly protective of me. They liked her just fine when she and I were an item. In fact, she and Daisy were like sisters."

Walker seemed surprised by that. "They were?"

"Yeah, you wouldn't know it by the way Daisy's carrying on now, would you?" Tucker said, not even trying to hide his disgust. "It all goes back to the fact that she found out about Mary Elizabeth and Chandler before Mary Elizabeth told me. I knew the two of them were friends. They liked to get together to talk politics, and old man Swan encouraged it. I guess somewhere along the way Daisy saw something that suggested to her it might be more than a casual friendship. She called Mary Elizabeth on it. The next thing I knew, Mary Elizabeth was telling me that she was falling in love with Chandler."

"Did Liz ever explain why she kept silent in the first place?" Walker asked.

"She told me that her relationship with Chandler had

been entirely innocent, but that Daisy's observation had made her take a harder look at the way she felt. She said she wanted the freedom to figure out how important the relationship might really be. It didn't hurt that her grandfather was encouraging things between them. Her grandfather liked me well enough, but I wasn't showing enough ambition to suit him, so he was pushing her toward Chandler. She'd always wanted to please him, and now she had a chance. I'm not sure if she even realized what a factor that was."

"Are you saying that in a weird way Daisy's pressure pushed her straight into Chandler's arms?" Walker asked.

"If I'm being honest, I'd have to say she probably would have ended up there, anyway," Tucker admitted, then sighed. "But knowing what I know about Chandler now, I've got to wonder if in time Mary Elizabeth wouldn't have seen him for what he was and made a different choice. Instead, the minute she gave Chandler an opening, he started rushing her straight toward the altar. They were married within months."

Walker's gaze narrowed. "You're not blaming your sister for the breakup, are you?"

"For a long time, a part of me wanted to," Tucker said. "But the bottom line is, Mary Elizabeth made the decision. She wanted what she thought Chandler could give her more than she wanted what the two of us had."

"Money? Status? What?"

"All of that, to some degree, but she says it was because she thought that married to him, she'd really be able to make a difference in people's lives," Tucker said. "Add in her grandfather's approval, the chance to live in Richmond, maybe even Washington, and the marriage was all but destined."

"What makes you think anything's changed?" Walker asked. "She could decide to go back to Richmond tomorrow and resume her life there. She'd made a life for herself, completely apart from Chandler. She must be on half a dozen charitable organization boards. She has been making a difference."

Tucker scowled at the question. "She says she's not going to go back," he said defensively. "That she wants to come home."

"And you believe her?"

"I'm hoping she's being honest with me," Tucker corrected. "And with herself."

"You're *hoping?*" Walker said derisively. "Isn't it awfully risky pinning your entire future on something you don't know for a fact?"

"I'm not pinning my future on Mary Elizabeth," Tucker insisted.

"Like I believe that," Walker retorted. "You're falling for her again. Your family can see it. I can see it."

"I'm helping her," Tucker corrected. "I'm trying to be a good friend."

"Sure you are. I'll make you a deal. You let me hook you up to a polygraph, and then sit there and tell me you haven't thought about hauling her off to bed. If you pass, I'll personally get King and Daisy off your case."

Tucker made an obscene gesture that told Walker exactly what he thought of that idea.

"Thought so," Walker said with a knowing smirk. "Now I suggest that you and I go to the marina, have a couple of beers, ponder the facts of this case and see if one damned thing makes sense." He gave Tucker a sly look. "And you can tell me all about your meeting with Selena Velez."

Tucker muttered an expletive. "You know about that?"

Walker shook his head at Tucker's shock. "Hell, I knew about it five seconds after you walked through the front door of the building down there. My men may be country lawmen, but they know their stuff, Tucker. Since you're the one who trained them, you ought to know that."

"I suppose it slipped my mind." Even with the prospect of being cross-examined about the unauthorized meeting he and Mary Elizabeth had had with Selena, the suggestion of going to the marina was the best offer on the table.

"You're on," he told Walker.

If nothing else, it would dull the temptation to go running out to Swan Ridge for another quiet evening with Mary Elizabeth. Walker was right about one thing—he'd long since lost his professional objectivity where she was concerned. The admission that he'd made to King that he still loved Mary Elizabeth was more truth than it was retaliation against King for his meddling.

And the prospect of getting her back into his bed was nagging at him like an itch that wouldn't quit.

Liz opened the door expecting to find Tucker on her doorstep. Instead, it was Anna-Louise and another woman who looked only vaguely familiar.

"Is this a bad time?" Anna-Louise inquired. "I took a chance that you'd be home and grateful for a little company."

"You were right. I'm going stir-crazy out here," Liz said. "Please, come in."

"Liz, this is Gail Thorensen. She owns the bookstore and café in town."

"Of course," Liz said, remembering the day she'd spent browsing through the latest bestsellers and mysteries. That was where she'd seen the other woman.

"Her husband's retired from the D.C. police force," Anna-Louise continued. "Andy's one of Walker's best friends."

Gail gave her an engaging grin. "Now that you know all of my dirty little connections to the cops, I hope you won't hold that against me. I begged Anna-Louise to bring me out here."

"Why?" Liz said. "Curiosity?"

"That, too," Gail admitted candidly. "But mostly because Anna-Louise and I have a proposition for you."

"Let's go in the kitchen, then. I've just made a fresh batch of lemonade and some cookies."

"Chocolate chip, I imagine," Anna-Louise said, then looked at Gail. "Tucker's favorite."

"Ah," Gail said. "Then it's true? The two of you did have a thing once?"

"A long time ago," Liz replied, unable to keep a note of wistfulness from her voice.

"Were you expecting him tonight?" Gail asked. "We don't want to intrude."

Before Liz could reply, Anna-Louise said, "I think we've got time. Last I heard, he, Walker, Andy, Bobby and Richard were all at the marina supposedly discussing the investigation. Since they haven't had a big break yet, my guess is they're drinking beer and talking about women. Primarily us."

"In that case, maybe we should get Daisy and Jenna over here," Gail said at once. "They should be in on this anyway."

Liz shook her head. "Jenna maybe, but Daisy won't come."

"Why on earth not?" Gail said. "Where's your phone?"

"She hates me for breaking up with Tucker years ago," Liz said, trying to prevent Gail from blindly walking into a brick wall, especially if she and Daisy were friends.

"Ancient history," Gail said breezily. "She needs to get over it."

Liz and Anna-Louise exchanged an amused look.

"Are you planning to tell her that?" Liz inquired.

"Absolutely. Besides, this is too important to let some old squabble get in the way. Hand me that phone." She punched in numbers, then grinned. "Daisy? This is Gail. Anna-Louise and I are starting a project, and we really need your input. Can you meet us now? Terrific." She winked at them. "Where? We're at Swan Ridge."

Liz could hear Daisy's explosion clear across the kitchen. She winced as Gail held the phone away from her ear. "Told you so," she mouthed.

"That's nonsense," Gail said briskly, when Daisy had finally wound down. "That was then. This is now. We're going to talk about a youth center for Trinity Harbor, and I think you need to be a part of it. Now, act like a grown-up and get over here. I'm not taking no for an answer."

The call to Bobby's wife went more smoothly. Jenna agreed at once and promised to be there in a half hour. When Gail hung up, she exaggeratedly dusted off her hands and grinned at them. "Piece of cake."

"Run any small countries lately?" Liz inquired with awe and respect.

"No, but my husband is a stubborn man. I learned a few techniques over the years for dealing with difficult people," Gail told her. "The bulldozer strategy works best in certain situations. That's how I managed to get my bookstore down here. After that, I used sweet talk to convince him to retire. He never stood a chance."

At the realization that Daisy was actually coming to her home after all these years, Liz was suddenly struck by an attack of nerves worse than anything she'd ever experienced entertaining on a grand scale for Larry.

"We should go into the den," she said. "And I think there's probably time to cut some fresh flowers and bake another batch of cookies. These are a little crisp around the edges. Maybe people would prefer iced tea. I could brew a pot."

Anna-Louise stopped her as she began to pace. "Whoa! The kitchen is just fine. It's cozier. And these cookies are delicious. I should know. I've just eaten three of them. The lemonade is perfect. Who doesn't like lemonade on a hot day?"

Liz sighed. "I'm stressing out for no reason, aren't I?"

"Sweetie, you might not win Daisy over in a single night, but this is a huge step toward mending fences," Anna-Louise assured her. "Just be yourself and don't expect miracles."

"I thought you were in the miracle business," Liz lamented.

"I think we can thank Gail for this one," Anna-Louise said. "She got Daisy over here."

"She's not here yet," Liz murmured, but just then the doorbell rang.

"Why don't I get it?" Anna-Louise said. "You try to stop hyperventilating."

Liz nodded, then caught Gail's gaze fastened on her.

"There really is bad blood between the two of you, isn't there?"

"On her side," Liz said. "There hasn't been a day in the last six years that I haven't missed having her for a friend. I wasn't just Tucker's girl years ago. I was a real part of that family. Even King treated me like one of them. Now he won't even look me in the eye, unless it's to tell me to steer clear of his son."

Gail nodded. "Then it's time to heal the wounds. We'll start with Daisy. Don't worry about a thing."

Liz gave her a wan smile. "Easier said than done." This was about more than regaining Daisy's trust. It was about solidifying her connection to all of the Spencers. Nothing would ever happen again between her and Tucker if she couldn't find a way to make peace with Daisy and King. Just the thought of trying to win over King was enough to make her shudder. First things first, she told herself. Daisy did have a soft heart. Liz just had to find some way to reach it.

She stood up, plastered a welcoming smile on her face and kept it there as Anna-Louise returned not only with Daisy and Jenna, but with two young people.

"This is my daughter, Darcy," Jenna told her.

"And this is Tommy, Daisy's son," Anna-Louise said, when Daisy remained stiffly silent.

Liz held out her hand and shook theirs. "I'm very glad to meet both of you."

"Okay, kids, cookies and drinks outside," Jenna said briskly, then looked at Liz. "Believe me, you don't want these two dropping crumbs all over your carpets. Do you mind if they go outside and prowl around?"

"Of course not."

Tommy headed straight for the back door, then paused, his expression awestruck. "You've got a pool," he said. "Can we go swimming?" He looked toward Daisy. "Please?"

"If it's all right with Liz, I suppose so. You can wear your shorts," Daisy said. "Shallow end, though. And no diving. Got it?"

"I don't have a suit," Darcy said, her expression dismayed.

Liz led her to the door. "See that room over there?" she asked, pointing toward the small bathhouse and pool room she and Larry had added when they'd first moved in. "You should be able to find something that fits in there."

"Awesome," Darcy said, a grin splitting her face.

"Last one in's a rotten egg," Tommy challenged.

"Not fair. I've got to change," Darcy protested, but she was already racing past him and out the door.

When they promptly heard a splash, Jenna sighed. "So much for changing into a suit. Darcy would rather win. If you're not careful, they're going to want to move in," she warned Liz. "Those two are like little fish. The second they spot water, they want to be in it."

Having the noise and commotion of a couple of kids underfoot appealed to Liz more than she could admit. One look at Daisy's face and she saw that she felt the same way. No one had ever craved motherhood and family more than Daisy. Liz knew some of the details about how Tommy—and ultimately Walker—had come into her life. There had been a lot of talk in Trinity Harbor at the time, and some had even reached her. She was glad for her, especially after the way that fool fiancé of hers had bailed on her years ago.

"Okay, let's get down to business, shall we?" Gail said briskly before the tension could start to mount again. "Anna-Louise, why don't you explain to the others what you and I have been discussing?"

The pastor nodded. "For the past year or so, ever since Darcy was injured by several young bullies here in town, I've been concerned that our young people don't have enough to do. They need a place where they can get together in a supervised setting and have some fun. We have programs at church certainly, but those don't suit all kids from all faiths. Hopefully, what Gail and I are talking about will bring them together, teach them about tolerance and getting along, and prevent the kind of mischief and trouble the kids were getting into back then."

"But it's been better," Daisy argued. "Once you, Bobby and Jenna talked to the parents, they've been taking a more active role in supervising their kids, haven't they?"

"True, but young people still need an outlet for all that energy," Gail said. "All kids do. So Anna-Louise and I got to thinking and came up with an idea for a youth center." She sat back and surveyed them expectantly. "So? What do you think?"

"I think it's a fabulous idea," Liz said at once. "What can I do?"

"We need people to put the design for it down on paper," Gail said. "That's where you come in, Jenna. The boardwalk has been a huge success. I think this can be viewed as an extension of that in some ways. Are you interested?"

"Absolutely," Jenna said eagerly. "I'd do anything that might prevent another kid from being hurt the way Darcy was. It wasn't just the physical injuries. Those healed. But the intimidation and the fear that resulted from that have taken a much higher toll. I'm definitely in."

"Okay, then. We're also going to need the land and the funds to build it," Anna-Louise said. "Liz, you have a real track record in Richmond as a fund-raiser, and Daisy, you have the right community ties to get the job done."

Liz held her breath at the outrageous suggestion. They wanted her to work with Daisy. She detected Anna-Louise's scheming all over this idea. The town might need a youth center, but the plan to implement it now and get her and Daisy to coordinate the effort was ingenious...and downright sneaky. How could either of them refuse?

Liz met Daisy's wary gaze. "I'm willing to give it a try, if you are."

Daisy had never been one to back down from a challenge. She met Liz's gaze with an unblinking stare. "Fine," she said tightly. "It's for a good cause."

Anna-Louise beamed at them. "Perfect. I'll tell Richard he can announce it in this week's paper."

Obviously, she didn't intend to give either of them time for second thoughts.

"Shouldn't we have the plans drawn up first?" Jenna asked. "I can make it a top priority, but I doubt I can have anything finalized for you to look at for a couple of weeks. And it would be even better if we had a site in mind, so I can make sure it all works together."

"I don't think we should delay the announcement," Gail said, clearly picking up on Anna-Louise's unspoken agenda. "We'll just promise that the complete plans will be forthcoming. It never hurts to get people excited early. Daisy and Liz will need to recruit volunteers for their committee as soon as possible. The more people working on something like this, the better."

"Absolutely," Liz agreed. "We want to start building momentum, getting people invested in the idea."

"That's settled, then," Anna-Louise said. "I'll tell Richard. Then we'll meet again in a couple of weeks to look over Jenna's preliminary plans. In the meantime, we can all be looking for a location that seems suitable. And Daisy, you and Liz can get together to begin formulating a strategy for a fund-raising campaign. How does that sound?"

Liz nodded, her gaze on Daisy. "I'll call you to set up a meeting."

"Whatever," Daisy said, her expression still unyielding.

Liz took small comfort from the fact that at least Daisy hadn't slammed the door on the whole idea. As the women were leaving, Liz managed to take her aside.

"Thank you for going along with this," she said. "I know you're uncomfortable with it."

"It's not as if I had much choice," Daisy retorted, casting a glance toward Anna-Louise.

"You could have said no."

"And let you throw my pettiness back in my face for years to come? Not a chance. Besides, it is a worthwhile cause, and you are an excellent fund-raiser," Daisy conceded grudgingly.

"We can make it work," Liz said.

"If we don't, it won't be for lack of trying on my part."

"Or mine. Good night, Daisy. I'm really glad you came tonight."

There was a flicker of surprise in Daisy's eyes at her words. "You really mean that, don't you?"

"Of course, I do. I've missed you."

Daisy held her gaze, still looking vaguely startled, then nodded and abruptly walked away. It wasn't much, Liz thought, but she was almost certain she had seen a softening in her former friend's attitude.

"It's going to be okay," Anna-Louise said, joining Liz after Jenna and Gail had left. "Daisy's got a big heart, and nothing's more important to her than family. As long as she sees you're not out to hurt Tucker again, she'll forgive you eventually."

"Thank you for dreaming up this idea," Liz said.

"I didn't dream it up for your benefit," Anna-Louise assured her, then grinned. "It's just a handy coincidence that we can kill two birds with one stone."

"Even so, I'm grateful," Liz said, giving her a hug.

Just then headlights cut through the inky darkness as a car approached the house.

"Don't look now, but more company's coming. Tucker, I imagine," the pastor said. "You have a lot of news to share with him, so I'll be on my way."

Liz stood on the porch as Tucker and Anna-Louise stopped and chatted quietly. When his gaze shot to Liz, she guessed that the minister had told him about Daisy's visit. He sprinted up the steps with a worried expression.

"Everything okay?"

"You heard that Daisy's been here?" she said.

"Yes, but not why. If she was on your case again—"

"She wasn't," Liz assured him, relieved that Anna-Louise hadn't shared all the details of the amazing evening. "Let's go out back. There's a breeze off the river."

"And a full moon," Tucker noted. "Want to walk down to the shore?"

She heard something in his voice she hadn't heard in years, the faint hint of a teasing dare, a touch of longing. "Should I bring a blanket?"

His gaze locked with hers. There was a flicker of hesitation, but then it was gone. "Sure. Why not?"

"There's lemonade left. You want some?"

"I'm not sure how well that would sit with beer," he said. "I'll pass."

"Okay, then, give me a second to get the blanket."

She stopped in the bathhouse, picked up an old quilt that had made many a trip to the beach, then joined Tucker on the lawn. To her surprise, he reached for her hand and held it as they walked through the damp, sweet-smelling grass.

"It's a beautiful night," he murmured, almost to himself.

"The prettiest I've seen in a long time," she agreed. "I'd forgotten how many stars you can see in the sky here."

He grinned at her as he spread the blanket on the cool sand. "Want to count them?"

It was a game they had played a million times in years gone by. Back then it had been an excuse to lie side by side, hand in hand, staring at the sky, content merely to be in each other's company. Sometimes it had led to more. Much more. Tonight, Liz would be grateful simply for the peace and companionship.

At least, that's what she told herself until the instant Tucker lowered himself to the blanket beside her and turned on his side to study her face. She barely resisted the urge to lift her fingers to his chiseled cheeks and that now-familiar furrow in his brow. The heat of his hard, lean body was reaching out to her.

"Do you know how beautiful you are with the moonlight splashing its silver light over you?" he asked, his gaze locked on her face. He, too, seemed to be struggling to keep his hands to himself. "God, I've missed you. Missed this."

"Tucker?" she whispered, a catch in her voice. "What's going on?"

"I realized something today." He caught a wisp of her hair, curled it around a finger, then released it with a sigh.

"What?"

"That I still want you, even after all this time, even after everything that's happened. You're in my blood, Mary Elizabeth. I don't know how to change that."

Some of that was the beer talking. She couldn't deny that, no matter how desperately she wanted to believe every word. Nor could she ignore the fact that there was a hint of despair and regret in his pretty words.

"But a part of you hates that, doesn't it?" she asked.

He sighed heavily, rolled onto his back and stared at the sky. "I can't deny that," he said, his voice sad. "I wish it were different."

"Me, too," Liz whispered, unable to stop the tears that welled up and slid down her cheeks. "Me, too."

19

If there had been a fancier place to take Frances, King would have opted for it, rather than the marina restaurant where his son would no doubt keep an eye on every move he made and report back to the rest of the family. Unfortunately, Bobby's menu was the best for miles, and King was determined that tonight he would see that Frances had only the best. He'd debated calling ahead and asking Bobby to prepare something special, but had concluded that Frances would simply view that as yet another of his fumbling attempts to control things, rather than let her choose her own meal.

He rang her doorbell promptly at seven, wearing his best suit, a starched white dress shirt and a tie. He seldom got this decked out, even for church. Frances's jaw dropped when she saw him. That alone was reward enough for the effort.

Of course, she had gone all out, too. He'd told her to wear something daring and she had. Her red dress had a slit in the skirt and a neckline that should have been outlawed. Damn, but she was a fine figure of a woman.

He had trouble believing they were the same age. She looked a decade younger.

"You look real pretty," King said, fumbling for words like a teenager on a first date.

Frances grinned. "You had a hard time spitting those words out, didn't you?"

"Only because I couldn't catch my breath," King said honestly. "You really do look amazing, Frances."

The pink that bloomed in her cheeks only added to the sparkle in her eyes. "Shall we go?" she asked.

"I just have one concern," he told her as they walked to his car. "I'm not sure I'm up to defending your honor against all the men likely to be gawking at you tonight."

"Oh, let 'em gawk," she said cheerfully. "It'll do my ego good."

King chuckled at the saucy comment. "You constantly amaze me."

"Only because you're finally starting to pay attention," Frances told him. "I haven't changed, King. *You* have."

"Of course, you've changed," he argued. "The new haircut, the new figure…" His gaze roved over her appreciatively. "That dress."

"All superficial," she said. "I haven't changed a bit from the first night you took me to bingo."

King grappled with the message until it finally sank in. She was trying to tell him that she'd been right in front of his eyes for years. It had simply taken him a long time to notice how incredible she was. That's what happened when a man started taking a woman—any woman—for granted.

For years he'd viewed Frances as a competitor, a smug kid who'd whipped his butt in a spelling bee in elementary school, then as the daughter of a man who'd always felt his family lineage was better than the Spencers'. King hadn't really looked at Frances in any other way until she'd been searching for a home for Tommy, and Daisy had set out to claim the boy. When King had objected, Frances had calmed him down. When he'd been about to do something that would strain relations with Daisy and later with Bobby, Frances had interceded with her instinctive wisdom. She was like an older version of Anna-Louise, sensible and steady as a rock. Lately, though, there was an edge of unpredictability about her that livened things up.

He glanced over at her, his pulse lurching at the effect of that red dress. She was sexy, too, by golly. She was going to keep his golden years from turning dull, that's for sure. Assuming, of course, he could pin her down and get a straight answer to his bungled marriage proposal.

He drove into the crowded parking lot at the marina, glad that he'd had the forethought to call ahead for a reservation. Not that Bobby wouldn't have seen to it that he got a table eventually, but he wanted tonight to go off without a hitch.

As he and Frances strolled through the restaurant, every eye was on them. King had little doubt that their presence here tonight, especially with Frances all dolled up in that provocative dress, would be the talk of Earlene's in the morning. Well, he could stand the ribbing he was bound to take. In fact, he was looking forward to it.

"My, my, don't you two look incredible?" Anna-Louise said as they passed the table where she was sitting with Richard. "King, I've never seen you look so dapper, and, Frances, you are stunning in that dress. You should wear red all the time."

King studied the preacher with a narrowed gaze. "You after something?"

Anna-Louise regarded him with an innocent expression. "What on earth could I possibly want?"

"That's what I'm wondering," King said. He turned to Richard. "You have any idea what she's up to?"

"All I know is that she was out at Swan Ridge earlier with Liz Chandler, Gail Thorensen, Daisy and Jenna," Richard said.

King's blood ran cold. "Daisy was out there consorting with the enemy?"

"King Spencer!" Frances protested.

King gazed into her condemning eyes and backed down at once. "Okay, okay, I won't get into all that tonight." He regarded Anna-Louise with an innocent look of his own. "So, how are things coming with that project of yours?"

"The youth center?" she asked.

"I don't know anything about any youth center," King retorted. "I was thinking about something a little more personal." He directed his gaze toward Richard. "She talked you into becoming a papa yet?"

This time the vehement protests came from both women. King winced at the chorus. He refused to back down. If Richard needed a little nudging along those lines, he was prepared to offer it. "Nothing like fatherhood," he told him. "And you don't want to wait too late for it, either. Take it from me, parenthood is not something for old people or sissies. It requires a lot of patience and energy."

"Especially when you insist on meddling in your

children's lives," Anna-Louise commented dryly. "King, do you suppose you could leave this particular topic to Richard and me?"

"Not till I've heard what he's got to say," King persisted. "So, boy, what's it going to be? You up to the task or not?"

Richard rose to his feet slowly and looked King directly in the eye. Anyone else would have backed down under that hard stare, but King didn't flinch.

"I know you think you run Trinity Harbor, King, but you can't control the lives of everyone in it," Richard said with a chill in his voice. "My personal life is off-limits. Try to remember that the next time you're tempted to stick your nose in where it doesn't belong."

King was about to respond that he had been consulted on the matter by one of the two interested parties, but one look at Anna-Louise's drawn expression warned him to stay silent. For once in his life he was smart enough to take the hint.

"I still say there's no time like the present to consider an important step like this, especially with a woman like Anna-Louise to be the child's mother. She's a born nurturer, and she's not going to be content with having a bunch of old geezers like me to look out for. She needs a baby." He nodded at Anna-Louise, satisfied that he'd done his part to help her get her wish. "You two enjoy your evening."

He turned to Frances, tucked her arm in his and led her to their table across the dining room.

"Why on earth would you get into such a personal topic with Anna-Louise and Richard?" Frances demanded the instant they were seated.

"That's confidential," he said prudently.

She studied him with a narrowed gaze. "And that's all you intend to say?"

"That's it," he said, scanning the menu. "The veal special looks good tonight. What do you think?"

"I think you'd be better off with crow," she said tartly. "I'll have the pork tenderloin."

He chuckled. "I imagine my son could even manage to make crow downright appetizing."

Frances feigned shock. "Why, King Spencer, I think that is the very first time I've ever heard you say something complimentary about Bobby's cooking."

"That's not true," he protested. "I might not understand his decision to make this his life's work, but I praise his skill all the time. Now let's forget all about my children, Anna-Louise and Richard, and concentrate on us."

She seemed startled by the suggestion. "That will be a first."

He shrugged. "Never let it be said that an old dog can't learn a new trick or two, given the right incentive."

"And the incentive would be?"

He opted for being plainspoken. This was one message he didn't want her to miss. Looking her straight in the eye, he said, "I want you, Frances. And I'm not going to quit until I get you."

She waved her menu to fan her suddenly flaming face. "Well, then, I suppose we'll just have to wait to see if you're up to the task."

King grinned at the challenge. "You know I am."

"I know nothing of the sort."

"Liar." He reached for her hand, brought it to his lips

and kissed her knuckles. To his satisfaction, her breath hitched. "That's just the warm-up, darlin' woman. You don't stand a chance."

"You should have seen the two of them last night," Bobby reported to Tucker over breakfast at Earlene's the next morning. "Daddy and Frances were making eyes at each other all evening long. And she was wearing this dress—this bright *red* dress—that just about had his eyes popping out of his head."

Tucker laughed. "Good for her."

"I'm telling you, if those two don't announce an engagement soon, I'll grind up the stemware behind the bar and eat it."

Tucker shuddered. "Sounds deadly."

"Which should prove how convinced I am that Daddy's fate is sealed," Bobby said. "So, where were you? I called several times to give you a blow-by-blow report of the events as they unfolded." He waved his hand. "Never mind. You were with Mary Elizabeth."

"Okay, yes," Tucker admitted defensively. "I did stop by after I left the marina."

"And?"

"And nothing," Tucker retorted. "We sat down by the river and talked for a while. That's it."

Bobby glanced up just then, and a grin began to spread across his face. "Maybe I'll try for another version and see if it matches up," he said, beckoning to someone behind Tucker.

Mary Elizabeth walked up to the table. Tucker's pulse began to thud dully. She could make a liar of him in two seconds flat, if she chose.

"Join us," Bobby suggested. "Tucker was just telling me all about his visit to you last night."

Her gaze narrowed. "Oh, really?" she said, slipping in beside Tucker until they were thigh to thigh. "And what did you tell him?"

Bobby held up a hand. "No, wait. I don't want you comparing notes. You just tell me what happened. I want to see how truthful my brother is being."

"Watch it, Mary Elizabeth," Tucker warned, amused despite himself. "Bobby seems to be all caught up in romantic gossip this morning. He's just been telling me all about our father's candlelit dinner with Frances last night."

"Don't try to distract her by changing the subject," Bobby protested. "Come on, Mary Elizabeth, spill everything."

Earlene arrived just then, plunked a coffee cup noisily on the table in front of Mary Elizabeth and filled it, grabbed up Tucker's plate, then left after casting a disapproving scowl at all of them. Mary Elizabeth sighed.

Tucker promptly took offense at Earlene's deliberate show of attitude. "I'll talk to her," he said grimly. "Let me out."

"No," Mary Elizabeth said. "Let it be. She'll mellow in time. I'm developing a thick skin and a renewed commitment to the virtue of patience."

"You're a customer," he protested. "Earlene should know better. Move, Mary Elizabeth. I want to have a few words with her."

She refused to let him out. "No, absolutely not. Forget about it, Tucker."

"She's right," Bobby added. "Let it go. You won't help matters by getting Earlene stirred up and causing a scene that everyone in town will hear about before nightfall." Apparently satisfied that he'd made his point, Bobby winked at Mary Elizabeth. "Come on, now. Let's hear all the good stuff."

Obviously relieved when Tucker sank back beside her, Mary Elizabeth propped her elbows on the table and rested her chin on her cupped hands. "Well," she began, regarding Bobby intently. "First we got this old blanket, and then we strolled down to the river. The sky was like black velvet sprinkled with diamonds, and the air smelled as sweet as honeysuckle."

Bobby made an exaggerated show of fanning himself. Tucker finally felt his tension ease as he listened to her spin her web around Bobby. To be truthful, her version was a whole lot more fascinating than his.

"And then we stretched out on the blanket, side by side," she said, her voice little more than a seductive purr now.

Bobby's eyes widened with anticipation. "Yes?"

She grinned. "And then we talked."

"Talked?" Bobby repeated.

She leaned back and poked Tucker in the ribs with her elbow. "Yes, that's it. We talked. Right, Tucker?"

"That's it," he agreed.

"Well, damn," Bobby muttered. "I had a higher opinion of you, bro. Maybe Walker and I need to have one of those birds-and-bees talks with you."

"Trust me, I have the birds-and-bees things down pat," Tucker said. He glanced at Mary Elizabeth, then intentionally held her gaze. "There's nothing wrong with building a little anticipation now, is there?" He watched the pulse at the base of her neck beat a little faster. She licked her lips, and suddenly his pulse was ricocheting wildly, too. He swallowed hard. "Well, Mary Elizabeth?"

"Anticipation is a beautiful thing," she agreed. "As long as a person remembers that there is a very fine line between pleasurable anticipation and teasing."

Tucker nodded, keeping his expression somber. "I'll remember that."

Bobby released a deliberately huge sigh. "Oh, my," he said with another wave of the menu to fan himself. "That was so…so… There are no words to describe it."

Tucker laughed. "Good. Maybe you'll be able to keep your mouth shut."

"Don't count on it. I live to spread tales about you, Tucker. I've waited a long time to get even for the way you taunted me about Jenna."

"Go for it, as long as Daddy's not on the shortlist to hear the news," Tucker said. "After that dinner you described him having with Frances, I'm not sure his heart can take much more."

Mary Elizabeth's expression brightened. "Let's talk about that. Are things heating up after all? When I talked to Frances, she was totally frustrated that King would never make a move."

Tucker stared at her. "You talked to Frances about her relationship with my father?"

She shrugged. "She was upset. We had a little girl-talk. I gave her a suggestion or two."

"Did any of them involve a slinky red dress?" Bobby inquired.

"Actually, no, but I must admit that had to have been a nice touch."

"Oh, yeah," Bobby confirmed. "I definitely think it did the trick."

"God bless Frances, is all I can say," Tucker said fervently. "If she can divert his attention from me for a while, more power to her."

"Trust me, bro. I don't think you were on Daddy's mind last night," Bobby said. "I'm pretty sure he was trying to figure out how to get Frances out of that dress."

"Please," Tucker protested. "The concept boggles the mind. I'd just as soon not have that particular image floating around in my brain all day long." He turned to Mary Elizabeth. "By the way, what are you doing in here at this hour? Were you looking for me?"

"No, you're just a bonus," she said, winking at Bobby. "I'm meeting Gail Thorensen for coffee. She called me after you'd left last night and suggested getting together before she opens the bookstore."

"More talk about the youth center?" Tucker asked.

"Actually, I don't think so. She was pretty evasive when I asked why she wanted to see me. She just said she'd had a brainstorm on the way home and wanted to run it by me."

"Uh-oh," Bobby said. "When any of these women get evasive, it means trouble, usually for us men."

"Especially Gail," Tucker noted. "I'll never forget how she maneuvered Andy into buying that property and helping her open a store more than a hundred miles from where they actually lived. The man was retired from the D.C. police force and living down here before he knew what hit him. Watch your step with her, Mary Elizabeth. She's sneaky."

"I doubt she'll try the same tactics on me that she used on her husband," Mary Elizabeth said, regarding him with amusement. "Besides, I'm up for anything that gets me out of Swan Ridge and back among the living."

"Glad to hear that," Gail said, arriving just then and nudging Bobby until he slid over to make room for her. "Because what I have in mind will definitely keep you occupied."

Tucker didn't like the gleam in Gail's eye one bit. "What are you up to?" he demanded.

"Just a little selfish request," she said innocently.

Then, in what Tucker was fairly sure was a deliberate attempt to keep them guessing, she waved Earlene over to ask for coffee and a cinnamon bun.

"Well?" Tucker prodded.

"Not till I've had my first sip of coffee," Gail said.

Thankfully the coffee and bun arrived at once, but then Mary Elizabeth decided she had to have one, too. Only when both women were happily drinking their coffee and eating Earlene's gooey, iced cinnamon buns did the conversation resume.

"Okay, here it is," Gail said, sitting back and regarding Mary Elizabeth with an expectant look. "How about coming to work for me?"

"In the bookstore?" Tucker asked before Mary Elizabeth could say a word. He tried to envision her working for minimum wage in a tiny little bookshop here in Trinity Harbor after hobnobbing with the elite in Richmond. He couldn't see it. As far as he knew, she'd never held a paying, nine-to-five job in her life.

"Of course in the bookstore," Gail said impatiently. "It's a respectable establishment."

"It's lovely," Mary Elizabeth said.

She emphasized her point by poking Tucker in the ribs again. At this rate he was going to have bruises.

"Never said it wasn't," he grumbled.

"So?" Gail asked. "Will you consider it? The hours

can be pretty flexible. I got my husband down here so I could spend more time with him, but it turns out I'm working all the time. I had no idea retail was so demanding. I could really use someone part-time to relieve the pressure. I have a couple of kids who help out on weekends, but they're too young and inexperienced to be left on their own."

Tucker watched the emotions registering on Mary Elizabeth's face. First disbelief, then worry, then the first faint spark of excitement.

"You're sure? This could backfire," she warned Gail. "A lot of people haven't accepted that I'm back." She glanced pointedly toward Earlene as she spoke. "In fact, I'm sure some are counting on me leaving. If I go to work for you, it will imply that I'm back permanently, and it might keep some of your customers away, especially with this cloud of suspicion hanging over my head."

"Oh, no one with any sense seriously believes you were responsible for your husband's death," Gail said, dismissing the problem as inconsequential. "I certainly don't, and neither does Andy. I'll take my chances. At least we can try it for a couple of weeks and see how it goes. Please. I really want to spend some time with Andy this weekend. It's our anniversary, and I have big plans." She grinned. "If you know what I mean."

"Then I will most definitely work for you this weekend," Mary Elizabeth assured her.

At this rate, she was going to be meddling in as many romantic relationships as his father, Tucker thought grumpily. He also felt a little nagging sense of shame at how readily this virtual stranger was willing to believe in Mary Elizabeth when he'd been fighting doubts off and on from the beginning, despite his instincts telling him she was innocent. Andy's defense of her, which he'd heard the night before, had also gone a long way toward reassuring him that his own instincts were sound.

Bobby shook his head. "See what I mean?" he said to no one in particular. "The woman is clever. Mary Elizabeth never stood a chance."

"Shut up, Bobby," Mary Elizabeth and Gail said in a chorus, then laughed.

Though he was relieved to see Mary Elizabeth so excited about something, Tucker was worried that she could be exactly right about Gail's plan backfiring. Even so, he couldn't bring himself to throw a damper on her enthusiasm. Besides, if she was happy working with Gail, she might really decide to stick around Trinity Harbor. That would make the plans he was beginning to formulate for the two of them go a whole lot more smoothly, once the timing was right.

Still, he glanced sideways at Mary Elizabeth. "You know anything about books?"

"Hey!" she protested.

"Well, as a kid you weren't much of a reader. You preferred climbing trees," he reminded her.

She gave him a coy grin. "Obviously you never snuck up to my tree house," she said. "That's where I kept my secret stash of books."

"Dirty books?" Bobby inquired hopefully.

She frowned at him. "Nancy Drew, if you must know. And the Hardy Boys. Louisa May Alcott. All the classics, including *Tom Sawyer* and *Huckleberry Finn*—which, by the way gave me great insights into how to get along with you, Tucker Spencer."

Gail beamed. "Oh, this is wonderful. You will be

so good at this, Liz. I knew my instincts were exactly right. Can you come with me now? I'll show you the ropes today and you can work a bit the next couple of days before I leave you on your own this weekend."

"Perfect," Mary Elizabeth said eagerly.

Tucker scowled, vaguely disgruntled by the fact that she was already taking off. "Hey, as long as you're here, I thought we could talk."

She hesitated. "Is there something in particular you wanted to discuss?"

To his disgust, Tucker couldn't think of one pressing thing to keep her right where she was. "No, go. I just hope you don't consider a cinnamon roll to be a nutritious breakfast."

A grin spread across her fact. "Thanks for caring about my eating habits, but I actually had breakfast at home hours ago. The cinnamon bun was dessert."

"It's only eight-thirty now."

"I know, but I got to bed early and woke up at dawn." She winked at Bobby. "That's what happens when there's nothing interesting going on in a woman's life."

Tucker sighed heavily at the clever way she'd managed to bring up their relationship again and the fact that he'd nobly left before anything could happen the night before. "You are not going to taunt me into changing my mind."

"Changing your mind about what?" Gail asked, regarding him with blatant curiosity.

"Never mind," Tucker said.

"Tucker thinks it is too soon for us to..." Mary Elizabeth leaned across the table toward Gail and said in a stage whisper, "Date."

He scowled at her. "Well, it is."

"Says who?" Gail asked.

"I know this town better than you do," he told her. "It wouldn't look right, and they'd hold it against her."

"And you?" Gail inquired. "Would they also hold it against you?"

"I am not thinking of myself," Tucker insisted. When Mary Elizabeth started to reply, he stopped her. "And you are not going to change my mind. Period."

"Bet I could," she teased as she slid from the booth. Laughing, she and Gail left.

"I'll bet she could, too," Bobby said.

"Oh, go to hell," Tucker grumbled.

"What? And miss all this?" Bobby retorted, grinning. "Not a chance. This is the most fun I've had in ages."

"Glad you're enjoying yourself. Maybe I'll mention to Daddy that I'm surprised you and Jenna haven't started adding to your family yet," Tucker said innocently. "Not that we don't love Darcy, but I think we're all anxious for a new little Spencer to join the ranks."

"I could learn to hate you," Bobby retorted.

"Me? I was just giving you a little something to keep in mind the next time you decide to start poking and prodding at me," Tucker said. "Surely you don't hold it against me?"

"Okay, okay, let's call it a draw," Bobby said, looking resigned. "You keep your mouth shut about babies around Daddy, and I'll keep mine shut about you and Mary Elizabeth. Deal?"

"Deal," Tucker said. "Isn't it nice how this all worked out? A pleasure having breakfast with you, Bobby." He slid out of the booth. "Thanks for treating."

"Hey, I didn't say I was buying," Bobby protested.

"Didn't you?" Tucker said. He took great satisfaction in Bobby's muttered oath as he left Earlene's, barely resisting the desire to give the woman a piece of his mind. Why spoil his mood? Seeing Mary Elizabeth, a free meal and irritating his brother all in one morning—what a great way to start the day!

20

Liz took to working in the bookstore as if it was what she'd been born to do. She loved opening the boxes that arrived from the distributor—it felt just like Christmas morning. She liked running her fingers over the foiled, embossed covers of the paperbacks, scanning the back-cover copy, even sneaking a peek at the first page or two of titles by her favorite authors. Invariably she set aside a huge stack of books she wanted to take home.

"At this rate, it will take you until closing to finish checking those books and get them on the shelves," Gail said, regarding Liz with amusement.

Liz cast a last longing look at a new thriller, then reluctantly put it aside and checked the five copies off on the packing slip. "How do you ever get anything done?" she asked Gail. "I want to read everything."

"So do I, which is why I don't let myself start. If I did, I'd be back in the café all day long with a book in my hands. The paperwork would stack up to the ceiling."

It was Liz's second week on the job. She'd worked the prior weekend completely on her own so Gail could celebrate her anniversary. Aside from jamming the cash register once and losing track of what she was doing a dozen times and having to start all over because she was chatting with the customers, she'd done okay. The receipts and the money in the register had balanced at the end of both days, and she'd gone home exhausted but happy.

The customers had been surprisingly tolerant of her mistakes and generous in their welcome. Many were tourists who had no idea who she was, but even the locals, aside from expressing some surprise at finding her behind the counter, had been pleasant. She'd told Gail on the following Monday morning that she thought it was going to work out. Gail, thankfully, had agreed.

To Liz's amazement, she had actually found herself a steady job, or rather it had fallen into her lap. Working in a bookstore might not be quite the same as serving on the boards of several charitable institutions, but it gave her a sense of purpose. And with the flexible schedule she and Gail had devised, she could still continue on several of those boards. It was the best of all possible worlds. She could actually envision a real future here in Trinity Harbor—with or without Tucker.

Hopefully with, she thought with a sigh, but the man surely was stubborn. If he pulled back from making love to her one more time, she wasn't sure she'd be able to restrain herself. She understood his reasons—all of them, including those he probably hadn't even admitted to himself—but it was damned frustrating watching him struggle to be noble when there was no need. She'd mourned the loss of her husband a long time ago. His death hadn't been the end for them. His affairs had accomplished that.

"Let's take a break," Gail said now. "It's three o'clock, and I could definitely use a cup of coffee and a biscotti as a pick-me-up. How about you?"

"I thought you were just chiding me about not getting these books checked in," Liz teased.

"You'll work faster once you've had some caffeine and a little sugar," Gail theorized, leading the way to the small area that had been turned into a café at the back of the store. There were a handful of tables and chairs, along with a few cozy, chintz-covered, overstuffed chairs for people who wanted to relax and browse through a stack of current newspapers and magazines kept for that purpose.

Gail poured them each a cup of coffee, plucked two chocolate almond biscotti from a jar on the counter, then sat in one of the overstuffed chairs and propped her feet on the coffee table. She sighed. "Ah, this is heaven. I had no idea how tiring it could be to stand on my feet all day."

"You could trade off with me more," Liz said. "I don't mind working the register."

"We need to talk about that. You're already putting in more hours than I'm paying you for."

"I'm not complaining," Liz said. "I didn't take this job for the money."

Gail chuckled. "That was pretty much a given, considering the salary you're getting, but I don't want to take advantage of you, Liz."

"Trust me, I love this, every aspect of it." Suddenly a chill swept over her. "You haven't had complaints about me being here, have you?"

"No, absolutely not," Gail reassured her. "If anything, the opposite. Everyone seems to be enjoying having the chance to get to know you again. I've had nothing but compliments. I'm just worried about taking up so much of your time."

"It's not as if I have a lot of things to do," Liz said, unable to keep the bleak note from her voice. "Tucker's still showing considerable restraint about spending time with me. And Daisy finally said she'd meet with me tomorrow to start on a list of prospective committee members and look at some property for the youth center. Frankly, I'm dreading it."

"Because?"

"Because she's made it plain that she's agreed to do this under pressure from you and Anna-Louise. Once we're alone, I'm not sure she'll manage to be civil, much less pleasant." She sighed. "It's not as if I expect her to forgive me overnight, but it's hard having someone who was once like a sister treat you as if you have a communicable disease."

"I could come along," Gail offered at once. "I'd be a buffer."

"Thanks, but sooner or later, Daisy and I have to deal with this. Besides, we're going during the day. You'll be here."

Just then the bell over the front door chimed. "I'll go," Liz said. "You keep your feet up."

She was halfway to the front when she realized with a sense of shock and dismay that the customer was Cynthia. Liz's steps slowed. Cynthia regarded her with a total lack of surprise. If anything, there was a triumphant gleam in her eyes at having caught Liz off-guard.

"What are you doing here?" Liz asked coldly.

"Looking for a book, what else?" Cynthia said, returning her gaze with an amused look. "Something with lots of lies and deception and sordid sex in it." She feigned innocence. "But then, you haven't written about your life with Larry yet, have you?"

Liz froze. Before she could lose it completely and tear the woman's hair out, Gail slipped between them.

"I think we have just what you want," she said cheerfully. "Right over here." She looked directly into Cynthia's eyes. "In fiction."

Cynthia allowed herself to be led away, but not before she'd cast a satisfied smirk in Liz's direction.

Liz sank onto the stool behind the register, her thoughts racing. Why was Cynthia back in Trinity Harbor? Was she here purely to torment Liz? Or was there another, more sinister reason for her reappearance in a town where she had no ties?

Only one way to find out, Liz decided, bracing herself for Cynthia's arrival at the checkout counter. A face-to-face confrontation with Larry's ex-lover was long overdue. Maybe if she'd faced Cynthia down years ago herself, rather than leaving it to Larry to handle, she would have maintained a better grip on her own self-esteem. She didn't intend to start a fight, but she would stand her ground.

In mere minutes Cynthia returned with Gail right behind her, a bestselling hardcover in her hand. Gail handed the book to Liz. "Can you ring this up, so our customer can be on her way?" she asked, giving Cynthia a pointed look.

"Certainly," Liz said, beaming an insincere smile at Cynthia. "Cash or charge?"

"Cash, of course," Cynthia said, her smirk still firmly in place. She handed Liz two twenties.

"I'm surprised to see you back in Trinity Harbor,"

Liz said, managing to keep her tone mildly interested rather than confrontational.

"I'm here to see a client," Cynthia volunteered.

"Oh?"

"Ken Willis is planning to run for Larry's seat in the legislature. He's asked me to coordinate his campaign. I imagine we'll be seeing quite a lot of each other, Liz. Won't that be fun?"

"As much fun as hives," Liz muttered under her breath, recalling the scene at Larry's funeral when she'd spotted Ken with several political party bigwigs. The speculation had been right. He'd seen an opening and seized it, even if his timing bordered on bad taste.

Cynthia apparently heard enough of her comment to get the gist of it. She laughed. "It's wonderful to see that you've managed to cling to your sense of humor. Few women would be able to after finding their husband murdered only a couple of months back."

"And few former lovers would want to work for the man who's intent on becoming his replacement," Liz snapped back as she handed Cynthia her purchase and her change. "But then, you always make the expedient choice, don't you?"

"Well, well, well, Ms. Goody-Two-Shoes has a bite," Cynthia retorted approvingly. "Maybe Larry didn't make such a dreadful mistake marrying you after all."

"Believe me, it was my mistake," Liz retorted. "Now, if you'll excuse me, I have work to do in back." She locked the register and walked away without so much as a glance at Cynthia. She could feel the dreadful woman's considering gaze on her just the same. It was several minutes before the bell over the front door rang to signal her departure.

When Liz got to the café, Gail regarded her worriedly. "What on earth was that about? Who is that woman?"

"She was Larry's campaign manager when he and I got married. She was also his lover, but I didn't stumble on that fact until I walked into his hotel room one evening," Liz explained.

"Oh, no," Gail whispered sympathetically. "I'm so sorry. What on earth is she doing here?"

"She says that Ken Willis has hired her to help him campaign for Larry's seat."

"Now there's a losing cause if ever I saw one," Gail remarked. "The man doesn't have two brain cells to click together."

Liz grinned at the blunt assessment. "But he is a charmer, just Cynthia's type. She can do great things for him."

"Do you suppose she'll go after him, the way she did your husband?" Gail asked.

"Oh, I'd bet on it," Liz replied. "I wonder if I should clue Arlene in, so she can be prepared to defend her turf."

"I've met Arlene Willis," Gail said. "Something tells me she can take care of herself."

Surprised by the hint of disdain she heard in Gail's voice, Liz regarded her with curiosity. "You don't like her much, do you?"

Gail hesitated, her expression thoughtful. "She just seems a little high-strung to me, a little unpredictable."

It had been years since Liz had spent any time with Arlene, but Gail's assessment didn't match her recollection. "Arlene was always a little on the quiet side in school. She stayed in the shadows."

"Those are the ones you always have to watch out for," Gail said.

Before Liz could ask what she meant, the bell chimed and Tucker strode through the store, his expression grim.

"What's wrong?" Liz asked at once.

"I just saw the Miles woman over at Earlene's. Since she had a bag from here, I figured she'd been in. What did she want?" He scanned Liz worriedly. "You okay?"

"Bloodied but unbroken, figuratively speaking," she assured him. "I handled her."

"You shouldn't have to," he said heatedly. "I can find some way to run her off. I'll get Walker to turn up the pressure, make things so uncomfortable, she'll be delighted to get out of town."

"Now there's a scene I'd like to see—Walker going toe-to-toe with Cynthia," Liz said. "But I think you should probably forget about it. She's here on business. She's working for Ken Willis."

"Son of a bitch!" Tucker said. "Now there's a combination that strikes terror in my heart. Let me guess. He has renewed political aspirations, now that his biggest rival is dead."

"Got it in one," Liz confirmed.

"Which raises an interesting question," Tucker said, his expression thoughtful. "Just when did Willis develop these ambitions, and how anxious is he to see them fulfilled?"

Willis was a lowlife, Liz reflected, the kind of kid who'd cruised through school with barely passing grades, the kind who preferred Cliffs Notes to texts. He was still taking shortcuts. He'd bought up a number of small businesses, but rather than trying to build them into successes, he'd run them into the ground, bleeding them of every cent they made. He'd accumulated more money than sense over the years. But a killer? Liz didn't think he'd have the stomach for it.

"Surely you don't think he could have killed Larry," she said to Tucker.

"He'd certainly have a motive, wouldn't he?" Gail asked, pouncing on the idea. "And he has quite a gun collection from what I've heard."

"You're right," Tucker said. "I've got the registration for all of them down at the station. I'd better get over there and fill Walker in. We can check that list and see if he has anything the right caliber, then try to get a search warrant to look for it."

He grabbed Liz out of her chair and planted a hard kiss on her mouth that snatched her breath away.

"Thank you, darlin'."

"Me? I think you're barking up the wrong tree."

"Well, until we know one way or another, steer clear of Cynthia and Willis. I'm going to try to get Walker to haul them both in for questioning."

"And set yourself up for harassment charges," Liz warned. "Tucker, be careful. Those are not two people you want for enemies, even if they had nothing at all to do with Larry's death. Ken's a mean, vindictive little thing, and Cynthia's claws can be deadly. She knows how to manipulate the media. You don't want her to go after you in print and on TV. She'll destroy your career."

"I can handle the likes of Cynthia Miles," Tucker said confidently.

He was almost out the door when Gail called out.

"Tucker, wait!" she shouted urgently. "I just remembered something. I knew I had seen that woman before, but I couldn't think where. It just came to me. She was here the day of the murder."

"In the store?"

"No, but she was here in town. I'd stake my life on it. I bumped into her, literally, coming out of the bank as I was going in. I apologized, but she never even looked at me. She was counting a big wad of cash."

Liz met Tucker's gaze. "Blackmail money from Larry," she said at once.

"Or the first installment on her pay for helping Ken Willis," Gail said. "Maybe he had reason to believe he'd be campaigning sooner than anyone else anticipated."

"What time was this?" Tucker asked.

"Just before closing, I'd say. Maybe one forty-five," Gail replied.

"And you're sure it was the day of the murder?"

"Absolutely. I'd just picked up the *Weekly.* I always grab that on my way to the bank to make my deposit. That's why I apologized, because I was glancing at the headlines and figured it was my fault that we'd bumped into each other."

Tucker nodded. "Thanks, Gail. That puts her right where we need her, here in Trinity Harbor and not down in Richmond, where she claimed to be."

Once again, he leveled a look at Liz. "Don't go out to Swan Ridge alone tonight, okay? Wait till I can go with you."

"Tucker, she's gotten what she wanted," Liz protested. "She apparently got money from Larry or Ken, and she's got a job with Ken. She's not going to do anything to me. What would be the point?"

"Revenge," he suggested in a way designed to make her blood run cold.

"Okay," she agreed, even though she wasn't entirely sure she bought his theory. "I'll wait for you."

He glanced at Gail. "See that she does, okay?"

"You've got it, Sheriff."

Liz scowled at her friend. "Traitor."

"No," Gail replied. "I'm a desperate woman who's finally found an employee who can help me run this place. I am not about to risk losing you."

"Okay, okay, you two," Liz relented. "I'll behave. Are you going to come back here, Tucker? Or should I meet you somewhere?"

"Meet me at Earlene's at five-thirty. We can grab a quick bite before we drive out to Swan Ridge."

Liz nodded. "Would that be like a date?" she inquired sweetly.

"If it gets you to stay put, you can call it anything you want," Tucker replied with a grin.

"Be still my heart," she said, putting her hand over her chest. "You are such a romantic, Tucker Spencer."

He winked at her. "Glad you're impressed, sweetheart. But just so you know, I'm saving my best stuff for later."

"Oh, my," Gail whispered as Tucker made a hasty exit. She grinned at Liz. "I think my eyelashes got singed from all the electricity racing around in here."

"He's all talk," Liz said, even though her heart was pounding just a little harder from the promising hint of desire in his voice.

"Honey, sweet talk like that sooner or later explodes into something downright dangerous," Gail pointed out. "If you're not ready for it, get out of the way."

"Oh, I'm way past ready," Liz declared, her gaze following Tucker as he crossed Beach Drive and met

Walker on the opposite side, where he'd just pulled into a parking space. The two men huddled for barely a minute before Tucker climbed in and the two took off toward Montross, lights flashing.

Liz's heart skipped uneasily. She might not take Tucker's theory entirely seriously, but it was apparent that Walker did. She exchanged a look with Gail. "I suppose it would be a bad idea to lock the door and make the customers knock," she said wistfully.

"I'll call Andy," Gail said decisively. "He can work security detail around here till it's time to close. He'll be ecstatic at having something to do that requires a weapon."

As it turned out, though, Andy was on his way to Montross to consult with Walker and Tucker, he told Gail when she caught up with him on his cell phone.

"Go," Gail said, after reporting what he'd said to Liz. "We'll be fine."

She hung up slowly. "He says he'll get someone over here. He doesn't think there's really anything to worry about, though. He's confident both Willis and the Miles woman are going to be tied up with a whole lot of questions for the rest of the day."

Liz wished she felt as certain about that.

"It's going to be okay," Gail assured her. "If Andy said he'd have someone come by to keep an eye on things, he will."

Not fifteen minutes later, a car screeched to a halt outside. Liz eyed the luxury sedan with astonishment, which only increased when King lunged out of the front seat and barreled inside toting a hunting rifle.

"What on earth?" she demanded, staring at him with alarm. "King, why are you here?"

"Andy called and said he was worried about some crazy person being on the loose. He asked me to come." His gaze narrowed. "Are you the crazy person?"

"No, of course not," Gail said, interceding. "Liz is working here. Tucker and Andy think there's been a break in the case. They're just being cautious, in case the people they suspect decide to make Liz a target."

Liz watched the range of emotions that crossed King's face—from disbelief to worry to outrage. She stood silent, waiting for him to say he didn't give two hoots whether she got herself killed or not.

Instead, he sank down in one of the chairs in the café, his gun resting across his knees. "As long as I'm here, I might as well have a cup of that fancy coffee I hear you brew in here," he grumbled, the comment directed at Gail.

"I'll get you a cup right away," she said.

While she was behind the counter pouring it, Liz stood her ground. King finally met her gaze. "Look, I may not be crazy about you or the way you treated my son, but I'm not about to let you get hurt and have *that* on my conscience for the rest of my days."

Liz bit back a grin at his grudging offer of protection. "Thank you."

"Don't thank me. I'd do the same for anyone in Trinity Harbor."

"I know that," Liz said. "I'm still grateful. And, King, just so you know, I did not kill my husband."

"So everyone seems to believe," he conceded.

"What do *you* believe?" she asked point-blank.

He held his tongue for so long, she thought for sure he was going to condemn her, but he finally stared straight into her eyes, his expression enigmatic. "The

Mary Elizabeth I once knew could never have done such a thing."

Liz felt the salty sting of tears in her eyes. "I'm still that same girl," she whispered. "A little older. A little wiser." She met his gaze as the tears slid down her cheeks. "And still very much in love with your son."

After what seemed an eternity, a deep, shuddering sigh rumbled through him and he held out his arms. "Come here, girl."

Liz let the sobs come as she was enfolded in King's solid embrace. It was like being held by her grandfather again. No, she thought, it was better, because not once did King tell her that her tears were wrong. He simply let her cry herself out, then handed her a clean, white handkerchief.

"I don't suppose you have any of those lemon drops you used to keep in your pockets?" she asked with a sniff.

King chuckled. "You still remember those?"

"You used to sneak them to me when my grandfather wasn't looking," she recalled. "He didn't approve of candy. He thought it was bad for my teeth."

"Oh, he was an old fool when it came to some things. Way too set in his ways," King declared, pulling a bag of candies from his pocket and offering it to her. "The best friend a man could have, but a hard man for a little girl who'd just lost her folks."

"I loved him, though," Liz said. "I still miss him."

"So do I," King told her. "He and I shared some good times together. We disagreed about most everything, but the man knew just where to go to catch fish."

Liz sucked on the tart lemon candy in silence, thinking

about this rare moment of peace between her and Tucker's father. Eventually, she risked a look into his eyes.

"King, can we start over?"

He reached down and took her hand between his calloused hands. "Darlin' girl, we already have."

21

Cynthia Miles was cool as a cucumber as she withstood Walker's pounding questions about her presence in Trinity Harbor on the day of the murder. Tucker was impressed despite himself. Her composure was apparently the result of all those press conferences she handled for her political clients. She was seemingly unfazed by the pressure.

Walker, however, was another story. He was getting irritated by Cynthia's calm responses and her ability to remain completely unflappable. Tucker shot him a warning look, but that was the most he felt entitled to do. He was being allowed to sit in thanks to Walker's goodwill. He didn't want to test that by criticizing or trying to take over.

Andy, however, appeared to have no such qualms. "Walker, could I see you outside for a minute?" he inquired in a tone that commanded his former detective to obey.

Looking thoroughly disgruntled, Walker followed Andy from the room, which left Tucker alone with Cynthia. The temptation to turn the screws just a little was too great to resist. There was one topic Walker hadn't broached yet: those unidentified fibers on Chandler's pants that suggested he'd been intimate with someone before his death.

"You told Deputy Ames a few minutes ago that you didn't blackmail Chandler to get that money he paid you on the day he was killed," he said.

"That's right."

"But you're not denying it came from Chandler?"

"No."

"Then what did you do for it?"

She regarded him blankly. "What do you mean?"

Tucker feigned a laid-back, mostly disinterested demeanor. "Was it for services rendered?"

"I hadn't worked for Larry for years," she retorted.

"I was thinking of something a little more personal," he said.

Her jaw dropped. She was on her feet and lunging for him before he could react. "Why you low-down swine," she shouted, raking her fingers down his cheek hard enough to draw blood.

Tucker had her hands behind her back and in cuffs before she could get in a second attack. Andy and Walker charged through the door in the same instant, guns drawn.

"What the hell?" Walker demanded, eyeing his suspect's cuffed wrists. Then he caught a glimpse of Tucker's bleeding cheek and winced. "Tucker, what went on in here?"

"Ms. Miles and I were just engaging in a little casual conversation," he said mildly. "She took offense."

"He accused me of being Larry Chandler's whore,"

she snapped. "I don't tolerate that kind of accusation from anyone."

Walker regarded Tucker with surprise. "You said that?"

"I just asked how she'd earned that money she got from Chandler. She drew her own conclusions."

"Maybe you'd better wait outside," Walker suggested, barely managing to hide his amusement.

"Sure thing," Tucker said easily. "I probably ought to get a tetanus shot while I'm at it. Maybe I'll wander on over to the doctor's office."

Cynthia lunged at him again, but she was too late. He closed the door between them, then grinned at Andy, who'd stepped out with him. "I seem to have upset the lady."

"Indeed," Andy said, regarding him suspiciously. "I've got to wonder why. You usually demonstrate a bit more finesse."

"Does she strike you as a woman who responds well to finesse?" he asked. "She's a street fighter. I wanted to see if I could rattle her."

"And?" Andy asked.

"I did. She wasn't with Chandler right before he died. I'd stake my badge on it. In fact, I pity the woman who was, if Cynthia finds her before we do." He looked at Andy. "I know you like hanging around in the thick of the action, but would you mind giving me a ride back to Trinity Harbor? I need to catch up with Mary Elizabeth. I have a feeling things are going to come to a head real soon. She could be in danger."

"I'll take you," Andy said at once. "But you don't need to worry about Liz. I called in the reserves."

Tucker stared at him. "Who?"

"Your father." He chuckled at Tucker's sharp intake of breath. "Of course, I didn't exactly mention to him that it was Liz he was going to be keeping an eye on. All I said was I wanted someone to keep watch at the bookstore. He thought he was going over there to protect Gail. He took to the idea with as much enthusiasm as if I'd asked him to guard the president. Any idea why?"

"Probably because he's been looking for an excuse to try her coffee," Tucker said. "He made such a big deal about someone from outside coming in to sell books and gourmet coffee that I'm sure he hasn't dared to step into the place since she opened."

Tucker tried to imagine an armed King and Mary Elizabeth under the same roof and shuddered at the image. "I hesitate to think what his reaction was when he found Mary Elizabeth working there. You know, Thorensen, for a smart man, you have some real dumb ideas from time to time."

"You know anyone else with a hunting rifle I could have called on in a pinch?"

"Half the town," Tucker said. "Any one of them would probably have been better than my father, under these circumstances." He glanced at the speedometer and noted they were doing precisely the speed limit. "Can't you make this car go any faster?"

"What kind of example would we be setting?" Andy asked.

"I don't give a rat's behind about setting an example right now. I'd like to get back there before those two kill each other."

"They'll be fine," Andy assured him. "Unless, of course, Gail has talked them to death by now, trying to make them see reason."

It was going on five-thirty when they reached the bookstore, which was locked up tight.

"I thought Gail closed at six," Tucker said, regarding Andy worriedly.

There was a pinched expression around Andy's mouth when he nodded. "She does."

"Then why the hell is this place all locked up?" Tucker demanded, trying to peer inside. He couldn't see a sign of anything amiss, but that didn't seem to stop his heart from pounding.

"Were you planning to meet Liz here?" Andy asked.

"No," Tucker said as his memory kicked in. "I told her I'd meet her at Earlene's at five-thirty. She must have gone over there."

"You check there. I'll take a look around inside and meet you in a minute," Andy suggested.

"Good idea," Tucker agreed, already jogging down the block.

But a trip to Earlene's proved futile, as well. She hadn't seen Mary Elizabeth, Gail or King all afternoon.

"Damn," Andy muttered when Tucker filled him in. "Everything inside the bookstore looks just fine. The register's locked up. The coffeepot's turned off, so they didn't leave in a hurry. Dammit, what the hell was King thinking? I told him to stay put."

Tucker punched out the number for Cedar Hill on his cell phone. When he got the answering machine, he left a curt message, then tried Swan Ridge and left the same message there.

"Where the hell could they be?" he asked Andy, trying to keep the edge of panic from his voice.

"I'll try our house," Andy said, dialing his own cell

phone, but hanging up a moment later in frustration. "Not there, either."

"You take your car and start looking. I'll pick up mine over by the bookstore and go the opposite direction. We can stay in touch by cell phone."

"Shouldn't we call Walker and see if he can spare some deputies to start looking?"

"He's got all of them combing the area trying to hook up with Ken Willis, but I'll let him know what's going on. At least they can keep an eye out while they're on the road."

Tucker placed the call, filled Walker in, then met Andy's gaze. "I really don't like this," he said grimly.

"I'm not so crazy about it myself," Andy agreed. "But there's one thing that's keeping me from panicking."

"What's that?" Tucker asked.

"Can you see anyone getting the better of your father when he's toting a rifle?"

Tucker considered the question. His father was a crack shot. He'd taught all of them to be comfortable and responsible with guns at an early age. Even Daisy could hit a target dead-center at a hundred feet. It was scant comfort, but at least some of his tension eased when he thought of all that.

"No," he admitted. "Daddy can hold his own."

"Then it's not likely that someone has taken all three of them captive," Andy concluded. "Let's hang on to that thought. We'll probably find them sitting around somewhere sipping lemonade."

As if they'd both reached the same conclusion at the same, precise moment, they both said, "Anna-Louise's."

Tucker punched out the pastor's number. The phone

rang and rang. Anna-Louise sounded breathless when she finally picked up. "This better be important," she grumbled.

"You okay?" he asked before he stopped to consider the likely cause of her attitude.

"Tucker? What's wrong?" she said, instantly sounding more alert and less grouchy.

"Are Mary Elizabeth, Gail and my father with you, by any chance?"

"No. I'm here with Richard," she said.

Her reply pretty much confirmed Tucker's guess. He'd heard about the baby project from Bobby. It was the worst-kept secret in town thanks to his father's big mouth that night at the marina.

"I haven't heard from them. Why?" she asked.

"Nothing to worry about," he told her. "Just call me if you do happen to hear from any of them."

"Will do."

"Sorry to interrupt whatever you were doing," he said, unable to keep the amusement from threading through his voice.

"You should be," she said cheerfully. "In fact, I'm going to cross Tucker off my list of potential baby names right now."

Tucker laughed as he hung up.

"You seem awfully cheerful for a man who just hit another dead end," Andy observed.

"You have to know the whole story," Tucker said, not willing to give away any of Anna-Louise's personal business, since there was apparently at least one person who actually didn't know that she and Richard had decided they wanted to have a baby. Everyone else was already starting to place bets on how quickly there would be an announcement about a pregnancy, especially since word was that they intended to give the matter their full attention.

"Ah, the baby plan," Andy said at once, grinning. "How could I have forgotten? You're right. It's the talk of the town. I'm still not used to the way everyone in Trinity Harbor knows absolutely everything about everybody's personal business."

"Except where we can find your wife, my father and Mary Elizabeth," Tucker said. "I guess we'd better hit the road."

Andy nodded, his smile dying. "Stay in touch."

Tucker jogged back to his car and set off through town, systematically going up and down all the side streets, then making another pass along Beach Drive from the northern outskirts of town all the way to the south, including several trips past Ken Willis's house. Nothing. Not one blessed sign of any of them or their cars, though he did pass several of his deputies in the vicinity of the Willis place.

There was one street he hadn't checked, he realized as he pounded the steering wheel in frustration: Primrose Lane, Daisy's street. He'd been so certain they wouldn't turn up there, given the way his sister felt about Mary Elizabeth. Well, it was way past time for long shots, he thought, turning back toward town.

Relief swept over Tucker as he spotted his father's car, Mary Elizabeth's and Gail's all lined up on the street in front of Daisy's. Relief quickly gave way to anger that they hadn't thought to fill him in on their plans to have an impromptu gathering. He had half a mind to keep right on driving, but then Andy pulled up beside him and he was stuck. If he took off now, everyone would make way too much out of it.

"I see you had the same idea I did," Andy said as he parked and climbed out.

"It's certainly the last place I expected to find them, especially Mary Elizabeth," Tucker said.

He walked inside half-expecting to find his sister and Mary Elizabeth at each other's throats with all the others sitting around watching the brawl. Instead, he found something damned close to a tea party. Daisy was passing around cookies just out of the oven, his father was teasing Mary Elizabeth over some childhood shenanigan, Gail was bustling around refilling glasses of iced tea. Even Tommy was underfoot.

"Well, isn't this just the picture-perfect family gathering?" Tucker commented irritably. "Guess everybody forgot to invite me."

Andy put a hand on his shoulder and squeezed. "Tucker's just upset because he expected to find Liz waiting for him at Earlene's."

Mary Elizabeth had the grace to wince. "I'm sorry," she said at once. "Your father was at the store, Daisy called to see what was going on because she'd heard he was there with a rifle and the next thing you know everyone was heading over here."

Tucker looked from his father to his sister. "I thought you two weren't speaking to Mary Elizabeth."

His father shrugged. "Changed my mind."

Tucker turned to Daisy. "And you?"

"I'm withholding judgment for the time being."

At least that was a softening in her attitude, Tucker thought, grateful that some good had come out of this mess, even if his heart was just now settling back into something akin to a normal rhythm.

"Cookie?" Daisy inquired, shoving the plate under his nose and wiggling it around so he could get the full benefit of the aroma of the gooey chocolate chips. "It'll sweeten your mood."

"Have one," Mary Elizabeth encouraged, "and come over here and sit by me."

Tucker took the cookie, but hesitated over the invitation, waiting to see what King would have to say on the subject.

"Oh, go ahead, boy. You're too old for me to have to tell you what to do."

Tucker chuckled despite himself. "Since when?" He slid a chair next to Mary Elizabeth and sat down warily, still expecting an acerbic comment from Daisy at least. But beyond a slight frown, she displayed no reaction to his choice.

Within seconds the boisterous conversation around the table resumed. He touched Mary Elizabeth's arm. "You really okay?"

She turned to him with shining eyes. "Better than I have been in years," she said. "I'm back with family."

Tucker laughed. "If you consider that a blessing when you're talking about this family, you might want to have your head examined."

"Nope," she insisted, leveling a look into his eyes meant to send heat spiraling through him. "This is the only one I want."

The look, the firm declaration, had the desired effect. Need shot straight through him. "You want to get out of here?" he asked, his gaze unwavering.

"Now?"

"Right now."

A satisfied smile began tugging at her lips. "And do what?"

"Whatever strikes our fancy," he said.

"You'll have to be more specific than that," she taunted.

Tucker felt heat climbing into his cheeks. "I can't say anything else in front of this crowd," he protested.

"They're not paying a bit of attention to us," she claimed.

Tucker knew better. They might be chattering away, but every one of them had half an ear attuned to his conversation with Mary Elizabeth. Because the goal was way more important than any momentary pangs of embarrassment, he leaned close and whispered exactly what he had in mind.

Now the color was blooming in her cheeks, but she scraped back her chair and stood in one fluid motion.

"We have to go," she said, sounding decidedly breathless as she reached for his hand.

"Now?" Daisy inquired with a speculative gleam in her eyes.

"This second," Tucker confirmed.

"About time," King noted.

"Stay out of this, old man," Tucker ordered without venom. "Daisy, take that gun away from him before he accidentally shoots somebody."

Daisy dutifully removed the hunting rifle from King's grasp, unloaded it and tucked it in the pantry. She kept the ammunition in her apron pocket. Tucker noted that she'd handled the weapon without the slightest unease. He knew then that if anyone came poking around to stir up trouble, either she or her father could handle it.

"Good night, everyone," Mary Elizabeth said from the door, then dropped Tucker's hand and went back to kiss King's cheek.

"Thank you," she murmured.

"Didn't have to do much," King replied.

"You did the most important thing of all," she told him. "You forgave me."

He glanced toward Tucker. "Just see to it that you make him happy."

"I certainly intend to try," Mary Elizabeth said, then followed Tucker outside.

He caught her hand and drew her to a stop. "Think you can do that?" he asked, looking deep into her eyes. "Think you can make me happy?"

She raised a hand to his cheek, then stood on tiptoe to brush her lips across his. Tucker's blood began to pound.

"What will it take to make you happy?" she inquired softly, her breath whispering across his skin.

"This," he said as his mouth closed over hers.

She tasted sweet, but the sensations ripping through him were dark and dangerous. His pulse ricocheted wildly. When the tip of her tongue slid along the seam of his lips, then invaded, he tensed, his blood roaring. He dug his hands into the soft flesh of her butt, pulling her tight against him, his hips grinding into hers, desperate for the one thing that had been missing from his life ever since the day she'd walked away.

He wanted—he needed—to be buried deep inside her, to feel her tighten around him with velvet heat.

Her soft moan of pleasure, rather than inflaming him, brought him to his senses. Much as he wanted to put an end to his longing, they couldn't do this here, right on his sister's front lawn. People in Trinity Harbor might recover from the scandal of him being back with Larry Chandler's widow only weeks after his death, but they wouldn't be so forgiving if he and Mary Elizabeth made a public spectacle of themselves.

Still holding her close, he ended the kiss, drawing in a ragged breath and putting a discreet amount of space between them, enough to cool the flames that had been about to erupt.

"It's less than a mile to my place," he said, as much to remind himself as her. "That's as far as we have to go."

Laughter sparkled in her eyes. "Surely we can do that," she said, though she managed to sound doubtful.

"Of course we can," Tucker agreed, though he still hadn't released her.

"Maybe we should walk," she suggested. "Cool down a little."

He watched her through hooded eyes. "How fast can you walk?"

She considered the question, then grinned. "Not fast enough."

Tucker drew his gaze away from her face long enough to glance from his car to hers. "Your car's closest."

"Yeah, but it's really lousy for parking along the way in case we decide we can't make it. I'm afraid the gear-shift between the seats could do some real damage."

Tucker stared at her, then burst out laughing. "I think once we actually get in the car, we can last long enough for a five-minute drive."

"You're not worried about having my car parked in front of your house all night long?"

He heard the serious note behind the teasing question. "No, Mary Elizabeth. From here on out, I'm not afraid of anything."

She reached into her pocket, then dangled her keys in front of him. "You drive. They're less likely to arrest you for speeding."

Tucker took the keys and led the way to her sports car. Mary Elizabeth was right. He made it to his place in record time with no sign of a sheriff's deputy on his tail. The night was definitely looking better and better.

He stepped out of the car and straight into a fist that knocked his head back so hard he thought his jaw might be broken. Mary Elizabeth screamed, but Tucker was ready for the second blow. He caught the man's arm in mid-swing, wrenched it behind his back and had him up against the car even as she rounded the back end with her purse swinging. Tucker caught that in mid-swing, too. The damned thing weighed a ton.

"What the hell do you have in here? Bricks?"

"I'd rather not say," she said primly, then peered down at Tucker's assailant, who was struggling fiercely against his grasp. Her mouth gaped. "Ken Willis, have you lost your mind?"

Tucker glanced down and realized that that was exactly who had attacked him. He jerked him upright and met his gaze. "I'd like to know the answer to that, as well."

Eyes flashing with fury, Ken scowled at both of them. "I've got nothing to say without my lawyer present."

"Fine," Tucker said, hauling out his cell phone and handing it to the aspiring politician. "Tell him we'll be waiting for him right here on my front lawn, where you attacked me. I'll spend the time it takes him to arrive deciding on which charges to press. Assault on a police officer comes to mind."

"You're on leave," Ken retorted.

"Oh, I'll bet I can make it stick," Tucker said. "Especially with a witness to say you were lurking in the bushes. For all I know it was attempted murder."

Willis turned pale at that. "Come on, Tucker. You know damn well I wasn't going to kill you."

"Do I?"

"You've known me all my life. I'm not capable of violence."

"My jaw disagrees," Tucker said. He wrenched Ken's arm a little higher behind his back until he yelped in pain. "What were you doing here, Ken?"

"Getting even," he said, his breath coming in gasps. "Dammit, let me go. You're hurting me."

Tucker eased his grip slightly. "Getting even for what?"

"For what all of you are doing to Cynthia. You're hounding her."

"The sheriff's department is questioning her about a murder. That's it. We'd be questioning you, too, but no one's been able to catch up with you, as far as I know. I'll have to check with Walker on that one. See if he still wants to haul your sorry butt in."

"I won't talk to him," Ken said. "I had nothing to do with Chandler's murder. Neither did Cynthia. She loved him, for heaven's sakes."

"Is that what she told you?" Mary Elizabeth said. "Did she happen to mention that Larry had moved on, that he didn't love her?"

Ken seemed vaguely shaken by that. "If you're talking about his marriage to you, everyone knew that was just a political move. Sorry, Mary Elizabeth, but it was."

Tucker saw her flinch as if she'd been struck, but her chin came up.

"Yes," she agreed. "That is exactly what it was." She looked him directly in his eyes. "So, Ken, when did you decide to make your political move and go after Larry's seat, before or after he died?"

"After," he insisted. "As long as he was alive, there was no point. He had a lock on it in this district."

"Which means you had quite a motive for wanting him dead while you were still young enough to handle the rigors of a campaign," Tucker pointed out. He retrieved his cell phone from Ken's grip and handed it to Mary Elizabeth. "Call Walker. He should be able to get a deputy over here in five minutes or less."

"Dammit, Tucker, I didn't kill anyone."

"I'm sure Walker will let you have your say," Tucker assured him, as a sheriff's car screeched to a halt. Tucker handed over the suspect. "If he gives you any trouble, remind him that I can still change my mind about pressing assault charges."

Deputy Bucky Harris stared at him, then obviously caught sight of his swollen jaw. "Boss, don't you want to file those charges now?"

"Not just yet," Tucker said, then cast a warning look at Ken. "I'll wait to hear just how cooperative Mr. Willis is when he talks to Walker."

"That's intimidation," Ken accused as he was led away.

"Could be," Tucker agreed. "I'm willing to let a judge decide, if you are."

Ken clamped his mouth shut and got into the police cruiser without further comment.

Tucker turned to face Mary Elizabeth, who lifted her hand to his injured jaw. "Are you sure you're okay?" she asked. "Let's get some ice on that."

"The ice can wait," he said. "We wasted enough time dealing with that weasel. I have plans for the rest of the night."

Her lips curved slowly. "Do you really?"

"Oh, yeah. Want to see?"

She sighed as he scooped her up, then buried her face against his neck. "Oh, yeah," she murmured. "Show me your stuff, Sheriff. I've been waiting way too long."

22

Even if Tucker hadn't been carrying her, Liz doubted if her feet would have touched the floor. Emotionally she was floating on air. Her life was finally coming together the way it should have—with the person it should have—years ago. She was in the arms of the man she'd loved practically her whole life, even during her ill-fated marriage to another man. She wasn't proud of the fact that she'd started comparing Larry's infidelities to Tucker's deep sense of honor and commitment within months of their wedding day and found him wanting, but it was the truth. It had just taken her way too long to admit it.

It was doubly unfortunate that tragedy had struck before she was able to finalize the divorce and go back to Trinity Harbor a free woman. She might be free now, but there were still a million and one questions to be answered about Larry's death and about the future. Thankfully, though, the only question that counted tonight was whether she and Tucker could recapture the passion they had once shared. Whether it would last this time or not didn't even matter, not at this moment. Being here, with him, was right…and long overdue.

Tucker hesitated in the foyer, gazing into her eyes. "Do you want dinner? Something to drink?"

"Later," she said at once. "Much later."

He laughed, clearly relieved. "Good answer," he said, as he strode down the hall to his bedroom.

The once-familiar room still had its hunter-green carpet and comforter that she had chosen. The seascapes she'd found at a boardwalk art show in Colonial Beach remained on the walls. And, she noted with surprise, a snapshot of the two of them continued to sit on the dresser. Had it been there weeks ago, on the night she'd crawled into his bed? She had been so distraught that night that she hadn't noticed her surroundings at all, at least not beyond Tucker's scent on the pillows.

"I got that picture out of my dresser drawer the day after you turned up here," Tucker said, answering her question without her having to ask. "I had put it away, but I couldn't get rid of it after you left to marry Chandler. How pitiful is that?"

She brushed the hair back from his forehead and kissed him there. "I think it's sweet."

"It is not sweet to pine for someone for six long years, even after she's chosen another man," he said with apparent self-disgust. "It's pathetic."

"Maybe you just knew in your heart that I'd come back," she told him. "I wish I'd had the strength to do it years ago, as soon as I knew what a mistake I'd made."

He gave her a wry smile. "Yeah, that would have been nice, Mary Elizabeth. It would have made the last few years a lot less lonely."

"I'm here now, Tucker. Let's not waste another second."

He lowered her to her feet then, her body sliding along his. She could feel the hard thrust of his arousal, and instantly her body was on fire, melting inside. Her fingers fumbled at the buttons of her blouse, but he brushed them aside, his gaze intent as he bent over the task.

The scrape of his fingers over her skin seared her, setting off a tingling that began in her belly and traveled lower, filling her with a sweet yearning.

He parted her blouse, then pressed a trail of hot, needy kisses along the curve of her breast, finally taking the lace-covered nipple into his mouth in a way that had her knees going weak.

"Oh, Tucker," she murmured, her back arching.

He flipped open her bra, sliding the satin and lace off slowly, provocatively, until her breasts were exposed to his dark, heated gaze. He circled the tips with his tongue, then drew the peak deep into his mouth in a suckling gesture that made her cry out. His gaze, filled with worry, flew to hers.

"No," she said. "More, Tucker. Please."

"Oh, there will be more," he promised. "Much, much more."

When he had her breasts damp and aching, his kisses roamed lower, even as he released the catch on her slacks and slowly, oh so slowly, lowered the zipper. The rasping sound, the skimming caress of his knuckles against her bare skin, had her most intimate muscles clenching in anticipation.

When his fingers slipped past the silky barrier of her panties and slid into moist heat, her hips moved restlessly and fire licked through her blood. A fleeting, teasing caress of the sensitive bud of her arousal almost took her over the edge.

As wondrous and demanding as the sensation was, Liz wanted more. She wanted this first time after so many years to be complete, with Tucker buried deep inside her. She wanted the two of them to come together, a uniting that was both sensual and symbolic.

Her breathing ragged, she backed away from his touch, smiling at his questioning look.

"Not just yet," she told him as she reached for the hem of his shirt and began easing it up. Her mouth followed along behind, pressing kisses to heated flesh that rippled over hard, tensed muscles.

"You're destroying me," he murmured, even as he surrendered to the assault.

"Good. That's the idea. I want you weak and under my spell," she told him, then ran her tongue around his masculine nipples.

"Isn't it enough that I've already admitted I've been under your spell despite the fact you'd left me?" he asked, groaning as she tweaked a crisp, dark hair on his chest.

She reached for his belt buckle, then slid her hand lower, inside denim and jockey shorts, stopping just short of making contact with his pulsing arousal. Her gaze locked with his, relishing the smoldering heat in his eyes.

"No, this is more what I had in mind," she said, clasping him and watching his eyes drift shut, listening to his breath hitch and his moan of pleasure.

"How am I doing?" she murmured.

"Uncle," he said, lifting her up and tumbling onto the bed with her. "I surrender."

Her plan to taunt went up in flames as need rocketed through both of them. Clothes flew off, arms and legs tangled, their bodies came together in a rush of desperate urgency. Each thrust of his body deep inside her had her hips rising off the bed to meet him, seeking the exquisite release that was tantalizingly just out of reach.

Just when she thought she might scream out in frustration, he slowed, met her gaze. Amazingly, rather than diminishing, the tension escalated until every nerve in her body was coiled with anticipation. Their gazes held, communicating everything—their passion, the years of lonely separation, the love that had never died.

And then he plunged into her once more, deeper than before, and the tension shattered into a million brilliant, sparkling sensations.

Liz was still trembling when Tucker's mouth covered hers in the sweetest, tenderest kiss they'd ever shared.

"I love you, Mary Elizabeth," he said, looking deep into her eyes.

Shaken more than she wanted to admit by the admission, she merely touched a hand to his cheek. The dark, masculine end-of-the-day stubble stirred whole new sensations. "Oh, Tucker," she whispered. "What did I ever do to deserve you?"

He grinned at that. "There are some who'd say I'm the lucky one. You're out of my league."

"Never," she insisted fiercely. "I never believed that. Don't you dare think it."

"A perfect match, then?"

She nodded happily at that. "A perfect match."

"We're still going to bump up against a few problems," he warned, his hand resting comfortably on the curve of her hip.

"They'll all be a piece of cake compared to what we've already been through."

He touched a finger to her lips. "I'm serious, darlin'. My family may have come around, but there's still going to be talk. I have voters to answer to."

"You're the best sheriff this county has ever had. Just let anyone try to say otherwise," she said heatedly.

"What are you going to do, punch them in the nose?"

"If necessary," she vowed.

"Then I'd have to arrest you."

She rolled to her knees and straddled him. "Would you use handcuffs?" she inquired curiously.

A laugh rumbled deep in Tucker's throat. "Don't even go there, please."

Liz leaned down and kissed the base of his throat, where his pulse was ricocheting wildly once again. "Conjuring up an interesting image, am I?"

"Oh, yeah," he said, flipping her and capturing her wrists and holding them above her head. "Something like this." He bent and began an assault on her breasts that had her writhing.

"Uncle," she whispered without much strength.

"Surrender's a damn sweet thing, isn't it?" he murmured, as he once again led her straight to the edge of a cliff and over in an explosion that left them both gasping for breath.

"It's entirely possible I will never move again," Liz said when she could finally speak.

"Then don't," Tucker answered readily. "I've finally got you back in my bed."

"I was here not that long ago," she reminded him.

"But I wasn't beside you." His gaze held hers. "As far as I'm concerned, there's no reason you ever need to leave."

It took the insistent ringing of the phone to finally jerk Tucker awake in the middle of the night. Mary Elizabeth was still curved tightly against him, her hand resting on his stomach. He was pretty sure he'd have been content to stay just like this for the rest of his life.

Unfortunately, whoever was calling at—he squinted at the clock and saw it was just after 3:00 a.m.—at this unholy hour had better have a damn good reason.

"What?" he growled into the receiver.

"You'd better haul your butt out of bed and get out to Swan Ridge," Walker said unceremoniously.

Tucker shot up onto one elbow, disturbing Mary Elizabeth, who murmured a protest, then rolled over and snuggled back into the pillow. "What happened?"

"Somebody just tried to burn the place down."

"How bad is it?"

"The fire department was fast. It hadn't spread much beyond the library, but there's a lot of smoke damage to the rest of the downstairs."

"A cover-up?" Tucker asked. "You think the murderer was afraid we might find something more if we did another search of the place?"

"Either that or it was pure spite," Walker said. He hesitated before adding, "There's one other possibility."

Tucker knew exactly where Walker was heading. "You think the perp might have hoped to trap Mary Elizabeth inside, don't you?"

"The thought crossed my mind," Walker admitted.

"Where are Willis and the Miles woman?"

"Both accounted for," Walker assured him. "Willis is safely tucked in at home. Cynthia Miles is at the motel. I've got men watching both of them."

"Well, hell," Tucker said, unhappy with the fact there the answer wasn't going to be so obvious. "I'll be there in ten minutes."

"You going to bring Liz along?"

Tucker supposed the question wasn't entirely unexpected, since everyone at Daisy's had seen the two of them leave together the night before, but the underlying thread of amusement in Walker's voice grated.

"I'll see if I can locate her," Tucker said wryly.

"Try rolling over," Walker retorted, then wisely hung up before Tucker could tell him what he could do to himself.

Tucker slowly replaced the receiver in its cradle, then turned to meet Mary Elizabeth's worried gaze. She was wide-awake and frowning.

"Something's wrong, isn't it?" she asked.

Tucker didn't even attempt to cushion the blow. "Someone set a fire at Swan Ridge. It's out now."

She swallowed hard. "How bad…how bad is it?"

"The damage is confined mostly to your grandfather's library, but we need to get over there."

Even though she blinked back tears, she nodded at once and shot out of bed, reaching for her clothes. Tucker went after her. "Mary Elizabeth."

"What?" she asked, shrugging away from his touch. "I'm okay."

He turned her to face him and saw the tears tracking down her cheeks. "You are not okay. This is more than anyone could be expected to handle and be okay. That room was…"

"It was where my husband was killed," she said vehemently. "It would never have meant the same thing to me, anyway."

He held her tight when she would have wriggled away. "But when you were a kid, all you talked about was how much you liked slipping in there while your grandfather was working, smoking his pipe." He felt a shudder wash over her and knew that he was right. She was more shaken than she wanted him to know. "Talk to me, Mary Elizabeth. Let it out."

For an instant, he thought she might remain stoically silent, but then she sighed and rested her head against his chest. The tears she'd fought to hold back were damp against his bare skin.

"The scent of his tobacco was still in the drapes," she whispered, her voice quaking. "They were dark and dreary and awful, but I didn't want to take them down because of that. Isn't that crazy?"

"We all cling to something that helps us remember," he told her. "After my mother died, I snuck into her room and found this scarf she used to wear. It smelled like her perfume. I kept it tucked under my pillow for months. Somehow, not one of the housekeepers King hired ever took it away when they changed the bed. It was always there until finally the scent faded and I put it away."

She regarded him with luminous eyes. "Do you still have it?"

"In my dresser drawer," he admitted. "I kept it with your picture."

Suddenly she chuckled. "White silk with splashy pink roses on it," she said, describing it perfectly.

"You've seen it?"

"When I was looking for a T-shirt to put on the night I came over here. I didn't see the picture. I was afraid the scarf belonged to a new woman in your life."

"No," he told her, regarding her somberly. "To one I didn't want to forget." He tucked a finger under her chin. "But you know something? You don't need things to remember the people you love. They're in your heart forever."

She sighed heavily. "You're right. I guess I'd forgotten that because I never had anything at all to remind me of my parents, and eventually I started to forget what they'd looked like, how they sounded."

"Because you were young when they died and your grandfather never did anything to help you keep them alive."

"He refused to bring anything back from Europe. And he wouldn't answer any of my questions. I think it hurt him too much to talk about them," she said. "I didn't see that then, but I understand it now." She kissed his cheek. "Thank you for reminding me that memories are more important than objects."

"Anytime."

"Tucker, I didn't say this last night because I didn't want you to think I was saying it just because you did, but I do love you."

"I know, Mary Elizabeth. In my heart, I always believed that you just got sidetracked for a while."

She nodded. "That's exactly right. I got sidetracked, but now I'm home."

A half hour later, when they got to Swan Ridge, they found the library was, indeed, a smoldering ruin. Aside from the scent of smoke that was thick in some of the closest downstairs rooms, the rest of the stately old house had survived intact.

As Tucker and Mary Elizabeth returned from their survey of the interior, Walker met them on the back patio.

"I see you found her okay?" he said, his eyes twinkling.

"Go to hell," Tucker retorted. "You find proof this is arson?"

"The fire chief has his suspicions, but can't say conclusively, at least not yet. I'm inclined to get the state police in here to make a final determination. It looks to me as if the blaze started smack in the center of the room, right where we found Chandler's body." He regarded Mary Elizabeth apologetically. "Sorry."

She nodded calmly, but she clutched Tucker's hand a little tighter.

"How far has word spread about those fibers you found and where you found them?" Tucker asked.

"Beyond revealing the fact that we have some forensic evidence, I haven't said a thing about them," Walker replied, his expression turning thoughtful.

"Which means that only a limited number of people know, or should know, what you have and what conclusions we drew."

"Didn't you toss that information in Cynthia Miles's face the other day?" Walker asked.

"I skirted around it," Tucker told him. "Besides, you're certain she was accounted for last night."

"Unless she slipped past my deputy, and if she did, he's not admitting it," Walker said. "I've checked with him to confirm that she stayed put. Ditto with the man I've got on Willis. He said the only person who left the house at all last night was Willis's wife."

Even as the words left Walker's mouth, Tucker muttered a curse. "Arlene Willis left home? What time was that? Did he see her come back?"

Walker had apparently leapt to the same conclusion. He was already punching a number into his cell phone. As soon as he had the deputy on the line, he bit out a string of terse questions, followed by a string of expletives that had Liz staring at him in shock and Tucker regarding him with commiseration.

"Mrs. Willis left the house at midnight. She's still not back," he told them. He called the station and told Michele to issue an all-points bulletin.

"If she's still in the area, we'll find her," he said, his expression grim.

Tucker turned to Mary Elizabeth. "Do you think Larry and Arlene knew each other?"

"She was beautiful. Her husband was politically ambitious," she said dryly. "Of course he knew her."

"Had he been having an affair with her?" Walker asked more bluntly than Tucker could have brought himself to.

Mary Elizabeth started to shake her head, then sighed. "I don't know. I thought down here he would be more discreet, but I was probably deluding myself."

"While everyone's out looking for Arlene, why don't you haul Willis back in for questioning?" Tucker suggested. "Maybe we've been asking all the wrong questions. We thought he might want Chandler dead because he wanted his job. Maybe it wasn't that at all."

He regarded Mary Elizabeth with sympathy, then said, "Maybe he wanted him dead because Chandler was involved with his wife."

23

Frances had been keeping King dangling for days now. He'd finally managed to pop the question the night they'd had dinner at the marina. He'd taken her for a walk along the water, kissed her thoroughly, and then, with the full moon shining down on them, he'd asked her once again to marry him. He'd been pretty pleased with himself at having the right romantic setting and mood for his declaration this time, but Frances had merely gazed at him thoughtfully and said she'd like more time to think about it. If anyone in his family learned about that, King would never hear the end of it. He was happier than ever that he'd kept his mouth shut about his intentions to propose.

"What the devil is there to think about?" he'd snapped, then retracted the question at once. He had to keep his eye on the prize and not get all caught up with having his pride hurt. "I'm sorry, Frances. You take all the time you want."

She'd regarded him with approval then, and suggested that perhaps in the meantime, he'd like to come home with her.

"Well, of course I'll take you home. I brought you, didn't I?"

To his astonishment, a little smile had tugged at her lips.

"I'm not sure you're grasping my meaning," she'd told him.

King was still reeling over that one, and over the fact that he'd turned her down. He thought it had been damned noble of him, telling her that she deserved more than a casual fling, especially since at one time he'd suggested the precise same thing himself. Since she still hadn't told him she wanted more than that, he was beginning to wonder if he'd gotten it all wrong yet again. Damn, but women were confusing!

At least Tucker and Mary Elizabeth seemed to be on the right track. And the talk around town about the two of them was dying down. King didn't have many worries left where they were concerned. He expected to have all of his children happily settled down before the year was out. Maybe this grandbaby project of his could finally get underway.

"What's on your mind, old man?" Pete Dexter inquired, sliding into the booth opposite him at Earlene's. "You look as if all those wheels in your head are spinning a hundred miles an hour."

"Just thinking about how life throws you a curve when you're least expecting it," King said, thinking of Frances again.

"Has that boy of yours gone and done something foolish?" Pete asked.

"If you're referring to Tucker, he doesn't do foolish things," King said crankily.

"That's not what you were saying when Liz Chandler first got back to town and dragged him into that mess," Pete reminded him.

"You all talking about the murder again?" Frank Davis asked as he joined them. "I hear they're about to make an arrest this morning. There was a fire over at Swan Ridge last night, and they're pretty sure they know who did that and how it's connected to the murder."

Alarmed by the announcement, King promptly pushed past his friend. "I've got to go."

"Where?" the two men demanded. "The fire's out."

"Not the one I'm concerned about," King said, knowing that Tucker and Mary Elizabeth were going to be caught up in whatever the heck was going on. No matter how things were shaping up, they were going to need people to stand by 'em, and he intended to be first in line.

"I thought you were meeting Frances here," Pete said.

"Did I say that?" King demanded irritably.

"No, but isn't that the way it's been lately?" Pete asked. "We haven't finished a conversation in weeks before you go slinking off to sit with her."

"Then today will be no different," King retorted, then hesitated. It was true he had been meeting Frances here most mornings. It wasn't like they had plans. It had just worked out that way. She might wonder where he'd gone off to. "If Frances comes in, tell her I've gone to Swan Ridge. Explain it's an emergency."

Pete and Frank shook their heads.

"When are you going to marry that woman and get it over with?" Frank asked. "Then you could have these conversations over your own breakfast table and leave us out of it."

King scowled. "Will you tell her or not?"

"Go," Pete said, waving him off impatiently. "We'll make sure Frances knows you're off meddling again."

King started to take exception to that, but he didn't have time to waste. If the Chandler murder case was about to come together, he wanted to be there to make absolutely certain that Mary Elizabeth wasn't the one behind bars. He was as convinced of her innocence as Tucker was, but he and his son had been wrong about her a time or two. He just prayed this wasn't another one of those times.

He was hurrying out the door when he ran into Frances. He gave her a thorough kiss that had her staring hard at him, then said, "I'm in a hurry. Pete will explain."

"If you're going to Swan Ridge," she said at once, "then I'm coming with you."

"You already know about the fire?"

"Anna-Louise called me a half hour ago—Richard heard about it on the police scanner. Actually, I was coming to tell you. We can take my car. It's closer."

King chafed at getting in a car with Frances behind the wheel. She tended to drive her sporty little convertible like a reckless teenager. It was a wonder she hadn't wrapped it around a tree before now. Unfortunately, it was right in front of Earlene's, illegally parked and running. His car was half a block away, since he tried not to park in a fire lane, the way Frances currently was.

"By all means," he said, climbing into the passenger seat and pulling his sunglasses from his pocket. Maybe if he closed his eyes, he wouldn't notice how fast she was taking the curves on the narrow, winding road to Swan Ridge.

Frances climbed behind the wheel, put the car into

gear and peeled out of her illegal parking spot. When she hit the outskirts of town, she glanced at him.

"You can open your eyes now," she said with barely concealed amusement.

"They're not closed," he lied.

"If a man fibs about the little things, he'll fib about the big ones," she said.

His gaze snapped open then, and he ripped off his sunglasses to prove it. "I have never lied to you, Frances. Never."

She regarded him with satisfaction, then nodded slowly. "In that case, the answer's yes."

"Yes?" he repeated. "What the devil was the question? Stop talking in riddles, woman."

She slammed on the brakes, turned and stared straight into his eyes. "Yes, I will marry you, King Spencer."

Mouth gaping, he stared at her. When her words finally sank in, he let out a whoop. "If I weren't in such a blasted hurry, I'd haul you over here and kiss you till your head started spinning," he declared.

She laughed, the happiest sound he'd heard in ages.

"I do love you, you know," she told him.

"And I you," he said, regarding her seriously.

"So," she said, "where's my ring?"

"Same place it's been for the past couple of weeks," he said. "In my pocket."

"Well?"

"You want me to pull it out while we're half-parked in the middle of the highway?" he asked incredulously.

She pretended to consider the question thoughtfully, then nodded. "Yes, I think I do."

King reached for the ring even as he glanced over

his shoulder and saw that cars were slowing to a stop on the road behind them. Let 'em wait, he thought as he plucked the velvet box from his pocket and removed the diamond inside. It caught the morning sun and sparkled brilliantly. Frances gasped.

"It's beautiful," she whispered. "I never expected anything so extravagant."

"I wanted something that suited you," he said softly. "And this captures the sparkle in your eyes."

Her eyes welled with tears. "King Spencer, sometimes you say the most romantic things."

She held out her hand and he slipped the ring on her finger, just as the horns behind them began to honk impatiently. People in these parts were used to slowing down behind farm equipment, but not to coming to a complete stop for no reason at all. He stood up and shouted at the closest driver.

"Pipe down. Can't you see I'm getting engaged?"

To his chagrin, it was Richard who poked his head out of the car, a grin splitting his face. He snapped a picture of the scene before King realized what he was about to do.

"Now that is front-page news!" Richard shouted back, giving him a thumbs-up.

King glanced at Frances and saw that her cheeks were flushed with embarrassment. "Nothing to worry about, darling woman. I have a feeling when push comes to shove, the fire at Swan Ridge and the arrest of Chandler's murderer are going to be bigger news than the two of us deciding to get hitched."

"Maybe so," she said, laughing suddenly. "But this traffic jam we're causing may just rate a headline below the fold. We'd better go."

"Not until I've kissed you to seal the deal," he said, tucking a finger under her chin and pressing a chaste kiss to her lips. "I'll do it right a little later."

He peered back at Richard. "Did you get that shot, too?" he hollered.

The *Trinity Harbor Weekly* editor leaned out and grinned. "What do you think? I keep telling you I'm a damned fine journalist."

"Not if you're more interested in snapping pictures of me and Frances than you are in getting out to Swan Ridge where the action is," King said, just as Frances sedately put the car into Drive and then shot down the highway, going full throttle and leaving Richard in her dust.

King laughed. Damned if this wasn't turning into the best morning of his life.

Tucker was getting tired of the sordid mess that was Larry Chandler's life. If their assumption was right and he had been mixed up with Arlene Willis, it was just one more example of Chandler's poor judgment and his humiliating treatment of his wife.

Over the weeks, as more and more things had come to light, Tucker was increasingly astounded that Mary Elizabeth had stuck with Chandler as long as she had.

As they waited at Swan Ridge for word on whether the police had brought in Willis or his wife, Tucker also considered something else for the first time. Given everything that Chandler had been up to in his personal and his professional life—the affairs, the shady business dealings—Mary Elizabeth had to have known that she would never be the only suspect in the case, not the way she'd implied the night she'd come to him for help.

All of which begged the question, why had she come to him, especially given their past history? Was it at all possible that she'd wanted something more than his help? It was something he needed to get into with her later. For now, he was just keeping a watchful eye on her as she roamed through the downstairs rooms at Swan Ridge, her expression increasingly sad.

Eventually she came to him, looking unbearably lost and alone. At least that's what he thought until he saw the glint of resolve in her eyes.

"I've come to a decision," she told him, her voice wavering. "Once this is over, I'm going to get rid of Swan Ridge. It's not really a home. It's a mausoleum."

Tucker's heart seemed to stop beating. "And do what?" he asked.

Her gaze met his. "That depends on a lot of things."

"Such as?"

She shook her head. "Now's not the time to talk about it." Suddenly her expression faltered. "Oh, my gosh, I was supposed to meet Daisy this morning to look at property for the youth center and to get our committee started. How could I have forgotten that?"

"Sweetheart, I'm sure she knows all about the fire. Walker came from home."

"I suppose, but I should call her. I don't want her to think I'm standing her up, not when we're just beginning to make progress with our friendship."

"Want me to call her?" Tucker offered, just as he glanced up and spotted a parade of people coming around the corner of the house. His father and Frances were in front, hand in hand, he noted. They were followed by Richard, and then by Daisy. He reached for

Mary Elizabeth's shoulders and turned her. "I don't think you have anything to worry about."

His sister's steps faltered when she saw Mary Elizabeth, but then her chin shot up, much as Mary Elizabeth's had earlier. She marched across the patio, reached up and touched Mary Elizabeth's cheek. "You okay? I would have come sooner, but I had to get Tommy up and take him over to Jenna's. Bobby's taking him and Darcy fishing this morning."

"I'm okay," Mary Elizabeth said, then added, "better now that you're here. I was just about to call you to apologize for forgetting about our plans to get started on the youth center project today."

"We can do that anytime," Daisy said. She nodded toward the house. "How bad is it?"

"Not as horrible as it could have been," Mary Elizabeth said. "I'll take you on the grand tour, though they don't want me in my grandfather's library. It's a crime scene, and they're not sure about structural damage."

"Whatever's damaged can be fixed," Daisy said, looping an arm around Mary Elizabeth's shoulders as they went off to survey the damage again.

"I'll come, too," Frances said, giving Mary Elizabeth's hand a squeeze.

As the three of them walked inside, Tucker thought about the irony of the situation. In the midst of losing a part of her past, Mary Elizabeth had finally found the friendships she'd been craving.

Tucker turned away and spotted his father watching the women as they left.

"So, Daddy, how are things with you and Frances?" he inquired. "Something seemed different just now."

"She accepted my proposal," King said, looking a little dazed. "Did it right out on the highway about ten minutes ago. She caused a traffic jam for at least a mile, since she came to a stop in the middle of the road to say yes."

Tucker laughed at the image. "Somehow that seems suitable."

"Doesn't it, though?" King agreed. "My life's certainly not going to be dull, that's for sure."

"I truly am happy for you," Tucker told him with heartfelt sincerity.

"Thank you, son. You think your brother and sister will feel the same way?"

"I know they will. Bobby will just be disappointed that he wasn't first on the scene. He kept thinking it was going to happen at the marina—even started a pool on it."

"He didn't?" King said, clearly scandalized at the thought. Then he chuckled. "Serves him right that he'll be the last to know." He shot a warning look at Tucker. "And don't you be the one to tell him, either. Let's wait and let him find out from the front page of the paper."

Tucker regarded him with confusion. "You're expecting coverage?"

King grinned. "Richard was in the car right behind us out on the highway. Unless Walker gives him a bigger scoop, he claims the engagement will be front-page news this week." His gaze narrowed. "So, son, what do you think? Am I going to get bumped off the front page?"

"If that's your way of asking if there's been a break in the case, I can't say. You'll have to ask Walker."

"That's a waste of time," King said, his disgust plain. "He's even more tight-lipped about police business than you are."

"A trait I sincerely respect," Tucker said. "Now if

you'll excuse me, I think I'll go wish Frances luck. She's going to need it."

"What about me?"

"She said yes. You've already had better luck than you deserve," Tucker told him, then gave him a hug. "Congratulations, old man!"

King regarded him slyly. "You hurry things along with Mary Elizabeth, and we can make it a double ceremony."

"You worry about your own love life. Leave mine to me," Tucker retorted as he walked away.

"Must mean you finally have one, at least," King called after him.

"I'm not talking," Tucker said emphatically.

His father's laughter followed him inside. Tucker wished he could be as cheerful about his prospects for the future. Instead, all he could think about was what Mary Elizabeth intended to do once she sold Swan Ridge and no longer had any ties to Trinity Harbor.

Liz needed some space. Every time she walked through the rooms at Swan Ridge, she was filled with an almost unbearable sorrow at the thought of leaving it behind. But there were almost as many sad memories here as good ones. And most of the good ones had to do with Tucker. She could make new memories with him, wherever they were.

Assuming he wanted a future with her. She didn't think that was an unreasonable leap of faith to take after what had happened last night.

She slipped out of the house, leaving Daisy and Frances pondering an idea she had had about turning Swan Ridge into the proposed youth center. Granted it wasn't in the center of town, but they could always offer a shuttle service, if need be. And the spacious, tree-covered grounds were perfect for running and playing. A baseball field and basketball courts could be carved out of the nearby land. There was already a pool in back, and there were more than enough rooms inside for crafts and other activities, even for classroom space. She had a feeling even her grandfather might have approved of that use for the stately old home that was far too big for a woman alone, or even one with the sizable family she contemplated having with Tucker eventually.

She glanced up at the cloudless sky as she strolled beneath the shadowy trees toward the Potomac. "So, what do you think, Grandfather? Would you mind very much if I did this for the town and for me?"

The wink of sunlight on the river seemed to answer her, or at least she chose to think it did. "All right, then. If everyone agrees, that's what I'm going to do."

"They say that talking to yourself is a sign of madness," a chilly feminine voice said from somewhere in the shadows.

Liz's nerves jumped, but she tried very hard not to react visibly. She recognized the voice, even though she hadn't heard it in years.

"Hello, Arlene," she replied evenly, as if she were welcoming company to her home. "Why don't you come out where I can see you?"

"I think I like this better," Arlene said. "I have the advantage, for once."

The unconcealed bitterness in the remark threw Liz. She couldn't ever recall being in competition with Arlene Willis, or Arlene Hathaway, as she had been back in high school.

"Is that why you set the fire?" she asked, amazed at how calmly she could ask the question. "To get even for some old slight?"

Arlene's laugh was brittle. "You've got to be kidding."

"Why, then?"

"It was just a little reminder," she said, finally confirming that she had, indeed, been the arsonist. "Something to make you sit up and take notice that I was going to take everything from you, the way you took it from me."

Genuinely puzzled, Liz said, "What did I ever take from you, Arlene?"

"My future," she replied with total seriousness.

"I don't understand."

"Ken and I had it all mapped out. He was going to go to law school, then run for office. He would have owned this county—if *you* hadn't ruined everything. Do you have any idea how I hated you for that? Instead of being important, the way we'd planned, people looked at us as losers after Larry trounced Ken in that first election. That destroyed Ken's self-esteem—he hasn't been the same since. And it's all because of you."

Alarm began to make Liz's palms sweat. Funny how she hadn't been scared at first, but now, hearing Arlene's crazed thinking, she realized she wasn't dealing with an old classmate who was rational, but one who was genuinely disturbed and dangerous.

"Tell me how I ruined things," Liz suggested, praying that if she kept Arlene talking, Tucker would eventually notice her absence and come looking for her. "What did I do?"

"You married Larry Chandler, an outsider with absolutely no ties to this region," Arlene said with the disdain many people felt about the "come-heres"—everyone who hadn't been born and bred in the Northern Neck and couldn't trace their ties back at least a generation or two.

"You legitimized him, you and your grandfather," Arlene went on. "He had money and charm, and after the wedding, he had the Swan family power behind him. Ken and I never stood a chance after that. I knew then that the only thing left to do was to destroy your marriage, the way you'd destroyed mine when you ruined our dream."

"How? By having an affair with my husband?" Liz said. "Were you one of the other women, Arlene? Was that part of your revenge, sleeping with my husband? How was that supposed to help Ken?"

"It was too late to help Ken. I wanted Larry for myself. I wanted to go all the places he could take me. I wanted what you'd stolen from me—the power, the success, the money."

Now Liz was totally confused. "Then why did you shoot him? You did kill him, didn't you, Arlene?"

Rather than replying, Arlene laughed. The sound was oddly shrill. It sent a shiver of foreboding chasing down Liz's spine.

Then Arlene stepped out of the shadows, and the day went from bad to worse. A bright glare momentarily blinded Liz, and the first hint of panic made her breath freeze in her throat as she tried to understand what had sent the blinding light into her eyes. Arlene shifted her stance until Liz could catch a clear glimpse of her.

The woman was holding a very deadly-looking gun, aimed directly at Liz's chest. Given what she had almost certainly done to Larry, Liz hadn't the slightest doubt in her mind that Arlene was perfectly capable of pulling the trigger.

24

Eager to offer his congratulations to Frances and bored with his role of observer rather than investigator, Tucker went inside and found Daisy and Frances had been joined by Gail Thorensen and Anna-Louise. They were deeply engrossed in an excited discussion about something. Normally he would have been curious about that, but he was more concerned because there was no sign of Mary Elizabeth. She'd been in an odd mood ever since she'd seen the destruction in her grandfather's library. He didn't think she ought to be left alone.

"Hey, ladies, where is Mary Elizabeth?" he asked, interrupting the conversation.

"She said she needed some space," Daisy told him. "Which probably means she headed down to the river, just the way she always used to."

Tucker stared at his sister with dismay. "And you let her go off by herself? How long ago?"

Immediately Daisy regarded him with the kind of concern that came from years of reading his moods.

"Of course alone. She went out about twenty minutes ago. Why? Is there a problem?"

"There's a damned killer on the loose," he retorted. "Yeah, you could say there's a problem."

"I'll find Walker," Daisy said at once.

Tucker was already running, cursing Mary Elizabeth's stubborn determination to go on as if nothing were amiss. What had she been thinking?—especially after that fire during the night. She had to recognize the danger.

Praying that he was being unnecessarily cautious, he stayed in the shadow of the trees, finally slowing his steps so that he wouldn't sound like a herd of elephants crashing through the woods and give himself away if a killer was with Mary Elizabeth. He was halfway to the river when he heard Mary Elizabeth's quiet, reasonable voice counterpointed against Arlene Willis's desperate, shrill tones.

"Hang in there, darlin'," he murmured to himself. "You're handling her exactly right."

He reached behind him and took his gun from the waistband of his jeans, even as he moved closer to the sound of their voices. When he finally caught a glimpse of the two women, his heart leapt into his throat. The heavy gun Arlene was pointing at Mary Elizabeth was beginning to waver in her increasingly unsteady grip. Her face was pale and drawn, her eyes filled with the primal desperation of a trapped animal.

Worse, Mary Elizabeth was smack in his line of fire, and he had absolutely no maneuvering room. From this point on, any move he made was likely to be spotted by Arlene, who was facing directly toward him.

If only he could somehow signal his presence to

Mary Elizabeth alone, he thought without much hope. He wasn't a great believer in the power of ESP.

"I really have no choice, you see," Arlene said to Mary Elizabeth, as if reasoning with a recalcitrant child and trying to explain why a spanking would hurt her more than the kid. "I have to end this here and now. You have to understand what you did to me, to my marriage. You were the one who drove me into Larry's arms. When Ken found out, he threatened to divorce me. That would have been the perfect solution, if only I could have talked Larry into marrying me, but he said he wouldn't, that he only loved you."

"But I was divorcing him," Liz said. "You would have had your chance, Arlene."

Arlene shook her head. "Don't you see, it didn't matter. He still loved you. He told me so that last night. He said he'd come back to Swan Ridge to convince you to try again. Even after he made love to me right there in your house, he still wanted you."

For one desperate second, Tucker wondered if there was time to get Willis in here to try to reason with his wife, but Arlene's obviously precarious mental state suggested there was no time to be lost.

"I can make it right," Mary Elizabeth was saying. "I can help you now. I can campaign for Ken, tell people that he's the man Larry would want to replace him."

"You're lying," Arlene scoffed. "You would never do that."

"Of course I would," Mary Elizabeth said quietly. "I've known both of you practically my whole life. Why wouldn't I help you? Put the gun down, Arlene, and let's talk about this, see what we can work out. Maybe we can be a team."

If anything, Arlene tightened her grip on the gun. “No way,” she said. “It’s a trick. Why would you do that when you know I came back that night and killed Larry? I’m not stupid, you know.”

“I know that,” Liz said. “Weren’t you the kid with the four-point average all through school? I know how smart you are, Arlene.”

For an instant Tucker thought he detected a hint of uncertainty in Arlene’s eyes, but then she shook her head. “No. I have to do this my way. It’s too late now. Everyone’s going to know I shot Larry. I’ll go to jail. It’s over for me, but at least I can make sure that you’ll never get what you want again.”

“It’s never too late,” Mary Elizabeth insisted, as if Arlene hadn’t just revealed herself as a murderer. “I ought to know. I’m getting a second chance with Tucker, a chance I didn’t deserve. You and Ken can have a second chance, too.”

Tears began to roll down Arlene’s cheeks, but she remained stubbornly defiant, utterly determined to complete the mission she’d set for herself of making Mary Elizabeth pay for some perceived hurt. Tucker hadn’t pieced together all of it, but it was obvious that Arlene saw herself as being in some sort of competition with Mary Elizabeth, a competition in which she had repeatedly come out the loser.

Come on, Mary Elizabeth, he thought. Keep her talking. With luck, this would drag on, Daisy would locate Walker and Tucker would have the backup he desperately needed.

In the meantime, though, the clouds that had been gathering on the horizon for the past hour turned darker. The wind kicked up, churning the river into a white-capped froth. They were in for a doozy of a storm. Tucker couldn't decide if that would work to his advantage or against him.

A sudden flash of light split the sky, and a rumble of thunder answered him. Already jumpy, Arlene whirled as if there had been a shot fired, her own gun shooting wildly, then falling from her hand. Mary Elizabeth instinctively dropped to the ground and rolled, grabbing the gun almost before Arlene realized she had dropped it. When she saw that Mary Elizabeth was holding the weapon, a resigned look spread across her face.

"Kill me," she pleaded. "Go ahead and shoot me."

Tucker stepped out then, handcuffs in hand. "No one's going to shoot anyone," he said, snapping them on her wrists, even as he surveyed Mary Elizabeth from head to toe to reassure himself that she was okay. She still hadn't lowered the gun, and her gaze was locked on Arlene.

"Darlin', give me the gun," he said quietly. "It's over."

Mary Elizabeth blinked as if coming out of a trance and handed him the gun, visibly trembling.

"Arlene set the fire," she told him, her voice unsteady. "She killed Larry, too. All because she wanted to get even with me for ruining Ken's political aspirations by marrying Larry in the first place."

Clearly shaken, Mary Elizabeth met his gaze. "How could anyone think that a *job* is more important than a human life?"

"She's obviously not thinking clearly," Tucker said. "The courts will make sure she gets some help." He spotted Walker and another deputy approaching the scene from opposite sides. "You can take over now," he told his brother-in-law. "Arlene's confessed to everything."

"You hear her?" Walker asked.

"I did," Mary Elizabeth told him. "She wanted me to know before she killed me."

"And I heard most of it," Tucker added.

Walker nodded, then glanced at Tucker. "Can you take Liz to the station to make her statement?"

"Will do," Tucker said.

Through all of this Arlene hadn't said a word. Tucker looked into her eyes and saw…*nothing*. It was as if a light inside had gone out. If he hadn't seen her leveling that gun directly at Mary Elizabeth, he might have felt sorry for her. As it was, he knew he would carry that image and his utter feeling of helplessness with him forever.

Only after Walker and the deputy had led Arlene away did Mary Elizabeth finally face him, her expression drawn.

"That's that, then," she said. "That chapter of my life is over. I can finally move on." Her gaze met his, her eyes shimmering with unshed tears. "I knew you'd find me in time."

"I don't like to think about how close I came to being too late," he said with a shudder, drawing her to him until her head rested against his chest. "I don't know what I'd do if I ever lost you."

She lifted her gaze to his. "You're not ever going to have to find out."

"Come on," he said, tucking her hand into his. "Let's go get that statement over with and go out on the town like two normal people."

"Do you think that's possible?" she asked wistfully. "Can we ever have a normal life?"

"I'm going to see to it," he promised. "Stick with me, Mary Elizabeth. Your troubles are over."

A smile played across her lips. "In that case, it could be that yours are just beginning, Sheriff."

Tucker laughed. "I can live with that."

Liz couldn't quite bring herself to celebrate that night, as she and Tucker strolled along the boardwalk with the happy sound of carousel music filling the air. Too many lives had been ruined. She counted herself lucky that hers hadn't been one of them, though she knew in time she'd have to face the guilt of knowing that in an odd way *she* had caused Arlene to focus on Larry and ultimately kill him.

But that struggle was down the road. Tonight she could only be grateful to be alive herself.

She glanced at Tucker and tried to gauge his mood. Everything he'd said earlier and over dinner tonight suggested that he was already envisioning the future, but he was holding something back, some doubt he clearly didn't want to get into. Finally, when she could bear it no longer, she drew him to a stop and looked him in the eye.

"Okay, what's going on in that head of yours?" she asked. "You've been acting weird all night."

"Nothing that can't wait."

"Tucker Spencer, don't make me drag it out of you," she retorted. "If we're going to have a clean slate, we need to erase every bit of this, including whatever lingering doubts are gnawing at you."

He regarded her intently, then shrugged. "Okay, then,

there's one thing about all of this that I just can't seem to shake."

"And it has to do with me?"

He nodded. "Come on over here," he said, leading the way to a bench at the edge of the sand. "Back at the beginning of all this, when you first came to me, why were you so determined to have my help? Why didn't you go straight to the police station or call nine-one-one?"

Liz debated trying to convince him that she'd been afraid, that she'd turned to him instinctively because she had believed she would be the primary suspect. But that was only a tiny part of what had taken her to his house that night. Telling him the rest would mean allowing herself to be vulnerable to him. But after he'd opened up and told her how he'd never stopped loving her, didn't she owe him the same?

"I was afraid," she began. "Not of being railroaded for Larry's death. I believe in the system, and I knew I wasn't guilty and that the truth would come out, no matter how long it took."

"Then what were you afraid of?"

"What the investigation would do to us."

He regarded her with confusion. "There was no *us*."

"I know, but the whole time I was in Europe thinking about divorcing Larry, I kept seeing your face. I kept remembering what we had, the kind of man you are. I wanted to come back here with a clean slate and see if there was anything left between us." She touched a hand to his cheek. "You were so much on my mind that when I found Larry that night, the only thing I could think about was coming straight to you, that you would keep me safe, that you would make everything all right."

Her lips curved. "And you did."

"I almost let you get yourself killed today," he said with self-derision.

She shook her head. "That was my fault. I took a stupid chance. I should never have walked away from the house knowing that Arlene wasn't in custody."

"I guess we've both made our share of mistakes, then."

She regarded him with surprise. "What was yours?"

"Letting you marry Chandler without a fight. If I'd fought harder, maybe I could have changed your mind and none of this would have happened. But my pride was hurt, and I took your decision as final." He looked into her eyes. "So, what about it? Do we get that second chance? After this, I think we can weather just about anything, don't you?"

Hope spread through her. "I want to believe that. I want to believe the past, all of the mistakes, are behind us."

"And the future's just beginning," Tucker said. "If you're sure it's what you really want. Do you want to be with me forever?"

"I'm more sure of that than of anything in my entire life," she told him. "Are you? Will you ever be able to trust me again?"

"I've known you were the woman for me since the fifth grade," he assured her.

"And your family?"

"They're already coming around. I spoke to Bobby earlier. He dropped off a batch of your favorite cinnamon rolls this afternoon. He told me Daisy's already planning a dinner to celebrate the way things have turned out."

"That leaves King."

"You won him over the other day." Tucker chuckled. "Besides, Daddy has his own romance to deal with. He's finally convinced Frances to marry him. I imagine she'll keep him in line. Besides, he'll be ecstatic once we tell him we're talking about having kids."

Liz felt as if her heart might burst with sheer joy. "Are we talking about that?"

Tucker lowered his head and captured her mouth. "We will be, but first things first," he whispered against her lips. "I could do this for a very long time."

"In a minute," she said, her expression suddenly thoughtful. "Maybe you and I should help Frances and your father along, make sure they take that walk down the aisle in the very near future."

"You want us to meddle in my father's love life?"

"Why not?"

Tucker's grin spread. "Why not, indeed? This could be the most exciting entertainment to hit Trinity Harbor in years."

"Except for one thing," she said.

"What's that?"

"This." She resumed the kiss she'd broken off, deepening it until it was darn close to X-rated.

"Hey, you two, take it off the boardwalk," Bobby grumbled, nudging the two of them apart. "This is a family venue."

"Go away," Tucker told him.

"Do I have to call a cop?" Bobby inquired, sounding amused.

Tucker sighed and looked up at his brother. "I am a cop. I'm officially back on active duty as of this afternoon."

"All the more reason for you to be setting a good example out here."

Tucker's gaze narrowed. "Tell me something, do you patrol out here every night?"

"Only when there's a rumor that someone in my family is making a spectacle of themselves," Bobby assured him.

Liz chuckled at Tucker's horrified expression.

"My God," he said to his brother. "You've turned into King."

Now it was Bobby's turn to look shocked. "Bite your tongue."

"It's true," Tucker said. "You're turning into our father."

"Did I hear somebody talking about me?" King asked, strolling up, hand in hand with Frances. Each of them was eating a grape snow cone, and the syrup had tinted their lips.

"Not a word," Bobby ordered Tucker. "Or I'll tell what I saw."

Liz couldn't help it. She burst out laughing. "You guys are too old to be tattling on each other."

"Especially when they have me around to do it," Daisy announced as she and Walker joined them.

"What the devil's going on?" Tucker grumbled. "Are we having a damned family reunion?"

"Somebody heard there might be something to celebrate," Daisy said. "We all came to find out."

"Aside from Daddy's engagement to Frances?" Tucker inquired slyly.

"Old news," King said. "I spread the word on that earlier. We're hoping for something a little more recent."

Tucker glanced at Liz. "Do we have anything to share?"

Amused at the finding herself almost engaged without ever having been formally asked, she shrugged. "Up to you."

His gaze narrowed. "You're not going to make a liar out of me later, are you?"

"For goodness' sakes, boy, haven't you gotten around to asking the woman to marry you yet?" King groused. "Want me to do it for you?"

"He's getting pretty good at it," Frances chimed in. "I made him practice several times on me."

"Come on," Bobby encouraged. "Ask her, Tucker. Here and now. I think it's fitting that a Spencer get engaged right here on my boardwalk."

Tucker uttered a resigned sigh and turned to face her. He tried his best to keep his expression somber, but his lips were twitching as he asked solemnly, "Mary Elizabeth, will you do me the honor of marrying into this impossible family?"

Liz gazed up at King and Frances and winked. "I'll think about it."

Tucker frowned at her. "Mary Elizabeth."

She laughed at his evident frustration. "Okay, okay, I'll marry you."

Bobby grinned at them. "What-say I commandeer the carousel, and we take a family ride and see if Tucker can catch the brass ring?"

Jenna pointed over her shoulder. "I think Tommy and Darcy are one step ahead of you. They've already got the carousel waiting." She reached for Liz's hand and led the way. "Bobby and I got the first ride and it brought us luck. I know it will do the same for you and Tucker."

A whole line of people had to step aside to let them pass. There were a few grumbles, but when they learned the Spencers were celebrating not one, but two, engagements, the crowd began to applaud in time to the organ music as the carousel spun.

Tucker sat astride a white horse with Liz in front of him. She leaned back against his chest.

"Aren't you even going to try for the brass ring?" she asked when they'd circled past it for the second time.

"Nope," he whispered in her ear. "I've finally got you right where I want you and I'm never letting go."

A whoop behind them settled the matter anyway. King had just latched onto the brass ring. He made a production out of passing it along to Frances, who handed it to Jenna, who passed it to Bobby. Eventually it made its way around to Tucker and Liz.

"See," he told her as she clutched it. "The best things in life always come to you, if you're patient."

Liz shook her head. "Not always. Sometimes you have to reach out and grab them."

"Care to go home and debate that?" he inquired.

"I wouldn't mind going home," she said. "But a philosophical debate is the last thing on my mind."

Tucker's gaze clung to hers. "In that case, what are we waiting for?" He signaled to Tommy and the carousel operator. "Stop this infernal contraption. We're getting off."

"Wonder where they're off to in such a rush?" Bobby inquired loudly.

"Better fish to fry," Tucker called back over his shoulder.

Then he took Liz's hand, and together at long last, they headed for home.

Epilogue

King wasn't one bit happy about the turn of events that brought him into church on a Saturday morning in October. He'd expected to walk down the aisle himself before his son got around to it, but Tucker and Mary Elizabeth were in some sort of rush. Frances had flatly refused to steal the limelight from them by scheduling their wedding until at least a month later.

No question, though, that Tucker was happy about something. King suspected he knew what it was, but darned if he could pry a thing out of his son or anyone else. He'd had the whole family working on it, but Mary Elizabeth and Tucker were as tight-lipped as any two people King had ever known.

As if that weren't bad enough, Mary Elizabeth and Frances had suddenly gotten to be thick as thieves. Every time he turned around, the two of them were looking at him as if they were about to dissect him under a microscope. If he were prone to hives, he'd be itching all over by now.

Tucker told him he was just getting his due after the way he'd meddled in all their lives, but King didn't see it that way. A conspiracy was a conspiracy, plain and simple, and he didn't like it one damn bit.

Of course, when Frances tucked her hand in his and looked up at him as if he'd hung the moon, he supposed he could forgive her for whatever she was up to. Something told him that whatever it was, in the end he was going to count himself the lucky one.

He listened to the solemn exchange of vows and felt his heart fill to overflowing. The words took on new meaning when he was contemplating saying them himself in the not too distant future. When he gazed at Frances and saw tears shimmering in her eyes, he could tell she was feeling the exact same way.

"Our turn next," he whispered, just as Anna-Louise pronounced Tucker and Mary Elizabeth husband and wife.

"I can't wait," Frances whispered back. "But there is something we have to talk about."

King's heart began to thud dully. "You're not backing out on me, are you?" he demanded, oblivious to the bride and groom, who were going down the aisle in a shower of flower petals.

"Not a chance," Frances assured him. "But Mary Elizabeth and I have been talking about planning something a little different."

"Different how?" King inquired suspiciously.

Frances frowned. "Maybe now's not the best time to get into this. We'll talk later."

She started out of the pew, but King held her back. "Tell me now," he commanded. "I'm getting old. I can't handle many shocks."

"Oh, stop it," she scolded. "You're only as old as you let yourself be."

"Tell me."

"Oh, for goodness' sakes, it's not like I want to get married jumping out of an airplane."

"Thank the Lord for that," King said, though he supposed he would have gone along with it if she'd insisted. He was of a mind to give Frances just about anything she wanted these days.

"I was thinking about..." She gazed at him hesitantly. "Well, I was thinking about the new bingo hall."

While King's head reeled, she went on in a rush.

"It's right on the boardwalk, which brought Bobby and Jenna together, and our first date was a bingo night over at Colonial Beach, and Anna-Louise has agreed if I can get you to go along with it." She regarded him with luminous eyes. "What do you think?"

King had envisioned a quiet church wedding with family and friends and neighbors. Something traditional and elegant, something befitting a Spencer.

"Of course, we'll want to do it soon," she raced on, as if she was afraid to stop and let King get a word in edgewise. "Because the fact is that Anna-Louise and Richard are expecting a baby, and she's going to want to take some time off, and I really want her to perform the ceremony, don't you?"

There were too many questions on the table for King to think straight. He focused on the least controversial first.

"Of course I want Anna-Louise to marry us. You say she and Richard are expecting? When's that? Nobody tells me anything anymore."

"I just told you." Frances flushed guiltily. "I don't think I was supposed to. Anna-Louise wanted to tell you herself, since you were the one who gave Richard a proper nudge in the right direction. Don't let on I told, okay?"

"Sure. Whatever," King said dutifully. "A bingo-hall wedding, that's what you really want?"

Frances nodded. "It is."

It would be the talk of the town, that's for sure. King began to grin. "Why the hell not?" he said, picking her up and twirling her around. "We're Spencers. We can do whatever we want. Trinity Harbor is our town."

"I am not a Spencer," she reminded him sharply, though there was a twinkle in her eye. "Not yet, anyway. My ancestry has just as big a claim on Trinity Harbor as yours does, but you don't see me throwing that fact in people's faces the way you do."

King laughed. "I am not going to get into a debate with you about whether your family or mine settled this town. Not on a day like today. Besides, once we're married, we can run this place jointly."

"From the sidelines, of course," Frances said.

"Of course," King agreed. "Isn't that what I've always done?"

Hoots of laughter greeted that remark. He looked up and discovered that the whole family had come back to see what was taking the two of them so long.

"Ungrateful brats, the whole lot of you," he accused.

"But we are Spencers," they all dutifully declared, even those who'd married into the family.

"Indeed," he said, a smile splitting his face despite his irritation. His chest filled with pride as he gazed at each of them in turn—Daisy and Walker, Tommy beside them, Jenna and Bobby with young Darcy and J.T., Tucker, his gaze locked on his beautiful bride, and the two he was willing to consider honorary Spencers,

Anna-Louise and Richard. His gaze finally came to rest on Frances, who would be officially one of them as soon as he could arrange it.

They were a fine lot, no question about it. And if a man had a loving—if occasionally disrespectful—family around him, what more could he possibly want? Yes, indeed, King considered himself blessed.

And while he was here in the church he'd attended all his life, he gazed heavenward and said a silent prayer that all of his children would one day know the richness of life that had been bestowed on him.

The sun, glinting through the stained-glass window, winked at him in response. Yes, indeed, it was a glorious day…and just the first of many, if he had anything to say about it.

Which he usually did.

* * * * *

Turn the page for a sneak peek at book one
in the beloved Chesapeake Shores series
THE INN AT EAGLE POINT
by #1 New York Times
bestselling author Sherryl Woods.

Available now from MIRA Books.

When Abby arrived, Jess was still wearing paint-splattered shorts and a faded T-shirt. Abby barely held in a sigh.

"Sorry," Jess said, her expression flustered. "I lost track of the time. I couldn't sleep, so I started painting at the crack of dawn, then someone called in a reservation—"

Abby cut her off. "Jess, we don't have time for this. You can't go to the bank like that," she said, trying not to lose patience. Jess was obviously tense enough without Abby yelling at her. "You know how important this meeting is. It's critical that we handle it as professionally as possible. Change, and do it fast, please."

"Five minutes, I promise. You go on ahead. I'll meet you there."

Abby nodded and drove off, relieved in some ways that she was going in alone. It meant she could say things that she wouldn't want to say in front of her sister—admit to Jess's failings, but stress that her sister had backup now and that things would be on track from here on out.

When they opened the door at Chesapeake Shores Community Bank, she walked in as if she owned the place, and headed straight for Lawrence Riley's office. She beamed at Mariah Walsh, who'd been working there as far back as she could recall.

"Abby, what on earth are you doing back in town?" Mariah asked.

"Visiting family," she said. "How've you been?"

"Same as always. Just a few more years on me."

Abby nodded toward Mr. Riley's office. "Is he in?" she asked. "I need to speak to him."

"What's it about?" Mariah asked, already picking up the phone.

"Jess's loans on the inn."

Mariah frowned and hung up. "Then you'll need to speak to Trace."

Abby felt her heart lurch at the mention of Trace Riley. It had been years since they'd seen each other, and it was ridiculous that hearing his name was enough to make her falter.

Trying to recover her equilibrium before Mariah could see how thrown she'd been, she said, "Trace is working here? I'm surprised." He'd always sworn that hell would freeze over before he'd work in a bank, much less for his father.

Mariah grinned. "He just started last week, and he says it's just temporary. He's in charge of the loan department."

Damn, Abby thought. Maybe that could work in her favor, but she doubted it. The last time they'd seen each other, she'd slept with him, had all but told him she was in love with him and then she'd taken off for New York without another word.

Over the months and years that followed, she'd convinced herself that she'd had no choice, that Trace was a distraction she couldn't afford. In fact, she'd had a whole litany of reasons that had made perfect sense to her at the time. She'd even told herself she was cutting things off for him as much as for herself.

Of course, she should have had the guts to tell him that in person. Instead, she'd taken the coward's way out, because he tempted her in ways she'd found all but impossible to resist. Had she seen him one more time, there was no telling what might have happened to her resolve to go to New York and start a career on Wall Street. She might even have been persuaded to stay with him right here. He'd obviously caved in to parental pressure, just as she'd always feared he might. That fear had made it impossible to trust all the pretty words he'd said, all the promises he'd made about their future.

Mariah gave her a knowing look. "His office is down the hall on the left."

Abby stiffened her spine and headed for his office. She tapped on the door, then walked in without waiting for a reply.

Trace was on the phone, his gaze directed out the window. Distractedly, he waved her toward a seat without even turning around. She breathed a sigh of relief at the reprieve. It gave her time to study him.

He looked good. Really good. The sleeves of his shirt were rolled up, revealing tanned forearms. The laugh lines that fanned out from his eyes were carved a little deeper now. His hair, thick and dark brown with golden highlights from the sun, was a little long and windblown. She grinned. She'd bet anything he'd ridden to work on his Harley. That bike had been his first major rebellion way back in high school, and the possibility that he'd never given it up gave her an unexpected sense of hope. That was the Trace she remembered, not a man who'd turned into a by-the-book banker like his dad. She could deal with that man, challenge him to bend the rules.

When he finished the call, he swiveled around and caught sight of her for the first time. Something dark and dangerous flashed in his eyes, but he kept his expression neutral. "Well, look who the cat dragged in."

"Hello, Trace."

"I'll bet you didn't expect to find me here," he said.

"It was a pleasant surprise, all right."

"Pleasant?" he inquired doubtfully.

"For me, yes. We were friends, Trace. Why wouldn't I be glad to see you again?" she asked, though she knew the answer. She'd just hoped to finesse her way past the awkwardness. The simmering anger in his eyes suggested that wasn't likely.

"Friends?" he echoed with a lift of one brow. "That's not exactly the way I remember it. Maybe my memory's faulty, but I thought we were more than that."

Heat stained Abby's cheeks. "It was a long time ago, Trace. A lifetime, in fact."

He hesitated for what seemed like an eternity, his gaze level, then finally he looked away and reached for a folder with an ominous red sticker on the front. "I imagine you're here about this," he said, his tone suddenly abrupt and very businesslike. "Jess has gotten herself into quite a mess."

Taking her cue from him, Abby opened her briefcase. "We're aware of that, and we're prepared to give the bank every reassurance that things will change from here on out."

"You'll have to do quite a bit of tap-dancing to pull that off," he said. "She doesn't have any management skills. I think that's plain. I have no idea why the bank approved these loans in the first place. I imagine they did it as a courtesy to your father."

Just then the door to his office opened again, and Jess stepped in. She frowned at his words. "You couldn't be more wrong, Trace. They did it because it was a sound investment. That's exactly what your father said when he called me to tell me the mortgage and the loan had been approved." She regarded Trace unflinchingly and added, "It still is."

"Not according to these papers I have in front of me," Trace countered. "It's time to cut our losses, and that's exactly what I intend to recommend to the board tomorrow."

"No," Abby said fiercely. "Not until you've heard us out."

She tried not to notice the alarm on Jess's face or the brick-red color that flamed in Trace's cheeks. Instead, she plunged on, throwing diplomacy to the wind. "If you have even an ounce of business savvy in that rock-hard head of yours, you'll see that this plan makes sense."

"Why should I believe anything you tell me?" he asked.

Abby swallowed hard. This was all going to blow up just because she and Trace had a history. Why hadn't Jess warned her? If she had, Abby would have stayed far, far away from the bank. But since she was in the thick of it now, she refused to let him goad her into backing down.

"Don't make this about us, Trace," she said quietly. "It doesn't reflect well on you or the bank."

Trace scowled at her. "Well, aren't you full of yourself? Trust me, you had nothing to do with my decision. It's all right here in black and white. People might lie, but numbers don't."

Abby knew he was right about that, but she wasn't giving up without a fight. She'd seen the flicker of guilt in his eyes when she'd accused him of letting his feelings for her get into the equation. She intended to use that to force his hand and make him reconsider.

She tempered her tone. "Will you at least hear me out? You owe us that much."

"Really?" he said quizzically. "How do you figure that?"

"You want to prove that you're making a totally unbiased decision, don't you? Then you have to consider all the facts. Otherwise, I'll have to insist on meeting the board myself, and you'll wind up with egg on your face after barely a week on the job."

Again, he gestured toward the file. "The facts are in here."

"Not all of them," she insisted. She handed him a set of the papers she'd spent all Sunday afternoon preparing. "Take a look. As you'll see, there's a new investment partner. Jess has more than enough cash now to make good on the loan payments and to capitalize the running of the inn for the first six months, longer if she's careful. There's a solid business plan on pages two and three. And on page four there's a plan for refinancing that egregious interest-only mortgage plan that should never have been offered in the first place. I think we could make a case that the bank was hoping she'd get herself into financial trouble just so they could foreclose and lay claim to the inn once she'd poured a lot of money into renovations."

Trace stared at her incredulously. "You can't be serious. You think this was the bank's fault?"

She smiled. "I do."

"You're crazy!"

"Want to test my theory in court? I think people are furious over the kind of lending practices that turned the whole industry upside down. I think we could make Jess into a very sympathetic victim."

Trace regarded her with a glimmer of new respect. "Not bad. You almost had me going there for a minute."

"I wasn't joking," Abby assured him. "My next stop will be a lawyer's office, unless I can make you see reason."

He looked taken aback. "I'll have to take this proposal of yours to the board," he said eventually.

"Of course. They meet tomorrow?"

"At ten o'clock," he told her.

"Then you should have an answer by noon?"

He nodded. "I'll meet you at the yacht club at twelve-fifteen and fill you in over lunch."

Abby hesitated. She could stay, had planned to stay, in fact, but with Trace involved it was too complicated. "Jess will be there, but I can't be. I have to get back to New York tonight."

His gaze clashed with hers. "You'll be there if you expect this to be approved."

"Why? This is Jess's business, not mine."

"You'll be there because I intend to recommend that the board approve this on one condition only."

Jess sat up a little straighter. "What condition?" she asked suspiciously.

Trace looked at her as if he'd forgotten she was even in the room. "That your sister take over as manager of the project."

"No!" Abby and Jess said at once.

"It's my inn," Jess protested. "You have no right to dictate who manages it."

"I do when this bank's money is involved and you have a history of failing to make your payments," he said, his gaze unrelenting. "Abby stays or it's a deal breaker."

"But the plan—" Abby began.

"Isn't worth the paper it's written on unless you remain involved," he said. "There's no assurance it won't be frittered away on who knows what before the next payment's due."

"Come on, Trace, be reasonable," Abby pleaded. "I need to get back to New York. I have a job. Jess knows what has to be done. I trust her."

"You're her sister. I'm her banker," he said. "Unless you agree to my terms, we'll proceed with the foreclosure."

He looked from Abby to Jess, then back again. "Well, what's it going to be? Will I see you tomorrow?"

Abby bit back the sharp retort on the tip of her tongue and nodded slowly, afraid of what she might say if she spoke. She held her breath, praying that Jess would be as diplomatic. When she glanced at her sister, she discovered Jess looked furious, but at least she remained silent.

For the moment, he had them both over a barrel and

they all knew it. Once the board went along with this insane plan of his, though, Abby was convinced he'd be satisfied with the victory. After that, she could make him see reason. She was sure of it.

Then again, she'd learned a long time ago that a man whose pride had been damaged could turn into a fierce and stubborn adversary. For now, anyway, Trace Riley held all the cards, so she and Jess were going to have to play the game his way...at least until she could come up with a new set of rules.

Outside the bank, Jess stood on the sidewalk, trembling. She whirled on her sister. "What the hell just happened in there? I thought you were on my side."

"Of course I'm on your side," Abby said, looking genuinely bewildered by Jess's attack. "This was all about keeping you from losing the inn."

"I might as well have lost it," Jess snapped. "He's put you in charge. Way to go, sis!"

Abby frowned. "Jess, calm down. Let's go to Sally's for a cup of coffee and talk about this. We need to plan our strategy."

"Strategy for what? Getting your name on the deed?"

"Jess!"

There was a flash of hurt in Abby's eyes. Jess was spitting mad and she needed someone to take it out on. Her sister was the most obvious choice, since she couldn't go back inside the bank and start pummeling Trace. Even in her fury, she knew that would be counterproductive.

"I'm sorry," she said. "It wasn't your fault. I know that. He just made me so furious."

"Join the club," Abby said dryly. "Why didn't you

tell me Trace was working at the bank and that he was involved in this? You knew, didn't you?"

"Not when I called you," Jess swore to her. "He hasn't lived here in years. Right before you got here, he came by the inn to look things over. That's the first I knew about him being back in town, much less working at the bank. I was afraid if you knew, you'd bail on me."

Abby lifted a brow. "Don't you know me better than that?"

"I had no idea how deep the bad blood ran between the two of you. You never said why you broke up with him. Everyone in town knew you broke his heart. What no one seemed to know was why, or if maybe he'd broken yours, too. You never wanted to talk about it."

"Okay, I suppose I understand why you didn't want to tell me I'd be dealing with a man I'd dumped."

"Let's not forget that I did try to tell you," Jess reminded her. "Dad arrived home, remember?"

Abby nodded. "I remember."

Jess extended an olive branch. "Want to go have that coffee, after all? I'll treat."

"With what?" Abby retorted. "Every penny you possess has to go into the inn. I'll treat."

Jess grinned. "Fine by me."

They were silent until they got to the café in the next block.

Jess studied her sister, then grinned. "Bet I know something you *don't* know."

"What's that?"

"Trace Riley still has the hots for you."

"You're crazy."

Jess shook her head. "Know something else? I'm almost a hundred percent certain it works both ways."

Abby drew herself up until her back was ramrod straight, her expression regal and dismissive. “You could not be more wrong.”

Jess wasn’t impressed by her sister’s performance. “We’ll see.”

In fact, watching the two of them trying to deny what was obvious to any observer might be just about the only amusing part of this entire messed-up situation.